Who Murdered Mr. Wickham

Carol Hutchens

DEDICATION

From idea to completion, this book has taken eight years to finish.

Many thanks to my family for their continued encouragement when the doubt demons attacked.

For my husband Larry who is always ready with his encouragement…even though he disliked the idea of murdering Mr. Wickham.

For Stan who enjoys the Jane Austen series as much as we do and gave technical advice.

For Aaron and Brandy who are always ready with words of encouragement.

For Colton and the joy he brings to our lives.

Chapter One

*I*t is a universally accepted truth that all newly wedded couples want to share their good fortune with their single relations, and thus Jane Bingley is looking forward to hosting her first ball tonight with great anticipation and apprehension.

Hopes of having Bingley to herself these first few months of married life have diminished quickly of late, for March was upon them and so was his family. The Hursts, Bingley's eldest sister and her husband along with his youngest sister, Caroline, arrived within the past fortnight in expectation of Jane's first ball as mistress of Netherfield.

It is no secret Bingley's sisters disapprove of his choice of a wife, but Jane hopes to gain their good graces. A task with no small import to Bingley and Jane's future tranquility, for Caroline, still unwed at seven and twenty, relies on her well-situated brother. Jane is certain she will have more time with dear Bingley if Caroline had a husband to engage her attention. Thus Jane intends to help Caroline, and her own beloved younger sisters, by finding love matches for them at the ball.

Still, plans for the ball keep Jane occupied and what a conundrum the event is proving to be for it is another universally accepted truth that March can baa as a lamb one day and roar loud as a lion the next. Travel to the ball could be treacherous in the case of the latter. Yet the London season begins at the end of the month, and Jane worries any delay of the ball will mean fewer guests for her first time hosting as Bingley's wife. Her matchmaking plans depend on as many eligible men as possible be in attendance.

In truth, this is her first time hosting any event due to their small country society. The shortage of local entertainment will attract more attention to the ball, but more important even than impressing her husband's sisters, is Jane's desire to see her beloved family.

Her dear Lizzy will soon arrive for her first visit to Netherfield since their double wedding. Yet, Jane's anticipation of Lizzy's arrival is not without dread for Jane fears Lizzy will not be pleased when she discovers Miss Mary King is to be a guest.

Jane had little choice in the matter for once Lady Lucas announced she had several guests, including some members of the militia, staying at Lucas Lodge, Jane extended them an invitation to the ball, as well. Thus the red haired young woman who once caused Lizzy such distress would be Jane's guest at the ball.

Even though she worried about her sister's reaction, Jane was convinced Lizzy benefited from learning of Wickham's fickle nature through his treatment of Mary King to get at her inheritance. Lizzy might even be comfortable with her old rival as they both escaped Wickham's grasp and Lizzy has Darcy.

Also, Jane dared not insult such long standing acquaintances of her parents as Sir William and Lady Lucas. Sir William Lucas was kindness itself and Lady Lucas was her mother's close confidant.

Thoughts of her dear Mamma brought to mind yet another concern. Mamma held strong opinions and would not approve of other guests arriving with Lady Lucas. Colonel and Mrs. Forester were among the guests staying at Lucas Lodge, and after their involvement in Lydia's elopement with Wickham, Mamma had nothing good to say of the couple. But Sir William opened his doors to acquaintances in the militia in his attempt to avoid the doldrums of winter, and Jane had no wish to offend a well-meaning neighbor.

Happily, two other guests at the Lodge were friends of the Bennets from when the militia had been in Meryton. Denny and Captain Carter would help even out the guests available for dancing. Perhaps one of them would seek a deeper acquaintance with Kitty or even Mary.

Truthfully, dark, hanging clouds trying to obscure the weak rays of sun were the least of Jane's concerns. Her parents and younger sisters were attending tonight's ball, and Lizzy and Darcy were due within the hour. However, the question none of them could ignore was whether Lydia and Wickham would attend the ball.

Jane wanted all her family to share her joy at finding such an agreeable husband, but having Lydia and Wickham present would stir old hostilities Jane wished to avoid. Her only hope was that Lydia had matured in the months since they last saw her, but truthfully, she held little hope.

She was saddened that a lack of funds and Wickham's commission in Newcastle forced Lydia to miss their double wedding, yet relieved as well at not having to listen to Lydia's complaints. Though even with Lydia's absence, not all had gone smoothly at the wedding, for Mary offered dissertations on any topic which came to mind and recitals on the pianoforte. But Aunt Gardiner had graciously taken Mary in hand during the festivities and kept her away from the guests and the pianoforte as much as possible.

Thoughts of the wedding reminded her how good it would be good to see Lizzy. Jane loved Mr. Bingley with her whole heart, but no one could take Lizzy's place as her confidant. She missed their late night conversations and long chats over cups of chocolate. Caroline and Louisa would never replace Lizzy as her most trusted advisor no matter how long they remained in the house. Even as much as she loved Bingley, she still needed to confide certain womanly concerns and missed Lizzy's presence desperately.

At the sound of footsteps in the great hall, Jane turned expectantly. The new arrival's identity did not disappoint her. "Oh, Mr. Bingley, have you ever seen Netherfield look so well?"

Charles Bingley smiled at his wife of four months and took her hands in his. "I cannot see beyond your beauty, my dear Jane. If you are pleased with your efforts, wife, so am I."

"Oh, Bingley, do stop distracting me, and mind your words. Your sisters or Mr. Hurst could appear at any moment." Jane feigned reserve, but in truth, she yearned to be alone with Bingley.

After kissing her hand, Bingley stepped away a respectable distance. "I think not, my dear wife. When last I last checked, they were resting in preparation for tonight's festivities."

"Even Mr. Hurst?" Laughter bubbled in Jane's voice. "He can outlast even the most tiresome guests."

"Unless he finds a bottle. I noticed him topping up his tea cup not long after our morning repast." Bingley's usual smile added a glint to his kind eyes. "I expect that is the reason he needs a rest."

"Oh, my dear Bingley, I do so want this ball to be a success."

"How can it not be, my Jane? You thought of everything."

"I did not give enough consideration to the season and the chance of bad weather. What if it rains or snows?" Jane peered out the window. "If only I had waited so long to give the ball."

"But my dear," Bingley turned from his perusal of the darkening skies, "you want to help your sisters find a husband before the season begins, and trust me, with two sisters I can assure you the most eligible singles will quit the country and leave for town as soon as the London season begins."

"Oh, Bingley, look. A carriage is approaching. They are here. Dear Lizzy and Mr. Darcy have arrived." Jane turned a flushed face to her husband. "Oh, Bingley, I do so hope they are as happy as we are."

⊂⊃

Later that evening Jane's insides were humming a not-so-pleasant tune by the time Lizzy joined her in the receiving line.

"Dear Jane, I am convinced I can never plan a ball half as well as you. Everything looks perfect." Lizzy's gaze brimmed with happiness as she looked at her older sister. "Did you ever imagine marrying for love could be so unequaled?"

Jane's lips tilted in a serene smile as she glanced toward the entrance. "Lizzy, do you think Lydia and Wickham will come?"

Lizzy made an unladylike sound and clasped Jane's arm in both hands. "Dear, sweet Jane, surely you do not imagine Wickham would miss the chance to borrow money from his new brothers-in-law."

Jane bit her lip to stop a smile in response to her sister's nonsense. "Lizzy, do not be unkind, though I must confess I dread their arrival almost as much as I look forward to seeing dear Lydia." Brow wrinkled, Jane turned an inquiring glance on Lizzy. "Do you think Lydia will be much improved now that she is married?"

"Are you inquiring if I think Lydia has stopped her forward ways and will act sensible at your ball? Then I must confess I do not. Lydia is spoiled and used to having her way, and lest we forget, she is not yet sixteen. Sadly, I fear Wickham cannot make a good impression on her."

"Dear Lizzy, you must know I could not avoid inviting Miss King."

"It makes no matter to me, Jane. As to the Foresters' presence, I fear you need be more concerned with what Mamma will say than

8

worry over any feelings I might have on the subject."

As if on cue, Mr. and Mrs. Bennet and their two unmarried daughters entered on a gust of cold air. Jane absorbed the sight of her beloved family as she rushed forward. "Oh, Mamma, Papa, it is so good to see you all."

"Dear Jane," Mrs. Bennet moved out of Jane's tight hug and lifted a hand to her hair, "you look as beautiful as ever, but take care not to wrinkle our gowns."

"Mamma, I have so much to tell you," Jane turned to her father, "and you, Papa."

Mr. Bennet arched a brow and gave his eldest daughter a peck on the cheek. "Now, Jane, I know full well your head is filled with womanly talk. Lizzy, my dear girl, you look well."

"Papa, Mamma it is lovely to see you again." Lizzy kissed both her parents. "Mary and Kitty, you both look nice."

"Kitty," Jane said, "you look lovely in this blue gown, but Mary, is that really a book tucked under your arm at my ball?"

"Thank you for the gowns, Lizzy." Mary turned a wise glance on Lizzy, "Kitty an I are most appreciative. It is said that it is better to give than to receive."

Jane and Lizzy exchanged smiles as Lizzy responded. "Then it is fortunate for you and Kitty that I know your sizes, isn't it Mary." Amid their laughter, a sudden silence filled the room and all eyes turned toward the doors.

More chilly air rushed in, announcing Lydia and Wickham's arrival. Lizzy turned rigid as she stood beside Jane, causing Jane to frown. Surely, Lizzy had put to rest any feelings she might have had for Wickham. With a man like Mr. Darcy for a husband, Jane could not imagine her beloved sister still felt slighted by Wickham's previous, fickle affections.

"Jane, I see marriage agrees with you," Lydia greeted loudly in her usual vocal way as she approached. "Lizzy, your grown must have cost as much as my husband's commission in his new regiment."

"Oh, Lydia, my darling girl," Mrs. Bennet rushed to hug her youngest daughter, "and dear Wickham, it is so good to see you."

At that moment, with her mother's face glowing with happiness and Lydia looking leaner without the usual fullness in her cheeks, Jane could see the resemblance between them. Her father often commented that Lydia's close resemblance to Mamma kept her out of more trouble than her good sense, which she was sadly lacking. Jane reached out to hug her youngest sibling. "Lydia, I am so glad you came."

"Are you, Jane?" Lydia turned to her with a wide eyed gaze. "When you sent no funds for the trip, we almost stayed away. Wickham said we could not manage the funds. Then he found he could not pass up the opportunity to get into Darcy's pocket." Seeming not to notice the look Jane and Lizzy exchanged on hearing her words, Lydia focused on Lizzy. "Now that you are married to Darcy, you can stop envying me my husband, Lizzy."

Then Lydia turned to Kitty. "You are looking well, Kitty. You must loan me that gown. It matches my eyes and all the men in Wickham's regiment will admire me in it."

"Sisters," Wickham's smile was easy and practiced, belying the lines of tension around his eyes, "it is good to see you again." He spoke to both Jane and Lizzy, but he focused on Lizzy. "I believe you have acquired a husband since we last met. Marriage suits you."

His slow drawl seemed to calm the storm left by Lydia's vexing comments, but he had ample time to practice. Or had he perfected the art before acquiring Lydia as his wife, Jane wondered as she rushed into speech before the glitter in Lizzy's eyes turned the greeting into a commotion. "Mr. Wickham, it is good of you to come and bring Lydia."

Suddenly Lydia's voice rose to a pitch they remembered from her younger days. "Jane, what is that sad looking woman doing here?"

Jane turned in time to observe Sir William, Lady Lucas and Miss King as they paused in the doorway. Sir William's wide smile contained no hint of the superior expression Lady Lucas had perfected since her husband's knighthood, but Jane's attention lingered on their guest. Mary King had inherited a fortune that lured Wickham from Lizzy's side early in their acquaintance, but seeing Miss King again, Jane guessed her worth was not all that attracted Wickham.

Lydia claimed Mary King's red hair was repulsive, but Jane noticed how light glinted off Mary's hair in the well-lit ballroom and decided the color was as attractive as her own, blonde locks, if not more so. Mary's natural coloring added a bloom to her cheeks that pale-complexioned females worked at achieving.

The look of determination on Miss King's face reminded Jane of Lizzy's oft seen expression, and she made up her mind to be more congenial to Miss King. After all, she was the hostess of this ball and she admired Lizzy's strong spirit.

⚮

Mary King's glance found her hostess and the entire Bennet family, including her former suitor, waiting in line to greet guests. Mary lifted her chin. Wickham and Lydia's presence made the evening more of a challenge than she expected. Lydia had shown her dislike the first night they had met and Wickham's quick attention made the situation worse. That she had inherited a great deal of money attracted Wickham. Why Lydia disliked her on sight she did not know.

Still, Mary did not give up easily. Inheriting a fortune had not opened all doors and Mary was determined to change the situation. Even before a great-uncle died and named her his heir, people considered her easy on the eyes. But, in truth, her pleasing looks only made her new life more difficult. Since acquiring wealth, Mary had learned some things never changed. Especially in as close a country society as this one.

The only people willing to accept her were fortune hunters and their hopeful relations. But Mary wanted more than a life based on riches. She wanted to be accepted. Given the chance, she would prove she was more than just a pretty face.

She was studying the classics and music, though she had told no one of her efforts. But she read each night before bed and when she was free during the day. She had heard Elizabeth Bennet's intelligence and beauty commented upon, and Mary wanted recognition as a woman of good sense as well.

"Miss King, you are most welcome to our home." Jane Bingley's smile was warm and friendly as she greeted Mary.

"Please, call me Mary. I hope we can become better acquainted now that I am moved to the area."

Jane concealed her surprise. "Then this is more than a visit for you? I had not heard the news. Welcome to Meryton."

"Yes, I am moving to my uncle's house." Mary confided.

"Alone?" Jane blurted. "Oh, do forgive me, Miss King, but I only meant will you not feel lonely?"

"I hope to become better acquainted with people in the area and make friends. Eventually, I plan to entertain as well."

"Oh, you must give a ball." Kitty edged closer to Jane's side. "Please say you will. Now that the militia has moved on, we have so few chances to dance and have fun."

Kitty's artless comments caused Jane and Mary to stare at each other in silence. Both were aware that before the militia left for Brighton, Wickham had thrown his attention to Mary and asked for her hand. For her part, Mary was certain word had spread about her great uncle's legal advisor stepped in and dissuaded Wickham from his pursuit. More than once, she had uttered a prayer of thanks for the timely intervention. Above all else, she had set her mind to marrying for true love. She had heard Jane and Elizabeth Bennet set their minds on marrying for love, and wanted that goal for her own. "I'll think—"

"Kitty, you must give Miss King a chance to settle and get to know people." Jane rushed to admonish her younger sister.

"That's what parties are for," Kitty insisted, showing her lack of maturity though she was not the youngest daughter in the family.

Before Mary could respond, a high pitched squeal filled the air.

Lydia rushed up and grabbed hold of Kitty's arm. "Look who has arrived." Then she pulled Kitty, still staring with her mouth open, toward the door to greet Denny and Captain Carter.

As was the norm for Lydia, she left an array of conflicting reactions in her wake. With his wife's noisy greeting of her old friends ring loudly in the room, Wickham smiled indulgently and turned his gaze on Mary.

Mary's brow arched. Wickham's look appeared to confirm the gossip she had heard. His satisfied smile could only mean he had spotted Mrs. Forester standing in line behind Denny, and was happy to see her, but Mary would keep the knowledge to herself.

Wickham's father-in-law was not as reluctant to share his opinion of the Foresters' presence. Mr. Bennet's brow wrinkled as he studied the new arrivals. "I knew there was a reason I should have stayed home with my books."

Mrs. Bennet was more vocal. "Oh, Jane, how could you invite the Foresters? You know they were responsible for my poor Lydia being banished from Brighton and she was so happy there."

"Mamma, please." Jane put a hand on her mother's arm and tried to distract her. "You are embarrassing poor Wickham." Jane wanted to include herself, but Mamma's regard for Wickham was her best chance of ending further unwanted comments. Despite the worry and disgrace surrounding Lydia's elopement with Wickham, her mother was as susceptible to Wickham's charm as Lydia. Which pointed to one more thing Mamma and Lydia had in common. Neither of them possessed good judgment in men. Though Jane thought her father an exemption, she and Lizzy had narrow escapes in their mother's attempts to see them married. Lizzy's near miss with their father's cousin was only one example.

Mary excused herself to Jane and moved across the room to join Lady Lucas. "I must thank you again, Lady Lucas, for inviting me to stay at Lucas Lodge while my uncle's house is prepared."

"It is of no consequence, my dear. Sir William and I enjoy the distraction of guests." Lady Lucas looked about the room. "If you will excuse me, my dear, I must confer with my friend, Mrs. Bennet."

Mary's cousin, Maggie, had acted as a companion for Miss Georgiana Darcy for some time, and should be here tonight. As Mary watched Lady Lucas join Mrs. Bennet, she wondered if she would have a chance to speak with Maggie.

"Did I hear correctly, Miss King, you have moved to the area permanently?" Wickham's low voice, close to her ear, was Mary's first warning of his approach.

"Mr. Wickham, how nice to see you again," Mary tried to hide her discomfort.

"Nice enough that you might be persuaded to renew our acquaintance, my dear Miss King?" As Wickham looked down from his superior height, his smile filled with confidence at how she would respond.

"Such a suggestion, sir." Mary revealed her surprise as her gaze rested on his handsome countenance, and again, she gave thanks for her narrow escape. "And you with a new wife, Mr. Wickham? Speaking of which, did I not hear Mrs. Wickham call you to come greet the Foresters?"

Mary watched color slash his cheeks and wondered how many of Wickham's conquests were in this room tonight. She was aware of four, although she was not certain she should include Elizabeth Darcy in that tally. For Mrs. Darcy had not had her wings singed by Wickham's advances, unlike other women encountering him.

"Ah, but you must be well versed on the situation, Miss King, as is everyone else in this county. And you must admit I am wise to keep distant from Colonel Forester."

"Who are the people entering the ballroom, Mr. Wickham?" Mary studied the elegant appearance of the two women and the man accompanying them. Her keen interest gave Mary witness the shorter woman's reaction when her gaze settled on Wickham. The woman's eyes widened in surprise, then the vast amount of creamy skin visible above the low neckline of her stylish gown began to pulse with the rapid beat of her heart. After a startled pause, Mary could not resist turning an innocent look on Wickham as she said, "Do you have another admirer, sir?"

"Ah, your compliment is much appreciated, Miss King, but alas, those ladies are Mr. Bingley's sisters. The gentleman is the husband of the elder sister. So, you see, as my wife's sister is married to Mr. Bingley, we are all family."

Mary would consume her elbow-length gloves for dinner if the looks exchanged by Wickham and the elder-Bingley sister had anything to do with innocent family relationships. "As you say, Mr. Wickham. Now if you will excuse me."

CREO

Jane noticed the sudden silence and turned toward the entrance to learn why her guests were staring. Then all became clear for Bingley's sisters stood in the doorway. Caroline and Louisa returned the stares of guests, proving they had had much exposure to such events. Caroline, the tallest by a head, attracted attention first with the drape and style of a gown in the latest London design. Standing beside her, much shorter and two years older, Mrs. Hurst flaunted as much skin as was acceptable in fashionable attire, thus attracting her own share of attention. Mr. Hurst, dressed in the latest London attire, followed the sisters, and looked as bored as if this were the end of the season before it had even started.

With a sigh, Jane turned back to the guests waiting for her attention. Much as she loved Bingley and wanted to love his sisters, the slight sneer on their faces as they observed the guests made it difficult. But she wanted so much for this evening to be a success. Perhaps she could find Caroline, Kitty and Mary a match and all would be well.

"Lady Lucas, it is a pleasure to see you. Lizzy is most anxious for news from Charlotte." Jane noted the vexed expression that flashed through the woman's eyes and wished she could take the words back. Despite being mamma's close confidant Lady Lucas and Mamma were competitive about finding suitable matches for their daughters. Even though her eldest daughter, Charlotte married first by accepting Mr. Bennet's cousin, Mr. Collins, after Lizzy had rejected him — thus giving Lady Lucas bragging rights — she still harbored resentment. That Jane and Lizzy married well probably did not ease the tension. "I am so pleased you and Sir William could come to-night."

Looking somewhat soothed by Jane's greeting, Lady Lucas managed a regal nod. "You are welcome, Jane. Everything looks quite acceptable for the event, I might add."

Oh, I wish you had not! Jane hid a wince and turned to the next guest in line. Sometime later Jane was pleased to find Mr. Darcy's sister in front of her. "Miss Darcy, it is a pleasure to see you. Are you late arriving?"

"I am sorry to say we are, Mrs. Bingley. Travel from town went slower than expected, but now we are warm and ready for the ball." Georgiana made a slight curtsy causing the skirts of her pastel gown to billow becomingly around her.

"You are most welcome to Netherfield. But surely, you did not travel alone?"

"Oh, no, my companion, Miss Brown, is with me. She asked leave to make use of your library. I said she could. I hope that is acceptable."

"Of course, and the fire in that room usually feels quite comfortable." Jane smiled. Mr. Darcy's young sister, though near in age to Kitty, Mary and Lydia, acted nothing like them. "Your brother and Lizzy have arrived, and Mr. Darcy is conversing with my husband."

"It will be nice to see Mr. Bingley again." Georgiana smiled shyly. "Charles is one of my favorite people. I think he is most fortunate to have found a wife as agreeable as he is."

"Oh, Miss Darcy, I think I shall love you much as Lizzy does, and your words have made me a friend for life. I do so admire my husband."

"Georgiana, is it you, all grown up, or perhaps my eyes play tricks on me?" A man in uniform declared.

"Do stop your nonsense, Cousin. Of course I am grown since your last visit. We rarely see you now that duty and the threat of war keep you away, Fitz." Georgiana turned a smiling face toward Jane. "Mrs. Bingley, do you know my cousin, Colonel Fitzwilliam?"

"Colonel Fitzwilliam," Jane offered her hand, "you are most welcome to Netherfield."

"Thank you, Mrs. Bingley. I was hoping my cousin could tear himself away from his new wife long enough to attend your ball. I have news I am most anxious to share with him."

Miss Darcy clasped both hands around the colonel's forearm

and sent him an engaging smile. "Oh, do tell me first, Cousin. My brother always gets the news before I do."

"This is nothing of consequence to concern your pretty head about, my dear. Just some words on the current state of events." Colonel Fitzwilliam turned to survey the room. "I say, is that Wickham over by the door speaking to Mrs. Hurst?"

"Yes," Jane murmured, following his gaze to the group chatting in the entrance, "Mr. Wickham is married to my sister Lydia."

"I beg your pardon, ma'am." Colonel Fitzwilliam bowed, "I had forgotten. Ah, Bingley and Darcy, so glad you arrived before I started chewing on my other boot. Good to see you."

"You are most welcome to our home, Colonel. Have you brought news of recent events?"

Colonel Fitzwilliam glanced around the room. "From the number of uniforms present tonight, I expect you have heard all I know."

"There are several militia men here, it is true," Bingley glanced at the guests, "but I believe most of them are guests of Sir William and we have not yet conversed with them. Come, have some punch, and tell us all. Right, Darcy?"

Mr. Darcy gave a nod and smiled at the Colonel. "By all means, you have our ear, Cousin."

Jane watched the three men walk away and smiled widely as Lizzy approached. "Look who has arrived, Lizzy." She need not have spoken because Georgiana gave a little squeal and rushed to give Lizzy a hug. Watching the warm exchange of the two new sisters, Jane felt a twinge of sadness. She glanced toward her own new sisters-in-law, still standing just inside the door.

Caroline Bingley was batting her eyes at a man Jane did not recognize, while a few steps away, her sister, Louisa Hurst, seemed in animated conversation with Wickham. At least her stiff posture and flushed cheeks indicated some aroused emotions, but all must be well because, Mr. Hurst was only a few steps away, casually studying his drink.

Still it saddened Jane on Lydia's behalf to see Wickham stand so close to another woman, even if it was Louisa. And, once again, she feared she would never enjoy the closeness with Bingley's sisters that Lizzy and Georgiana enjoyed.

Chapter Two

Though thoroughly entertained by Lydia playing the role of superior female in possession of a husband and jealous wife in turn, Mr. Wickham took advantage of an interruption by Caroline to excuse himself from Louisa Hurst.

As usual, he was able to hide any discomfort in his expression with a pleasant grin on his face. He meandered through the crowd, watching the dancers and spied his young wife, loudly conversing in a far corner of the ball room, and was thoroughly entertained by Lydia playing the role of the superior female, in possession of a husband, and jealous wife in turn.

After a few minutes, the musicians stopped for a break and he left the ballroom for a breath of fresh air. Too many members of his wife's family were in the room for him to experience the pleasure he usually enjoyed at such events. Of course, the fact that he was now a married man, in attendance with his wife, accounted for some of the missing excitement. Everyone present knew of his new status as Lydia Bennet's husband.

The darkness in the formal gardens suited his purposes much better, and he paused to take in a deep breath of the crisp night air.

The chill did not deter him. Soon he expected to find the warmth he needed and did not worry about the cold. With the darkness of the night and hedges grown taller than his head bordering some of the paths, he appreciated the convenience of the space. Not since his youth, when he and Darcy romped through the formal gardens at Pemberley, had he admired the rambling paths and heavy growth of a garden so much. And to confirm his opinion on the joys of the darkness, a breathless feminine voice called his name out of the shadows.

"Wickham, are you there?"

"I am here, Madam," Wickham turned toward the shadowy figure as Mrs. Forester floated toward him, but, even in the dark, her light-colored gown revealed abundant curves he longed to hold again. After the regiment had moved to Brighton, and without the small-town gossips watching every move to feed their need for news, he had enjoyed Mrs. Forester's company to the fullest.

Even though she was the wife of his commanding colonel at that time, he visited her, alone, quite freely and often. Of course, Lydia's arrival as a guest of the Foresters provided an excellent excuse for his continued and frequent visits, but she had become infatuated, and the colonel more watchful. If only he had not miscalculated, and been forced to encourage Lydia to conceal the true target of his affections.

"How is it that you are outside on this cold night, Mrs. Forester?"

"For shame, Wickham," Mrs. Forester said with a breathless giggle as she came nearer. "You know full well why I risk catching a chill to walk in this garden. Oh, my dear, it has been so long since you last held me in your arms. I thought I would die of desperation when we danced earlier."

"Ah, Madam, I feared you had forgotten me, and turned your affections to another."

"Do not tease me so, dear Wickham. Can we not find a secret place and be alone for a while?" She moved close in the dark as clouds covered the moon, and pressed her body against Wickham so their curves fit as one. "Do say you have missed me, sir."

"I can not deny my feelings for you know me too well, my dear, but we must use caution."

"Why? You want to be with me, do you not?" She whirled toward a rustle in the bushes and gripped the front of Wickham's uniform in both hands. "What was that? Did you hear something? I dare not let my husband find me alone in your company again. I must go, dear Wickham." With a swift turn and a whirl of skirts, Mrs. Forester disappeared into the night.

Wickham rolled his eyes and stared at the sky as an icy moon peeped past the clouds. Why, had she fled just when her lush feminine curves were almost in his hands? Could she not tell he needed her warmth more than ever? With a shrug of regret he turned back the way he had come, but before he could take a step, another flash of pale gown appeared out of the shadows. Had she returned? Would she dare take the risk to be with him after all? But unless she had grown much taller in the last few moments, it was not her. And then the shadow spoke.

"Ah, there you are, Mr. Wickham. I saw you leave the ball room." Caroline Bingley floated to his side. "It is very warm in there with all the dancing do you not agree?"

"Indeed it is, Miss Bingley, and the cold air is refreshing."

"You are describing yourself, I think, sir. After taking a turn with all those stuffed shirts, dancing with you was a pleasure. Though how you stay out of trouble with those wondering hands of yours, I do not know."

"Yet here you are, ma'am, all alone with me in the dark. Why is that, I wonder?"

"Do not let my presence go to your head, my dear Mr. Wickham." She paused and looked over her shoulder. "Did you hear something? Are we not alone?"

Wickham rolled his eyes and released a sigh. He had grown weary of dealing with jittery females this evening. The ballroom was populated with women eager to dance, but leery of experiencing the danger of his arms. He longed for a warm and willing woman in his arms, and not his wife's inexperience.

"Of course we are alone. Though, I am certain there is a rabbit or two about on this chilly night. Are you not cold, my dear?"

"Always looking for an opportunity, right Wickham? That is the reason I wanted to speak with you, sir." Caroline Bingley stepped closer and lowered her voice. "I would like your assistance in a little activity you might find amusing."

"Indeed, ma'am, I am all that is curious. Pray tell me how I can help."

"I ask only because I thought you would enjoy the game, as you were once attracted to Eliza Bennet."

"Ah, you refer to Mrs. Darcy, do you not? It is common knowledge that at one time, before I formed an attachment to her sister, I did think Miss Elizabeth Bennet and I might be more than friends. But alas, she had no fortune, you see, so I turned my attention elsewhere."

"Yet you married her youngest sister, who has even less to recommend her as the perfect wife than Eliza."

"You speak of my wife, ma'am." Pride, and his refusal to admit his mistakes or his feelings for Darcy's wife forced Wickham to speak in a firm tone. In truth, he had no doubt Lydia was much more accommodating as a spouse than Lizzy would ever be. Lizzy had a mind of her own and would not bend easily to a man's will, but that was all in the past, and circumstances forced him to turn away from those thoughts.

The bushes along the path rustled again and Miss Bingley rushed into speech. "I am not here to discuss your wife, Mr. Wickham. I am come to ask you to assist me in making Darcy jealous. He is tied to Eliza, but if you, the most handsome man here — after Darcy — seemed taken with my company, I might make a dent in his controlled emotions."

"My dear Miss Bingley, are you suggesting..." Wickham paused as sounds came from the other side of the bushes, "I do believe you are correct, Miss Bingley. I believe we are not alone."

The rustling grew louder. Miss Bingley glanced around, then rushed into speech. "Please do as I asked. I must go." She turned back the way she came, and almost slammed into her sister. "Louisa, whatever are you doing out here in the cold?"

"I expect the same as you, Caroline, getting a breath of fresh air." Mrs. Hurst glanced over her sister's shoulder. "Good evening, Mr. Wickham. We are saddened to be deprived of your presence of late. I hope you will remedy the situation while we are all visiting in the area."

"If it were my choice, ma'am, you would never suffer from the lack of my presence." Wickham left unsaid the words they knew as well as he did. He was no longer welcome at Pemberley where they had first met. "Perhaps, I can make amends for that oversight, and sooner than you might imagine." He stopped speaking because a loud rustling in the bushes to the right drew their attention.

A swift heartbeat later, Mr. Hurst burst through the greenery. "I say, wife, what are you doing out here in the dark?"

Mrs. Hurst stared at her husband, astounded he had left liquid refreshment long enough to come out of the house. However, she quickly surmised his appearance did not bode well for her if she responded incorrectly. "I came with Caroline to enjoy the fresh air. Did you not get overheated, sir?"

"Caroline?" Mr. Hurst turned his head from side-to-side and blinked as Caroline stepped closer. "Oh, thought you were a shadow, m'dear. This garden is full of people out taking the air." He lifted an arm in a swiping motion and almost lost his balance. "That Colonel Forester almost trampled me over in the dark." He pointed in the direction where earlier, Wickham and Mrs. Forester had heard a rustling in the hedge.

"Oh, Hurst, how you carry on when you are in your cups. Do take a long respite in this night air to clear your head." Mrs. Hurst grabbed her sister's arm. "I must escort Caroline safely inside. I declare, her skin is quite chilled." With those words, Mrs. Hurst tugged Caroline along the path.

Mr. Hurst stepped closer to Wickham and peered at him from wide eyes. "I am on to you, sir. You think you can smear your charm around and do as you please, but I am aware of your tricks."

"Pray tell, sir, of what are you speaking?" Wickham stiffened the least bit. Not that he had any fear of a man twice his age and already half in his cups, but a loose tongue could put him in an uncomfortable situation with Lydia.

Mr. Hurst's body seemed to wind around in his shoes before he steadied himself and pointed a shaking finger in Wickham's face. "My wife, sir. I am speaking of my wife and I am warning you to stay away from her." His body did that winding motion again and he frowned. "My wife. Where is she? She was standing right there not more than a minute past."

"Mrs. Hurst and her sister went back inside, sir." Wickham looked down from his considerable height at the shorter man. "Might I suggest you should do the same?"

"Suggest all you want, you...you —"

"Hurst, you do not seem well. Would it not be better if you returned to your wife?"

"Ah, yes, m'wife. I warn you, Wickham. I mean what I say. Stay away from my wife or you will regret it until your last breath." Mr. Hurst stumbled as he turned around. "I must find some refreshment to warm my insides. Blasted cold. Feel it all the way to my bones." He wandered off down the path, mumbling as he went.

◌◌◌

On the other side of the shrubs, sheltered by the tall overgrown bushes, Kitty covered her mouth to conceal her gasp. How could Mr. Hurst threaten Lydia's husband in such a manner? Hand clutched to her chest, Kitty tried to think of what she must do. She had followed Denny to the garden, hoping to spend some time with him, but lost sight of him in the shadows. The moon half covered by clouds and soft glow from the windows was not enough to guide her around the garden. So far the evening was a disappointment, and hearing this conversation made things worse.

To start, Lydia and Wickham arrived late — so she had no time to converse with her sister before the ball. Even when she entered the ballroom and was amongst all those officers, Lydia seemed vexed. Kitty had missed Lydia since she and Wickham relocated to the north. They exchanged letters, but Kitty longed to hear all the news her sister left out when writing, for Lydia never had the patience or attention for her correspondence. But all evening Lydia was either clinging to Wickham's arm or delivering insults to anyone unfortunate enough to speak to her.

Kitty was of the opinion that marriage had made no improvement in Lydia's disposition, and she longed for the fun and laughter she found in Denny's company. However, speaking to her old friend had proved difficult. Denny arrived with the guests from Lucas Lodge and seemed to have time only for Mrs. Forester.

Kitty stomped her foot, frustration making her forget she was hiding from the men on the other side of the hedge. But it was so unfair. Lydia went to Brighton last summer and she was younger than Kitty. Now some of the militia were here at Jane's ball, but no one would talk to her. She wanted fun the same as Lydia did. But what vexed Kitty even more than the lack of interest from guests was being ignored by her old friend Denny, while he gave his attention to Mrs. Forester, who was already married.

Why did Mrs. Forester encourage single men like Denny and Captain Carter when she already had a husband? Colonel Forester was their commanding officer, and not as pleasing in his appearance and personality, and Mrs. Forester gathered other officers around her with smiles and giggles. Couldn't she be happy with the status of being a colonel's wife?

And now, to add to her unrest, Kitty mulled the threat she had overheard Bingley's bother-in-law deliver to Wickham. Even Jane with her calm disposition would be unhappy at learning Wickham and Mr. Hurst had exchanged harsh words at her ball.

Whatever would poor Bingley think of such an exchange? He was as good-natured as Jane and by far the friendliest of her sisters' new husbands, and Kitty dreaded to think what he might say when he learned about this incident.

Perhaps she should keep what she had heard to herself. Yet to what end, if Mr. Hurst was sincere in his threats to Wickham? She dared not ask her mother what to do, for Mamma would react with a fit of her nerves and ruin the ball. Papa would only pat her on the head and tell her to be a good daughter. Kitty clenched her hands in her skirts as she sighed. Life had been so dull since Lydia left for Brighton. Even her elopement with Wickham proved little distraction after she was found safe. When Lydia married and moved to Newcastle, Kitty had even less to do to occupy her time. And now, repeating Mr. Hurst's threats to anyone would bring only disbelief and censure upon her head as a silly, overly-imaginative female.

Ohhh! Where was Denny, anyway? She had lost sight of him in the shadows and now see what a state she was in. Why could the clouds not blow away and allow the moon to shine bright on Jane's ball? Why did it have to be so dark? And cold? Why could Denny not turn his attention to her now that Lydia was married?

Kitty shivered and caused limbs of the hedge she was leaning against to shake. Fearful of revealing her presence and bringing a lecture upon her head, she decided to give up the search for Denny and return to the house. Perhaps she would find Lizzy and ask her what to do. Lizzy might lecture her for being foolish enough to come out in the dark alone, but after a sisterly warning, Lizzy would tell her what to do.

Some short distance away, Caroline Bingley came to a halt in mid-stride and jerked her arm from her sister's grip. "Louisa, do stop this rapid pace and explain yourself. Why claim you left the ballroom with me, for you know quite well you arrived on your own?"

"Caroline, what are you thinking?" Louisa snapped, "I said the first words in my head. You know full well how Hurst can vex me. He spends all evening emptying his cup, refuses to dance and ignores my conversation, but let me step out for air and he follows like a devoted servant."

"Did you want your husband's attention? I should think that the last thing you wanted." Caroline sniffed. "After all, you did not marry a man with a countenance as pleasing as Darcy's or Mr. Wickham's. Though, I dare say, you wish your husband had half Wickham's charm."

"You are right in thinking I would change Hurst if I had a choice, but for the time being, I must make amends for my swift departure or I might well regret my actions before the morrow dawns." Louisa turned to retrace her steps, then paused and looked over her shoulder. "Go along inside, Caroline, your skin is really quite chilled."

"What of you, Louisa? You do not even have a shawl."

"Pray do not concern yourself, my dear. My blood is quite warm." Louisa hid a smile behind her glove before remembering it was quite dark and Caroline could not see her face as she hurried away. It she had her wish, she would get warm quite soon.

Cৎৎৎৎৎৎৎৎ

Colonel Forester eased down the path so as not to encounter another guest in the dark. Almost stepping on Mr. Hurst was bad enough. Yet Hurst was so full of drink, perhaps he would not recall the incident. It seemed possible, for Hurst was so far in his cups he made no effort to lower his voice while threatening Wickham. Still, Forester felt a certain amount of sympathy for the man's ire. He also found himself searching for results on this dark night, but fate was not in his favor. He was so focused on discovering his wife's whereabouts that he had ignored the need for stealth and barreled into Hurst. Still, some measure of satisfaction was his, for he had not found his wife in Wickham's arms as he had feared.

Though, in truth, he had not discovered his wife's whereabouts at all. Since the militia moved to Brighton , he had suspected his wife fancied Wickham more than was considered proper. But he would be the first to admit his young wife was easy on the eye. He was not the least surprised she was the center of attention where ever the militia were stationed.

He had reservations, however, about her becoming too familiar with one of his officers, in particular. Wickham's attention troubled him. For that reason, he suggested his wife invite Lydia Bennet to come with them to Brighton. But his plan ended in failure. He and his wife suffered embarrassment when Wickham used the opportunity to slip away to London with Lydia, while she was under their guardianship. Despite their subsequent marriage, and Wickham's new commission in Newcastle, he was never really sure of his wife's feelings for Wickham.

In his opinion, commanding officers must maintain an air of authority and status. Yet his encounters with Wickham cost him both, as his actions tonight proved, for he was tiptoeing around Mr. Bingley's garden in the dark, looking for his wife. And worried where he might find her.

CRBD

Denny slipped behind a tall hedge soon as the weak moonlight revealed Colonel Forester in the shadows a few feet away. He had followed Mrs. Forester when she left the ballroom, but took the wrong path and lost sight of her in the dark. Only the light color of her gown stood out in the odd shaft of light from a ballroom window. The moon was quickly becoming obscured by clouds and provided little light. If not for the white trim on Colonel Forester's uniform, in two more strides Denny would have been nose to nose with his commanding officer.

Not daring to move a muscle, Denny stood rigid and listened to sounds in the night as he waited for Colonel Forester to go past. Earlier, he almost walked into Mr. Bingley's sisters and now his superior officer was roaming around the grounds. There must be more people in this garden than in the ballroom.

Finally, the colonel passed and Denny eased out of hiding to continue his search. He wanted to meet Mrs. Forester alone. This might be their only chance for one of their secret rendezvous while they were away from Brighton.

CRBD

Across the garden, in the opposite direction, Lydia trudged through the dark. She was determined to discover who Harriet was meeting. To that end, she kept her focus on the pale figure ahead of her on the path and held her temper. Harriet better not meet Wickham. Or Denny either, for she knew Harriet's flirtatious ways, and did not wish to find her old friend entangled with his commander's wife.

She had enjoyed Harriet's company when the militia was stationed here in Meryton, and overjoyed when Harriet asked her to travel to Brighton as her companion. However, she was not fond of that woman's actions now that she had married one of Harriet's special favorites. A fact well concealed even though she learned later that her presence provided some distraction for Harriet's actions. Lydia sighed as she stomped down the path. Now that Wickham was her husband, she resented Harriet's attempts to continue her acquaintance with him.

She felt the need to protect Denny, as well. He was always an enjoyable companion when she needed a dance partner, before she had married Wickham, and she could not bear to watch him fall under Harriet's spell.

Surely, if Colonel Forester knew of Harriet's flirting, he would not tolerate his wife's actions. Though how a man could reach his rank and not use the eyes in his head to see what was happening with his own wife, was beyond Lydia's understanding. Therefore, it was up to her to protect Denny and Wickham. Truthfully, she delighted in thoughts of denying Harriet pleasure, as well. When she met up with Harriet, Lydia intended to speak her mind while they were alone in the garden. At least, she thought they would be alone, but when she paused to determine where the figure she was following had turned, she heard a squawk from the other side of the garden. But that noise sounded more like a surprised female than of any animal she was familiar with.

Lydia stopped and stared into the night. She was about to reach the conclusion she had lost sight of Harriet, when a hand took hold of her arm. Letting loose a screech, Lydia jerked her arm free. But as her vision adjusted to the darkness, her nose twitched at the familiar scents of lavender and vanilla that brought visions of her sister to mind. "Lizzy, you gave me a such fright. Why are you prowling around in the dark? Why did you not alert me to your presence?"

"I followed you from the ballroom." Lizzy glanced about the garden. "I confess, if I had not had you in my sight, I would not venture out with all these moving shadows. What are you about? Are you meeting Wickham?"

"Not that it is any concern of yours, but in you must know, I was following Harriet." Lydia huffed. "And it wasn't very nice of you to give me a fright, but since you are here, we may as well walk together for I am not ready to return." Lydia sighed. "Really, Lizzy, why are you out here alone? I thought you would cling to Darcy's arm now that you succeeded in catching him for your husband."

"Is that your view of matrimony, Lydia? Your husband is a catch, same as holding a pole in a pond to lure a fish."

"Don't put on your airs with me, Lizzy Bennet. I know you wanted Darcy." Lydia cast a frustrated glance toward the last place she had seen Harriet's shadow. It was too late to catch the woman now and she blamed Lizzy. "For all your claims that Darcy didn't interest you, I saw the way you watched him at socials. You think you are so much better than I am because I ran off with Wickham, and you waited for Darcy to beg for your hand. Well, I found the man I wanted and I went after him. What is so wrong about that?"

"Lydia, please, I followed you out here to have a conversation, not ponder over past mistakes."

"So, you do think you are better than me." Lydia whipped her skirts out of the way and rushed down the path at a fast clip. "I knew what you thought." She stopped abruptly and whirled to face Lizzy. "Just as I know you once had feelings for my husband. Do you care for him still, Lizzy? Is that why you try to make me look bad?"

Lizzy struggled for a calm tone. "Lydia, do be sensible. I always wished to marry for love, as you well know. Do not doubt my feelings for my husband."

"You were making eyes at my husband, before you met Darcy." Lydia snapped. "Now, leave me alone, Lizzy. I came outside for a reason."

"What reason would that be?" Lizzy put a hand on Lydia's arm. "What are you doing, Lydia? Surely, you are not considering a liaison outside of marriage. Please think of what you are doing, Lydia. You could lose all with such behavior."

Lydia whirled to face Lizzy and barked a laugh. "I am married now, Lizzy. I do not need your lectures."

"Perhaps not," Lizzy stepped in front of her, "but you will listen to what I have to say about my husband."

"What? Are you warning me off Darcy?" Lydia let loose a fit of giggles. "Oh, Lord, Lizzy, you are so funny. I knew there was a reason I missed being at home."

"You do, really? Oh, my dear Lydia, we have missed seeing you too."

"Well, forget I said that. I am married to Wickham now and I love him."

"I know you do, and that is why it is important that you to understand what I have to say. We all wish that your circumstances were better. I want to help when I can. But Lydia, you must stop Wickham from asking Darcy for money."

"Why should I? Darcy is married to my sister. He has more money than he needs, and goodness knows Wickham and I never have enough. What does it hurt to remind Darcy he has a responsibility to help his family?"

"Lydia, please —"

"Oh, Lizzy and Lydia," Kitty gasped as she bumped into Lizzy.

"I was so busy looking behind me, I would have missed you if you hadn't been arguing."

"Kitty, why are you out alone in the dark?" Lizzy demanded.

"Silly," Lydia snickered, "Kitty, are you still afraid of your own shadow? I am surprised you would venture out here on you own, if indeed, you are alone."

"Lydia, that is not fair." Kitty whirled in her older sister's direction. "Lizzy, make her take it back. She thinks she is better than me just because she married Wickham, but we all know — "

"Kitty, Lydia, that is enough. You have been apart months, can you not enjoy each other's company for one night without fighting? Jane will be disappointed if you argue at her ball."

"I am a married woman, now." Lydia tilted her chin up. "I do not miss such childish chatter."

"You would not act so haughty if you knew what I just heard," Kitty retorted.

"I am finished with this childish game." Lydia whirled around and stalked off toward the house. "I will see you inside."

Determined to have the last word, Kitty called, "Watch your step, Lydia. You never know who might be lurking in the bushes."

"Hush, Kitty. You know how Lydia is when she is vexed." Lizzy took hold of Kitty's arm. "Come, we should return to the ball and on the way you can tell me what you heard."

"I will Lizzy, but you will not be pleased, in the least." Kitty locked arms with Lizzy, happy to have a sister to chat with instead of facing Mary's condemnation all the time. "I followed Denny out of the ballroom — "

"Kitty, you know — "

"I only wanted to talk to him. And Lydia followed him too." Kitty stopped and stared at her sister's shadowy features, dully illuminated by the half-covered moon. "Lizzy, I think Lydia still has feelings for Denny. I know she married Wickham, but she knew Denny first; and I am not convinced but what she regrets her choice of husbands."

"You must be mistaken, Kitty," Lizzy insisted. "Not long before you appeared, Lydia declared her love for Wickham."

"Then why is Wickham chasing after another woman who already has a husband?" Kitty tilted her chin up and strode forward, happy for once that she, not Lydia, was the one to shock Lizzy. "I just heard Mr. Hurst warn Wickham to stay away from his wife, if you doubt my word."

CRSO

Jane sent her husband an affectionate glance as he approached. "How go things with you, dear Mr. Bingley? Do you think our party is a success?"

"Rather well, I do believe, my dear." Bingley glanced about the room, his usual convivial smile across his face. Guests were meandering around the room during the rest from dancing. "Several of the gentlemen are partaking of the refreshment and discussing the news Colonel Fitzwilliam has to share about the recent conflicts. Pity Colonel Forester is not around to give his views on how things were in Brighton." His glance roamed the room, again. "Have you seen him?"

"Many guests left the room, perhaps to stroll in the garden to cool off after dancing." Jane's lips twitched. "Mrs. Forester departed and so did Lydia. I am certain Colonel Forester accompanied them, as it is very dark outside." Jane glanced around. "I think Lizzy must have joined them, as well."

"It is frightfully warm in here," Bingley tugged at his neck cloth, "even for a cold night the room heated quickly. I say, wife, have you spoken with Caroline about your plan? I do hope she will let go her ridiculous attachment to Darcy now that he is married to your sister."

"I beg to differ with you, husband." Jane arched a brow and aimed a teasing smile at her beloved. "Caroline's reaction is not as outrageous as you seem to suggest. Lizzy's Mr. Darcy is handsome and has deep pockets, and that is enough to turn most female heads."

Bingley allowed a smile to acknowledge Jane's teasing tone. "But not yours, I pray, dear Jane."

"Never fear, Mr. Bingley. I am quite content with your attentions, dear husband." Jane flushed with pleasure at being able to say the words so true. From the moment her dear Charles and Mr. Darcy entered the room on the first night they met she had not given Mr. Darcy, or any other man, a second glance.

"Your kind words turn my head, my dear." Bingley's smile slipped as he reverted to the subject of his sister. "Yet, to put a finer point on the subject, the fact is, Darcy never gave Caroline any indication he favored her attentions. He invited us to visit Pemberley, and spent time in my various abodes as well, but beyond those occasions, he never sought her out. Yet, Caroline set her hat at him from the first encounter."

"Do not be so harsh in your judgment of Caroline, dear Bingley. The female mind works in mysterious ways, and I dare say half the women in this room wanted Darcy's attention that first evening we met. Do you recall that social at Meryton?"

"How could I forget, my dear Jane? You were the loveliest creature I had ever set eyes on and I fear I showed my attraction to all in attendance."

"Now you are flattering me, dear sir." A shy smile brought warmth to Jane's face as she glanced about the room. "I do so hope the guests taking air will return soon. The room seems less enjoyable with so many . I noticed that Denny and Captain Carter have departed as well, and now I cannot see Mary King. I wanted to speak to her when we were on our own, to make her feel welcome."

"Despair not, wife, I am certain you are only missing the chance to converse with Lizzy. As as to enjoyment," Bingley nodded toward the end of the room as a burst of laughter erupted from the gentlemen gathered there, "your ball sounds a success. Now I fear I must rejoin the gentlemen for it sounds as if I am missing all the fun."

೦೪೭೦

Captain Carter eased through the shadows as if he were on a training mission with his troops. Caution seemed the wisest choice since he had heard whispers and rustling in the hedges and lost sight of Denny at the same time. Denny's career in the militia would be on the line if he were caught in a compromising situation with Mrs. Forester, but Carter planned to use restraint in searching for Denny to protect his own position. He would be well advised to act with care as there were so many people afoot in the grounds on this dark, chilly night.

Lydia and Kitty had departed from the ballroom after Denny, and only the Lord knew of their intentions. Because they had departed separately, Carter did not worry too much about them encountering Denny, except, like Mrs. Forester, Lydia was now a married woman. That seemed not to affect her familiarity with Denny, but then neither did Mrs. Forester restrain herself from enjoying Denny's attentions. Even Wickham had received favorable smiles from that lady, and considering the circumstances of Wickham's departure from the regiment, Carter could barely contain his own surprise.

Though, after he considered the situation, he acknowledged that

Lydia had not been received so warmly by either Mrs. Forester or the Colonel. Nor had the Colonel done more than greet Wickham with a nod. Carter assumed the colonel still held Wickham responsible for the uproar following his elopement with Lydia.

Frankly, Carter could understand Colonel Forester's reaction. Things had not been as usual in the regiment since that incident. Some of the men muttered comments as to the colonel's handling of that situation. Even officers of the regiment pushed social boundaries and showed questionable familiarity with Mrs. Forester. In Carter's personal opinion, the colonel's command had weakened because of his association with Wickham.

This gathering was the first social event with all involved being in the same place, and only served to show the strained relations still remained. Worse even, young Denny had blundered into the midst of a situation he seemed not to comprehend when he turned his attentions to Mrs. Forester.

In Carter's opinion, their current stay at Lucas Lodge was only one example of Denny's lack of observation. His own position would be safer if he kept his distance from all involved in these events, but Carter could not ignore the danger to his friend.

Denny's actions threatened his best interests, as previous dealings with Wickham had proved. Wickham had borrowed money from his friends, and had the poor judgment to take his insult to Denny even further. On one furlough, before Lydia arrived in Brighton, Wickham had made familiar overtures to Denny's sister, Peggy. Had it been any other officer in the regiment besides Denny, fleeing to Gretna Green with that young woman for a quick marriage ceremony was all that would have saved Wickham. Yet Denny's easy manner prevailed. He managed to soothe matters over, and Peggy married one of his associates she had favored before Wickham appeared on the scene.

Lost in contemplation, and totally out of sight of Denny, Carter gave a start of surprise when Miss King spoke his name from a nearby shadow. "Pardon me, Miss King, but the hedges grow so tall and the night is so dark, I took no notice of you standing there."

"No reason to apologize, Captain Carter. It seems reasonable that two people should have the same inclination to take cool air after the exertions of dancing, do you not agree?"

"Indeed I do, Miss King, and may I add I consider it my good fortune that we are of the same mind." The dark night hid her features from him, but Carter could imagine the glow in her green eyes, and visualize light reflecting on her bright, red hair as he had notice earlier in the ballroom. In all honesty, the very sight of Miss Mary King sent a stinging sensation through his chest. And that was a feat few females had ever managed as he keep his feeling to himself.

He kept his guard alert, allowing only light flirtation—as with his previous associations with Lydia and Kitty Bennet—and concentrated on his future in the militia. Carter did not consider himself among the group of officers who took their position as lightly as Wickham and Denny seemed to do. "And speaking of the dancing, may I take this opportunity to compliment you on your skilled execution of the steps, Miss King? A finer form on the dance floor I have rarely observed."

"I am convinced your exertions must have addled your brain, kind sir, for I am certain my efforts would attract no notice if the Bennet sisters were dancing."

"You are quite mistaken, Miss King, if you are under the impression that your dancing skills were not noticed. For you must recall, only two Miss Bennets are present tonight, and to my knowledge, Mary Bennet never dances. So I am certain you have no competition."

Her voice bubbling with laughter, Mary replied. "How gallant you are, Captain Carter. I am not the least offended by your calling the situation to my notice." She glanced over her shoulder and shivered at the surrounding blackness of the night. "Shall we continue our walk together, so as not to risk bumping into each other in the dark?"

"I would be delighted." Carter offered his arm. Denny would have to look after his own head on this night. "Though, I would not mind bumping into you in the dark, Miss King."

They were so occupied in conversation Mary forgot her earlier suspicion that Captain Carter might have followed Lydia Wickham to the garden. In fact, she was so focused on his charm, she paid no notice to Colonel Forester standing in the shadows as they walked along the path. Indeed, Mary was so impressed with Captain Carter's easy presence, she forgot her need to constantly act the proper lady, and allowed herself to relax enough so that she enjoyed the captain's company immensely.

Chapter Three

*S*uffering from the lack of Lydia's attention long as she could stand, Mrs. Bennet was ready to insist on a conversation with her youngest. "My dear Jane, have you seen Lydia or Wickham?"

"No, Mamma They departed to take a breath of air some time ago, and I have not seen them since." Jane shared her mother's impatience, but for different reasons. How could she find a match for Kitty if she remained absent from the ballroom half the night? Of course, Kitty would have followed Lydia out to the garden. Evidently so had Caroline, leaving Jane of two minds as to whether to even concern herself with organizing matches for them.

"I so wanted time to visit with my dear girl before Wickham takes her back up north to that awful regiment. You know well as do I, Lydia preferred to stay in Brighton with her friends, but nothing would do except Wickham change regiments."

"Mamma, surely you must see it was not possible for Wickham and Lydia to remain in Brighton after all that happened." Jane sent an urgent glance around the room, wishing for Lizzy's support, but her sister seemed to be absent from the room, as well. "Where is Papa?"

"Where do you think? I a quite certain he has found a secluded spot to read a book. You must recall what he is like. For my part, my poor nerves will not tolerate so much reading. I cannot understand how he finds such contentment in books." Mrs. Bennet raised a lace handkerchief to fan her face. "Lizzy is very like him, you know. Always reading, and filling her head with nonsense. Always with that little smirk on her face, as if she knows something no one else does. And I can tell you, Jane, it is not complimentary to her countenance at all. Why I would much rather dance and enjoy myself, as dear Lydia does, than ruin my eyes reading a book."

"Mamma, perhaps some refreshment would do you good. Can I get you a refreshing cup of tea?"

"Tea? Really Jane, I will thank you not to speak to me as if I were in my dotage." Mrs. Bennet's chin angled high. "If you must know, I was once the belle of gatherings such as this, Jane, and not that many years hence. Now, I would like to speak to my dear Lydia, but a great number of your guests seem to have departed the ballroom. Really, Jane, you must plan your socials to be more entertaining."

"I am certain the guests will return soon. Much refreshed by the night air and ready to dance the night away." Jane concealed a sigh as she glanced around the room. In truth, she found hosting the party taxing, even without Mamma's comments adding to her disquiet. Not that far past, she enjoyed strolls in the garden during a ball. But, now she was the hostess, and she longed for the guests to resume dancing as proof they were enjoying themselves. "Have you had a chance to converse with my Aunt Gardiner?"

"Of course, and with my sister Phillips, as well. And, if you must know, Jane, I am quite fatigued from conversing with my sisters." Mrs. Bennet flapped her handkerchief in front of her face. "Tell me, Jane, do you not think Darcy should help Lydia and dear Wickham? After all, he has ten thousand a year. Surely he can do with a thousand or two less and not miss it at all. Why, he could even assist your Papa, if he were so willing. I cannot think why he should do otherwise, now that he has married Lizzy."

"Mamma! Please do not approach Mr. Darcy —"

"Approach him? Really Jane, you are beginning to sound as judgmental as Lizzy. Who said anything about approaching him? I cannot imagine conversing with such a high-nose as Mr. Darcy. But your Papa could if he set his mind to it, and why should he not?" Mrs. Bennet's voice rose in competition with the music, as the musicians resumed playing at the other end of the room, and Jane wished for nothing more than to melt into the floor.

"Mamma, please —"

"Do not 'Mamma please' me in that tone young lady. You could help our dear Lydia, as well. Mr. Bingley may have only five thousand a year, but surely that is more than enough for him to share with Lydia and poor Wickham."

"Mamma, please—"

"Jane, my dear, this is such a lovely party."

"Lovely? How can you say such nonsense, sister?" Mrs. Bennet huffed. "Half the guests are absent from the room, and now there are hardly enough people to dance."

"Oh, Aunt Gardiner, I am so happy to see you." Jane cast a loving glance at her favorite aunt, and prayed her presence would distract her mother. "How are my dear cousins, for I am certain they are much grown since last I saw them?"

"Sister, Jane is distressed so many of her guests have departed to the garden," Mrs. Bennet's voice seemed to carry over the entire ballroom. "This is her first ball, you know, and she has not yet learned that being a hostess includes keeping her guests entertained."

Jane exchanged glances with her aunt and sighed. To the best of her memory, Mamma was always the guest at social events. Jane feared losing her good nature if she stayed hear more of Mamma's comments. Perhaps she and dear Bingley should take a stroll in the garden, as well, but she knew it was not possible. She must remain accessible to her guests, added to which, she had not yet had a chance to speak with Miss King. "Oh, but Mamma, I am quite happy for my guests to entertain themselves."

"Of course you are, my dear, and very sensible I might add." Mrs. Gardiner quickly agreed. "Now, do feel free to go about your duties, for I shall I visit with your mother and catch up on the rest of her news."

"What duties does she have pray tell, sister? Bingley has enough servants so Jane need never lift a hand. I was just saying to her, before you joined us, Bingley and Darcy could help her family if they would." Mrs. Bennet sniffed.

ဢ

After urging Caroline to return to the house, Louisa hurried back along the path, where they had left Hurst with Wickham and kept a watchful glance ahead. If she was careful, she could avoid her husband in the dark night, and continue with her original plan. Soon she spied Mr. Hurst, weaving his way unsteadily along the path towards her. Quickly, she stepped into a deep nook between two tall hedges and held her breath until Mr. Hurst passed. Giving him ample time to disappear in the darkness, she continued along the path and spotted a light figure in the darkness that could only be a female in a light colored gown.

Again, she ducked into a crevice in the hedges. Pausing to push limbs out of the way of her vision, Louisa focused on the figure capturing her attention. She had not a doubt that she was observing Mrs. Forester, for that woman was wearing the lightest-colored gown at the ball, as if she were unmarried. However, much to Louisa's distress, Mrs. Forester was soon joined by a man in uniform. Clenching her fingers on a sprig of hedge, Louisa strained her sight to identify the dull figure with the bright white bands indicating his garb. It was not Colonel Forester she was certain, for he was not as tall as this figure. And the intensity of the couple's attention in each other hinted that this was not a couple bored by years of marriage.

Even so, Louisa could not move until she identified the man with Mrs. Forester. After several thudding heartbeats, she began to breathe again, for she determined the man was not Mr. Wickham. Of that she was quite certain, for Wickham was much taller. Then she heard the low, masculine laugh, and identified the voice. Mrs. Forester was with Wickham's friend, Denny. They were standing very close together. Definitely a secret meeting. How very interesting, Louisa sniffed. She knew a thing or two about clandestine meetings. Still, she had no time to speculate on this encounter, for she, too, had an assignation planned for this dark night.

Easing out of the hedge and onto the path, she looked back over her shoulder to make certain Mr. Hurst was long departed. Then, convinced she was safe, she hurried on her way back to where she had first encountered Caroline and Wickham.

To her delight, there he still remained. His shadow was tall and dark in the deep of night. There was no light to show her the glimmer in his eyes or allow her to feast on the charm of his slow smile, but she recalled his actions from earlier encounters, and the memories were enough to heat her blood with longing. "Ah, there you are, sir. Do I find you alone at last?"

Wickham reached for her hand, erring from his target only enough to brush his fingers against her breast. Enjoying the gasp indicating her quick response, he brought her hand to his lips. He took his time, allowing the heat of his breath to warm her gloved skin. "Finally, we are alone, my dear. I feared you would not return."

"How could I stay away, my dear Wickham? It has been so long," Darkness added to the passion in Louisa's whisper. "Though, this garden is as populated as the ballroom was earlier, and I fear we have no privacy."

"You need not fear, my dear. Perhaps others are as intent on escaping prying eyes as we are."

"Oh, Wickham, you make our meeting sound so enticing. Though, I made several attempts before finding you alone, it is worth the effort." Louisa gasped as his fingers traced the low neckline of her gown. His touch brought forth her groan of pleasure. "Oh, please, do not stop, I beg of you, dear sir."

"My dear, I am all yours for the moment and ready to follow your smallest command."

"Then let us be gone from this place, and find a nook for privacy, dear sir, for I wish to have you alone with no eyes prying into our activities." Louisa covered his wandering fingers with her hand and pressed into her chest.

"That has been my wish since I observed your arrival in the ballroom, my dear. Come, I will find us a quiet corner where we can be undisturbed while we share our hunger." Wickham grasped her hand and led her to a secluded nook in the hedge which he had discovered earlier. Once convinced of their seclusion, he turned to take her lush curves in his embrace.

СЗВО

Caroline glanced at the stairs leading up to the ballroom as she passed through the front entrance. Facing Darcy and his adoring new wife again, turned her stomach sour and made her want to delay returning to the ballroom as long as she could. Though she should have assisted Louisa in soothing Mr. Hurst's ire, she could not bring herself to do so. She found Hurst's desire for drink as distasteful as his behavior and wished to avoid the encounter. Thoughts of warming her cold hands by the library fire seemed a good option, before she retired to her room to repair her hair from all the snags in the bushes.

The twigs hanging from her hair and gown were her only reward for thinking she could gain Wickham's assistance in making Darcy regret his choice of a wife. Though Wickham had not refused her request, she could hear the hint of amusement in his voice and imagine the knowing smile on his face in response to her appeal. Yet, in her opinion, Wickham was a waste of manhood. It was a shame, actually, for he had a handsome countenance and enough charm to lure widows out of their sorrow, but his sense of privilege left him lacking.

Still, had he been in possession of a fortune equal to that which she inherited, she could imagine trying to seek his attention. However, her father left her well situated, and Wickham possessed no funds to secure the future, to her slight regret. Perhaps it was just as well he married Lydia Bennet. She might have lowered her standards and acted drastically when Darcy spoke of Eliza's hand.

∽∾

Maggie Brown assisted Miss Georgiana Darcy with her preparations in dressing for the ball, and then was left to her own devices. Normally, she would accompany Miss Darcy to the ball, but tonight she was not needed as Mr. and Mrs. Darcy would be present. It was a relief for Maggie feared coming face to face with Mr. Wickham almost as much as she longed to see him. It was her greatest desire to converse with him in private, but not in a ballroom full of women wearing fine gowns.

Not that she was ashamed of her status. To be perfectly honest, she was thankful for her position in service with the Darcys as Miss Georgiana Darcy's companion. Georgiana was one of the most accommodating people she had every encountered, but Maggie had no wish to be compared with women dressed in finery the likes of Miss Darcy's or Mr. Wickham's quickly acquired wife.

After Miss Georgiana left the room for the ball, Maggie straightened her belongings, then made her way down to the library. Earlier, she had secured Miss Darcy's permission, and was glad she had when she opened the library door. A warm blaze glowed in the fireplace, and Maggie soaked up the warmth, for the night was as cold as her aching heart. If only she could huddle under the covers with her cousin Mary, as they had as children, and talk over her fears. But even that comfort was denied her for Mary's new position in society was precarious at best, and revealing their relationship could hamper Mary's acceptance in society.

It was true, Mary longed for recognition as the heiress she was, but her acceptance by local society meant far more than invitations to the proper socials. Establishing Mary's position in the county was important to both their futures.

After standing in front of the fireplace until she finally felt warmed from the chilling trip to Netherfield, Maggie searched the long walls of shelves for something to read. Selecting a volume of poems, she settled in a wing chair in a distant corner so she wouldn't appear too presumptuous if any of the Bingleys' guests entered the room. She preferred reading novels. but, many older libraries in the homes they visited rarely contained the current volumes she enjoyed. Still, not all was lost, as she could share her readings with Miss Georgiana on their next walk.

She was well into the pages of the book when the door opened, and the sound of rustling skirts approached the fireplace. Forgetting caution, as she was not a guest, Maggie peered past the wing chair and locked glances with Miss Caroline Bingley. Jumping to her feet as soon as she recognized Mr. Bingley's sister,, Maggie made a slight curtsy, "Begging your pardon, ma'am. I hope you do not mind my reading one of your volumes."

"Who are you?" Caroline Bingley looked down her long nose at Maggie. Then said, as if they rarely met, which was not the case at all, "Ah, yes, Miss Darcy's companion. So you like to read, Miss –"

"Miss Brown, ma'am. Yes, I find a good book to be relaxing."

"And you have nothing better to do than sit in front of the fire this night and read? I dare say Miss Darcy is too young to under- stand how to manage her servants."

"I asked Miss Darcy's permission, ma'am, as we are away from Pemberley, and did not cart all our studies for the trip."

"Mm." Miss Bingley's glance roamed over Maggie as if she were examining something from the back of a horse, "I am certain with Miss Darcy's sweet disposition she was amenable. However, in my opinion, you should have duties to keep you occupied, but, as these books belong to my brother and Miss Darcy is his guest, I suppose you might as well make use of them. Goodness knows, I have no need to do so." With that comment, Miss Bingley whirled on her heels and departed the room.

Maggie slumped back down in the chair and gulped a breath to calm her shaking limbs. The likes of people such as Miss Bingley made Mary's acceptance into society questionable. And Maggie, through no intention on her part, had almost caused a scene that could harm Mary's chances if their connection became known. Still, Miss Bingley had given her permission, if somewhat reluctantly, for Maggie to use the library, and the night was long. So she tucked her knees in the chair under her skirts and picked up her book.

ᏣᏆᏋᏅ

Lydia returned to the ballroom and headed directly to her older sister. "Jane, I do hope you are not planning to lecture me as Lizzy has done." Lydia glared at Jane as she brushed a leaf from her skirt. "Pray tell me what is wrong with asking Darcy to help Wickham? After all, Darcy is the one who ruined Wickham's chance of claiming the living he was promised by old Mr. Darcy."

"Lydia, please. Perhaps you are not in possession of all the details."

"I know what my husband has told me. Old Mr. Darcy promised him a living —"

"As a clergyman, Lydia. A position similar to the one our cousin, Mr. Collins, holds," Jane kept her tone low, but firm. "Can you imagine Wickham being happy in such a role?"

"Oh, my word," Lydia burst into a fit of giggles. "Was old-man Darcy out of his gourd? Even on his best days, Wickham does not have the temperament of a clergyman."

"Then you should understand why Mr. Darcy withdrew his support —"

"I certainly cannot. Surely a man of Darcy's position, and deep pockets, could find something for —"

"Lydia, my dearest girl," Mrs. Bennet called from a short distance away, "come and talk with me and your Aunt Gardiner. We have not seen you for so long."

"Oh, Mamma," Lydia glanced at the couples stepping to the music and turned back, "I want to dance and have fun. Talking is for old women." Lydia whirled to stare at the dance floor. "Now, where is Denny? I cannot see Carter or Wickham, either." Lydia added her husband's name almost as an afterthought.

Jane and Mrs. Gardiner exchanged glances.

"But, my dearest girl, we will have no time to visit, if you dance. Come tell me about your life up north." Mrs. Bennet coaxed her youngest child to her side. "Sit and tell me how much you like being married to dear Wickham."

Mrs. Gardiner left her chair and moved to Jane's side. "My dear, I fear the shine has left Lydia's interest in her husband. How long do you think it will take her to accept that she cannot throw a husband away like an old toy?"

"Oh, Aunt Gardiner, I do so fear for her future."

"Do not waste your time and good humor, my dear. Lydia is one of those people who always land on a soft cushion. Has not Mr. Wickham avoided all his past responsibilities? And he will continue to do so in the future, or I miss my guess."

"But to live with so little expectation of life seems a waste—"

"It is said that a life without hope—"

"Oh, Mary, dear, do come tell me about what you are reading now." Aunt Gardiner said as she steered Mary toward the waiting chairs.

CRBO

Captain Carter paused as he and Miss King entered the front door and glanced down the hall to see Caroline Bingley come out of the library and head toward the stairs. Glad they had no reason to interrupt their moments alone, he turned back to his companion. "Miss King, I thoroughly enjoyed our encounter in the garden. May I secure a dance before your card is filled?"

"Indeed you may, Captain Carter, for I, too, enjoyed our conversation." Miss King paused and lifted her chin to look in his face. Candle light from the chandelier overhead revealed a determined sparkle in her eyes. "I hope we can meet again while you are in the neighborhood."

"It would be my pleasure." Carter turned toward the stairs, reluctant to end their time alone, but elated that she had spoken so openly. Rarely had he felt as much at ease in female company as he did with Miss King. Yet he had heard from local gossip about the fortune she had inherited. Could she be unspoiled by the event because, like him, she had not had the advantages of some of the guests at this ball? Regardless, he hoped to pursue the enjoyment they had shared and see what occurred.

As they entered the ballroom, Lydia pranced over, and stopped in front of them, with a pout on her face. "Carter, where have you been? I haven't had a chance to converse with you since we arrived, and I have so missed your company. You must move north to join Wickham's new regiment. Then we can have fun as we used to."

"Mrs. Wickham—"

"Carter, do stop that nonsense. You always called me Lydia. Why change when we are such friends?"

"Very well. Lydia, do you remember Miss King?"

Forced to acknowledge the woman at Carter's side, Lydia's smiling expression transformed into a frown. "Of course I remember Miss King. She distracted my Wickham's affections from my sister Lizzy last time she visited the area." Lydia tossed her head and sniffed. "I suppose I should thank you, Miss King. If you had not interfered, my sister might be married to my husband." Lydia collapsed in a fit of giggles. "How droll that sounds. Can you imagine how miserable Wickham would be if he were married to Lizzy."

"Then perhaps we are all fortunate with the way things worked out for everyone." Mary King replied in an even tone. "If you —"

"Especially you, Miss King, since everyone knows that Wickham was interested in you only because of your fortune."

"Lydia —"

"Do stop worrying, Carter, for Miss King knows I speak the truth, do you not, Miss King?" Without waiting for a response, Lydia continued. "And you are still searching for a husband, I see." Lydia eyed the hand Mary still rested on Carter's arm. "Do you suppose there is some quality you lack, even with your vast source of inherited funds?" Not pausing for breath, Lydia turned to Carter, "Have you seen Denny? I am dying to dance."

"Perhaps Captain Carter will oblige you." Mary King withdrew her hand from the strong arm at her side and kept her tone even, while refusing to look for the captain's reaction to her words. Lydia Wickham's attitude reflected the adversity she faced for wanting to join polite society in this county. Perhaps she should move away and start a life somewhere far from Hertfordshire.

Yet she could not Mary acknowledged to herself as Lydia latched onto Captain Carter's arm and tugged him toward the dance floor. Her cousin could not leave the respectable position she now held because of her personal obligations, and Mary would not leave Maggie to face her future alone. She had offered Maggie a home, but her cousin insisted they would become targets for gossip if any word was discovered of their connection. Mary accepted Maggie's opinion for she knew her cousin was correct. They were bound by mores that examined a single female's actions with close scrutiny, and observers were only satisfied when they dragged out some matter worthy of the local gossips.

She and Maggie must bide their time until such occasion as she was accepted in the social status she desired, then she would assist Maggie. Keeping apart until that time was their only option. Maggie insisted this was necessary. She had no wish to bring unwanted censure upon Mary's actions as they were close as sisters.

For her part, Mary would not rest until she could improve Maggie's lot in life. When she considered of how close she had come to the same fate as her dear cousin, Mary shuddered. It was difficult to believe they were both attracted to the same man. The fact that he had almost destroyed Maggie's life was unthinkable.

"Ah, Miss King, at last I have found you alone," Jane Bingley said as she arrived at Mary's side. "I am so happy you came to our ball this evening. Are you returned to the area to stay?"

"I am currently visiting Lucas Lodge." Mary said as she blinked her astonishment at the contrast between the two sisters. Jane Bingley was soft spoken and kindness itself. Yet, only minutes earlier, her youngest sister had lashed out at Mary with no provocation other than the fact that Wickham had once favored Mary with his attentions. "But I want to thank you for the kind invitation, Mrs. Bingley. I am happy to be here."

"Please, you must call me Jane, Miss King, for I hope that we can be friends."

"Friends?" Caroline Bingley scoffed, pausing as she passed them. "Really, Jane, there is no such thing as friendship between ladies of a similar age, for they all want to attract the attention of the single males in their company. Do you not agree, Miss King?"

Mary King studied Caroline's smooth hair and careful grooming. Miss Bingley must have taken a circuitous route by her room before returning to the ball, for Mary had seen her leave the library looking ruffled and wearing sprigs of the hedge in the garden.

"I agree there is competition among females of a marriageable age, but how can it not exist?" Mary replied, with a determined tilt of her chin. "With so many young men serving in the militia, the chances of finding a proper match are greatly diminished. However, as Mrs. Bingley is in possession of a husband, I feel forming a friendship with her is quite possible."

Jane smiled warmly at Mary and turned to her sister-in-law. "As you can witness, Caroline, not all females feel the need to compete."

"So you say, Jane," Caroline cast a glance around at the guests, "but I do not believe your observation to be truthful, and I have my own sister as proof. Ah, there she is now, though she appears to be wearing some sort of twig arrangement in her hair. I must see if I can be of assistance."

Mary King's glance followed Caroline's tall, elegant figure as she strolled across the room toward her sister. "I fear I will never measure up to the expectations of some people in this county."

"Have no worry, Miss King, for I share similar feelings." Jane smiled as Mary King sent a startled glance in her direction. "I have discovered that marriage does not bridge all gaps. My upbringing in this county is a point my husband's sisters object to, but I hope I shall win them over with time."

"I do so admire your confidence, Mrs. Bingley."

Jane smiled. "It is not confidence, Miss King, but desperation. For I am determined to be a wife of which Mr. Bingley can be proud, therefore, I must make a good impression on his sisters."

"How can you, when they act so superior —"

"It is only their upbringing, Miss King. If you and I had been raised with riches, I am certain we would act as Bingley's sisters do and look down our noses at all who dare to grace our presence."

Jane and Mary exchanged glances and then burst out laughing.

Mary sobered first. "You would never act in such a way, Mrs. Bingley. I have known you but a short while, yet I am certain you would never belittle even the poorest acquaintance."

Jane's smile reflected her pleasure at the kind words. "I believe we are bound to be friends, Miss King. Do say you feel the same, for I miss my sister, Lizzy, now that she has married and moved away. I could well do with a local companion."

Mary King met Jane's gaze earnestly, "I do so hope I will be in the area long enough to become better acquainted with you, Mrs. Bingley."

"Are you thinking of leaving, Miss King?"

"I would if I were free —"

"Please, do consider that attitudes can change, Miss King. Pray give us a chance to prove we are not all so full of ourselves that we can ignore new acquaintances. I fear I shall despair of my own lot, if you believe such past behaviors to be a measure of our society."

"How can that be, Mrs. Bingley, for you were raised in this county and are accepted by all."

"Before my marriage, that was true, Miss King. Nevertheless, now I find I face the same issues as you do. As Bingley's new wife, I must start afresh, for my husband's associates do not hold me in the same regard as those whom I have known all my life. Yet it is my greatest wish to earn their good opinion for my dear Bingley's sake, as well as my own."

"I desire the same acceptance, Mrs. Bingley —"

"Oh, Denny, there you are," Lydia squealed as she rushed past them to grab Denny's hand, as he returned to the ballroom. "Why have you been gone so long and why do you look so ruffled after a sedate stroll in the garden?"

Denny's face filled with color as he saw that Jane and Mary were gazing at him as was Lydia. "Come dance, Lydia and I will tell you of my tussle with a wild hedge."

Giggling carefree as a girl, Lydia clasped her arm in his and skipped so she and Denny quickly joined the other couples on the dance floor.

"I had hoped marriage would improve Lydia's behavior," Lizzy murmured to Jane as she joined them at the edge of the dance floor, "but I fear she is not much changed."

"Lizzy, do you remember Miss King?"

"Yes, of course," Lizzy gave a nod to Jane's companion. "How do you do this evening, Miss King?"

"Very well, thank you, Mrs. Darcy. May I offer my congratulations on your marriage?"

"Thank you. I am most happy."

"Then can I hope you do not bear me the same grudge as your sister, Lydia, because of my earlier association with Mr. Wickham."

"On the contrary—"

"Did I hear someone mention Mr. Wickham?" Mrs. Forester joined them and stretched to her tip-toes to scan the room. "I have not yet had a chance to regain his acquaintance since he moved north. Has anyone seen him? He was taking air in the garden, but it was so crowded I did not have a chance to converse with him for more than two words."

"I am afraid I have not seen him." Jane was quick to respond as she put a calming hand on Lizzy's arm. The summer before, Lizzy's tour of Derbyshire with their Aunt and Uncle Gardiner had ended with news of Lydia's elopement with Wickham, leaving Lizzy's acquaintance with Mr. Darcy greatly strained. Considering Lizzy's strong feelings about Lydia's lack of supervision on the trip to Brighton in the company of Colonel and Mrs. Forester, Jane was convinced Lizzy would regret any show of her disregard for the couple. "How are you enjoying the ball, Mrs. Forester?"

"Oh, it is quite splendid, thank you. I feared we were in for a dull visit to Lucas Lodge, after our social life in Brighton, but you rescued us from boredom, Mrs. Bingley, and I am most appreciative."

"It is good you could attend this evening, Mrs. Forester. Are you enjoying your return to our district?"

"Colonel Forester needed a rest from his duties, but, for my part,

I am as happy in Brighton as I have ever been in my life." Mrs. Forester acknowledged, adding very quietly, almost to herself "except for one difference." She looped her arm with Mary King's. "Come, Miss King, let us find you a partner to dance with while you tell me how well you knew Mr. Wickham."

"I wonder, does she mean she missed female companionship," Lizzy breathed as she and Jane watched Mrs. Forester tug Mary King across the floor toward Lydia and Denny, "or Wickham's company."

"Lizzy," Jane admonished with a half laugh. "I am certain she means she missed our dear Lydia's company."

"Dear Jane, must you always insist on thinking the best in everyone?" Lizzy's smile was affectionate as she hooked arms with Jane. "I am certain Mrs. Forester meant a little of both. How do you suppose she acquired all those twigs stuck in the back of her gown?"

"Lizzy," Jane exclaimed on a smothered laugh, "do be serious. You know how overgrown the hedges are. I am quite certain Mrs. Forester has a perfectly respectable explanation for looking so ruffled." Jane glanced about the room and almost choked on a laugh, "Same as Mrs. Hurst has. Now, let us forget the guests. Do tell me how much you like being Mrs. Darcy."

"I am certain that no matter how those ladies acquired enough branches in their gowns to inspire speculation, you, my dear Jane, will come up with a perfectly reasonable and very kind explanation."

"I do wonder why Mrs. Hurst remained outside so much longer than her husband. Mr. Hurst returned some time ago." Jane turned to look at her sister. "Lizzy, do you suppose he might have caused her to fall as he staggered back inside?"

"There, Jane, this is exactly what I expected. You can think of only the best of people, while I, on the other hand, suspect Mrs. Hurst was not alone after her husband returned to the house."

"Lizzy, please," Jane struggled for she was near to collapse with laughter, "this is why I have missed you so much. You know my faults and yet you turn them into a source of amusement."

"My dear Jane, someone as sweet and accommodating as you has no faults. I, on the other hand, have a talent for doubting that people speak the truth or act innocently all the time. I am convinced Mrs. Forester's gown was not so wrinkled before she went to the garden." Lizzy laughed and tugged on Jane's arm in an effort to remove the frown forming on her sister's face. "Now, tell me about being Mrs. Bingley."

Chapter Four

Sometime later, Jane rushed into speech as her husband approached. "Oh, Mr. Bingley, it is a success, do you not think." Bestowing a satisfied smile on him, Jane turned to survey the groups of guests trying to converse over the noise of the music and couples swirling about the floor. Yet, not all guests seemed to be enjoying themselves. Across the room, Mrs. Hurst seemed in serious conversation with Caroline, and Jane recalled her rushed return to the ballroom.

Bingley's eldest sister had quickly joined a chattering group of women, though Jane had observed Mrs. Hurst rarely had time for female company. Something about the speed of her return to the ballroom puzzled Jane. Louisa and Caroline usually made a point to enter a room slowly to gain the most attention. Much as she was reluctant to admit it Lizzy's comments could be right, Jane knew Louisa usually only paid attention to other women long enough to sneer at their mode of dress.

Jane drew a deep breath. "With the exception of your sisters, everyone seems to be enjoying the ball."

"My dear Jane, you must disregard my entire family." Bingley glanced to where Mr. Hurst was standing near the drinks table, before he turned to smile down at his wife. "You are the one I want to make happy. My sisters must make their own entertainment."

"Dear Charles," Jane frowned as her gaze returned to Mrs. Hurst, "I have no wish to offend you, but is it possible Louisa might have a previous acquaintance with Mr. Wickham?"

"I cannot know, dear wife." Bingley glanced about the room. "They have met at Pemberley and at our wedding, I suppose."

"But Charles, Lydia and Wickham were not at the wedding."

"Perhaps they met when we visited Darcy. Other than that, I cannot say. Is it important, my dear?"

"Not at all," Jane's cheeks warmed as she returned the intimate look in her husband's gaze. She loved the way his eyes caressed her with only a glance, and made her skin feel warm. Her mother would not approve if she but knew how much Jane enjoyed marriage relations with her husband. Yet, Jane wanted none of the marriage arrange endured by her parents, but one filled with love. She had dreamed of marrying for love, yet there were times when she was at a loss as to how to handle the deep emotions her husband aroused. "Mr. Bingley, I'm so happy —"

"Help! Come quickly, help!" cried a woman standing in the doorway. "Please, come. I think he is dead."

"Who the dickens is that?" Bingley demanded as he rushed toward the woman.

"Miss Darcy's companion," Jane gasped as she tried to keep pace with his long stride. By the time they reached the sobbing woman, Mr. Darcy, Colonel Fitzwilliam, and Mr. Bennet were by their side. Jane turned to look for Wickham, surely as a member of the family, he would rush to their aide as well, but she could find no glimpse of him in the ballroom.

"Try to calm yourself, Madame," Bingley urged as he approached the distraught woman. "What is the problem?"

"He is dead," she screeched. "I know he is dead."

"Woman, who are you?" demanded Mr. Bennet. His brow wrinkled, showing his displeasure that someone would upset the calm routine of his evening.

"I am Maggie," she sobbed, "Maggie Brown, sir." She twisted her hands in the dull grey of her modest dress. Her face was the color of clotted milk. Her red streaked eyes were wide with fear.

"She is Georgiana's companion," Mr. Darcy said as he approached the distraught female. "Miss Brown, try to regain your calm and tell us what the matter is."

"I found him. On the floor in the library," Miss Brown's words ended in a loud sob. "He is dead. I know he is dead."

"Who is dead?" Bingley held out a protective arm to shield Jane from the response, as if the deceased man might reach out to grab her. "Who did you find?"

Eyes wide, brown hair bobbing loosely above her death white face, Miss Brown gasped. "It is Wickham. Wickham is dead."

Jane shuddered and slumped against Bingley.

A scream sounded. The guests gathered around to hear Maggie Brown turned as Lydia let out another screech. "It can't be Wickham," she cried. "Why would he be in the library?"

"It is Wickham." Miss Brown held her head high under the shocked gazes turned in her direction. "There is no doubt. It is Wickham's body on the floor." Then she gasped, but in the shock, no one seemed to notice she left off the 'mister' or her sudden confidence of his identity.

Lydia whirled toward her sister. "You did this, Lizzy," she finger was shaking as she cried, "you wanted him and he chose me. You killed him. I know you did."

"Lydia, please," Lizzy ignored gasps from guests. "You have suffered a shock—"

"Daughter, watch your tongue," Mr. Bennet spoke in a strained tone as he sent an impatient glare at his wife.

"Oh, my poor, dear Lydia," Mrs. Bennet ignored Mr. Bennet's accusing glare and rushed to Lydia's side. "No one understands how she feels. It is her nerves making her say such things. I know well the results of being controlled by emotions." She cast a stinging glare in Lizzy's direction, "Though I must say some people are not content until they ruin things for those around them."

"Mamma, please," Jane cried as she rushed to her mother's side. She understood the look of pain on Lizzy's face. They had heard these critical remarks since Lydia was born. Nevertheless, she could not understand the mean twist to Lydia's mouth. If Lydia had burst into tears, it would make more sense. "We can not know for certain—"

"Correct you are, Mrs. Bingley. Best everyone hold your tongues until we know more," Mr. Darcy said. He took a protective step toward Lizzy, but she lifted her chin and shook her head. Mr. Darcy held her gaze then turning to Bingley he continued, "We must check the body."

"I am not certain that is a good idea, Will." Colonel Fitzwilliam sent Mr. Darcy a warning glance. He sensed his cousin was ready to rush to the scene, but Darcy needed to keep his distance. Especially with the victim's wife accusing Mrs. Darcy of the murder. "Who is the local authority in charge of this district?"

"We need to confirm there is a body before we send for the authorities," Mr. Darcy insisted. He needed to do something to keep from shaking Lydia to force her to take back the words she said about his wife. How could even a wife as young and spoiled as Lydia imagine Lizzy wanted Wickham after all this time?

Darcy knew better. When he first met Lizzy, she had been fond of Wickham, but things changed after Wickham ran off with her youngest sister. It was then that Darcy explained how Wickham had tried to ruin Georgiana's life. He apologized to Lizzy for keeping the facts quiet when he might have prevented Lydia's downfall. However, the people here knew nothing of that incident. From their expressions, they might believe the careless words Lydia spoke in her shocked reaction at learning of her husband's death.

"Darcy, you must listen to Colonel Fitzwilliam." Mr. Bingley stepped away from Jane and straightened his shoulders. "This is my house. I will check on the body."

"One minute if you please, Mr. Bingley," a voice sounded from the back of the group. All heads turned as guests moved aside to make room for Sir William to push to the front of the group. "I am the local magistrate. I will check the body first."

"Mmm, are you quite certain?" Mr. Bennet said, knowing Sir William's reluctance to face unpleasant circumstances. After a pensive look at Sir William's face, and in complete understanding of his friend's wish to avoid such incidences, Mr. Bennet continued. "Right you are, Sir William, but I suggest we need several eyes upon the scene." He glanced at his youngest son-in-law. "Bingley, I believe you are correct. You should assist Sir William."

"Right," Mr. Bingley paused for a second, and turned to his friend. "Darcy will accompany us. We will check the library with Sir William and report back directly."

"I would be most grateful for the assistance." Sir William gave a quick nod.

"He is dead, I tell you. He is dead." Miss Brown insisted on another sob.

Lydia's cries added to the noise of whispers and murmurs from the guests. "No, he cannot be dead. Not Wickham." She turned to stare at the people gathered around her and seemed to gather her temper. Hands on her hips, she glared at them. "What do any of you care? You chased us away."

Gasps escaped from watching guests and shocked expressions covered their faces.

Lydia pointed a trembling finger at Mary King. "Did you kill him because he ended your engagement and married me?"

Miss King squared her chin and held Lydia's accusing stare. "It was not I. If you must know, I was pleased when Mr. Wickham lost his regard for me."

"I doubt that," Lydia gave a snort and her furious gaze settled on Kitty. "Was it you, Kitty? You were infatuated with Wickham and tried to attract his attention just because I wanted him."

"Mamma," Kitty whimpered, "I could never hurt Wickham."

"Hush, Kitty," Mrs. Bennet snapped. "Leave the poor girl alone."

Still furious, Lydia turned and her glare settled on her former friend. "Harriet Forester, was it you? From your first arrived in Meryton, you flirted with Wickham, and you a married woman."

"Of course I was friendly to dear Mr. Wickham. You were both my friends," Mrs. Forester clasped her husband's arm as she returned Lydia's glare, but her voice faltered. "I could never hurt him."

Lydia's gaze flickered and darted about again, "Don't look down your nose at me, Caroline Bingley. I watched you flutter your eyes at Wickham this very night. Your sister made eyes at him too." Lydia raised her voice, glaring at the guests as she voiced accusations. "Any one of you could have killed my poor, dear Wickham."

"Lydia, please, you do not know what you are saying. Mamma, please help me get Lydia—"

"Not this time, Jane. I will speak." Lydia jerked her arm away from Jane's grasp. "Do not act the sweet big sister tonight. My husband is dead and you cannot know my pain." Lydia whirled and rushed down the stairs toward the library.

After a horrified breath, Jane followed. This was her house. Her ball and her sister suffered pain she could not imagine. There was no way she could stand by and allow Lydia to rush into danger. Nor could she wait for the men to give their approval to move about the house, after Lydia plunged down the stairs alone. If a murderer was in the building, Lydia was in danger, and not thinking straight.

In fact, after Lydia's display of emotions, Jane feared her entire family would be suspected of murder. She must do something. Calming Lydia seemed the best option. At the bottom of the stairs, Jane caught up with her sister. "Lydia, please wait. Seeing the body will only distress you more."

"I have to see him. Can you not understand?" Lydia cried. She whirled away from the library door and turned tortured eyes on her elder sister as tears rolled down her face. "I am but sixteen years old, and they are saying my husband is dead. What am I to do? Where will I go if my poor Wickham is dead? Can you imagine going back to our parents' house, and acting the dutiful daughter after I have been married and lived on my own? Oh, Jane, please tell me what must I do?"

Gathering Lydia in her arms, Jane hugged her sister tight, but she had no words of advice to calm Lydia's pain.

⋄⋄

Mary King watched Lydia's headlong flight down the staircase, with Jane following on her heels, and turned to study expressions on faces around her. She had been blamed with murder same as other guests, and she dare not ignore the accusations. Her position in this county was fragile at best. One hint of unacceptable behavior could exclude her from polite society completely. She must find a way to remove all suspicion from her name before local gossip put an end to all she hoped to achieve. Unlike many guests around her, some standing rigid, barely turning their heads as they glanced around avoiding all eye contact, she had the prospects of two other people to consider. However, before she could form a plan, Mrs. Bennet's loud sobbing filled the air.

"My poor Lydia and dear Wickham. He was charm itself and did not deserve to die so young. Oh, my poor girl. What will become of her without dear Wickham?" Mrs. Bennet fanned her face frantically with her handkerchief and gasped. "My poor nerves, I feel one of my spells coming on. Lizzy, make yourself useful. Fetch my smelling salts."

Mary King heard snickers and turned to see Miss Bingley and her sister exchange glances. The extreme pallor of Mrs. Hurst's complexion caught Mary's attention, but before she could gather her thoughts as to why Mrs. Hurst looked the color of old sheets, Mrs. Bennet whirled to confront Colonel and Mrs. Forester.

"You," Mrs. Bennet pointed a shaking finger toward Colonel Forester, "the entire fault of this event rests with you. You lured my poor dear Lydia away from home to be your wife's special companion, and failed to protect her innocence. Instead of treating Lydia as the young girl she is, you allowed her to copy your wife's loose relations with members of the militia while she was in Brighton, and now look what has happened."

"I say, madam, I respect that you are overwrought because of the shock of this sad occasion, but I must insist you not speak of my wife in such a manner." Colonel Forester put a protective hand on his wife's arm.

Mrs. Forester peeped up at him with what Mary King could only describe as a guilty look, but said nothing. In fact, she did not have a chance, for now that Mrs. Bennet had everyone's attention, she seemed determined to hold court on all the issues rambling around in her head.

"It is true. My poor nerves trouble me more than most people understand." Mrs. Bennet sniffed a pitiful sound and angled a glance at her audience. "But you sir, have not explained your actions, nor the behavior of you wife."

"Mamma, please," Lizzy pulled at her mother's arm, "Kitty has gone to fetch your salts. Do come and have something to drink to calm yourself. We must think of Lydia."

"Well, of course, I am thinking of Lydia. I know not what will happen to my poor girl now that she is without a husband. Lydia was right, you know. You saw it with your own eyes if you will but admit the truth. That Miss King wanted dear Wickham, just as you did at one time, Lizzy, and you know what I say is true."

"Mamma, please," Lizzy grasped her mother's arm and tugged her toward the ballroom, "all that happened a long time ago."

Mrs. Bennet pulled away from Lizzy's grasp and reared back to glare at her. Twin patches of red filled her cheeks. Her eyes glared with temper. "It was not all that long ago, missy, and pray do stop any pretense that you were not interested in dear Wickham. Why, you and half the women in this room vied for his attention." Mrs. Bennet glanced around as Lizzy urged her toward the refreshment table. "Why, even that Mrs. Hurst was making eyes at Wickham earlier this very night, and her a much married woman."

"Sister, sister," Mr. Gardiner moved to Mrs. Bennet's other side, and took her arm, "I fear your nerves are at risk if you continue these worrisome observations. Come, have some food while Kitty attends to your salts."

"Oh, Brother, my nerves do visit me so when I am unsettled at times like this," Mrs. Bennet cast an accusing glare about her, "especially when someone at Jane's ball wanted poor Lydia's husband dead."

"Come, sister," Mr. Gardiner urged Mrs. Bennet toward the chairs on the far side of the ballroom from the guests now staring at her with open distaste.

As Mr. Gardiner led Mrs. Bennet away, Mary King heard sighs escape from the group around her. No doubt, they were all glad Mr. Gardiner had taken control, before Mrs. Bennet accused everyone in the room of murder. Yet, how much of what Mrs. Bennet said was true? Moreover, what was Mrs. Hurst's connection to Wickham? For that matter, how well did Caroline Bingley know Mr. Wickham?

The few times Mary had crossed paths with Miss Bingley, she learned Caroline had little time for anyone she considered her social inferior. Would that include Mr. Wickham? Mary had to admit Wickham's charm had overcome her own good sense. Perhaps Miss Bingley could say the same. Whatever the explanation, she was determined to clear her name and intended to listen for any mention of Caroline Bingley, or Mrs. Hurst's dealings with the late George Wickham.

⋐⋑

In the library, things were not going well.

George Wickham was indeed, dead.

His body lay face down on the rug. Closer inspection revealed a stab wound in his back, but there was no weapon in view.

"Charles," Darcy turned to Bingley after the men stepped away from the body, "before we commence further, do you notice anything out of order in the room?"

Glad for the opportunity to remove his gaze from the body stretched on the floor, Bingley surveyed the room.

The library was long and narrow. Three walls were filled with shelves of books broken only by the door to the hallway on one long wall, and the fireplace dividing the room in half on the opposite wall. The fourth wall was broken by windows, the dark hangings closed against the night.

The affect from walls of books and the dark green velvet drapes left the room darkened by shadows, except for the flames blazing in the fireplace and light from candles burning about the room. Chairs and sofas were spread around the room, inviting occupants to sit and read. Jane declared the library perfect, her favorite place to spend a cold winter day. What would she think now, if she saw Wickham's body on the rug to the left of the fireplace?

Forcing his attention back to the events at hand, Bingley examined the room for anything pointing to the identity of Wickham's killer. Who would do such a thing? Knowing the worry and unrest Wickham had caused Jane's family, he could not claim a liking for the man, but who wanted Wickham dead? In Bingley's opinion, Wickham did not have a confrontational bone in his body.

Wickham could look a person in the eye and charm the last coin from their pocket, and they would never notice. He won his battles with smooth charm and the ability to converse in such a manner that made one think he was telling the truth, no matter what he said.

Bingley walked about the room, studied objects on tables and position of the furniture. Finally, he admitted that the servants could better answer Darcy's question as to anything being out of place. Taking care not to step on any object that might be on the floor, he considered how Jane would deal with this unpleasantness. Not as her mother would, of that he was certain. Most likely, his mother-in-law had the entire ballroom in an uproar by this time, but he suspected Jane would contain her emotions.

Early in their acquaintance, Jane's quiet control almost caused him to lose any hope he might win her heart. He had moved to London and contemplated giving up this residence completely. However, a chance word from Darcy sent him on a wild ride, which ended in a double wedding with the Darcys.

An familiar scent twitched at his nostrils. Bingley stared through the shadows as he approached a table next to an armchair in the corner near the windows. Situated so it was not immediately obvious to anyone entering the room, the nook offered a quiet refuge for one weary of events going on in other parts of the house. He often sat here when he needed to escape the demands of Caroline and Louisa. Someone else had done so not long past, for as he leaned to examine the table he found the source of the odor attracting his attention.

"Darcy, someone has left a pipe, still warm and smoldering."

Darcy and Colonel Fitzwilliam crossed the room to Bingley's side. "Leave it as it is," Colonel Fitzwilliam said, "authorities might find the position useful."

"I say, Colonel, you sound very knowledgeable on the subject of solving crimes." Bingley eyed his guest curiously.

"Indeed you do, Cousin." Darcy studied the colonel, as well. "Perhaps you should lead the charge to discover who committed this deed."

"I am flattered by your confidence in me, Will, but this matter is best left to the local authorities," Colonel Fitzwilliam said. As cousins and constant playmates in their youth, both men called the other by names even their own parents did not use. Mr. Darcy was Will to his cousin, and Colonel Fitzwilliam became Fitz.

"I agree with Darcy," Bingley responded as he eyed the cousins, so alike and yet different in his opinion. "You seem to know the subject, Colonel."

"How did you acquire a skill such as this, Fitz?" Darcy stopped his contemplation of the pipe's location and turned to study his cousin.

Colonel Fitzwilliam responded with a slow grin. "Long nights with time to read after hours of exhausting duty can add knowledge on many topics."

"My word, Fitz, have you been reading Samuel Johnson's book of words, again?" Darcy's voice rose. "How will you ever claim a wife if all you do is read in your spare time?"

"I don't have time to engage in social events, Cousin. The war keeps me occupied if you recall."

"Here, here, I say, gentlemen, Mr. Bennett and I have a solution to our problem." Sir William regarded the three men expectantly as he joined them. "As Mr. Wickham was in uniform, and Colonel Fitzwilliam and Colonel Forester are commanding officers, we believe it is they who should take charge and start the investigation immediately."

Colonel Fitzwilliam shook his head and held up both hands. "I cannot agree, Sir William. We should send to London for the authorities if you are not up to the task."

Looking distinctly uncomfortable, Sir William shuttered, and then attempted to regain his good nature. "Not at all, Colonel Fitzwilliam. However, I have no wish to intrude in military issues. As Mr. Wickham was in neither of your regiments, it seems only proper for men of the rank of colonel to take charge of investigating a military man's murder."

"Sir William has a point, Fitz." Darcy sent his cousin a speaking glance. "With a murderer in our midst, time is of the essence." Darcy surveyed the other men in the room. "What say you, Charles?"

Bingley squared his shoulders as he glanced at the men waiting for his response. "I agree with Darcy. We should handle this matter with the utmost haste. Since the colonels are on hand, we should al-

WHO MURDERED MR. WICKHAM

low them to solve the case."

"Of course we would need to confirm that both of you are free of any suspicion as to your own involvement in the murder." Sir William rubbed his hands together as his voice boomed in the silence of the room. "As the person responsible for this deed could be one of the guests in this house, it seems sensible to confirm that the two men in charge of solving the murder are absolved of any suspicion."

The library door banged open. Lydia Wickham burst in the room in a whirl of skirts, followed by Jane, and demanded in a loud voice, "Is it true? Is my poor Wickham dead?"

The men standing in the corner, turned toward the body on the floor.

Lydia rushed to stand beside Wickham's body, fell to her knees and sobbed as she laid her cheek against his. "Who would do this to my husband? Who would kill my dear Wickham?"

Despite the arched brows, indicating the men gathered in the room could think of many reasons for this crime, Jane's heart poured out at the sound of her sister's pain. She moved to Lydia's side but her father and Bingley were there first.

Mr. Bennet clasped hold of Lydia's arm and urged her to her feet. "There, there, child. Time for tears later. For now you must not spoil the space around the body for there might be signs lying about to give hints of who did this."

"But he is dead. My poor Wickham is dead." Lydia sobbed broken heartedly as they steered her away from the body. Then mid-sob, she jerked her arms free and stomped her foot as she glared at the men in the room. "Not one of you cares. You stand around when someone did this to my poor Wickham." Her fierce glare landed on Darcy. "You did this to him, Darcy. I am sure you did." She gulped air. "You could not forgive him for thinking your precious Georgiana really cared for him, and now you have killed him."

"Hush child," Mr. Bennet gave Lydia's arm a firm shake, "you are like your mother. When your nerves overtake your good sense, your tongue flaps out of control, and you give no thought to what you say. Darcy is a member of this family. He has no need to wish harm on Wickham."

"Someone wanted to hurt my husband. You must find who did this." Lydia's accusing stare stabbed each man in turn. "My Wickham did not deserve to die like this."

Observing the anguish on Jane's face, Bingley stepped close to

Lydia and spoke, though his good sense warned his words were better left until later. Yet time was of great importance and Lydia did not act the usual grieving widow. Her temper was in fine form, and he needed to ease the concern from Jane's face. She could chide him later if she believed him insensitive to Lydia's situation. "Mrs. Wickham, can you think of anyone who wished your husband ill?"

"Oh, no," Lydia wailed with renewed sobs, "I will never really be Mrs. Wickham again. My husband will not be here to hold me at night to keep me warm—"

"Lydia—"

"Child," Mr. Bennet spoke over Jane's attempt to steer Lydia's comments to appropriate matters. "Control yourself. Have you any response for Mr. Bingley? Can you think of anyone who wished to harm Wickham?"

Lydia seemed to gather herself up to meet the occasion as she observed the men from tear-drenched eyes. "Half the people at this ball were vexed with Wickham." She sent Mr. Darcy a glare. "My sister's husband is a good place to start. Or Colonel Forester."

"Lydia, please," Jane said as she stepped forward. Then she caught sight of Wickham's body stretched full length on the rug and her head started reeling. What distress Lydia must feel. Jane clenched her fists and turned away. She needed to help her younger sister. "After this shock, you cannot know what you are saying."

Lydia whirled about to face Jane. "It is easy for you to say I should stay calm. You still have Bingley. What am I to do without Wickham? Who did this to me? Who wanted my husband dead?"

Jane kept her eyes away from the body on the floor and took hold of her sister's arm. "Come, Lydia, let us depart so questions can be asked."

Chapter Five

After Jane steered a sobbing Lydia from the room, Bingley turned to his guests. "Gentlemen, for the sake of all concerned, we must solve this matter without delay. Much as it pains me to admit such a fact, the murderer could be in our midst. No one should leave this house until the issue is settled."

"Right you are, Bingley," Darcy turned to the colonels, both looking official in their red and uniforms, "which of you wants to answer questions first?"

"I fear I must speak with my wife without delay," Colonel Forester said. "When Sir William asked me to accompany him to the library, he did not explain why my presence was required immediately. I would be remiss if I did not speak with my wife as this investigation is likely to take some time. News of Wickham's death was most distressing for Harriet as the Wickhams were particular friends of hers."

"Of course you should speak with her, Colonel Forester. Please send our sympathies to her." Bingley gave a slight bow as he held the door for the colonel to depart. "We will send for you directly, when we finish speaking with Colonel Fitzwilliam."

When the door closed behind Colonel Forester, all eyes turned to Colonel Fitzwilliam. Shoulders squared, chin angled, he met their questioning stares. "Gentlemen, I am aware of your concerns on this matter, and agree to assist you in any way that I might. What questions do you wish to ask?"

Bingley spared a glance in Darcy's direction, then stepped forward to assume his role as host. "Sir William, as the local magistrate perhaps you will question the officers."

"Oh, um, quite right, Mr. Bingley, quite right," Sir William said as he moved his portly figure forward to join them in front of the fireplace. "Um, Colonel Fitzwilliam, perhaps you will enlighten us as to how well acquainted you were with Mr. Wickham."

"Of course, Sir William. Unlike many of the guests, I have known Wickham since we were in knee pants." Colonel Fitzwilliam looked at each of them. "When my family visited the Darcys at Pemberley, Wickham was always there because his father worked for the estate. The three of us played together, roaming the woods and enjoying our youth."

Sir William cleared his throat with a loud rumbling sound. "You must be distressed, sir. I am sure his murder came as a shock. So, you have always been friends with Mr. Wickham?"

Bingley prepared to endure the dull ramblings of Sir William just as the magistrate asked a very pointed question. Bingley exchanged a startled glance with Darcy as Fitzwilliam answered.

"In all honesty, Sir William, I cannot claim as much. After we reached our majority, our paths went in different directions. Darcy and Wickham went to university and I joined the militia. Our lives changed."

"Ah, I see," Sir William arched bushy brows, his mild mannered expression suddenly alert, "Colonel, am I correct in assuming that you had not the funds to attend university?"

"Sir William, I must protest such questions. What does Fitzwilliam's monetary status have to do with Wickham's murder?" Darcy demanded as he faced Sir William.

Sir William hooked his thumbs in his waistcoat pockets, and studied Mr. Darcy and Colonel Fitzwilliam for several long ticks of the clock. "Am I correct in assuming Mr. Wickham lived on the estate, and that he was the son of an employee?"

"Yes, of course, but Fitz explained as much," Darcy said as he nodded toward Colonel Fitzwilliam. "I cannot see how such facts have any connection with Wickham's death."

"I merely inquire on such matters to discover if Colonel Fitzwilliam might foster any ill will toward Mr. Wickham since, obviously, your family funded Mr. Wickham's education. Yet Colonel Fitzwilliam, a close relation by your own admission, did not receive the same benefits."

"That is a ridiculous assumption, Sir," Darcy turned away, only to stop abruptly and turn back to face the magistrate again. "But pray, do continue so we might discover the person guilty of this murder and be rid of these ridiculous claims."

"Right," said the mild mannered Sir William as he turned back to the colonel, "now where was I? Ah, yes, Colonel Fitzwilliam, did you hold any resentment toward Mr. Wickham for his good fortune at having the opportunity to attend university?"

"Not in the least, Sir William. As the second son of an earl, I was aware I needed to make a living for myself. University seemed a waste of time when I could establish a career. Wickham and I grew up as friends, and, though it is true we were less so in the recent past, I had no reason to wish him dead."

"Am I correct to assume you were not on good terms at his death?"

"You are not mistaken, Sir. In fact, we have not been on amicable terms for some years past."

"Yet, you both wear the uniform and serve to protect your country. How did this parting of ways happen? Did Mr. Wickham resent your rank even though he attended university?"

"Why should Wickham resent my position? He had the opportunity to acquire an education, and claim a post as a clergyman if he chose. His refusal of the position led to his need to join the militia as a means to survive."

"Perhaps you harbor ill will towards Mr. Wickham on a personal level, Colonel?" Sir William's raised brows seemed to indicate he knew of Wickham's hapless past, and a loud gasp echoed in the room.

Bingley dared not react for fear of alerting Sir William to tension, he was certain had no bearing on the current situation. He risked a glance and saw Darcy's face was dark with contained emotion. Muscles bulged along his jaw. Aware of Darcy's ability to keep control of his emotions, the evidence of his friend's distress filled Bingley with dread.

This line of questioning was not acceptable. Darcy should not be made to suffer again the pain of discovering his childhood friend's betrayal. Bingley refused to remain silent and allow details concerning Darcy's sister be discussed with strangers. The last thing Darcy needed was for his sister's name to be exposed in this manner, even if

Wickham was lying dead before them, and could do no further harm.

Bingley stepped forward as he spoke. "Colonel Fitzwilliam is a ranking officer in the militia, Sir William. Do you think it is necessary to draw this inquiry out any longer?"

"I'm satisfied," Mr. Bennet spoke in a tone so firm, each occupant of the room reacted in surprise.

Sir William turned to stare at his old friend with a wide-eyed expression, then clearing his throat in a noisy rumble, the portly gentleman said. "Um, perhaps I strayed too far off the point with my inquiries. Forgive me, Colonel."

"Not at all, Sir William," Colonel Fitzwilliam said. "You ask no more than I might have done myself. Shall I go request Colonel Forester's presence?"

"Do we need continue —"

"Yes, Sir William, we most definitely do." Mr. Darcy intoned over the magistrate's tentative suggestion. They should question Colonel Forester, if for no other reason than to get Fitz out of the room before one or both of them turned their ill-humor on the bumbling, but well-meaning, magistrate. "We should treat Colonel Forester to the same level of questioning as Colonel Fitzwilliam."

"Yes, indeed, Sir William, I totally agree," Mr. Bennet said. "I have not experienced such riveting entertainment since my wife's nerves last attacked. Though it is a pity such diversion was at the cost of Mr. Wickham's demise."

Tension eased slightly as Colonel Fitzwilliam departed the room. Bingley sighed as he closed the door behind the colonel, having more reason than most to desire this incident to be finished. His wife's entire family was accused of wanting Mr. Wickham dead, and now Darcy's cousin had barely escaped the same charge.

Jane would never invite guests to this house again, for fear of being shunned after this event. And making Jane happy was his aim for the rest of his days. That meant solving the question of her family being involved in Wickham's murder.

"This is unacceptable," Darcy muttered as Bingley reached his side. "This magistrate is willing to drag my sister's reputation out for public speculation after all the effort we went to in order to protect her from such."

"Calm yourself, Darcy, for you are close to reverting to your ways of old. Think of your wife. Did you not promise Lizzy you would attempt to give people a chance to make a favorable first impression?"

"It makes no matter. I cannot allow such free public examination of my younger sister's actions. This is insufferable —"

"Ah, Sir William," Bingley spoke louder than necessary to cover Darcy's words as the magistrate joined them. "Darcy and I were just speaking of how thorough you were with your questions to Colonel Fitzwilliam. Are you quite certain you have no wish to conduct the investigation?"

"Ah, Mr. Bingley, thank you for the kind comments, but I fear solving this case is not for me." Sir William's good-natured laugh rumbled from deep in his portly chest. "However, I am conscious of the weight of my responsibility, and I do appreciate your confidence in me, kind sir. But I have no wish to continue beyond these immediate interviews." Sir William said as he gazed toward the body. "I have no taste for murder."

"Takes the stuffings right out of you, eh, Sir William?" Mr. Bennet clapped a hand on his friend's shoulder as he approached and heard the magistrate's words. "I will say one thing after observing you in action, Sir. My sympathies are with any man standing before you, if you ever decide to give this position your full attention."

Darcy and Bingley exchanged a swift glance. Both were aware this was as close as their father-in-law would venture toward censuring his friend for casting doubt on the Bennet family's involvement in this crime.

Sir William, however, seemed to miss the message entirely. His chest puffed in pride at what he considered his friend's high regard, Sir William blustered. "My dear Mr. Bennet, you are not in any danger of having to waste your sympathy, I assure you. Magistrate duties on a level such as that would drain me of all good will. Ah, there you are, Colonel Forester. Good of you to join us at last. Please, take a seat."

As they all returned to their previous positions, Bingley said in a solicitous tone, "Colonel, how did you find Mrs. Forester? I do hope she is holding up well after the shock."

"Not good, I must confess." Colonel Forester joined Darcy in front of the fireplace. "Not very good at all. She has such tender emotions as I am sure most women are at this sad event."

"Indeed it is a sorrowful event, Colonel. Indeed it is." Sir William cleared his throat with impressive authority, no doubt, based on the praise he had received while waiting for the colonel to appear. "Now, how well were you acquainted with Mr. Wickham?"

"Quite well, Sir William, as you might recall from the time we spent in Meryton. At that time, Mr. Wickham was under my command and a frequent guest at the same social events my wife and I attended." The colonel glanced at Mr. Bennet before he continued, "I would go so far as to claim we remained close, until certain events occurred, making it impossible for Wickham to remain in my regiment."

"Rightly so, Colonel, but can you explain how those events affected your acquaintance with Mr. Wickham?" As Sir William voiced the question, all the air seemed to escape from the room. For long ticks, no one moved.

Bingley turned a questioning glance on the magistrate, but Sir William seemed unaware of the deep wounds his question probed.

Mr. Bennet sent his old friend a glare that should have stopped even a dedicated thief in his tracks.

Darcy's response was only slightly better. The fury in the glance Darcy sent Sir William was so powerful, Bingley expected to see bodily harm. However, the magistrate continued to stare at Colonel Forester as if he were about to pronounce a guilty sentence, causing Bingley to release an uneasy breath.

"It most certainly did affect our relations, Sir William." Colonel Forester sent Mr. Bennet an apologetic glance. "My poor wife was almost delirious with disappointment when Mr. Wickham and Lydia left Brighton to join a regiment up north. My home was very unsettled for quite some time after the Wickhams departed. Lydia was a particular friend of my wife's. In fact, both the Wickhams were in her close circle of acquaintances and their absence was disappointing."

"Is that all, Colonel?" Sir William probed, "You never felt any warmer emotions for Mrs. Wickham than friendship?"

"I say—"

"Sir William," Bingley raised his voice over Mr. Bennet's objection, as he exchanged a stare with Darcy. Jane had shared some of the events surrounding Lydia and Wickham's marriage with him, but he strongly suspected the details were not common knowledge. "Perhaps we should focus on the murder and not such personal issues?"

"Yes, yes of course, Mr. Bingley. Quite right," Sir William cleared his throat. "Colonel, was there any reason that you might have harbored ill will toward Mr. Wickham?"

"There was not, Sir William."

Bingley and Darcy exchanged relieved glances at the change of subject, but Sir William was already at the door. "Then I suggest we turn these inquiries over to the officers."

Colonel Fitzwilliam appeared outside the door and prevented Sir William's departure when he said. "Have you finished questioning the Colonel?"

"Yes, yes," Sir William thundered in his booming voice. "Come in, Colonel Fitzwilliam. I am just taking my leave."

"Could you delay for a time, Sir William, and indulge us with a bit more of your company," Colonel Fitzwilliam said as he brushed past the magistrate and entered the library. "If all is ready for us to proceed, I have a suggestion. While you were speaking with Colonel Forester, I made a list of the most unlikely guests. Might I suggest we eliminate those people first, and then move on to more serious candidates." Colonel Fitzwilliam glanced at the four men. "Also, I suggest we ask Mr. Bingley to assist us in the questioning as neither of us actually know all the guests."

"What of the woman who found the body?" Demanded Colonel Forester. "Should we not question her first?"

"I checked on Miss Brown while I was in the ballroom," Colonel Fitzwilliam said. "She is still sobbing and in no fit state to answer questions clearly. After surveying the unfamiliar faces present, it is my opinion that Bingley's assistance is necessary, if he is willing."

"Yes, of course." Bingley swallowed, unwilling to admit he was unfamiliar with many guests at the ball. Yet, if he could assist in removing Jane's family from fault, it was his duty to do so. "As you wish, Colonel Fitzwilliam. How can I be of assistance?"

"Colonel Forester, would you care to view the list or shall we proceed as I suggested?"

"By all means continue, Colonel Fitzwilliam. You have obviously spent more time thinking about this matter than I have. Let us commence as you suggested."

Colonel Fitzwilliam turned as Darcy, Mr. Bennet and Sir William prepared to leave the room. "Gentlemen, when you reach the ballroom, please send Mrs. Bennet, Mrs. Phillips, and the Hursts to speak with us."

"Mm, I suppose it is a good sign that my wife is first on the list, though I am probably a more likely suspect for murder, especially when her nerves act up."

"One moment, please, Mr. Bennet. Your comment reveals a weakness in my plan." Colonel Fitzwilliam turned to Colonel Forester and continued. "I fear I overlooked the obvious step we should take first. Colonel Forester, we should delay acting on the list of names, and eliminate these gentlemen before we proceed further."

"Indeed, I believe you have a good point." Colonel Forester studied the men in question and gave a nod. "Sir William, perhaps you will speak with us first? If you other gentlemen will wait outside in the entrance hall, please."

Bingley opened the door and prepared to step into the hallway with Darcy and Mr. Bennet, when Colonel Forester spoke. "Please remain, Mr. Bingley, and observe our conversations if you please."

Bingley sent a questioning glance toward Colonel Fitzwilliam, but he nodded in agreement with Colonel Forster. Bingley closed the door behind Darcy and Mr. Bennet and turned back to the room.

"Sir William," Colonel Forester gave a slight bow to his host at Lucas Lodge, "I trust you do not mind answering your own questions, sir." Without waiting for a response, he launched into his first query. "How well were you acquainted with Mr. Wickham?"

"Not well at all, Colonel. Though we attended many of the same social functions, in all honesty, I cannot say I ever exchanged one word with Mr. Wickham. When he attended socials, he spent his time with young ladies. Before his marriage, of course."

"He was known to you before his marriage to Mr. Bennet's daughter?" Colonel Forester persisted.

"I must object to your words, Colonel. To say I knew Mr. Wickham is incorrect. I only observed him at events."

"You held no ill will toward Mr. Wickham, though he showed no interest in your own daughters?"

"My dear, Colonel, the youngest of my daughters is not yet out of the school room, and my eldest daughter was attached to her husband. Mr. Wickham's choice of a wife was no concern of mine."

"Very good, Sir William," Colonel Forester gave a nod, "precisely what we wanted to hear."

Sir William seemed to shrink, much as a pigeon whose feathers had been soothed. "Very good, then. Very good indeed."

"On your way out, would you ask Mr. Darcy to join us, Sir William?" Colonel Fitzwilliam gave a nod to the elder man and turned to Colonel Forester. "I am not at all convinced I care for this type of work."

Colonel Forester folded his hands behind his back, no doubt enjoying the warmth from the fireplace, and stood erect. "Quite right, but as leaders in the militia, we have dealt with worse, have we not? Ah, Mr. Darcy, please have a seat."

"Darcy, how well did you know Wickham?" Colonel Fitzwilliam demanded before Darcy's body touched the chair.

"What is this, Fitz? You know, full well we grew up almost as close as brothers." Darcy glanced at Colonel Forester, then turned his focus back to his cousin. "You are also aware that all changed at university."

"Ah, so you quarreled with Mr. Wickham, sir?" Colonel Forester demanded.

"Not at all, Colonel. I only meant we went our separate ways. I concentrated on my studies as my father expected. Wickham, on the other hand, turned to more social activities, and our paths rarely crossed."

"So you have no conceivable reason to murder this old friend of yours?" Colonel Forester insisted.

"After returning from university, we had a disagreement. In fact, Wickham was quite vexed with me for a spell, but that was sometime ago. I had no reason to wish him harm."

"How was the matter between the two of you settled?" Colonel Forester demanded.

Darcy cast a frustrated glare at Colonel Fitzwilliam before responding. "My father left provision for Wickham to have a living as a clergyman. Wickham refused the position from a lack of interest, but insisted he was due the funds set aside for his post. I disagreed, believing he was owed no funds if he rejected the position my father arranged for him." Darcy shrugged. "But as my father thought well of Wickham when we were young, I decided to give him the funds and be done with the matter."

"That was your only disagreement?"

Darcy sent Colonel Fitzwilliam a glance. The clock ticked twice, before he responded to Colonel Forester's question. "We had another encounter."

"Could you explain, sir?"

Bingley observed the angle of Darcy's jaw and turned a glare on Colonel Forester as he rushed to speak. "Must we pursue this, Colonel? I assume Colonel Fitzwilliam knows the details of these events, and is satisfied there was no threat from Mr. Darcy."

Colonel Forester studied each man in turn, "I fear we must proceed, considering both Mr. Darcy and Colonel Fitzwilliam know of the incident." He turned to focus on Darcy. "Sir, elaborate on this situation, if you please."

"My...sister became infatuated with Wickham. When I learned of the situation, I became concerned about the seriousness of his intentions, and intervened before Wickham eloped with her."

"And you held Mr. Wickham responsible for the affair?"

"Of course, I did. Wickham was older and knew what he was doing. My sister was not yet out of the schoolroom. Any responsible brother would object to such an arrangement." Darcy's words were forced, but his control was in a firm grip as he stared at the colonel. "That happened some time ago, Colonel. Wickham has since been involved with several other women and chosen a wife. The situation with my sister has long been settled."

"Or perhaps you were waiting for an opportune time to satisfy your family's honor."

"Sir, you —"

"Colonel Forester, I must insist you allow this issue to rest. My cousin has nothing to hide and much to lose if he had acted as you imply. I suggest you are overstepping your authority and should cease these questions." Colonel Fitzwilliam squared off as he faced the other officer.

"Perhaps, you are correct, Colonel." Colonel Forester paced in front of the fireplace as he stared at his audience. "But in my opinion this is a crime of opportunity. I will bow to your judgment, Fitzwilliam, and allow the matter to rest for now. We have yet to question the guests, and can delay a decision until such time as we have done so. Mr. Darcy, you may go."

As the door closed behind Darcy, Bingley turned to Colonel Forester. "Colonel, I must insist you show courtesy to my guests."

"You wish us to spare the feelings of someone who might be a murderer, Mr. Bingley?"

Bingley clenched his teeth but remained silent. What would Jane think of the insensitive questions put to Darcy and possibly the whole assembly? Doors to all local society events would close to them. Yet some good had come from the event. Darcy had held his pride in check, and responded to the Colonel's questions. That showed progress on his friend's goal to give people a chance to make a good impression, surely. "I wish to discover the culprit as well as you, Colonel. But as the host of this ball, I must insist you use restraint with your questioning."

"Ah, Mr. Bennet, come in and have a seat."

Mr. Bennet cast a sardonic glance toward Colonel Forester. "You sound as if this were a social occasion, Colonel. Yet you stirred the pot deep with both Sir William and Darcy."

"Mr. Bennet, I am convinced you will agree we need to find the person responsible for Wickham's death. And is it not true, sir, that you have more reason than most to want Wickham dead."

"How did you reach that interesting conclusion, Colonel?" Far from appearing unsettled by the claim laid against him, Mr. Bennet aimed a lively gaze at the officer before turning to look at Bingley. "What say you, Bingley? Have you ever witnessed any occasion in which I expressed ill will toward Mr. Wickham?"

Bingley covered his humor at the question behind a blank expression. He, better than the other two men in the room, knew of the Bennets' intense relief when Lydia was finally married to Wickham. "I can say with all good conscience, sir, I have not."

"There, you heard the words yourself, Colonel. I had no reason to wish Wickham harm." Mr. Bennet settled in his chair with a contented tilt to his lips. "In fact, now that you mention the subject, I will admit I was truly in Wickham's debt."

"Come sir," Colonel Forester persisted, "everyone knows Wickham ruined your daughter's reputation when he ran off with her. And he made matters even worse when their marriage was not immediate."

"Yes, I can see why you would think that was so," Mr. Bennet's calm expression remained in place, "but tell me, Colonel, are you in close acquaintance with my wife? No, well, sir, her life's ambition is to find husbands for her daughters. Do you not think I was well pleased at news Lydia had found a husband? Believe me, sir. Wickham was charm itself, from the first moment we met." Mr. Bennet hunched his shoulders. "How could I not like the man who granted one of my wife's dearest wishes? As to having a reason to wish harm on Wickham, I dare say I worried about Lydia's circumstances less than I should have. And things ended just as well, because Wickham charmed us all."

Colonel Fitzwilliam stepped forward. "I have observed your wife and daughters at previous social events, Mr. Bennet. Considering the deportment of your younger daughters on those occasions, I find I am quite satisfied with your response." Colonel Fitzwilliam turned a glare on the officer still leaning over Mr. Bennet. "What say you, Colonel Forester?"

"Very well, then," Colonel Forester backed away and paced back and forth in front of the fireplace, "who is to be questioned next?"

CŗꙴꙎ

"Miss Brown," Colonel Fitzwilliam purposely spoke in a soothing tone so as not to upset the troubled female sitting before him with swollen red eyes and pale countenance, "please accept our apologies for your inconvenience. However, we do require more details about what happened in the library if you feel able to recount your experience."

Miss Brown sat rigid and angled her body away from the area where Wickham's body still lay on the rug. "I have explained to you all that I know, Colonel." Miss Brown smothered a sniff in her handkerchief, and dabbed at tears rolling down her cheeks. "I fell asleep after Miss Bingley left—"

"Miss Bingley? Pray tell us, more, Miss Brown. Are you saying Miss Caroline Bingley here in the library?" Colonel Forester said in a firm tone.

"Well, yes, she was—"

"When?" Colonel Forester demanded.

Colonel Fitzwilliam frowned at Forester's abrupt tone and turned to Georgiana's companion as he said in a calm voice. "Take your time, Miss Brown. Try to recall—"

"Oh, I could not forget such an encounter, Colonel. Miss Bingley was none too pleased with finding me in the library, and she went into great detail to tell me so."

Bingley winced and then gave a shrug when the colonels glanced at him, for Caroline treated the house as her own as he knew full well.

"Why would she reprimand you, Miss Brown? What were you doing?" Colonel Forester's tone was insistent.

Color filled Miss Brown's cheeks. Tears dried on her cheeks as she lifted her chin to look at the colonel. "Not a thing I ought not to do, sir. Miss Georgiana gave me leave from attending the ball, as Mrs. Darcy was to be a guest. Miss Georgiana also said it would do for me to come here to search for a book to read." Miss Brown turned to Bingley. "I hope I did not over-step my bounds, sir, but Miss Georgiana said —"

"Not at all, Miss Brown, please accept my apologies for my sister's misinformation."

"If I understand this correctly," Colonel Forester frowned, "your mistress is a guest in this house?"

"Yes, sir, that is true. Miss Georgiana Darcy."

"Have you ever been in this house before?" Colonel Forester's frown deepened as he stared at the woman sitting primly on the edge of her chair.

Miss Brown's brow wrinkled as she glanced from one man to the other. "No, sir, this is our first visit to Mr. Bingley's home."

"In that case, I am muddled. How did you know Miss Bingley's identity? Perhaps it was Mr. Bingley's wife or his other sister who spoke to you."

Frowning, Miss Brown glanced at Mr. Bingley before responding to the colonel. "I am familiar with Miss Bingley because she accompanied her brother and Mrs. Hurst on a visit to Pemberley."

"Did you encounter Miss Bingley at that time or have a disagreement with her?" Colonel Forester leaned in as if ready to attack.

"Colonel Forester, how is this —"

"I was merely trying to establish a reason for why Miss Bingley might react so strongly at finding Miss Brown in the library. Surely, Colonel Fitzwilliam, you find it as strange as do I that Miss Bingley should become so vexed over a woman reading a book."

Colonel Fitzwilliam gave a slight nod and said. "Please continue, Colonel."

After a pause to clear his throat, Colonel Forester resumed his questions as he loomed over the stiff-backed companion. "Why was Miss Bingley so vexed at finding you in this room, if you have never spoken to her before tonight? Did she have plans to meet someone?"

"I would not know her plans would I? I told Miss Bingley that Miss Darcy gave me leave to look for a book." Miss Brown's chest heaved fast as a pigeon's breast, "But still Miss Bingley reckoned that the working class should have no time to read and all but told me to leave."

"Yet you stayed in the room," Colonel Fitzwilliam's tone encouraged Miss Brown to continue, "even after Miss Bingley made no effort to conceal she was vexed by your presence?"

"Indeed I did, sir." Miss Brown turned to Mr. Bingley and

rushed to add. "No offense intended to your sister, sir. But the fire was warm after getting chilled on our travels and Miss Georgiana had no need of me while she was at the ball."

Colonel Fitzwilliam gave a nod as he said, "Did Mr. Wickham enter the library before Miss Bingley left? Did they meet?"

"Oh, no, sir," Miss Brown sounded confident. "Miss Bingley left soon as she finished telling me her opinion of finding me here and then I was in the room alone."

"How is it that a man was killed in the same room and you know nothing about the incident, Miss Brown? Where were you sitting?" Colonel Forester's words grew deadly quiet. "Explain how you went undetected by Wickham or the killer."

"I sat over there in that wing chair in the corner." Miss Brown's voice quivered as she turned and pointed to a chair in the far corner of the library, in the opposite the end of the room from the door.

His face almost as red as his uniform, Colonel Forester exchanged a glance with Colonel Fitzwilliam and rolled his eyes, but said not a word more.

Colonel Fitzwilliam turned back to Miss Brown. She looked young and vulnerable with her face swollen from crying and he disliked pressing her to speak of the events, but a murder had occurred in this room. In a soft tone, Fitzwilliam encouraged her to continue. "What happened then, Miss Brown?"

"Well, I fell asleep, didn't I?"

∞

"My nerves, oh, my poor nerves," Mrs. Bennet gasped as she flapped a handkerchief in front of her face and glared at the men awaiting her response. "Colonel Forester, I can not think how you expect me to know who killed my poor Wickham. Colonel Fitzwilliam I know you are Darcy's cousin, but you show none of his pride. Therefore, I trust you will find the person guilty of this murder and punish him for this deed. My poor Lydia is now without a husband to take care of her." Mrs. Bennet buried her face in the square of lace in her hand.

Colonel Fitzwilliam managed to keep his tone calm, regardless of Darcy's mother-in-law's raised voice, and tried again to discover if the woman knew any information that might help them identify the killer. "Do try to calm yourself, Mrs. Bennet. We must ask these questions so we can confirm your innocence and find the guilty person."

WHO MURDERED MR. WICKHAM

"If you ask me, it is Colonel Forester who should be questioned." Mrs. Bennet sniffed and sent a look of dislike toward Lydia's former friend. "It was he who allowed my poor Lydia to run off to Gretna Green."

"Believe me, madam, I knew nothing of your daughter's plans until all was done, and, if you will recall, I sent word to your husband immediately."

Mrs. Bennet rolled her expressive eyes and tightened her lips. "I am quite certain your wife was aware of Lydia's intentions and could have stopped her, had she tried."

"I assure you, Mrs. Bennet, my wife would have moved the entire regiment to prevent that elopement if she had but known of your daughter's plans in time."

Bingley noted the vehement tone in Colonel Forester's voice and exchanged a glance with Colonel Fitzwilliam. This was not what he expected. By the time Colonel Forester finished his questioning, Bingley suspected his guests and family members would be furious with him and the colonel. "Colonel Forester, I fear Mrs. Bennet is still unsettled by the night's events. She needs to rest."

"Oh, my dear, Mr. Bingley, how thoughtful of you." Mrs. Bennet turned a glare on Colonel Forester. "As for you sir, I wished no harm on my poor, dear Wickham. Can you make the same claim?"

Colonel Forester's glance was so grim, Bingley was certain his recruits would be shaking in their boots, but not so with Jane's mother. Nevertheless, Bingley frowned when the colonel's voice boomed loudly.

"Mrs. Bennet, we have heard enough. Send in Mrs. Phillips as you leave."

"Why would you question my sister?" demanded Mrs. Bennet, proving she was not afraid of the colonel's show of temper. "She barely knew dear Wickham. Sister knows nothing about his murder or she would have told me by now."

"Madam, that is for us to decide. Now, if you would tell her we are waiting, please." Colonel Forester turned his back and stared into the fire.

Mrs. Bennet cut him a glance and sniffed. "You could put a uniform on a pig, and he too would stomp on my poor nerves." She rose and flounced to the door. "My dear, Mr. Bingley, I know not how you can stand this inquisitive behavior."

CBEO

"Sister said you wanted to see me, Colonel, but what can I tell you?" Mrs. Phillips gasped in a breathless voice as she entered the room. "I barely knew Mr. Wickham, even though he married my dear niece. Lydia reminds me so much of her dear mother when they were of an age. Still, I am informed you wish to ask questions."

After a few words, the men ushered Mrs. Phillips out and called Mr. Hurst to enter. Bingley tried to conceal his consternation as Hurst stumbled into the room. "What, Wickham is dead? But I saw him in the garden, not more than an hour since."

"Did Wickham leave the garden before you returned, Mr. Hurst?" Colonel Forester's tone was mild as if accustomed to dealing with men too far in their cups.

Mr. Hurst leaned back in his chair. "Now that you make mention of it, I seem to recall I returned to the house because I was thirsty. Walking the grounds builds a need for refreshment in a man of my years, you know."

"What of your wife, sir?"

"Eh? My wife? Nay, she never touches the drink. Too hoity toity if you ask me." Mr. Hurst squinted as he recognized his brother-in-law. "Right, eh Bingley?"

"Do you wish to remain while we question your wife, sir?"

"What? Oh, yes. 'Course. Bring her in." Mr. Hurst settled in the chair and was snoring by the time Mrs. Hurst entered library and took a seat beside him.

Bingley noted the lack of color in his sister's face and felt a pang of sympathy for her emotional state as she sent a glance toward the muslin covering Wickham's body.

Mrs. Hurst angled sideways to avoid looking in that direction again and dabbed at her eyes as she aimed her questions to Colonel Fitzwilliam. "How do you expect me to help, Colonel?"

Colonel Fitzwilliam paused, reluctant to broach the topic to one of Darcy's frequent guests, or perhaps conscious of the fact that Mrs. Hurst's brother was listening to questions about how she might be connected to the murdered man. Nevertheless, he stalled only for a breath before he continued. "Mrs. Hurst, how well did you know Mr. Wickham?"

Louisa Hurst lifted her head and managed to look down her nose, even though Colonel Fitzwilliam stood over her. "I encountered Mr. Wickham at Pemberley and at socials, locally, when we were visiting my brother."

Colonel Forester stopped pacing and stared down at Mrs. Hurst. "You do not claim a long standing association with Mr. Wickham, such as Colonel Fitzwilliam here?"

"Whatever are you implying, sir?" Mrs. Hurst stared at Colonel Forester with wide eyes.

Recognizing his sister was in a temper, Bingley rushed to respond before she could vent her opinions on the unsuspecting military officers. "Colonel Forester, my sisters and I were not acquainted with Mr. Darcy as children. We have known him but a few years past."

"Ah, so, no long standing disagreements with Mr. Wickham in your past, Mrs. Hurst?"

"Certainly not, sir!" Mrs. Hurst gasped, as if he had accused her of some social blunder, and cut a glance at her brother. "Bingley was always too easy-going to argue with anyone, and we were not acquainted with…Mr. Wickham."

The break in her voice was barely noticeable. In fact, Bingley was almost certain neither of the colonels took it for anything other than an affected speech pattern. However, Bingley knew different. He frowned as he considered reasons for his sister's unexpected emotion.

Not realizing anything of significance had occurred, Colonel Forester made a dismissive sound and clasped his hands behind his back as he announced in a loud voice. "Madam, you may go and take your husband with you."

By the time Bingley and Louisa coaxed Mr. Hurst awake and out of the room, Colonel Forester's patience had disappeared. "This night has no end and I am certain you agree, Colonel. And another point," Forester paced in front of the fireplace, "we have not asked one question of Mr. Bingley and yet he hears all that is said on the subject."

"Now see here, Colonel," Fitzwilliam did not attempt to keep the amazement out of his voice, "Once you are around Bingley enough, you will learn he has not a mean bone in his body."

"Be that as it may, we should question him."

"A waste of time, as are most of the questions we have asked so far this night. But if you insist, then ask Bingley anything that you will."

"Uh, no matter. It is my belief the murderer is long gone by now. Possibly a passing highwayman, looking for easy pickings and

Wickham tried to prevent his theft."

Colonel Fitzwilliam fought the urge to laugh. "Surely you jest, sir. I would suggest Wickham was slippery as a snake and much more likely to slither away into the night than to confront a robber."

"Quite right you are, Colonel. Wickham did not have the persistence to stand up for his beliefs, if he had any."

"Oh, he had beliefs a plenty," Colonel Fitzwilliam snapped, "but all to do with him prospering at the expense of others, regardless of how his actions affected them."

"You did not think very highly of Mr. Wickham, Colonel."

Fitzwilliam aimed a grim glare at the colonel. "You were his commanding officer for a time, Colonel. Can you say you would give Wickham a favorable mention?"

Silence reigned in the library for long ticks of the clock. Each man turned and stared at the body. Flames flickered in the fireplace. Fitzwilliam stared at the blaze and said. "I think we would have been better to keep this room cold, considering there is a body in here, but it is too late now."

"Clear vision often comes too late, Colonel." Forester kicked at a spark that landed on the hearth. "Often it comes after it is too late to correct that which is already done. On this night, we can at least rectify this one error. When the blaze burns out, we will adjourn to another room, if you wish. Now, who is next on your list?"

After interviewing Bingley, which Colonel Forester insisted was necessary, then Jane and the Gardiners, they learned nothing to lead them to the culprit. The Gardiners were almost as kind in nature as Mr. Bingley and much too mild mannered to harbor any ill feelings against Wickham. Even after questions about his part in arranging his niece's wedding, Mr. Gardiner cast not one ill word against the deceased Mr. Wickham.

"Your wife is next on the list, Colonel." Fitzwilliam looked at man he had only come to know this evening. Two Colonels and two men in the wrong place at the wrong time was his assumption.

"Ah, she may be too overwrought to speak coherently for Lydia and Wickham were very dear to her."

His response did nothing to unsettle Fitzwilliam. In fact, as Fitzwilliam stared in the flames, he acknowledged he had anticipated such a response. In Colonel Forester's place, he too would want to protect his wife from such gripping emotions. "Then, sir, I suggest we go over what we have learned and form a new plan."

Chapter Six

Much later, the three men entered the ballroom, and Colonel Fitzwilliam concealed his relief at escaping the library. He had breathed all the stench of death he could stand. Encounters with foreign forces left memories he would as soon forget, and the evening spent so near Wickham's body brought the horrors of war to his mind.

Yet the environment in the ballroom, that had filled with music three hours earlier, was almost as gloomy as the scene in the library.

Guests gathered about the room in clusters. Men sat around the card tables playing whist, or conversed with women, and all had an opinion as to who had murdered Mr. Wickham.

Fitzwilliam and Colonel Forester planned to mingle with guests and listen for any comments that might assist in identifying the murderer. Bingley was in complete agreement with the plan as he was anxious to check on Jane.

As the colonels approached, Caroline Bingley was quick to voice her solution to the crime, and glanced at her sister for reinforcement. But Mrs. Hurst's face twisted in anger and she refused to acknowledge them. Caroline turned back to the colonels and pointed a finger at Fitzwilliam as she said. "Colonel Forester, if you are looking for someone with a reason to murder Mr. Wickham, you need look no further than your companion."

Colonel Fitzwilliam sent a resigned glance across the room to where Darcy watched the encounter with an arched brow and turned back to the disgruntled sisters. One thing Fitzwilliam had confirmed during his acquaintance with Bingley's sisters was their lack of the good nature so enjoyed by their brother. Another point was Caroline Bingley's obsession for Darcy's attention. Even as a poor relation, compared to Darcy's deep pockets, Fitzwilliam had been a target for her attention, though he had noticed Caroline was more interested in Darcy's reaction to her overtures than in his own interest in her. Yet he had endured her flirtation as they were both guests of Darcy's and as such, Fitzwilliam did not wish to express his aversion to her actions.

Not that Darcy noticed, or cared, about Caroline's attempts to attract him. Darcy's lack of response earned Fitzwilliam her ill humor as proved by her present actions, so Fitzwilliam kept quiet and allowed Colonel Forester respond.

"Miss Bingley, Mrs. Hurst," Colonel Forester gave a slight bow in their direction and turned his gaze on Caroline. "Are you referring to Colonel Fitzwilliam, ma'am?"

"Absolutely, Colonel, and if you intend to identify the murderer, then you need search no further." Caroline aimed a slanted glance at Fitzwilliam to detect his reaction to her words. "I assume the colonel has informed you of his role as a joint-guardian of Miss Georgiana Darcy?"

"Your comments are quite helpful, ma'am, for I had no knowledge of such an arrangement." Colonel Forester's brow wrinkled as he glanced at Fitzwilliam. Then he turned back to Caroline and lowered his voice as he inquired. "Begging your pardon, ma'am, but do apprise me as to how such a fact is relative to Mr. Wickham's untimely demise."

"Colonel Forester, surely you are aware Darcy has enough funds to arrange any actions he should choose. I am merely suggesting that, perhaps, Colonel Fitzwilliam added some funds to his own pockets and removed an embarrassment for the family. Or perhaps he possesses some of Darcy's famous pride and he acted out of honor." Caroline paused as she sent a glare across the room toward the object of her heart's greatest desire.

Fitzwilliam was relieved to note Darcy focused his attention totally on his wife as guests milled around them. Perhaps she was incensed by Darcy's lack of attention, for Caroline lowered her voice to a confiding tone and continued to share details with Colonel Forester. "Everything was kept very quiet, mind you, and few people ever heard that Mr. Wickham once tried to elope with dear Miss Darcy."

A gasp sounded loud in the low hum of conversation filling the room. Colonel Fitzwilliam looked about to locate the source, but was unable to determine if the sound came from a pale- faced Georgiana or from a pink-cheeked Lizzy as she glared at Caroline.

Either source was possible for since Lizzy had married Darcy she devoted her free time to his sister. In return, Georgiana had formed a strong bond with her brother's wife, making the three of them a close-knit family.

As one of Georgiana's guardians, Fitzwilliam appreciated Lizzy's devotion to his young cousin and felt nothing but admiration for Darcy's choice of a wife. Fitzwilliam had encountered few people with a temperament as sweet as his ward's and he was relieved to see her so happy.

Glancing about the room in an attempt to clear his mind of Caroline's unsettling claims, Fitzwilliam's attention settled on his hosts for the evening. It occurred to him that Bingley and his wife, Jane, were two people who possessed dispositions as pleasant as Georgiana's. But reality returned with the accusing tone of Caroline's voice and he found it difficult to accept that with her unkind manner of speaking, Caroline was indeed Bingley's sister.

Forcing any trace of his thoughts from his expression, Fitzwilliam managed a polite tone and a slight bow as he said. "Miss Bingley, I cannot tell you how disappointed I am to learn you have formed such a low opinion of me since last we met."

"Oh, but you are quite mistaken, Colonel Fitzwilliam. My opinion of you has not changed in the least since the moment we first met."

"Ah, then you must forgive me daring to think otherwise on previous occasions when you made a point to seek my attention." Fitzwilliam hid his expression with a formal bow.

Colonel Forester paid no attention to polite manners and demanded, in an astounded tone, as Fitzwilliam straightened to his full height. "Sir, is what Miss Bingley says in fact true? Are you Miss Darcy's guardian?"

"It is true, I share the role of guardian with Mr. Darcy, but I have no notion why such information matters in the circumstances of Mr. Wickham's death."

"As you observe, Colonel Forester, all is not as it seems," Caroline's tone hinted at dark secrets as she spoke to the colonel. "Perhaps before you disregard the value of my contribution, you should consider how such information coming to light would reflect serious neglect by two such gentlemen as Mr. Darcy and Colonel Fitzwilliam. News that they allowed the young girl under their protection to be whisked out of their care and off to Hamsgate, would reflect poorly on both gentlemen."

"Correct you are, Miss Bingley. This matter needs further examination," Colonel Forester retorted.

Colonel Fitzwilliam acknowledged the comment and accompanying glare from his fellow officer with a nod, "Of course, Colonel. And it shall be scrutinized at great length, but not in front of the guests." Fitz sent a slight bow toward the Bingley sisters. "Ladies."

⊗⊗⊗

Lizzy turned to Darcy and murmured only for his hearing. "Oh, I cannot think how Bingley could be related to such a woman. Caroline is up to her games again. Surely we cannot allow her to cast doubt on members of your family without responding."

"We must, my dear." Forcing his jaw to relax, Darcy lifted a shoulder and removed his gaze from the source of the loud comments. Instead he turned his attention to the more pleasant sight of his wife's face. "There is more to be lost than gained by acknowledging Caroline's nonsense."

Darcy's mood lightened as he studied the disgruntled expression on his wife's face. In the few months since their marriage, his heart had never been as content, and his younger sister had blossomed under Lizzy's attentions. He would not allow vengeful statements to destroy this pleasant state of affairs, but neither did he wish Georgiana's lack of judgment to be ridiculed if her plans to elope with Wickham became public knowledge.

He must ignore the source threatening his family's happiness. Bingley would not object if him cut Caroline cold. Previous encounters with Caroline had proved her aim was to gain his response, and he vowed she would get no such satisfaction from him. Still, if she persisted with these inane comments, she would force him to act. For the time being, however, more urgent matters demanded his attention.

For one, his dear Lizzy was unaware of how serious the allegations against members of her own family were, and he intended to keep her free from worry. He must find a way to disprove claims against the Bennets before they damaged his wife's contentment. Normally, Fitz would assist him in his efforts, but, while his cousin was solving this crime, Darcy intended to protect his family in his own way.

"But Mr. Darcy—"

"Dear wife, have I not requested you to use my Christian name?"

Lizzy smiled as she lost herself in his eyes. "I know, Will, but it is a habit learned from early childhood. Mamma always calls our father Mr. Bennet, and I feel compelled to call you—"

"Husband, dear, or Will, if you please, wife."

The warmth in his brown eyes tugged at Lizzy's heart. She had always dreamed of marrying for love, but never realized the joys awaiting her when she did so. Darcy was different when they were alone. His eyes filled with a teasing light she had never witnessed in public. Not even with Georgiana did he show his emotions as he did with her. Had she guessed at the depth of Darcy's emotions, she was not convinced she would have acted any more circumspect than Lydia had with Wickham. However, as strong as her feeling were for Darcy, Lizzy maintained some semblance of proper behavior in public. Still, she would do anything to please him.

"Dear Will," Lizzy breathed. Then she peeped past his shoulder to confirm that her mother could not hear the endearment. However, her mother was attempting to speak with Lydia. For Lydia was a moving target, pacing the floor, sometimes stomping her foot, or staring at the guests. Poor, Lydia. Being a widow so young was unthinkable. "How goes the quest to find Wickham's murderer?"

"We must ask Bingley." Darcy glanced some feet away, where his friend hovered near his wife. Darcy would rather avoid intruding on their time together, but he dared not, and urged Lizzy forward. "Charles, what say you about the situation?"

"Oh, Lizzy," Jane rushed into speech as soon as Lizzy and Darcy reached them. "They have accused our family and Bingley's of being suspect in Wickham's murder. What are we to do?"

"What nonsense." Lizzy clasped Jane's hands in hers. "Tell me, exactly what they said."

"I cannot recall every word, but it seems they believe all the Bennets have good reason to want Wickham dead, but especially you, Lizzy."

"The colonels have reason to suspect Caroline," Bingley added when Jane paused for breath, "and I expect we will hear Louisa and Hurst accused as well."

"How can this be?" Lizzy looked at Darcy then turned back to Bingley. "Do they not have other suspects for this crime?"

Color filled Bingley's face as words spewed from him. "Most of the guests in fact, but our families were named. Of course there is no truth to this."

"What of Lydia?" Darcy asked. "Do they suspect her of the deed as well?"

Lizzy whirled toward him. "Surely you cannot mean Lydia killed her own husband?"

Darcy lifted a shoulder as he glanced about the room. "It would not be the first time a wife has killed her husband. I would look there first, if I had the duty."

"Where exactly would you look, Will?" Colonel Fitzwilliam appeared at Darcy's side. "What have I missed?"

"Colonel Fitzwilliam, pray do not pay any heed to Mr. Darcy's words. He only suggested possibilities." Jane replied.

"What theory have you now, Will?" Colonel Fitzwilliam eyed his cousin. "Pray, tell me if you have a solution to this crime, for, as yet, we have no answers."

"It is not a solution, but pure tomfoolery and not to be considered." Lizzy ground her teeth as she glared at her husband. "I cannot think how you could suggest such a thing."

"I merely suggested if the rest of the family is under suspicion, then why not Lydia?" Darcy kept his voice calm amongst the tightly wound nerves he had set on edge by his casual comment. "It was only an observation."

"Yet one to ponder," Colonel Fitzwilliam turned to study the young widow with a thoughtful glance, "though I must confess we have so many prospects, I doubt this one will be unexpected."

⊰⊱

Across the room, Mrs. Forester was in fine form as she lifted her chin to stare at the colonel. "Well, husband, pray tell, who murdered dear Wickham."

"It is difficult to say." Colonel Forester turned to gaze about the guests, and then focused his attention on his wife. "For all I know, you could be guilty of the crime."

"How droll of you to suggest such a thing, but do whisper the name of the guilty person in my ear."

"If I but knew." Colonel Forester reached to pluck a leaf from his wife's long locks. "My dear, how is it that you go outside to take the air and come back wearing a bouquet of leaves on your person?"

"Oh, do stop with your foolish talk and tell me, Forester. Who is guilty of this murder, for I want to give him a piece of my mind before you haul him off to the gaol?"

"Mm, yes, the murderer robbed you of one of your favorites, did he not, wife?"

"How do you know the murderer was a man?" Mrs. Forester arched a shaped brow. "Perhaps the crime is the results of a lover's tiff. Are you questioning women as well?"

"Wife, do you dare suggest that Mrs. Wickham might have murdered her husband?"

"Oh, how delightful of you to reach such a conclusion, my dear, for even I had not considered such a possibility." Mrs. Forester beamed up at the colonel. "Do you think it is a solution? We know Lydia well enough. Do you consider her capable of such an act?"

"Do you suppose his wife could do this thing? Or perhaps it was you, wife. For you were better acquainted with Wickham than ever I was."

Mrs. Forester tapped her toe as glared at the colonel. "Could not any wife or husband on occasion find the passion to commit such an act?" Not waiting for a response, she swept a hand over her hair and gazed around her. "This gathering has become even more uninteresting than evenings at Lucas Lodge, and I swear, all our acquaintances have deserted us."

"Stop swearing, wife, it is not good manners."

Mrs. Forester tapped his chest with her finger and sent him a flirting glance showing her mood had improved. "And how, pray tell, do you expect me to avoid doing so when I live surrounded by militia men?"

"Wife, you should be a good influence on my men, not the other way round." The colonel sent her an affectionate glance. "Save your games for later, my dear. Now, I have duties to perform." He turned to search the crowd. "What happened to Denny and Captain Carter? They are usually at your beck and call for entertainment."

"Oh, poof," Mrs. Forester tossed her head. "Denny is attending the poor widow and Carter was with Miss King, last I saw him. So it is up to you, husband." She leaned against the colonel's arm and pressed her body close. "Play a game with me, and take the boredom out of this wasted evening. Let us guess who murdered Wickham."

"Perhaps it was Denny," the colonel nodded toward Denny,

who stood on the other side of the room beside Lydia, "since he was one of your close circle and knew the Wickhams well."

"Oh, how you go on, Colonel." Mrs. Forester trilled, though an unbecoming expression coverd her face as she watched Denny bend to speak in Lydia's ear. She whirled back to face her husband. "What possible reason could Denny have for doing such a thing?"

"He was friends with the wife before Wickham arrived. And let us not forget he is a trained militia man, and would find the task easier than some ordinary person."

"You and Carter are trained as well, and so is Colonel Fitzwilliam. Does that mean that any one of you could have murdered poor Wickham?"

"Of course not, I was only trying to indulge you in a game. Is that not what you wanted, wife?"

"Oh, I do so enjoy party games. Pray continue, husband. What reason could Denny have for murdering his friend Wickham?"

"An unpaid loan, perhaps? As close as the two men were, I suspect Wickham borrowed from Denny. He asked for loans from everyone else of his acquaintance."

"Perhaps debt was the cause," Mrs. Forester tapped her chin, "but it does not seem reason enough to kill. Murder seems such a violent act. There must have been intense passion inside the person responsible."

Colonel Forester frowned as he glanced at his wife. "You make a point that deserves consideration, my dear. Perhaps it was an act of passion, jealousy, mayhap, or —"

"Jealousy," Mrs. Forester's brow arched as she laughed, "really, husband, are you not reaching too far to find a cause? For why would Denny be jealous of Wickham?" She fluttered her handkerchief as a shield as she considered the possibility. Jealous. Could it be so? Was dear, sweet Denny so troubled over her previous encounters with Wickham that he would commit such an act of violence to win her attentions? Oh, surely not, for, after further consideration, she was quite certain Denny was unaware of her relationship with Wickham.

Unless, the two of them were great friends, as her husband stated. She supposed Wickham might have been indiscreet and spoken of his liaison with her. Though he could not have made such a misstep, for word would have traveled around the whole of Brighton had he done so. If Denny committed this deed, it was because of something he learned at this ball, but what? Did he suspect she had gone to the garden to meet with Wickham, and only turned to him as a last recourse? Would that provoke him to murder?

"My dear, have you not noticed how fond Denny is of Mrs. Wickham? Indeed, I believe they were great friends even before Lydia set her eye on Wickham?"

"So you keep saying," Mrs. Forester sniffed. "What nonsense you do go on, Colonel. If this is your idea of creating a game for my entertainment, you have failed."

Colonel Forester rocked on his heels, determined to regain his wife's good humor. "Perhaps the other young lady you mentioned is responsible."

"Oh, that red-headed, Miss King did claim Wickham's attention for a time. Um," Mrs. Forester tapped her chin, "yes, she could be the murderer. I have heard it said that people with red hair have a temper to match. Now there is passion for you, sir. A woman scorned."

"You think such could happen, wife?" Colonel Forester studied the female in question as Miss King stood conversing with Lady Lucas. "Still, did we not hear that she was the one who ended the arrangement with Wickham, and not the reverse?"

"Such gossip is rarely true, sir. Perhaps she actually expected the match to occur. I heard she all but snatched Wickham from Lizzy Bennet's snare."

"Ah, do I detect that you do not care for Lydia's sister, my dear?"

"She is too full of herself, by far. Not as much so as that Caroline Bingley, but she has a haughty expression about her, as if she can tell what you are thinking. Now there is a woman who could commit a crime of passion, husband."

Colonel Forester frowned as he glanced at the target of their discussion. "I am not so certain you are correct, my dear. Mrs. Darcy has too much at stake to commit such a careless act, and for what reason?"

"Wickham rejected her favor when he turned to Miss King, of course. Yet, his lack of interest in her did not end there, for he added even more insult to her considerable pride when he married Mrs. Darcy's youngest sister. Can you imagine her shame?"

"Ah, but you are overlooking one very important point, my dear. Mr. Darcy is well-heeled, while Mr. Wickham borrowed from all his acquaintances just to have enough funds to survive. Regrettably, in this matter I fear you are mistaken."

"Then we must reconsider Miss King as a likely suspect." Mrs. Forester turned to stare at the woman holding her attention. "Look at her big blue eyes and tiny little person. Why, she looks no more than a child playing dress-up. No wonder Wickham turned her away. He wanted a real woman to get his arms around."

"You seem very certain of that fact, my dear."

"Oh," Mrs. Forester turned a heated gaze on him, "is that not what you whisper in the dark, husband? Are we not still playing a game?"

"Perhaps you have not heard that Miss King inherited a fortune? Why go for a wastrel such as Wickham, when she could choose a man more worthy of her attention?"

"Oh, really, husband. You speak as if she were someone to admire." Mrs. Forester sniffed as she peered at him. "Did you not notice Wickham's countenance, or the length of his leg, and the charm he practiced so well? I for one, sir, would say Wickham was far from being the wastrel you describe."

CRED

"My dear, Miss King," Lady Lucas spoke in a low voice so as to not be overheard, "have you noticed the Foresters seem to find your presence uncommonly fascinating?"

"Indeed, I have made note of their interest, Lady Lucas." Mary cast a casual glance to the other side of the room, in the couple's direction, and saw that both the Foresters had their gazes locked on her person. "It seems quite unusual—"

"It is but fact, my dear, for I have been aware of their interest for some minutes past, and I can not help but wonder why." Lady Lucas turned to her youngest houseguest, "Indeed, it seems odd as you are all guests at Lucas Lodge. Have you not engaged the Foresters in conversation this eve, my dear? Could that be the cause of their attention?"

Mary pretended interest in the cup in her hand and tried to keep a tide of color from rising to her face. Indeed, red hair was no handicap in her estimation, but the burden of the fairnee of skin accompanying her coloring was hard to deal with at times such as this when she needed to keep her thoughts secret. "I confess, I have not exchanged pleasantries with Mrs. Forester, ma'am."

"No matter, my dear." Lady Lucas lowered her voice and cast a glance in Mrs. Forester's direction. "If you were of the opposite gender and blessed with a good countenance, I dare say you would have ample opportunity to speak to the lady."

A gurgle of laughter caught in Mary King's throat. On a night of such disastrous events, it would not do to appear merry, but Lady Lucas had cast Mrs. Forester's character in such correct detail, Mary found it difficult to contain her mirth. "How you do go on, Lady Lucas. Yet casting humor aside, do you not think we are being somewhat unkind to speak of Mrs. Forester in such terms?"

"Not at all, my dear," Lady Lucas said as she warmed to her topic. "I have it on good authority that young Mrs. Forester was so eager to improve her status in life as to accept the offer from Colonel Forester, a man years her senior, when her heart belonged to a local young man in her county."

"But marrying to benefit her status in life does not condemn her to ridicule, surely." Mary glanced around the room. "I can observe couples who give evidence of such matches in this room alone."

Lady Lucas followed Mary's gaze as she glanced toward the group surrounding Lydia Wickham. "I can see where your thoughts are aimed, Miss King, but rest assured, the elder Bennet daughters were nothing if not ladylike in their actions, regardless of their younger sister's behavior or their mother's. Pray do not misunderstand me, for Mrs. Bennet is a special friend of mine. After all, they are s leading family in the county and Sir William and I are quite fond of them. Not for one anything would I compare Jane or Lizzy with Mrs. Forester."

"Ah, Mrs. Forester," Mrs. Phillips said as she appeared beside Mary. "What was that you were saying, Lady Lucas, for all the room is chattering of Mrs. Forester's actions on this eve. What have you to add?"

"Really, Mrs. Phillips," Lady Lucas said as she sent Mary a sidelong glance. "I was only saying to Miss King that Colonel and Mrs. Forester are staying with us at Lucas Lodge because they were such favorites of Sir William's when the militia was stationed locally. But pray, do tell us all you have heard."

"Um," Mrs. Phillips examined each of them with an intense gaze before continuing, "yes, so I seem to recall. In those days, between Lydia and Mrs. Forester, no social event was lacking laughter. I know this to be true from my own social."

"Yes, of course, Mrs. Phillips, but do tell us the latest news." Lady Lucas leveled a gaze on the woman. "For you must have heard details from your dear nieces."

"Well," Mrs. Phillips leaned close and lowered her voice, "it has been observed by several guests that Mrs. Forester had two assignations on her recent visit to the garden—"

"No!" Lady Lucas managed a look of surprise, despite the words she shared with Mary earlier. "You cannot be serious."

"And neither was with her husband." Mrs. Phillips concluded with a satisfied expression on her face.

Mary swallowed the lump in her throat as she observed her companions. This was how easy it was to assassinate a person's character. "Perhaps Mrs. Forester was only greeting acquaintances on her walk about the grounds as she went searching for her husband."

Lady Lucas and Mrs. Phillips turned to stare at Mary.

"My dear Miss King," Mrs. Phillips rushed to speak, "your response is much kinder than I was lead to believe what was expected of you. Yet I fear I must prove you wrong for Colonel Forester left the ball after his wife did so, but before two other men who also followed her from the room. And," Mrs. Phillips paused, though she looked ready to burst as she whispered, "she was observed hiding in the bushes with another man when Colonel Forester passed close by."

"Oh, do tell, us more Mrs. Phillips," Lady Lucas exclaimed, "for I have so missed womanly conversation since my dear Charlotte married and removed from Lucas Lodge. Though Charlotte was not the best person to converse with on such topics, I must admit. She would much rather conduct a discourse on some book she was reading, and though Sir William is quite vocal, he does not speak of such events that interest a woman. I believe men do not see the importance of noting the exact actions of a person's behavior."

Mary lifted her cup to cover the smile trying to break from her lips. Sir William would prattle about on any topic, but as his wife affirmed, he was not a gossip. Indeed, he was often so busy talking he took no notice of his surroundings, and these women were alert to the actions of everyone around them.

"Perhaps the gentlemen have more important issues to discuss than whether someone is wearing the latest fashion." Noting the frowns greeting her statement, Mary quickly added, "But I dare say, women would suffer without such details and where would fashionable society be without adoring followers?"

"You are so astute, Miss King," Mrs. Phillips studied Mary with an exacting eye as if to determine if she were being made a mockery of, or if indeed, Mary actually meant the words she spoke. "I cannot think why my nieces chose not to spend more time with you. Perhaps, now that my dear Jane has returned to the county, that situation will change."

Mrs. Phillips' words fostered hope in Mary's heart, but she dared not show how much she wanted such connections. "You are too kind, Mrs. Phillips — "

"And not at all forthcoming for one with so much news to share," Lady Lucas added with barely concealed frustration at the interruption in their topic. "Now, Mrs. Phillips, what have you to tell us about Mr. Wickham's murder?"

"Well, since you asked," Mrs. Phillips said as she glanced around to make certain no one was listening. "I should not speak ill of the dead, but there is a search for Wickham's killer, so I will repeat what I have heard. Some of the guests think perhaps Mrs. Forester intended to meet Mr. Wickham in the garden."

"No!" Lady Lucas sounded aghast.

"Why would anyone think such a thing? Mrs. Forester is a married woman, with a husband in the militia." Mary kept her voice low, though she knew full well why people might make such assumptions. When she was once the focus of Mr. Wickham's attention, he often suggested they should stroll in the garden. On those occasions, he seemed more interested in things other than good conversation, much to her regret.

"Well, few people know this," Mrs. Phillips lowered her voice to a near whisper, "but when the regiment was located here in Meryton, Mrs. Forester and Mr. Wickham were quite friendly. That was before he turned his attention to my niece, Lydia, of course."

"Of course, Mrs. Phillips," Lady Lucas nodded in quick agreement, "for who could believe Mr. Wickham would look at another once his interest was fixed."

Mary swallowed the gasp trying to erupt from her mouth and tried to conceal her disbelief from her companions. Indeed, had Wickham not switched his attentions from Miss Elizabeth Bennet to Mary as soon as news of her inheritance was public knowledge? With that fact in mind, Mary could well believe Wickham turned his attentions from his wife to another woman.

 beginning

Denny backed away as Lydia's family gathered close to offer comfort, and went to join Captain Carter at the refreshment table. "I noticed you strolled in the garden with the comely little red-head."

"Get that condescending tone out of your voice, Denny, and use your good sense." Captain Carter surveyed the space around them for anyone listening. "There will be questions about Wickham's murder, you can be sure."

"I am aware of that, Carter." Denny filled a cup with punch and took a long gulp. "But why should I be concerned?"

"Where is your head, Denny," Captain Carter said as he straightened to his full height. "It will not take long for someone to discover you argument with Wickham."

"Wickham owed me more than I can spare, as he did you and half of our regiment."

"Even so, we are the only two of his friends here and likely to be accused of the murder. And you forget the little matter of his affair with your sister."

"Do not mention Peg's name in the same breath as Wickham's," Denny faced off against Carter, illustrating the disadvantage of his shorter height and ill temper, "if you are my friend."

"That I am as you well know, but how long do you expect it will take the colonels to discover you are now enjoying Wickham's former lover?"

Denny set his cup on the table with a loud clatter. Shoulders squared, fists clenched, he faced Carter. "You are in no position to mention his attachments, after your recent walk in the garden with the lovely Miss King."

Carter clenched his teeth as he glared down at his friend. "Do not ever refer to Miss King in that manner again, Denny, or I might not be responsible for my actions."

Denny's shoulders slumped. A shadow of his usual grin stretched the corners of his mouth. "Correct, as usual, Carter. I apologize for my loose tongue. Miss King has done nothing to earn my careless remarks. If anything, she showed remarkably good judgment by giving Wickham the boot when he cast his attentions towards her. It does me no credit to admit I am consumed with wanting for his other interest, yet she is here in the same room, and I must not go near her."

"Can you not see this puts you in danger of being accused of this murder?" Carter shook his head, and slowly refilled his cup. "I am concerned for your best interest, my friend. That is all."

"Wickham owed you funds, as well. You were even in the garden tonight, as was I." Denny paced away a step and turned back. "You, too, were in the company of another female Wickham favored. How am I in any more risk of being blamed than you?"

"Your recent confrontation with Wickham will come to light, and there is the matter of your insistence on pursuing the woman he went out to the garden to meet."

"How can you know this?" Denny lost his attempt at recovering his good humor. "Perhaps their meeting was unexpected. Or have you even considered she might have arranged to meet me."

"And perhaps, suddenly, I have pockets as deep Mr. Darcy's." Carter exclaimed. "Use your good sense, my friend. Wickham left the ballroom without his wife in tow. You know what that means, for you are as aware of his ways, as am I. Perhaps even more so, as you were once inseparable companions."

"That was before — "

"He tried to seduce your sister?"

"Leave Peg's name out of this." Denny struggled to unclench his teeth and ease the tension from his fists. "The incident with my sister was settled. Any issues I had with Wickham was over the debt owed me — "

"My point, exactly," Carter said as he refilled his punch cup. "Even without your current complications, past events could complicate your efforts at proving your innocence." Carter took a long drink from his cup.

Denny picked up his discarded cup. He gazed about the room, though he was careful not to focus on the face of the woman pulling at his heartstrings. If word of their connection reached his superiors, all would indeed be lost. "I do believe you are correct as usual, Captain Carter."

That Denny used his rank alerted Carter to his friend's troubled thoughts. "I am sorry about Wickham's demise, but 'tis even more regrettable that we happen to be in the county when his death occurred."

Chapter Seven

Colonel Fitzwilliam mixed with the guests, standing in groups discussing the murder, but heard no hints to assist with solving the crime. He was so intent on his self-assigned endeavor to discover information, he even joined the group surrounding Sir William.

Fitzwilliam, like Sir William's captive audience, hoped to learn new information. Standing with his back stiff, his reserved patience in full force, Fitzwilliam soon realized the mild-mannered magistrate was entertaining his audience with long-winded descriptions of the same topic, repeatedly.

Finally, when he could keep his expression blank for not a minute longer, Fitzwilliam move to speak a few words with the grieving widow, after which, he approached his host. "Bingley, I have mingled among the guests, and from the comments I overheard, I concerned that recent events have put you in a most difficult position. I think I speak for Colonel Forester, as well as myself, when I say everyone would understand if you are inclined to forego the remaining investigation into this matter."

"Why would Bingley withdraw his assistance, Colonel?" Jane examined her guest with intense interest. In any group of men, Colonel Fitzwilliam would claim notice, even without his known connection to Mr. Darcy. In the encounters she and Bingley had had with him, since Mr. Darcy and Lizzy had become a couple, Colonel Fitzwilliam had earned her approval with his calm manner and commendable behavior. She was relieved Colonel Fitzwilliam was on hand to take charge after this tragic event.

In fact, considering her good opinion of him, perhaps she should regard him as a possible match for one of her...but no. The idea of contriving a match between this competent officer and one of her sisters was not possible. There was Caroline, however. And considering the colonel's blunt suggestion that Bingley bow out of the investigation, he seemed a perfect match for her sister-in-law. Curbing her flare of emotions with her usual calm demeanor, Jane keep her tone firm. "After all, Colonel, this is Bingley's home."

"I beg your pardon, Mrs. Bingley —"

"My dear, Jane," Bingley touched her arm, "I believe you misunderstood. For I am quite certain Colonel Fitzwilliam spoke only out of kindness."

"Just so, Bingley," Colonel Fitzwilliam said as he acknowledged Bingley with a nod. "As several of your family members were mentioned in an unfavorable light, I thought it prudent to offer you the choice before resuming our examination."

"Pray tell me, Colonel, what member of my family is accused of this murder?" Jane's low tone did not reveal her roiling emotions, but her insistence left no doubt of her interest. "I must ask that you explain."

"Jane, my dear," Bingley began in a soothing tone, "do not —"

"No, Bingley, your wife is correct in calling me to task as I mentioned the subject in her presence." Colonel Fitzwilliam turned his full attention to Jane. "Mrs. Bingley, I assure you the utmost care will be given to our efforts to reveal the truth of this matter. You must expect some unpleasant questions to be asked, but please, do not overly concern yourself."

"You avoided my question, Colonel Fitzwilliam. And with charming manners, I might add, but I must ask again. Which members of my family do you hold as suspect?"

"Everyone at this ball is being questioned, Mrs. Bingley."

"That is not an answer I can accept, Colonel."

"Jane, my dear —"

"No, Bingley, your wife has a right to inquire about what happens in her home. Perhaps the two of you have not had time speak and you have not informed your wife of our investigation. For that omission, I beg your pardon, Mrs. Bingley. Now I will beg my leave, so Bingley may tell you of recent events." Colonel Fitzwilliam bowed and walked away at a swift pace.

Jane turned a worried gaze on her beloved. "Pray tell me, Charles, what ever did the colonel mean?"

Bingley looked lovingly into her wide eyes and wished for privacy to sooth her fears, for her use of his given name in public revealed to him how worried she was more than words could have done. "Let us stroll to the refreshment table, my dear."

"Oh, I could not swallow a drop." Jane sent an anguished glance toward Lydia, now sitting in a chair with her face crumpled. Their mother stood over her, flapping her hands as fast as her lips moved. "I could not consume a bite of anything."

"You are the hostess, my dear. Surely it is appropriate for you to check that the needs of your guests are being met." Bingley took hold of her arm as he glanced toward her family. "The distance will give us a chance to speak without anyone hearing our words."

More precisely, he wished to move away from Mrs. Bennet. For he had yet to witness her speak in other than the piercing tone echoing in his head at present. Moreover, she reacted to all that she heard by blurting the first words to enter her head. His words on conversations in the library were for Jane's ears alone, so he urged her forward. After a deep sigh, Jane complied, and they moved toward the long tables at the back of the room.

After they confirmed there was an ample selection of food, and the punch bowl brimming, despite Mr. Hurst's frequent refills, Bingley pulled Jane to the quietest spot he could find in the great hall. Finally, he could delay the news no longer. "All members of your family, and my own, are possible suspects of this murder."

"So you said earlier, but how can this be," Jane turned wide eyes on him, "Mamma, Papa, and Kitty? They would not have the faintest knowledge of how to commit this crime. Nor Mary, an you imagine such a thing, Charles? Suspect Mary? Who quotes Fordyce's sermons as easily as most people repeat gossip."

Bingley's indulgent smile warmed his face as he looked down at his wife. "I notice you did not mention Lydia. Lizzy either, for that matter."

"Spare me the levity, please, Charles. Be serious for I am in fear for my family's safety. Are Lizzy and Lydia's names on the list? For you must know, better than any of the men trying to solve this crime, that neither of my sisters could commit such a deed."

"Mary's name has not been mentioned, of course, but I fear Lydia and Lizzy will be questioned." Bingley paused, and then added words he dreaded for her to hear, "As will your parents."

"Oh, Charles, what are we to do?"

"That is not all, my dear. Caroline and Louisa are on the list, as well. Even Hurst." Bingley observed the aforementioned man as he staggered past them on his approach to the punch bowl. Hurst refilled his cup, sloshing half the contents down his waistcoat with his shaky attempt to lift the cup to his lips. Bingley released a gusting breath. "The man cannot walk straight, much less keep sober long enough to handle a murder weapon."

"Whatever will we do, Charles? I am so frightened." Jane turned a concerned glance toward of her family. "It is beyond my comprehension to even consider Lizzy or father guilty of such a crime. And Mamma's nerves are so devoted, I can not imagine she could remain calm enough to swat a fly. As for Lydia," Jane shook her head and sighed, "I confess I have no knowledge of the dark side of passion. I have heard of the frightening aftermath of such emotions, but I cannot believe Lydia capable of such. Above all else, Lydia truly loved Wickham." Jane chewed her lip as she surveyed her family, and whirled back to face her husband. "We must do something, Charles. This is our home and our ball. We invited these people. We must do all we can to save our family."

"The colonels are trying to do just that, my dear."

"On that point, dearest Charles, I fear you are mistaken. The colonels aim to discover who murdered Mr. Wickham. They have no care if the process tramples a good name. We have more at risk. The good names of our family will suffer if word spreads that they were suspected of Wickham's murder. You must help me, Charles, please. We must do all that we can to discover who committed this murder."

"I understand your intentions, my dear." Bingley's gaze drifted to where his sisters were standing on the other side of the room, then to Darcy and Lizzy adding their presence in support of the Bennet family. "All those we hold dear are threatened by what occurred in our home. I believe you are correct in your assumption. Indeed, we must act. I shall ask Darcy —"

"Please, Charles, no! You must not speak of this to Darcy." Jane grasp hold of his arm as he moved to turn away. "Did you not say Darcy was also under suspicion? Will it not cast more doubt on him if he helps and we offer forth another name? Please, Charles, we must do this on our own. That is the only way we can remove suspicion from Lizzy and Darcy."

CRED

"Miss Darcy," Mary King gave a slight curtsy to the young girl, "you must be exhausted by your constant care of Miss Brown, and I fear you have had no chance to seek comfort from your brother during this time." Mary glanced down at Miss Darcy's companion. "Please allow me to be of assistance. I will sit with Miss Brown so you may stretch your legs and confer with Mr. Darcy."

"Miss King, is it not? How kind of you, but it is no trouble to sit with Maggie." Miss Darcy sent a familiar glance to her companion, "I dare say she has suffered far worse from me in the past."

"Not at all, Miss." Miss Brown met the gaze of her mistress. "I find I am quite calm, at the moment. Pray, do speak with Mr. Darcy and discover what news he might have."

Miss Darcy cast a longing glance toward her brother and Lizzy, and then said in a soft voice as she turned back to her companion, "If you are quite certain, Miss Brown."

The young girl's skirts swished away in a manner unsuited for the somber occasion, as Miss Brown glanced at Mary King. Jaw tightened, she forced her words to a whisper. "Mary, what can you be thinking? You should not come near me. The danger is too great. Did we not agree we must do noting to arouse curiosity?"

Mary grabbed a handful of her skirt and fell inelegantly into the chair next to Miss Brown. "Do stop fretting, Maggie. We agreed to maintain our distance at this ball, but that was before you found Wickham, dead." Mary glanced at her cousin in time to see tears roll down her face. "Oh, Maggie, I am sorry. After all that has happened, I was not aware you still loved him so much."

"Hush, Mary." Maggie swiped at her tears and sent a cautious glance around the crowded room. "Already, you are taking a chance by sitting with me. I beg you not make mention of the past, for someone might be listening." Maggie turned her cousin. "Why have you acted so?"

"I could not witness your pain without offering comfort. It must be dreadful to be the one to find Wickham's body like that."

"No words can express my pain, Mary. To discover I was asleep, not ten paces from where he was murdered, stirs fear in my heart. But even worse is the vision of his dead body, for I fear it will fill my head the rest of my days."

"Maggie, I pray you will not feel harsh toward me, but I must ask. You did not do this deed, did you?" Mary paused as she heard

Maggie's swift intake of breath. "I asked, for you are my dearest cousin and I love you, but I must have the truth, or I fear I cannot go on."

Maggie clasped a hand to her heart and turned a tortured glance on Mary. "I can scarcely fathom why you ask me such a thing."

Mary squared her shoulders and met Maggie's offended gaze. "I dare so because the colonels have made it obvious they think I am guilty of this crime."

"But that is not possible. For what reason would they think such a thing?"

"I am not as bothered by their intentions as much as I am by my thoughts. It grieves me to confess I suspected something was amiss when Wickham focused his attentions on me." Mary paused, conscious of the discomfort she was about to inflict. Yet she was a suspect in Wickham's murder and dared not ignore the topic. "The colonels think I nurtured hurt feelings after he turned his attentions elsewhere."

"If only they were aware of the aftermath of that situation, they would believe you happy to be rid of Wickham's attentions."

"Ah, 'tis true, I am sure." Mary sighed, "Yet I dare not give an explanation for fear of casting suspicion where it cannot easily be denied. However, my continued silence implies guilt and could be the ruin of both of us. For that reason, dear cousin, I must ask if you have been forthright in all you have told me."

"You question my words?"

"Oh, Maggie, the outcome of this situation affects more than our personal feelings. I must know that I am justified in fighting for our future."

Maggie's clamped lips showed she was vexed, but a heartbeat later she forced emotion-filled words from her lips. "I did not harm him. Considering all that he meant to me, how could you dare suggest I could murder him —"

"Ah, I heard the word murder." Colonel Fitzwilliam stopped in front of them, and studied each of them in turn. "It seems the situation is much as I feared when Miss Georgiana informed us that Miss King was sitting with her companion." He gave a slight bow. "Ladies, I fear I must ask you not to discuss the events of this evening."

"Oh, but Colonel Fitzwilliam," Mary stood and turned wide eyes on the handsome officer, "it is not what you might think. I was trying to console Miss Brown and stop her tears. Yet she is tender hearted and insists she cannot soon forget the murder."

"I share her aversion for these events completely." Colonel Fitz-william studied his ward's companion for long moments. "However, until the crime is solved, I would prefer Miss Brown kept any impression of the events to herself. Therefore, I have asked Miss Mary Bennet to sit with Miss Brown until Miss Darcy returns." He held out his arm. "Miss King, could I offer you some refreshment?"

Mary exchanged a glance with her cousin, then took the colonel's arm. "I would like something to drink. Though must admit, Colonel, I am most unnerved in your presence, as you are leading the investigation into this crime."

"Why should my efforts affect you so, Miss King? Do you have reason to suffer guilt over Mr. Wickham's death?"

"Ah, pray do not try to suggest guilt where none exists, Colonel." Mary smiled up at him. "However, the thought of being interviewed by, not one, but three fine gentlemen, two of whom are in full-dress uniform, sets my poor heart pounding."

"Miss King, may I inquire if your admiration for a man in uniform is the reason for your attachment to Mr. Wickham? For I must confess, I can see no other reason why a young woman of your countenance would settle for a man with his character, when there are officers ready to trip over themselves for your attention."

"Really?" Mary opened her eyes wide as she stared around the room. "I see no such gentlemen, sir." Some of the tightness in her chest eased as the colonel smiled down at her. Oh, he was quite good, this colonel, and very handsome. She must watch her step or else she would find her shoe in her mouth with him around. "Do you jest, Colonel?"

"Are you avoiding my query, Miss King?"

"Not at all, Colonel. However, as a man, I cannot expect you to understand. But Wickham was a dashing figure in his uniform, which I am sure you have heard from other women present, and his charm was second to none I have ever encountered. So when he turned his attentions to me, it was difficult to keep a sane thought in my head."

"Ah," Colonel Fitzwilliam acknowledged with a nod, "I thought as much. Now, I am afraid you must forgive me for leaving you at the refreshment table, Miss King but Captain Carter has arrived." He turned and motioned Captain Carter to their side. "Captain, would you be so good as to see that Miss King gets some punch to revive her spirits, and take care she is not left alone to mull over the night's sad events." With a tilt of his head and a slight smile, the colonel departed.

"So, we meet again, Miss King. How are you coping with events of the evening?

"As well as one could expect I believe, Captain. And you?" Mary accepted the cup of lemonade Carter offered and, again, noted how kind he seemed. After her experience with Wickham, and her escape from what would surely have been a disastrous match even without dear Maggie's involvement, she avoided men in uniform. Yet with war approaching and many young men departing to serve King and country, she had few encounters with men who were not in the militia. Captain Carter, for all his quiet ways, was as handsome as Colonel Fitzwilliam and the sadly-departed Wickham, yet his charm was warm and believable. "If I recall correctly, you and Mr. Wickham were close friends."

Captain Carter seemed to stand straighter and studied her with such seriousness that she wondered what she had said wrong until he said. "If I may speak truthfully, Miss King, and not be accused of speaking wrongly of the dead, Wickham was friends with anyone who would loan him funds."

"Captain, I must confess your words surprise me."

"Because I speak bluntly, ma'am?"

"On the contrary, Captain, it is the fact that you spoke the truth. For I have discovered honesty is a quality it is difficult to find among men in uniform." She smiled under his warm gaze, and felt the coldness around her heart ease. "If I may speak as truthfully in return, sir, it is a relief to encounter a man of honor, and one who does not excuse the actions of other men because they wear the same colors. For, I found Mr. Wickham's actions less than honorable on occasion."

"You must take care of what you say, Miss King. For, as I warned Denny earlier this night, the walls have ears."

"I quite agree, Captain." Mary glanced around the room at the groups of guests and tried to keep the eagerness building inside her out of her voice. "But I am curious, sir. Why did you feel the need to caution Mr. Denny? Were he and Mr. Wickham not great friends? Surely, he is not one accused of this deed."

"Ah, Miss King, you must remember, all is not as it seems."

"Oh, do tell, Captain. I am making an effort to seal my mind against this night's events, and your comment promises much distraction. Pray tell me, was there a disagreement between Mr. Wickham and Denny?"

"There are things I should not mention in your presence, Miss King." Captain Carter reached for a biscuit from the tray near him. "Some topics are not acceptable to speak of in front of a lady."

"Ah, now I understand. Mr. Wickham and Denny fought over a female."

"Not exactly and, if you will forgive me for saying so, Miss King, you should not be so forthcoming with your knowledge of such things."

Color rose to Mary's cheeks. This man she barely knew was trying to protect her, yet Wickham had acted the opposite. He had lulled her into thinking he cared for her and had asked for her hand in marriage, while, at the same time, he was carrying on an affair with another woman. She learned the truth too late to save her cousin from a broken heart, but she had salvaged her own. Yet, from she knew of this man, she was convinced Captain Carter would never repeat Wickham's behavior. "You are quite right, Captain, but females learn these things from men who are not as honorable as you. Did Denny care very much for the female in question?"

"Aye, it was his sister." Captain Carter sent her a guilty glance. "There, now you have charmed the truth out of me with your flattery, Miss King. What manner of friend am I, to possess such a loose tongue?"

"A very good friend, Captain, for you made it most difficult for me to uncover the truth. But pray, do not leave me in suspense. How did the tale end?"

"Denny was fortunate enough to rescue his sister in time, but alas, he never recovered the funds he loaned to Wickham. Neither have several other men in our regiment."

"So Mr. Wickham lived on loans and spread his debts among his fellow service men. Tell me, Captain, do men in the militia earn enough to support themselves and the likes of Wickham?"

"Not from their service pay, Miss King, but many chance what little they have, and all they can borrow, on games of chance."

Mary made a mental note to add bad debts to the possible reasons for Wickham's murder. Lydia Wickham's accusations against her made her uneasy. Everyone present heard Lydia's claims, but though Lydia had accused others of the crime as well, if certain facts were discovered, Mary would appear to have more reason than most for wanting Wickham dead.

In her heart, Mary knew she could never murder anyone, not even Wickham. Yet, she would need all her wits about her if she disproved Lydia's claims. Moreover, since Colonel Fitzwilliam acted promptly to remove her from Maggie's presence, Mary was more frightened that ever. But she was determined to fight for her life and that of her cousin. And to that aim, she was left with only one choice. She had to discover the truth about Wickham's murder. "Is that the reason you warned Denny to be cautious before he spoke?"

"Not entirely," Captain Carter stared at the punch cup in his hand, "I thought it prudent to caution Denny because he has been less than sensible in forming a recent liaison."

"Ah," Mary could hardly control her excitement, "you are referring to his assignation with Mrs. Forester, in the garden."

"How did you know this, Miss King, for I know you have not coaxed me into revealing these details?"

"Do not fret, Captain. If you will recall, I was also in the garden tonight and I saw many interesting events going on in the dark as I am sure you did, as well."

"You have relieved my conscience, greatly, Miss King. For while I do not agree with Denny's choices, I have no wish to be disloyal. Still, I fear his actions put him in an untenable position."

"Quite right, Captain, unless we find others who stands to gain if Denny is blamed for the crime." Would Captain Carter forgive her for using his concern for Denny to gain knowledge of what he knew? Yet, even if he did not, she was left with little choice in the matter. She had to find information to protect herself and Maggie.

"I agree, Miss King." Captain Carter paused as he considered her words. "And to that end I will add that Mr. Bingley's sisters had a very active evening in the garden, as well."

"Really, oh do tell." Mary glanced at the women in question. Of all the guests present at the ball, surprisingly, she had not considered the possibility that Bingley's sisters might be involved in the murder. "Pray tell why you suggest such a thing, for I observed Miss Bingley, as well as, the Hursts in the garden. Do you suggest they attacked Mr. Wickham?"

"I have no reason to believe such. Yet they each met with Wickham, but the interestingly enough, they met him separately."

"Oh! But how can you know this?" Chills chased over Mary as a new thought occurred to her. She liked Captain Carter, and for that reason, she had not considered that he might have reason to want Wickham dead. Nevertheless, standing in the middle of a roomful of guests, anyone of who could be the murderer, she eyed the man beside her, whose quiet charm had lured her to feel comfortable with him. Surely she had not misread Captain Carter's character so badly. After the incident with Wickham, she used caution in dealing with others. "Ah, you were watching out for Denny, were you not?"

Carter gave a nod. "Denny ignores caution when he is involved like this. I thought only to protect him from his own folly."

"This sheds light on why Mrs. Hurst had twigs caught in her gown upon her return." Mary sent him a thoughtful glance. "Yet, Miss Bingley had not a ruffle out of place."

"Did you not observe her leave the library, as we returned from the garden?" Carter raised a brow. "Yet she returned to the ballroom some time after we arrived. Who is to say she did not use the time to restore her appearance and remove any hint of her activities?"

"You are very observant, Captain. I made no notice of Miss Bingley's departure from the library or her return to this room. How is it that you were so aware of her actions?" Mary tilted her head to study him as she continued. "Do you have an attraction for Miss Bingley, or perhaps you were still watching out for Denny's best interests. Tell me, did Denny return with twigs attached to his person as several of the women appear to have done?"

A smile tilted the corners of Carter's mouth. "It pains me to admit as much, but indeed he did, Miss King, and I fear I know the reason why."

"What do you fear, Captain Carter?" Jane Bingley said as she joined them. "Is there anything I can assist with to ease your mind?"

"Mrs. Bingley, I thank you, but there is nothing about which to concern yourself. I was merely recanting some of our mishaps in the militia for Miss King's benefit." Captain Carter smoothed over the topic and glanced around the room. "I notice the colonels and Mr. Bingley have departed the room. Are their examinations of guests underway once more?"

"I fear this is so, Captain." Jane released a sigh. "There, I have used the word as well. Yet it seems we all have fears on this night. Your fear is for mistakes made while you were training, while I fear I invited a murderer into our midst for my first ball." Jane managed a weak smile as she turned to Mary. "And you, Miss King, are you fearful this eve?"

"Not as long as the Captain remains in the room to watch over us, Mrs. Bingley. However, may I say you should fear not for you ball, as it was a beautiful evening until the news turned bad, and that was out of your control."

"Oh, thank you, Miss King. You are so kind. There is one event occurring this night I am grateful for," Jane smiled at them, "and that is the chance to become better acquainted with you." She glanced from Mary to Captain Carter. "When I approached, you seemed agitated over something. I do hope nothing more is amiss?"

ೞ

Jane turned away slowly, convinced she had missed information that would prove her family innocent, but could not remain conversing with Miss King and Captain Carter for very long. She needed to speak with Bingley's sisters, and discover how they were dealing with recent happenings. Bingley told her of his concern after he observed Mrs. Hurst's agitated state, so Jane slowed her steps as she approached the sisters. "Louisa, Caroline, I pray all is well with you."

"What nonsense you spout, Jane." Louisa snapped before Caroline could respond. "If you and Charles had a brain between you, you would realize we are all ruined for any future society events."

"This worry has brought about your agitation?" Jane kept her tone calm under Louisa's glare. Objecting to the comment would only make Louisa more vexed. Moreover, Louisa only voiced the assumption Jane had often heard from acquaintances. Because she did not vex easily or hasten to defend her beliefs, people assumed she did not have the good sense to take part in conversations. Their conclusion was misguided to say the least. She and Lizzy often discussed events in exacting detail and, while Lizzy was quick to voice her opinion, Jane preferred to think a situation through before forming an opinion.

Lizzy often said she wished for one measure of Jane's caution, after she voiced hasty comments she had later regretted. And there were times Jane wished to be more outspoken like Lizzy, as she had on the occasion last year when she feared she had lost Bingley because she had controlled her emotions. Still, it was her nature to search for the meaning behind a person's words. She wanted to understand why a person reacted as they did, and what they meant by comments that tumbled from their mouths without thought.

Louisa's summation of Jane and Bingley's abilities was hurtful.

Yet Jane knew Louisa was fond of her younger brother, and would do nothing to endanger her enjoyment of Bingley's deep pockets. Thus Jane was alerted that there must be another cause for Louisa's disquiet. "Is worry for your status in society all that concerns you this night, Louisa?"

"How could that not be reason enough for concern, Jane?" Caroline exchanged a pointed glance with Louisa. "Someone you invited to your ball committed murder." Caroline's voice dropped to a consoling tone. "You are acquainted with a murderer, so naturally Louisa and I are concerned. Can you not see what this means to your chances of acceptance in London society?"

"With concern for our guests weighing on my mind, I have had no time to think of society. Truthfully, when I witnessed your distress I assumed you must be acquainted with Mr. Wickham." Jane remained calm despite the emotions roiling inside her, but it was difficult. Lydia had lost her husband, yet Bingley's sisters were only concerned with their status in society. This night's events could blot her chance of acceptance in some circles, but there was more at stake than her social standing. "Bingley mentioned that you made Mr. Wickham's acquaintance at Pemberley."

"Great heavens," Louisa's voice rose as if she were about to burst into song and she locked glares with Caroline. "Of course, we met Mr. Wickham. But to imply he was more than a casual acquaintance is insulting. Really, Jane, I thought better of you than to have you imply such a thing."

"Louisa," Caroline's tone would sweeten a pot of tea, yet a warning lurked underneath her words, "do calm yourself. Jane, you must overlook my sister's agitation. Of course we knew Mr. Wickham well enough to greet him by name." She glanced at Louisa and her expression changed to that of a sly fox. "Louisa is unsettled at knowing we bumped into Mr. Wickham in the garden, and she fears we might have been the last to see him alive." Caroline flicked a glance at Louisa. "If you must know, we worry the murderer was nearby and we might be in danger."

"If you spoke to Wickham in the garden, how did he seem?" Jane asked as she reflected on their words. They might have brushed by the murderer if they spoke the truth. However, Wickham's state of mind concerned her more at the moment. Had he arranged to meet with his killer? Was this death an accident? Was Wickham the intended victim?

"Whatever can you mean, Jane?" Louisa snapped. "Really, with such naive thoughts as this, I wonder what you and Bingley can find to discuss when you are alone."

Ignoring Louisa's repeated suggestion, that she possessed no intellect whatsoever, Jane grew more intense in her need to clear her family of blame. "Was Wickham alone?"

"Alone?" Caroline scoffed, "Of course Wickham was alone. If you seek to discover if his wife was with him, then rest assured she was not. However, I did see Mrs. Wickham on another path in the garden. She was speaking with your sister, Eliza."

"Did Mr. Wickham seem agitated or concerned for his safety?"

"Really, Jane," Louisa gave a derisive snort, "do you intend to assist with this investigation as Colonel Fitzwilliam has done? I feel I must warn you. Assuming the duty of solving this murder has not improved the colonel's disposition, and, frankly, I have serious doubt such that actions will add to your own character. Be advised, Jane. Best leave solving this murder to the colonels and turn your concern to the guests."

Jane clenched her gloved fingers, but kept her tone steady. "I merely search for words which might ease my sister's pain. Lydia has suffered much this night. I thought only to seek some source of comfort."

"How admirable, Jane." Though Caroline's tone implied otherwise, she exchanged a glance with Louisa, and said. "Perhaps we could help. Mr. Wickham seemed his usual, congenial self, all charm, and good humor. However, we only exchanged a passing greeting with him. In truth, now that you bring the matter to my attention, I do believe we left Mr. Wickham in conversation with Mr. Hurst."

"I see," Jane glanced at Louisa's husband. He sat slouched in a nearby chair, head back, eyes closed, and mouth hanging open, with his legs sprawled out in a very inelegant pose. In Jane's estimation, Mr. Hurst was deep in his cups, but the need to remain polite kept her from saying so. "Do you have any recollection as to how long they conversed?"

"Really, Jane," Louisa said with a snort, "how you do go on. How could we possibly know how long they conversed? The garden was cold, so we returned directly to the house."

Jane considered the possibility that Louisa may have also visited the punch bowl too often on this eve. Her strident tone and unladylike manner made Jane wonder if punch, or annoyance were to blame.

"Ah, Louisa, I fear Jane is not satisfied with your response." Caroline turned a teasing glance on Jane. "I am all astonishment at your persistence in this matter, Jane. However, you must take caution. If you insist on asking questions, you must prepare for unpleasant responses. To be quite frank, our encounter with Mr. Wickham was truly objectionable."

"Whatever do you mean?" Jane's heart pounded against her ribs as she waited for their response. How was she going to explain this to Lydia? Then another, more unnerving possibility occurred to her. If Wickham insulted Bingley's sisters, Jane knew her husband would never accept such behavior. Had Bingley... No! It was not possible. Her dear Bingley was not capable of such violence. She was convinced his calm demeanor could not conceal anger strong enough to end in murder. She had no doubt Bingley could never do such a thing. As further reassurance, she recalled he had been in the ballroom all evening.

In which case, if Louisa or Caroline's honor required defending, then the actions must have come from Mr. Hurst.

Jane turned her gaze to the man slumped in the chair, obviously inebriated, and acknowledged she would get no response from him. However, the suggestion would not leave her head. Could Mr. Hurst be the murderer? Judging the width of his shoulders and possible strength he might use against Wickham, Jane guessed it was possible. She tore her gaze from him and turned to face Louisa and Caroline. "Did Mr. Hurst follow you back to the house?"

Bingley's sisters exchanged an intense glance. Finally, with a hint of color tinting her cheeks, Caroline said, "I know not, for I was chilled and returned to the house directly. But I believe Louisa still needed the fresh air."

Considering this, Jane directed her gaze to Louisa, "Did you observe anyone unusual, or perhaps hear anything that seemed out of place at the time?"

"Jane, you astonish me." With a huff, Caroline flounced toward the chair beside Mr. Hurst. However, she did not sit, but whirled to Jane and demanded in a slightly raised tone. "If you are going to exclaim over every little incident of the evening, should you not turn your attention to Miss Brown? I find it unacceptable to discover one of the servants reading in the library as if they were a guest in this house. Yet when I returned from the garden and stopped to warm by the fire, there she was, making free use of Bingley's library."

"Neither Bingley nor I mind if someone borrows a book." Jane tried to comprehend the annoyance underlying Caroline's words. Surely she had misunderstood. Caroline could not wish to embarrass Georgiana or Mr. Darcy over such a matter. Usually her reaction was the opposite. More than once since making Caroline's acquaintance, Jane had observed her attention focused on Lizzy's husband. "What was Miss Brown doing in the library?"

"If you insist on the details," Caroline glanced at Louisa through her eyelashes, then turned to Jane and lowered her voice. "She—"

"Jane, what does it matter what the woman was doing? She is a servant and has no right to make free with the house as if she were a guest." With a loud sniff, Louisa flounced down in the chair beside her husband. "I completely agree with Caroline. You have no control over your household."

Since Louisa and Caroline had hired the staff before Jane even met Bingley, their comments were yet another insult, and Jane would have left the conversation there, but for the fact that Caroline had discovered Miss Brown in the library where Wickham was murdered.

Taking a deep breath, Jane said, "I fear I must insist—"

"If you must know, she was reading a book. Though I cannot claim to understand why you suddenly have an interest in the actions of one of Mr. Darcy's servants."

Chapter Eight

*A*fter her conversation with Captain Carter, Mary King drifted toward the women gathered around her cousin. Lady Lucas and Mrs. Phillips were listening eagerly as Miss Georgiana Darcy recounted what she had discovered while conversing with her brother and Mrs. Darcy.

"Oh, Maggie, it is so dreadful." Miss Darcy fell in the chair next to her companion. "The colonels believe Lizzy murdered Wickham in a fit of jealousy." She turned wide, innocent eyes on her companion. "It cannot be true. Pray tell me you did not see Lizzy in the library, for I know she is true to my brother. I have witnessed them together as have you, Maggie. Please, can you not speak to the colonels and inform them they are wrong."

Miss Brown reached for Georgiana's hand. "Calm yourself, please —"

"This cannot be I assure you." Mrs. Phillips rushed to agree with Miss Darcy. "My niece could never do a thing so unspeakable."

"Mrs. Phillips," Lady Lucas said thoughtfully, "pray remember, this could well be a crime of passion. Once deep emotions are stirred, I am certain none of us know of what we are capable."

"Upon my word, Lady Lucas, you claim a close association with my dear sister, yet you stand there and dare to suggest her daughter capable of such a thing?"

"You misunderstood my words, Mrs. Phillips. I merely suggested we should consider all possibilities. We all agree Mrs. Darcy was never shy about sharing her feelings on any subject. Who is to say her emotions did not get the best of her on this occasion?"

"Lizzy is the model of correct behavior and decorum." Miss Darcy blurted.

"Have no fear, Miss Georgiana." Miss Brown again laid a calming hand on her charge's arm. "These ladies are only searching for a reason why poor Mr. Wickham died." Her chin trembled as she tried to calm the young girl at her side. "You must take no offense at what you hear this night, for much talk is speculation."

"Excellent advice, Miss Brown," Mrs. Phillips declared. "To suggest Lizzy still cared for Mr. Wickham is beyond belief. Anyone can see how besotted she is with Mr. Darcy. Moreover, Lady Lucas, I fear you are misinformed in this matter. And for my part, I find it most difficult to believe you would even think such a notion, considering how close Lizzy and your Charlotte were."

Lady Lucas looked down her nose at the gathered group. "Sometimes, familiarity can blind one to the truth of a person's real character."

"Truth?" Mrs. Phillips puffed up like a rooster ready to attack, "I believe there are more facts missing than you seem willing to admit."

"Whatever can you mean, Mrs. Phillips?" Lady Lucas seemed taken back that Mrs. Phillips failed to wither under her scornful glare.

"I sense that you desire Lizzy to be guilty of this crime and I cannot help but wonder why such a thing could be so." Mrs. Phillips studied the woman who had flaunted Sir William's knighthood since moving to the county. "Could it be that you are displeased because Lizzy married above the status Charlotte achieved, and you wish her brought down by false accusations?"

What response Lady Lucas might have made went unheard as Colonel Fitzwilliam chose that moment to join the group, much to Mary King's disappointment. If Mrs. Phillips was correct in her assumptions, then Lizzy Darcy suffered the same false claims as Mary. Could they work together to discover the real culprit of this crime?

"Ladies," Colonel Fitzwilliam said as he studied the group, "did I hear correctly as I approached? You have a theory on who committed this murder?"

"You must pay us no mind, Colonel. We were only speculating on events," Mrs. Phillips rushed to reply.

Lady Lucas cast a glare at her companions and said. "Really, Colonel Fitzwilliam, have you no news for us? It is most distressing to imagine one of our neighbors might have committed such an act."

Upon hearing her emphasis on the words, 'our neighbors', Miss Georgiana gasped. "Cousin, pray tell these ladies there is no chance Lizzy committed this deed."

"Dear Georgiana!" Colonel Fitzwilliam moved to her side and asked in a soothing tone. "What has put such a notion in your head? Do not trouble yourself on this subject. Darcy will keep his wife safe."

"Even if she is guilty of committing this crime," Lady Lucas demanded with a darting glance at the other ladies. The color in her cheeks and squint of her eyes gave hint of her temper.

"My good lady," Colonel Fitzwilliam turned a level gaze on her, "pray tell what put such a notion in your head?"

"If you must know, Colonel, Lizzy Bennet's attraction to Mr. Wickham was obvious to anyone at the same social gathering, before he turned to Miss King. Ask my Charlotte of her attachment if you need further convincing. Pray be not deceived by her ladylike airs. She is as likely to be seen trudging through muddy lanes as any servant in the county. And I must say, Colonel, I fear no matter how hard you try, you and Mr. Darcy cannot protect Lizzy from this charge."

"Lady Lucas," Lizzy said as she arrived to hear the overwrought woman's claims. Her chin was angled in a determined manner as she continued in a firm tone. "I could not help but hear my name. I was aware you did not favor my attachment to Charlotte, but your disapproval exceeds even my imagination. As for my fondness of walking to enjoy the beauty of our surroundings, I cannot accept that habit as a blot against my character."

"Mrs. Darcy," Colonel Fitzwilliam turned to his cousin's wife, "allow no comments such as these to distress you. Everyone is searching for a solution to the events of this night so they might understand why it happened."

"How kind of you to say, Colonel Fitzwilliam, but tell me, have others tried to malign my character this night, as well?" Lizzy turned a glare on her mother's good friend. "For if they have, I wish to be made aware —"

"Oh Lizzy," Miss Georgiana jumped up and rushed to her sister-in-law's side, "I beg that you will not listen to such unkind words."

"Lizzy," Mrs. Phillips added quickly, "your poor mamma's nerves will be overtaxed if she learns of these claims. Pray do keep your own council on these matters."

"I must depart, ladies." Colonel Fitzwilliam gave a slight bow, but his glance rested on Lizzy as he continued, "Perhaps it would be best if you discussed some matter of fashion for the rest of the evening." Then he turned and walked away.

"Ohhh," Lizzy ground out as she stared after his departing figure, "how could he listen to such nonsense?"

"Mrs. Darcy," Mary King took a step closer to Georgiana and Lizzy, "perhaps I could have a word—"

"Oh, Lizzy, what will my brother say when he hears these claims?" Georgiana threw herself in Lizzy's arms and clung to her. "I could not bear to lose you—"

"Miss Georgiana, please, calm yourself so as not to distress Mrs. Darcy." Miss Brown took Georgiana's arm. "Come, let us get some refreshment. You must be ready to collapse after this long night."

"She is fine with me, Miss Brown," Lizzy smiled and hooked her arm through Georgiana's. "I think she will do better after a few words with her brother." Lizzy turned to Maggie, "I am certain you are the one who needs substance after your experience."

"Thank you, Mrs. Darcy," After a curtsy, Maggie glanced around as the other women drifted away. Lady Lucas departed first, no doubt wishing to avoid another tangle with Lizzy. Mrs. Phillips gave Lizzy a long glance then trailed behind Lady Lucas, no doubt hoping to mend fences with the ranking lady in the county. Maggie turned to the remaining member of the group and said quickly, "Miss King, perhaps I could accompany you to the refreshment table?"

CB℘

As Lizzy led Georgiana away, Maggie stepped close and forced Mary to turn away from her attempt to speak to Mrs. Darcy. Turning toward the refreshment table on the other side of the room, Maggie kept watch of the other guests as she said. "Mary, whatever are you thinking? Why did you approach Mrs. Darcy in such a manner? Are things not bad enough, but you risk my position and the good pay packet I need to live on by speaking with my employer's wife at such a time?"

"Calm yourself, Maggie, or you will attract attention," Mary whispered as she walked past groups of guests, but disappointment twisted her insides. She had never claimed a friendship with Mrs. Darcy, and especially not after Wickham turned from Lizzy to pay attention to her. His disregard of Lizzy's fondness, should have alerted Mary to his character for he quickly turned his attentions to her when local gossip revealed she had inherited a fortune. But Wickham's charm had clouded her judgment, as she suspected it had Lizzy's for a time.

Yet now, Wickham was dead and even with his actions clouding their past, Mary felt she needed to align herself with Lizzy to fight the claims against them. She had almost succeeded in capturing Lizzy's attention, before Miss Darcy interrupted.

Walking faster, Mary said. "I need to speak with her that is all."

"Mary! I beg you, please do not speak to Mrs. Darcy. I know better than most the affection with which Mr. Darcy regards his wife. To vex her is to turn his good opinion aside, as well, and I cannot be without employment."

Mary glanced about them before whispering. "Why are you so certain you will have a position to go back to after events of this night?"

"Whatever do you mean?" Maggie gasped. "Surely you do not believe Mr. Darcy will dismiss me because I discovered the body. I cannot even consider such a possibility."

"When the body you discovered was that of Mr. Wickham, anything is possible." Mary sighed. "Maggie, need I remind you that once your connection to Wickham is revealed, you could be dismissed immediately?"

"Mary, do not speak such words, I beg you. I must have employment if I am to keep my son —"

"Hush, Maggie," Mary cast a careful glance around them, "as Captain Carter reminded me earlier this evening, on this night the walls have ears. Surely, the vile words from Lady Lucas proved such to be the case."

Maggie glanced over her shoulder as if suspecting the murderer was behind her. "If that be the case, why did you attempt to speak with Mrs. Darcy? And do not deny the fact. You were intent on making conversation with her, even before Lady Lucas cast slurs on her character. But I can assure you, Mrs. Darcy is all that Miss Georgiana claimed and more. I would be fortunate to work in that house the rest of my days."

Mary studied the selection of biscuits, then selected one for her plate. "I only thought to suggest we compare notes to solve this murder as both our names have been bandied as possible suspects."

ॐ

After much debate on her plan, Mary finally convinced Maggie to return to the company of her young charge. Left to her own devices, Mary trailed through the guests, in her renewed attempt to enter into a discussion with Mrs. Darcy. However, it was not as easy as she had hoped.

Mrs. Darcy stood with Mr. Darcy and Georgiana on the outskirts of a family group, gathered around Lydia Wickham. Mary's courage almost deserted her at thoughts of another confrontation Lydia this evening. After the venom Lydia spewed earlier, and the suspicion her claims cast on Mary's character, Mary was not certain she could hold her tongue if Lydia started ranting again. Yet, disproving the false claims was of the utmost importance to her future and Maggie's, so she had no other option but to attempt the conversation.

Approaching the group on Georgiana's side, Mary managed to smile as she said. "There you are, Miss Darcy. I do so appreciate the loan of your companion on my trip to the refreshment table. Miss Brown was a great comfort, but I sent her back to your corner seat. I feared keeping her away too long and infringing on your kindness. And to be quite truthful, her concern for you is upmost in her thoughts and she wished to return to your side."

"Thank you, Miss King, I am happy with Miss Brown." Georgiana glanced at Lizzy as she said, "I am in excellent hands now, but I am certain there are things Lizzy and my brother wish to discuss in private."

Despite the Darcys' objections, Georgiana took her leave. She had only taken a few steps, when she met Miss Brown, who was coming in search of her. Georgiana took hold of her companion's arm, and urged Miss Brown back to the familiar corner they had occupied most of the evening.

Miss Darcy's quick reaction left Mary standing on the edge of the group, near Mrs. and Mr. Darcy, but too close to Lydia for Mary's comfort. Deciding not to risk drawing the widow's attention, Mary turned away. Hopes of speaking to Mrs. Darcy denied yet again, Mary stared about her. What now? Her attempts to speak to Mrs. Darcy had ended in failure, but she refused to accept that state of mind. She was no more a murderer than she believed Lizzy Darcy to be, but how could she prove that fact?

"Miss King," Jane Bingley approached with a smile, "would you escort me to the refreshment table? I find I am famished, but I have no wish to trudge through this crowd alone." Jane hooked her arm in Mary's and urged her away from the Bennet family. "If we appear to be involved in deep conversation, perhaps no one will stop to ask if we have any news."

Mary glanced over her shoulder. The intense expression on Mr. Bingley's face as he watched them walk away, made her wonder how innocent Jane Bingley's actions actually were. Lizzy was speaking intently with Mr. Darcy, and did not appear to notice their departure, so perhaps Jane was acting only as a good host as Mary had been left standing alone after Miss Darcy dragged Maggie away. So Mary smiled as she replied. "I am happy to oblige, Mrs. Bingley."

"Oh, Miss King, do call me Jane." The kindness and sweet smile most often associated with Jane, covered her face. "I want us to be friends."

"I would suggest you call me Mary, but with your sister called the same name, I think confusion could reign. But, please, call me Mary King, and do let us be friends." With a lighter step, Mary almost skipped toward the refreshment table. This was twice Jane had voiced her wish for them to become better acquainted. Once could be good manners, but repeating her intent surely meant she was sincere. "How are you maintaining your calm manner with all that is going on?"

"In truth," Jane paused and turned to Mary, "I am sorely distressed. You must have heard by now that all of my family are suspects for the murder."

"But are we not all to be questioned?" Mary tried to remain calm. Perhaps Jane knew more than she did. "Pray do not worry, Mrs. Bingley." Then at Jane's quick look, Mary added in a tentative voice. "I mean, Jane."

"To be quite frank, I am greatly concerned." Jane lowered her gaze to her gloved hands as she added, "Lizzy could not commit such an act. Yet Colonel Forester and Colonel Fitzwilliam consider her a possible suspect, just as they do Mr. Darcy and the rest of my family."

"We cannot all be guilty of the murder," Mary struggled to keep her tone even as excitement rushed through her, "yet this is all we hear. Perhaps we should leave the colonels to question the guests and try to discover who murdered Mr. Wickham ourselves."

"I am happy you say such, Mary, for I had the same thought myself. But my husband fears I will only make matters worse."

"How can things get any worse, Jane? The last I heard most of your guests are suspected murders. We must mount our own search for the murderer."

CRISIS

"Pray do not concern yourself, dear husband." Lizzy stepped closer to him and put a hand on his arm. "Georgiana is handling the situation quite well. It is as if she has only distant memories of Wickham from her childhood." Lizzy gazed after the young girl and Miss Brown as they returned to their corner seats. "I fear I can not say the same for Miss Brown. Her complexion remains the color of clotted cream."

"Indeed, it must have been quite a shock when she discovered the body." Darcy mused, but his attention rested on Jane and her red-haired guest as they walked away, rather than his sister's companion.

"I have no doubt it was, but even Lydia's countenance has improved by now, yet Miss Brown still appears as pale as the dead." Lizzy frowned. "Was she acquainted with Wickham?"

"Darcy, your attendance is required, if you please." Bingley sent his wife's favorite sister a smile. "Sorry to intrude, Mrs. Darcy."

"Dear Mr. Bingley, I insist you call me Lizzy or I will think you do not approve of me as a sister." Her teasing smile brought color to Bingley's face and Lizzy quickly changed the subject. "Truthfully, it is no bother, for I was about to abandon my husband so I might check on Lydia."

As Lizzy moved away, Bingley urged Darcy in the opposite direction. "Come, Darcy. I do not wish the ladies to overhear."

"What now, Charles?" Darcy demanded in an agreeable tone. "Has yet another of your guests come to a grisly end?"

"Do not even mention the possibility in jest. I am counting on your level head, Darcy." Bingley sighed as he considered his next words. "I fear all this talk of murder has put suspicious in my head, and I wish your opinion. Much as I regret voicing the words, I must ask. Have you made notice of Miss King?"

"Sorry, Charles," Darcy drawled. "My attention was focused on my wife, not your charming guests. Come, Charles, stop dithering. What has happened to put you in such a state?"

"I blame my suspicious behavior on a body having been found in my library." Bingley paused and glanced around the room. "But Miss King was very keen to speak with Lizzy after your sister departed. When Lizzy paid no notice, Miss King appeared...well, trite as it may sound, the poor woman seemed lost."

"Lost? In this room filled with your guests?" Darcy demanded. "Really, Charles, how is it possible you are so suspicious of your own guests?"

"It is not a situation I would wish for," Bingley angled his chin and ignored the heat to his cheeks, "but someone murdered Wickham. We know not that it was a guest. Yet no mention has been made of a stranger hanging about the house or grounds."

"A very good point, my friend. Do forgive my attempt to lighten your mood." Darcy gazed about the room. "What action do you suggest?"

"It pains me to reach this point, but I suggest we post guards at the door to keep the guests contained." Bingley released a deep breath. "But I fear Jane will never forgive me if I follow through with the suggestion."

"Ah, but if the guards are there to protect the guests, I am certain Jane would approve. In fact, I would not be surprised Sir William made the suggestion himself."

CB80

Lizzy watched Darcy and Bingley walk away, then moved to stand near her sister's chair. "Lydia, how are you feeling?"

"How do you suppose your sister feels?" Mrs. Bennet's quick retort was accompanied by a glare that would bring a strong man to tears. "Her husband is dead and a guest of Jane's is responsible—"

"Mamma, please. We do not—"

"Mamma, pray do not cast the blame on Jane," Lydia's defense surprised all within hearing. "Jane and Lizzy are my only hope of mixing in society and I should not like them vexed."

"Vexed?" Mrs. Bennet rolled her expressive eyes and gave a snort. "Who said anything about vexing your sisters? I simply stated the truth. Poor Wickham—"

"Mammaaa," Lydia wheeled in a tone she had perfected long ago, "pray do not remind me with every breath. I am fully aware my poor husband is dead."

"Oh, Lydia." Lizzy motioned for Kitty and Mary to vacate the chairs beside Lydia and sat down as close as possible. "I know you are suffering from all that has happened, but please try to clear your head and consider the matter. We must discover who did this deed. Now that your first shock has passed, can you recall anyone who wanted to harm Wickham?"

When Lydia's expression started to slip into the obstinate look from her youth, Lizzy quickly added. "I ask out of concern for your safety. What if the murderer intends to harm you, as well? Moreover, we must consider Jane. Her chance at gaining acceptance from Bingley's sisters and society might be ruined if this murder goes unsolved."

"Jane! All you care about is Jane!" Lydia cried. "What about me? My life is ruined. And you care nothing for how I feel."

"Oh, Lydia, of course I am concerned for you. Yet the questions must be answered. I believed you would feel less vulnerable speaking with—"

"Lizzy, do stop pestering poor Lydia in her time of need. If you must involve yourself, bring her some refreshment, and stop asking senseless questions." Mrs. Bennet turned to her younger daughters. "Mary, fetch my smelling salts. I feel one of my spells coming on."

"It is often said—"

"Mary! If you repeat one more quote, I—"

"Mamma, please!" Lizzy observed stares from guests closest to them and clenched her jaw. Nothing had changed. Mamma married off three daughters, but that feat still failed to improve her disposition. Even faced with Lydia's loss, she made demands. And poor Jane lived so near their parents, she likely heard more complaints than a new wife needed.

"Please what, Lizzy?" Mrs. Bennet's cheeks filled with spots of color. "I notice you have not overcome that obstinate streak since your marriage to Mr. Darcy, and I must say it is not becoming in the least."

Lizzy clenched stood and clenched her hands in the folds of her gown as she took herself off at a swift pace. If ever she was a mother...

CЗ8О

"Colonel Forester, this will not do." Fitzwilliam's words bounced off the walls of books as he stared at the other officer. "You, sir, may return to Brighton, but these guests must face their neighbors on the morrow, and you must not alienate them. We are obliged to question them, but not at the cost of their good names."

"Why must you put such importance on a good name?" Colonel Forester demanded as he rocked on his heels in front of the fireplace.

"Should we call Sir William from the ballroom and ask this question of him?"

"Nay, his ramblings make me long for a battle."

"From what I have heard, his title was earned for his good name. So I ask you, Colonel, why ruin a name it takes a lifetime to earn?" Fitzwilliam studied the other officer as he prowled about the library.

In their recent absence, the servants had moved Wickham's body to a room at the back of the house where it would remain until authorities arrived. Candles burned bright and the fire crackled with warm flames, but the stench of death still hung heavily in the room.

If he could have retreated to another room, he would have, but common sense warned it was better to question the suspects at the scene of the crime. Fitzwilliam took a deep breath and added in a low voice. "For some of us, a good name is all we possess."

"I beg your pardon, sir." Colonel Forester gave a slight bow. "I could not agree more. Until we are cornered, we know not what we will do to protect that name. If I offended you, Colonel Fitzwilliam, I apologize. I had no intention of doing so."

"You did not, 'tis events of this eve that gall me. Murder of a man in uniform is unacceptable." Fitzwilliam paced the room, careful to avoid the dark stains of Wickham's blood on the floor. Much as he had wanted to strangle Wickham when he tried to lure Georgiana away from the safety of her family, he would never wish this outcome on the man. He deserved a good thrashing for his conniving ways, or perhaps a round of fisticuffs, but never murder. "Who are we to question next?"

"The time we spent taking refreshments gave the guests a chance to—"

"Compare their account of the events." As he finished the colonel's thought, Fitzwilliam raked a hand through his hair. He wanted this thing done. Wanted Darcy and Lizzy free from suspicion. "I assume you observed all the whispering while we were in the ballroom, as well?"

"Ah, yes, indeed, but I expect most of the guests are similar to my wife. She insisted on hearing details of what we had learned. No doubt most conversations concerned the same topic." Colonel Forester turned and stared in the flames. "Let us continue with Miss Bingley." With unexpected compassion, Colonel Forester turned to Bingley. "Sir, if you would rather not be present for this interview we understand."

"Not at all, Colonel." Bingley's face paled slightly, but his voice remained steady. "I will fetch her directly."

⚜

"Miss Bingley, how kind of you to join us," Colonel Fitzwilliam said a short time later when Bingley escorted his youngest sister to the library.

"Really, Colonel, you make it sound as if I had a choice." Caroline sniffed and glared at the colonel as she jerked her arm from Bingley's grip. "Is this interview in response to the comments I made earlier to Colonel Forester?"

Fitzwilliam expected her reaction to being questioned. What unsettled him was Bingley's sympathetic glance in his direction. As the younger brother, no doubt Bingley often suffered from the sharpness of his sisters' comments. "Our questions concern the murder of Mr. Wickham, and nothing more, Miss Bingley. Perhaps your answers can assist our efforts to identify the person responsible?"

Caroline turned and focused wide eyes on Colonel Forester, as if Fitzwilliam had remained silent. "Colonel Forester, I will repeat what I said the ballroom. If you want the murderer, you need look no further than Colonel Fitzwilliam."

"Miss Bingley," Colonel Forester's tone rose in objection to her smirk and the note of delight in her voice, "a former member of my regiment is dead. I must insist you consider the serious nature of this situation and respond accordingly."

"I am nothing if not profound, Colonel Forester." Caroline glared at Fitzwilliam with dislike. She suspected him of warning Darcy against forming an attachment to her and that was unforgivable. "But I must insist on an explanation as to why I am being treated in this manner in my own brother's home." She turned a pointed glare toward Colonel Fitzwilliam. "And why must I be subjected to insults from this man?"

"Must I remind you again of the grave nature of this event, Miss Bingley? To investigate this murdeer, we must question all guests present, including Colonel Fitzwilliam. Now, let us proceed without further issue. Who did you converse with during your time in the garden?"

"Really, Colonel, how do you expect me to recall such insignificant details about a stroll in the garden?" Caroline's attempt at humor seemed out of place in the otherwise silent room. "The garden was so populated I saw many guests, even you and your wife."

"My wife?" Colonel Forester glanced at Colonel Fitzwilliam and cleared his throat. "If you saw my wife, surely I would remember seeing you."

"How could you when you were on the other side of the garden from where I spotted Mrs. Forester?" Caroline arched a well-shaped brow. "And you, sir, were definitely not with you wife when I saw her."

"What exactly are you suggesting, Miss Bingley?"

"Only that you were walking without your wife when I observed your presence, Colonel." Caroline's intolerant sigh sounded over the crackling flames in the fireplace. "As half the guests in attendance were in the garden at that time, Colonel, I cannot imagine why you are questioning me on their whereabouts. When last I saw Mr. Wickham he was in the garden, alive and well. Very well, indeed, from what I observed, for he seemed more popular than any other attraction of the evening."

"What do you imply by that comment, Miss Bingley?"

"Really, Colonel Forester," Caroline's mouth stretched in a knowing grin, "a man with your experience must know what I imply?"

"You are in fine form, Miss Bingley, considering the serious events that happened in this room but a few hours past." Colonel Forester's cheeks matched the red of his uniform. "Had you have no feelings for Mr. Wickham?"

"I am, of course, saddened by his death, but I had no reason to wish Mr. Wickham dead, if that is what you imply." Caroline brushed at something on her skirt. "In fact, his demise is a great loss for Mr. Wickham was blessed with what most men lack."

"And what might that be, Miss Bingley?" Fitzwilliam had remained silent until Forester's face turned so red he appeared ready to collapse, so now he stepped forward to risk the slicing from Caroline's tongue.

"Oh, that question is quite easy." Caroline fluttered her lashes as her lips twisted in a sly smile. "It was charm, Colonel Fitzwilliam, a quality both you and Darcy seem to lack. But Mr. Wickham was a master at using his charm. He could —"

"Was the power of his charm the reason we found a note from you note in his pocket?"

"Why, Colonel Fitzwilliam, you sound vexed." Caroline stretched her long-elegant neck and pinned Colonel Fitzwilliam with a cunning glare. "Is there any reason I should not exchange notes with Mr. Wickham?"

"One or two things come to mind. His wife is sister to your brother's wife, for one. But other than that, Miss Bingley, none whatsoever, except for the fact that you asked him to meet you in the library. Considering the fact that his body was found in this room, I believe you understand why the meeting place alone is enough cause suspicion." Colonel Fitzwilliam raised a brow as he held her stare.

Failing in her attempt to stare Fitzwilliam down, Caroline finely turned to her brother and snapped. "Do stop pacing, as if you fear I am soon to hauled off to the gaol, Charles. I did not meet with Wickham as planned so you can breath easy."

"What changed your arrangement, Miss Bingley? Your note seemed quite insistent."

Caroline turned a glittering gaze on Fitzwilliam, "Um, yes, Colonel, now that I see the obstinate angle of your chin, I do notice your likeness to Darcy. You and Darcy are of a similar disposition. You appear upstanding and honorable, yet each of you have a broomstick for a backbone."

"Caroline—"

"It is of no matter, Bingley." Fitzwilliam said as he returned his attention to Caroline. "Do enlighten us, Miss Bingley. If your meeting was important enough to put it in writing, why did you not meet Mr. Wickham as planned?"

"Oh, but I did." Caroline fluttered her lashes as a secretive smile twisted her lips. "But not in this room I suggested." Brows arched over eyes gleaming with satisfaction, Caroline waited for the reaction to her next words. "I stumbled upon Wickham in the garden, along with half the other guests," she turned to look at Colonel Forester, "including Mrs. Forester."

"Now, see here—"

"Did you encounter Mrs. Hurst on your stroll?" Fitzwilliam demanded over Colonel Forester's objection.

"Of course, I saw my sister and Mr. Hurst." Caroline watched the colonels exchange a glance, then added in a purring tone. "I also saw Mrs. Wickham and your precious Eliza Darcy."

Fitzwilliam hid his reaction to her taunting remark with a quick question. "Who else you observe in the garden?"

"Have you no interest in who Mrs. Darcy was with?" The crinkle of Caroline's gown sounded loudly in the near silent room as she leaned forward eagerly. "Have no fear for I shall gladly enlighten you. Eliza was talking to her sisters, Lydia and Kitty."

Fitzwilliam kept his gaze fastened on her face and chose to ignore the reference to Darcy's wife as he continued. "You were observed leaving the library after you returned from the garden. Yet you claim you did not meet with Mr. Wickham as planned."

"I am not yet in my dotage, Colonel. In fact, my memory is quite good. If you have any doubt as to that point ask my sister or Charles. Now, as I informed you earlier, I talked to Mr. Wickham in the garden, hence there was no need to meet him in this room as arranged. However, since you insist I recollect every occurrence, I do recall stepping into this room to warm by the fire. And before you ask if anyone can give evidence I did so, that Miss Brown was in here when I arrived."

"Yet the party is upstairs on the first floor. Why come in this room if you were not meeting Mr. Wickham?"

"Really, Colonel, is it not obvious? It was quite chilly in the garden and my dress is thin. I wanted to warm by the fire before returning to the ballroom. And as I am quite certain you will ask, when I left this room I decided to freshen up before joining the guests."

"Mmmm, so you came in here because you were aware of the warm fire kept in this room. What was Miss Brown about when you entered?" Fitzwilliam asked.

"Now that you make mention of her," Caroline's scathing glare turned on her brother, as if he were at fault in her discovery of Miss Darcy's companion, "Miss Brown was curled in a chair, reading a book as if she owned the house. Do servants not know their place any longer?"

"Miss Brown is not a servant. She is Miss Georgiana's companion." Fitzwilliam responded forcefully.

"Are you quite certain of that fact, Colonel? Mr. Darcy pays her does he not? And as such is the case, Miss Brown is a servant and has no right to make familiar with my brother's home."

"Ah, yes, Miss Brown recalled you saying so, quite vehemently, Miss Bingley." Fitzwilliam turned to Colonel Forester. "Have you any more questions for Miss Bingley?"

Colonel Forester's voice rumbled loud as he said. "Aye, I have but one more question, Miss Bingley. If you saw Mrs. Forester, as you claim, with whom was she speaking at the time?"

"Is it your intention to examine your wife's actions as well as all the other guests, Colonel? Or is this information of a more personal nature?" Caroline's taunt echoed in the sudden silence of the room. "I cannot think it matters in the least, but as you insist on knowing, I believe she was conversing with Mr. Denny. However, with the moon peeping from behind clouds and the shadows so dark, it was difficult to be certain. Perhaps it was Captain Carter...umm, no. Captain Carter was with Miss King. Yes, now I do recall seeing the uniform. Mrs. Forester was with Mr. Denny."

Chapter Nine

*A*s the door slammed behind Miss Bingley, Colonel Forester turned to Fitzwilliam. "We need to speak with Denny."

"I disagree, Colonel. I suggest we question Miss King before we query members of your regiment." Fitzwilliam kept his tone mild, but the colonel's agitation with Caroline over his wife's whereabouts was obvious. Forester needed time to regain his composure, and Fitzwilliam found he was curious to learn more of Miss King's involvement in events.

Lydia Wickham's quick accusations against Miss King remained foremost in his mind, as did her claim that Lizzy Darcy had murdered her husband. It was hardly likely the women worked together to murder Wickham. Fitzwilliam wanted to discover the reason Lydia Wickham was so quick to target her blame. However, after this latest interview with Miss Bingley, he was not convinced Colonel Forester shared the same intent after observing the flushed color in the colonel's face when Caroline Bingley mentioned Mrs. Forester's presence in the garden. Fitzwilliam was not pleased with the possibility that he was the only one with total focus on identifying the murderer.

"I say, Colonel," Colonel Forester squared his chin showing disagreement, but after a long stare at Fitzwilliam he gave a curt nod. "Very well, Bingley, if you would fetch Miss King.

ભ૪

Miss King's appearance as she entered the library was all that any man could desire in a female. Her petite form and easy grace spoke of good breeding, even if she had not been privy to a fortune until her uncle died. Her red hair, which Miss Bingley found so unfavorable, was very becoming, Fitzwilliam concluded. Many females present tonight should follow Miss King's example on how to conduct oneself as a lady, Fitzwilliam decided as he acknowledged her presence with a slight bow. "Please, have a seat, Miss King."

Miss Kings' cheeks blossomed with a becoming hint of pink, adding a startling emphasis to the bright blue color of her eyes, as she settled in a chair near the fire. "You wished to make inquiries of me, Colonel Fitzwilliam?"

"We must, I fear." Fitzwilliam suddenly felt he had both boots in his mouth as he turned his attention to the other two men. "We were informed that you are currently a guest at Lucas Manor, along with Colonel and Mrs. Forester. Might I inquire how long you have been acquainted with Sir William and Lady Lucas?"

"Since my schooldays when I visited my uncle," Miss King's expression revealed her surprise at the question.

Her forthright manner of response earned Fitzwilliam's good opinion. After dodging and bending in attempts to decipher Caroline Bingley's comments, Miss King's precise response was refreshing. Bingley seemed to agree, for he observed Miss King with a fascinated expression that gave Fitzwilliam a new thought. "So, you must be well acquainted with the Bennets."

"No," Miss King's cheeks flushed a deeper rose color, "actually, I only met the Bennets after my uncle passed away."

"That seems unusual considering the small county and your acquaintance with Sir William. How can this be?"

"Colonel," Miss King's wide eyes held nothing but honesty, "my uncle led a quiet life and I was not yet out of the schoolroom. Therefore, I did not attend social events when I visited him."

"I see, then you must have met Mr. Wickham about the same time you were introduced to the Bennets." Fitzwilliam paced a step away and turned. "I mention this because it is common knowledge that your introduction to Mr. Wickham severed his attachment to Miss Elizabeth Bennet. Is that correct?"

More color rushed to Miss King's cheeks, yet she held her head high as she returned his gaze. "Colonel, I knew of no—"

"Miss King." Fitzwilliam stopped pacing and kept his tone even. "I need to inquire whether you harbored any ill will toward Mr.

Wickham because he turned his attentions from you, and married Lydia Bennet."

"Colonel," Miss King's laugh was a soft, melodious sound in the grim surroundings of the room, "pray do not think harshly of me for speaking bluntly of the dead, but I wished to be rid of Mr. Wickham's attentions. When I discovered his interest was in the funds I inherited rather than in me, I enlisted the help of my uncle's solicitor to end the engagement. Therefore, I can honestly say I harbored nothing but good will toward Mr. Wickham and his wife."

"Yet Mrs. Wickham —"

"I cannot think as to why Mrs. Wickham spoke the words she did. Perhaps the shock of hearing that her husband was dead rendered her senseless for a moment. Is it any wonder she spoke such nonsense? After she had time to regain her calm, I am convinced she would not have made such claims. I regret my presence caused her discomfort, but I must remind you that she made the same charge against her own."

With a nod, conceding her words were true, Fitzwilliam asked, "Did you speak with Mr. Wickham in the garden this night?"

"Colonel, I did not observe any sign of Mr. Wickham's presence in the grounds while I was there."

"Then you cannot be certain Mr. Wickham ever left the house?"

"I observed Mr. Wickham leave the ballroom." Miss King paused as she studied the two officers through her lashes. "I also noticed a number of guests followed him out —"

"Miss King, for one who claims no interest, Mr. Wickham seemed to attract much of your attention. Do you have an explanation as to why you were so observant of his actions, if you truly harbored no ill will for his past behavior?"

Color drained from Miss King's cheeks. "I was...I needed —"

"Do continue, Miss King." Fitzwilliam encouraged in a mild, yet slightly suspicious tone.

"Actually, Colonel, it was one of Mr. Wickham's friends who was the focus of my attention. I observed Mr. Wickham's movements merely because of who left the room after his departure."

"If this is true," after remaining silent for a considerable time, Colonel Forester's tone sliced through the room, "then I insist you identity of those guests, Miss. King."

Fitzwilliam focused his attention on Colonel Forester. The colonel's tone was badgering rather than an attempt to gain Miss King's cooperation. Fitzwilliam wondered why the colonel would use such a sharp tone to a fellow guest at Lucas Lodge. Had something occurred before Sir William's party reached the ball?

Intent on finding answers to these new questions, as well as identifying the murderer, Fitzwilliam kept his voice low as he said, "Take time to gather your thoughts, Miss King. I am certain you wish to find the murderer's identity as much as do we."

"How can you be so certain of that point, Colonel?" Colonel Forester rocked on his heels as he studied Fitzwilliam. "Perhaps this young woman has something to hide."

"Colonel Forester, I beg you to keep a civil tone when speaking to my wife's guests." Bingley stepped forward before Fitzwilliam could object to the colonel's implications.

"This meandering line of questioning must cease. We need to identify the person responsible for this crime. The killer could strike again while we ask the guests senseless questions, and I have no wish to deal with the consequences. My wife is in that ballroom without my protection." Colonel Forester angled his chin, obviously daring either of them to deny his words as fact.

"I agree wholeheartedly, Colonel" Fitzwilliam said. "However, we accomplish nothing if we alienate the guests. Surely you are in agreement that we need their cooperation."

"We need details that will identify the murderer and we need them now."

"Very well, Colonel. As you are correct in your concern and wish only to prevent more harm, I will reply in turn. If it will assist your investigation I admit I followed Captain Carter from the ballroom." Miss King's cheeks deepened in color but she held her head high.

"Did Captain Carter follow Mr. Wickham?" Colonel Forester demanded as he leaned over her.

"I should think not." Miss King frowned. "Captain Carter was one of the last to leave the ballroom."

⋐⋑

"We accomplished nothing." Colonel Forester slapped his hand against his thigh after the door closed behind Miss King. "An heiress pursued by a fortune hunter, who then broke her heart. No news in that, unless Miss King harbored enough anger to wish Wickham harm."

"I find that hard to believe." Colonel Fitzwilliam eyed the other two men. "Miss King seemed more uncomfortable admitting to her interest in Captain Carter than any details of her affair with Wickham."

"Women are known for being fickle, Colonel. As a man with a wife, I assure that fact is true. Miss King could have been head-over-heels for Wickham and led us to believe otherwise when confronted. Why else would Lydia Wickham blame her for the crime?" Colonel Forester rocked back on his heels as he concluded with a satisfied nod.

"Colonel, you forget you and Mrs. Forester were also blamed for the crime." Fitzwilliam paused as he studied the other two men. "No, gentlemen, I suggest it happened as Miss King described. The shock of hearing of Wickham's death resulted in Mrs. Wickham's harsh claims. No offense intended to your wife's sister, Bingley, but that is my conclusion of the situation."

"I am in agreement, Colonel." Bingley nodded. "I am certain Lydia would never say such words against Lizzy in normal circumstances."

"If one of the women Wickham courted and discarded did not commit the murder, what cause do we have for this crime?" Colonel Forester demanded. "In my experience, Lydia Wickham says exactly what is on her mind. At least, she did so for the months she stayed with us in Brighton, before she ran off to marry Wickham. For that reason, gentlemen, I consider Mrs. Darcy and Miss King the main suspects."

"We cannot proceed with charges of murder when the claims against the two women are based purely on the words of a grief stricken wife." Colonel Fitzwilliam insisted.

"I agree with Colonel Fitzwilliam." Bingley threw his shoulders back and stepped forward to defend his wife's family. "Neither woman possesses the temperament of a murderer. I am quite certain Mrs. Darcy could not commit this crime."

"Dare you risk the safety of your wife, based on this assumption?" Colonel Forester shook with barely-suppressed emotion as he faced them. "Were you at Mrs. Darcy's side the whole of the evening, or were you with your wife, Mr. Bingley?"

"Gentlemen," Fitzwilliam said in the voice he used to command his men, "we must not vent our frustration on each other. Do reconsider your opinion, Colonel, for I agree with Bingley's assessment of Mrs. Darcy's character. I have known my cousin's wife but a short time, but I do not believe her capable of murder."

"Ah, but this is where I have the advantage over you, gentlemen. I have firsthand knowledge of Lydia Wickham's behavior and she holds no thoughts in her head, but blurts them for all to hear." Colonel Forester raised his finger for emphasis, "Also my wife and I are house guests along with Miss King. I believe I can claim a more knowledge of her character, as well. With those facts in mind, it is my opinion that Mrs. Darcy and Miss King remain the main suspects."

A tense silence followed Colonel Forester's declaration.

Fitzwilliam and Bingley studied each other in disbelief. Colonel Forester insisted Darcy's wife committed the murder but they each had reason to prove she did not.

"Why would Lizzy...Mrs. Darcy do such at thing?" Bingley demanded in a rush of words. "Begging your pardon, Colonel, but I must disagree. Mrs. Darcy speaks her mind. If a thing irritates her, she makes no attempt to hide her emotions, as my dear wife is known to do. Nor does she have a fit of temper as Lydia and her mother do. Mrs. Darcy confronts the source of her irritation."

"Precisely!" Colonel Forester exclaimed, rocking back on his heels. "It might have escaped your notice, but we attended the ball the evening Mrs. Darcy's younger sister tried to play the piano, despite all attempts to dissuade her. I clearly recall Mrs. Darcy's expression and witnessed her humiliation as guests reacted to her sister's lack of skill. Based on that account, I believe she confronted Wickham on his betrayal of her affections. Perhaps she intended no harm, and was overtaken by emotion. Upon my word, sir, how can anyone be certain of what they are capable when emotions take control? Therefore, I stand firm in my belief that Mrs. Darcy or Miss King is the murderer we seek. Both have the temperament. Have you not noticed the fire in their eyes as proof of their depth of emotion?"

"How can you imagine, such?" Bingley stared at the colonel. "What does Mrs. Darcy gain by bringing harm to her sister's husband?"

"It is possible she had no mind of such actions. Perhaps Wickham forced his attentions on her. The confines of marriage did little to contain his passion, as we are all aware."

"I must disagree, Colonel. Bingley's thoughts are more to the point. Mrs. Darcy would not respond in such a manner. She might slice Wickham to the quick with her words, but not in an act of violence. Lizzy married Darcy only a few months ago. They have a life-time ahead of them." Colonel Fitzwilliam studied the two men. "Why would she take such a risk?"

"Ah, but did she not marry a man she once professed to hate? That is the gossip repeated to my wife. Perhaps her true affections focused on Wickham. Or having gained knowledge of his character, could it be she had no choice but to defend herself." Colonel Forester pursed his lips. "You must have observed how Wickham reacted to women. He charmed them and, poor souls that they are, few women resisted his attention. Perhaps Wickham attempted to pursue his previous relationship with Mrs. Darcy."

"Such a suggestion is not possible!" Colonel Fitzwilliam stalked across the room and back. "Compared to Darcy, Wickham had no chance—"

"Wickham could not compete with Darcy on any level." Bingley blurted.

"Ah, but you must attempt to think as a woman might, if subjected to his charm. Mrs. Darcy was attracted to Wickham before he turned to her sister, Lydia. Perhaps she missed his charm, which I am told Mr. Darcy lacks." Colonel Forester sent them a knowing glance. "Mrs. Darcy would not be the first married woman to seek excitement outside her marriage."

"You are out of line, Colonel."

"That idea is offensive, Colonel, and disrespectful." Bingley added to Colonel Fitzwilliam's objection. "My wife's sister would never contemplate such behavior."

"Unless she had a good reason." Colonel Forester held up a hand. "Consider the humiliation she must have endured when Wickham turned his attentions to Miss King's fortune. Even worse, Wickham lured her younger sister into disgrace before marrying her. Imagine the blow to Mrs. Darcy's pride when Wickham did not return his attentions to her after ending his affair with Miss King. Instead, Wickham turned to her younger sister. Gentlemen, I am convinced this is a crime of passion, and I suggest Mrs. Darcy is the murderer."

"So you disregard your earlier suspicion of Miss King and turn all blame on Darcy's wife? How can you suggest such a possibility, Colonel?"

Colonel Forester's face twisted in thought as he considered Fitzwilliam's question. "You are correct, Colonel. I offered only one possible solution. Either of these women could be guilty of this crime."

"Unbelievable," Bingley muttered as he stomped across the room. "Wickham was tall, with wiry strength, while both women you hold suspect are of small stature. How could they commit this crime?"

"Mr. Bingley," Colonel Forester's face eased into a pleased expression, "has described the reason I believe this to be a crime of passion. How else could anyone get close enough to murder a man trained in the militia, if not by pretending to embrace him?"

CZ80

To diffuse tension, Colonel Fitzwilliam suggested they halt the questioning for a short time. He needed to warn Darcy of Forester's claims. Colonel Forester agreed to the delay and rushed to check on his wife with the concern of a devoted husband. Mr. Bingley also seemed relieved and hurried to find Jane to relate the latest news.

"Lizzy is not a murderer! That cannot be," Jane insisted upon hearing Bingley's report. "She did not care a whit for Wickham after he turned to Miss King. Whether you agree or not, I am of the opinion Lizzy was attracted to Darcy from the night they first met. However, Lizzy's pride prevented her from admitting her interest when Darcy acted standoffish. Do you not recall how aloof Darcy acted, Charles? He was puffed up and looking down his nose —"

"My dear Jane," Bingley laid a soothing hand on her arm, "pray do not distress yourself."

"How can I not?" Jane's cheeks filled with the heat of her emotions. "Where is the colonel now? I must disabuse him of this notion at once."

"Fear not, dear wife," Bingley replied in a calm tone as he nodded toward Lizzy and Darcy standing with the colonel. "I suspect Colonel Fitzwilliam is relaying the details to Darcy as we speak. They will shield Lizzy from Colonel Forester's claims."

For all her calm nature, Jane turned to glare at Colonel Forester as he hovered over his wife several feet away. "Has he not done enough to ruin my family without claiming that Lizzy murdered Wickham? Really, Charles, I am quite certain Colonel Forester has reached the wrong conclusion."

"Rest assured my dear, Darcy will defend Lizzy —"

"How can he do so when his deeds are doubted as well?" Jane clutched her husband's arm as she pleaded. "Oh, Charles, they are our family. We must prove —"

"My dear, you must not concern yourself. Allow the colonels to inquire into these matters. The danger is too great and I will not have you exposed to risk. Come and walk with me as we consult with our guests."

"Oh Charles, if only I could depend on them but, as the colonels are not in accord, I cannot rest with knowing Lizzy is under suspicion. I need to help clear her name. You converse with the guests. I must consult with cook about food and drinks."

"Jane, please allow Caroline to handle the details, she is accustomed to dealing with cook."

"Oh, Charles," Jane angled her chin to look in his eyes, "do you not see that as a problem? Caroline is still in charge of all that goes on in this house, but I am your wife, and I intend to make you proud."

"But Jane, I believed you were happy for Caroline to continue to handle things about the house."

"It saddens me to admit I was, Charles, and that only added to the problem. I stood back, willing for others to make my decisions, much as my parents did when I was at home. If no other good comes from this night, my eyes have opened to the need for us to take charge of our lives. I want to take my rightful place at your side as your wife. Therefore, I must share the responsibility as well as the joy." Color filled her cheeks as their eyes tangled for long moments. "This night has taught me a lesson. Now I will speak to Cook. You must share with Mr. Darcy all that you know and learn what he thinks should be done."

Even so, Jane left the ballroom reluctantly. All she wanted to do was close herself and Bingley in their bedchamber and forget the rest of the world, but that was not going to happen. Until she proved Lizzy was innocent of this crime, she could not enjoy her husband's love or any other pleasant events. Thoughts that Lizzy or Miss King might lose all because of false claims made her stomach roil.

More determined than ever before in her life, Jane hurried downstairs, turned to the back hallway, and made her way to the kitchen.

CB&O

A short while later, Lizzy took her seat and glanced around the library as she said, "Why have they called us all here?"

All the members of her family were gathered in the room where

Wickham died. Kitty and Mary sat huddled together in a large chair. Lydia sat near-by and spread her skirts on the chair as she stared about with wide-eyed, as if unaffected by the crime. Mamma settled on one end of a sofa, while Jane sat at the other end. Bingley stood directly behind Jane, one hand on the back of the sofa as if to offer his support. Her father lounged in the wingback chair opposite the sofa and Lizzy suspected she was the only person in the room aware of his tension. Certainly her mother never seemed to notice the slight twitch to his right eye when he was worried.

Darcy stood in front of the fireplace, hands clasped behind his back. He, too, kept his reactions to events from marring his countenance. When they first met his stern control kept her from understanding the depth of his emotions, but not any longer. She knew he was ready to spring to her defense from the way he took notice of every detail in the room.

Most of his attention focused on the two officers leading the investigation. Even Darcy's favorite cousin held himself rigid, but Lizzy supposed Fitzwilliam must appear detached. Her situation could worsen if Colonel Fitzwilliam showed favorites during the investigation of Lydia's claims. Lizzy was confident her activities this evening would prove her innocent. Indeed she dearly hoped that would be the true. She prayed there was no added reason for her mother to fall into a another fit of nerves.

She glanced about and noticed Colonel Forester was studying her family as if they were a group of recalcitrant troops in need of discipline. "Colonel, why do you call all my family here if you only have questions for me?"

"We assumed you would feel more comfortable with your family present." Fitzwilliam said before Colonel Forester could respond, which was just as well Lizzy decided, as she noted the scowl on Colonel Forester's face.

"Then let us begin," Colonel Forester demanded as he turned a grim glance on Lizzy. "Mrs. Darcy, were you angered by Mr. Wickham's actions when he lured your sister, Lydia, to elope with him?"

"Wickham did not lure me." Lydia giggled. "It was all my idea. I wanted to surprise my family by being the first one married, and me the youngest."

Ignoring her sister's comment, Lizzy angled her chin high as she met the colonel's stare. "I was quite vexed with Wickham's behavior."

"Lizzy —"

"Were you jealous of Mr. Wickham's affections for your youngest sister?" Colonel Forester demanded, ignoring Lydia's attempt to interrupt.

"Not at all, Colonel. I was worried his actions would ruin Lydia's reputation and that of the rest of my family as well."

Lydia made a snorting sound. "You were afraid you would lose your chance with Darcy. You had no concern for me or the rest of our family." Lydia watched Lizzy and Darcy exchange a glance and raised her voice even more. "Well, you have Darcy now, Lizzy, and I hope you are satisfied."

Colonel Forester watched the exchange with a gleam in his eye. When Lydia went silent, he gave a nod of agreement. "Perhaps Mrs. Wickham is correct. Were you concerned only for your own reputation, Mrs. Darcy? After all, a man of your husband's standing would hardly choose to marry a woman with a tarnished reputation."

"Colonel Forester —"

"Do not concern yourself, Darcy. I will respond to the question." Lizzy sent her husband a half-smile then turned to the colonel. "I was deeply concerned for Lydia's future, but also for my father's safety. I feared for his health if he pursued the couple to protect Lydia's honor. You are also correct in assuming I feared for Jane's future and my own. Wickham's careless actions could have ended Mamma's goal to marry off her daughters and my family's chance for happiness."

"What nonsense is this?" Mrs. Bennet sputtered as she glared at Lizzy. "Ruin our family's future? I was thrilled to have a daughter married at last. Lydia is younger than you, Lizzy, and not as pretty as Jane, but she found a husband, first, did she not?"

"Now, who is being silly?" Lydia blurted as their mamma stopped speaking. She sent Darcy a challenging glance and turned back to Lizzy. "A little gossip would not keep Darcy away if he really loved you. Look what my Wickham did for me."

"What?" Kitty and several other voices said at once.

Lydia turned a surprised glance on them and responded patiently. "Why, he turned his back on all his friends and the regiment and took me to London, of course."

"He ruined your reputation by running off without marrying you first." Vexed emotions echoed in Lizzy's voice.

"Wife, do allow the colonels to get on with their questions."

Darcy's words rang with caution as his gaze bored into Lizzy's with an unspoken warning to control her emotions.

"Ah, so you did have strong feelings against Mr. Wickham for his actions with your sister." A satisfied gleam glowed in Colonel Forester's eyes as he rocked on his heels.

Lizzy's jaw set in a determined angle. "It is true. I harbored hard feelings towards Wickham for what he put the family through, at first."

"You expect us to believe your feelings changed after some time had passed?" Colonel Forester held her stare with a grim glance.

"That is exactly what I expect." Lizzy lifted her chin and glared at the colonel. "Lydia and Wickham came to Longbourn on a visit and he talked all of us around."

"A more charming son-in-law I never expect to have," Mr. Bennet said. Crossing his hands over his mid-section, he turned a bland glance on Colonel Forester. "As his former commanding officer, Colonel, I expect you experienced some of Wickham's smooth-talking skill at one time or another. I am certain you understand his ability."

"Um, yes, of course," Colonel Forester mumbled as he turned back to Lizzy. "So, Lydia and Wickham visited the family and you forgot his past transgressions?"

Lizzy arched a brow as she replied. "We agreed it was best to say nothing more for Lydia's sake."

"How droll," Lydia said between giggles. "Why did you worry about me? I was the one married, not you."

"Is it possible," Colonel Forester continued as if Lydia had not spoken, "you met Wickham tonight for the first time since your marriage?"

"Yes." Lizzy's tone clinked cold as ice pellets.

"Were you happy to reunite with Mr. Wickham?"

"I was very pleased to see my sister. Lydia missed our wedding, and it has been some time since we last saw her." Lizzy locked gazes with Jane as they recalled their hopes and fears for Lydia's adjustment to married life.

"Ah, but seeing Lydia also meant seeing Mr. Wickham, did it not?" Colonel Forester demanded.

"I suppose—"

"Perhaps you were eager to take your revenge? It did not take you long to arrange a meeting with Wickham in the garden, did it?"

"Lizzy Bennet—"

"Wickham is mine, Lizzy, and do not forget that." Lydia's outburst interrupted her mother's objection.

Colonel Forester ignored Mrs. Bennet and Lydia, as he demanded, "As soon as Mr. Darcy left your side in the ballroom, Wickham appeared did he not?"

"I am sure I do not know—"

"Mrs. Darcy, I insist you answer the question. Wickham joined you and engaged in conversation as soon as your husband walked away, is that not so?"

"We talked—"

"And arranged to meet—"

"Wickham was only trying to regain my good opinion—"

"Why is that, Mrs. Darcy? Why would your brother-in-law feel the need to renew his association with you?"

"We were being polite for the sake of Jane's ball, Colonel, and nothing more." Lizzy's glare flamed hot as she met the colonel's stare. "And yes, I did arrange a meeting in the garden—"

"Ah, ha—"

"—with Lydia," Lizzy continued, her voice steady even with the gloating expression on Colonel Forester's face, "and only Lydia."

"It is true." Lydia sniffed. "Lizzy ordered me to meet her in the garden so we could have a conversation without being interrupted. Some discussion that turned out to be. She scolded me, same as always. I should have paid her no attention and stayed away."

Colonel Forester eyed Lizzy as he continued, "You left the ballroom alone, but met with Lydia in the garden? Good story, Mrs. Darcy, yet there was still time enough for you to murder Mr. Wickham."

The only sound in the library came from the gentle crackling of the fire and gasps from the occupants. Jane watched muscles bunch in Darcy's jaw. Lizzy clenched her hands in the fabric of her gown, but neither of them made a sound.

Was it finished then, Jane worried. Would Colonel Forester declare Lizzy was Wickham's murderer? Even thought of such a thing was abhorrent to Jane. Could no one speak a word in Lizzy's defense? What would happen to Lizzy...to Darcy...if they charged her with this crime? Life would never be the same if they took Lizzy away. Jane released a shuddering breath. How could she wrap herself in the warmth of Bingley's affections if her favorite sister was not there to share her joy? This must not happen. Lizzy would never hurt anyone, especially her own sister's husband, but how could she prove Lizzy was innocent?

A loud crackle sounded in the fireplace, and suddenly, all those gathered in the room seemed to snap out of a trance.

"Well, that does it then," Colonel Forester clasped his hands behind his back as a satisfied expression covered his face.

Bodies shuffled around Jane as her family straightened in their chairs and stared at the colonel. Murmurs escaped, as one by one they sensed approaching doom. Muscles bulged along Darcy's jaw as he exchanged a tension-filled look with his cousin.

As if activated by Darcy's silence, Colonel Fitzwilliam stepped forward and spoke for the first time since accusations against Lizzy began. "Colonel—"

"This is not right," Kitty's voice sounded on a breath, her words squeaky as a little girl's voice. "I was with Lizzy when we met Lydia in the garden."

Jane watched disappointment line Colonel Forester's face as Kitty's words echoed in the quiet room. He seemed determined to blame Lizzy for this crime, but why? All his questions focused on Lizzy's actions and her reasons for wishing Wickham harm, all of which Jane knew to be unfounded. Now, her dear, giddy sister, Kitty, had saved Lizzy.

"My apologies, Madam," Colonel Forester made a stiff bow toward Lizzy and scrubbed a hand over his face, "I only wished for this crime to be solved."

"Mrs. Darcy," Colonel Fitzwilliam's voice rang with authority, but his tone softened as he continued, "why would you go to the garden at night without Darcy?"

Lips clamped, her expression tightened from Colonel Forester's assertions, Lizzy glanced at her husband. "Darcy knows I am not helpless. He was talking with someone across the room. I saw Lydia leave the ballroom and I followed to meet with her. I wanted a chance to speak to her alone."

"Why was it important that Mrs. Wickham be alone? I take it you mean without her husband's presence?" Colonel Forester said.

Lizzy lifted her chin as she replied. "Lydia is my sister. I have not visited with her in months. What other reason would I have for seeking her company?"

"Perhaps the two of you were making plans." Colonel Forester rocked on his heels, ready to attack again.

"It is as you suggest, Colonel. We were making plans for Lydia to visit Pemberley."

Jane frowned. From Colonel Forester's comments this evening, she concluded he had never liked Lydia. Perhaps he had not been in favor of Lydia accompanying his wife to Brighton. But if that were the case, why had he not refused his wife's request for Lydia's presence? Surely, he did not imagine Lydia, three years younger than his wife, was a bad influence. If anything, Jane believed the opposite. For all of Lydia's forward ways in dealing with Denny and his friends, she actually had no real experience of being alone with a man until she went to Brighton to visit the Foresters.

"Taking a stroll in the cold, evening air seems extreme for such an innocent conversation." Colonel Forester stared at Lizzy. "Tell us, Mrs. Darcy, what did you really want to talk to your sister about?"

Jane watched as color fill Lizzy's cheeks. Oh no, she knew that expression. Colonel Forester would get no response from Lizzy by badgering, and why was Lizzy so unforthcoming? Could she not explain why she needed to speak with Lydia instead of adding to the colonel's suspicion of her actions?

Lizzy studied Darcy's tight expression for several heartbeats, and finally, her chin angled, she returned the colonel's glare. "It is as I said. I wanted to visit with Lydia."

"Oh, what stuff and nonsense," Mrs. Bennet blurted the words into the tense silence following Lizzy's comment. "You could have talked to Lydia all evening had you so desired. Tell the colonel what you were doing."

"Mamma," Lizzy exclaimed, her expression not hiding her impatience with her parent. "It is true. I wished to speak to Lydia and it seemed easier to talk without the music and chatter around us."

"Stuff and nonsense is right." Lydia said, glaring at Lizzy with a pouting expression on her face. "Why not tell them the truth?"

"I only wanted to speak with you."

"Same as all the times you would seek me out for a conversation at home?" Lydia made a snorting sound and turned to the colonel with her chin angled stubbornly. "It is true Lizzy wanted to talk to me in private, but not about a visit. She —"

"Lydia, please," Lizzy said, "you need not do this."

"What do I care if they know? Wickham is dead. It matters not," Lydia said as she sent Lizzy a defiant glare. A smirk covered her face as she turned to Darcy. "Lizzy warned me to stop Wickham from asking Darcy for money."

"Did she threaten you?" Colonel Forester demanded eagerly.

"Lizzy? Threaten me, her own sister. How droll." Lydia's giggles filled the stunned silence of the room. "I lived with Lizzy's bossy ways and stubborn manner all my life, but she never threatened me. Why would she? She married a man of wealth. Wickham was lucky to have two pence in his pocket. Why would she threaten me?"

"But she warned you off," the colonel repeated helpfully.

"She said we should not trouble Darcy over matters of money." Lydia turned wide eyes on the colonel. "She offered to help when she could, and so she should. She is my sister."

"You are satisfied she intended no harm?"

"Lizzy would not hurt an insect. Have you not seen her tromping through the fields on her nature walks? Really, Colonel, if you must blame someone for Wickham's murder, you need to look farther than Lizzy."

The entire room seemed to revive at once as those present sighed with relief.

Mr. Bennet stood slowly and surveyed the colonel with a calculating glance. "Colonel Forester, your murderer is gaining ground, as you sniff the wrong trail." With a smirk revealing his wicked humor, Mr. Bennet walked to his wife's chair and to the surprise of his daughters, he offered his hand. "Come, wife, we must return to the guests before the good Colonel decides you too are guilty of Wickham's murder."

"Me," Mrs. Bennet screeched as she took his offered hand, "why would I harm Wickham? Why he was charm itself and reminded me of men in uniform I knew in my youth. I fancied a militia man more than once before we married, you know."

"So you keep reminding me." Mr. Bennet steered her out the door. Mary and Kitty followed, looking dazed.

Darcy stopped in front of Fitzwilliam. "You were very quiet, cousin."

"I thought it best if the colonel tripped over his own suggestions. Had I defended Lizzy, he might have continued badgering her."

"Point taken, but Mr. Bennet's words are correct. The killer gains a head start with all this wasted time."

"It is a matter foremost in my mind."

Lydia flounced to a halt in front of Colonel Forester. "Really, Colonel, you were most unkind to Lizzy."

Colonel Forester bowed. "I accepted the duty to discover who murdered your husband, my dear."

"Then perhaps you should speak with your wife." Lydia said with a sly glance. "Surely you are aware she fancied my Wickham above all the militia men in Brighton? Have you not wondered why she is so vexed with me?" Lydia burst into giggles. "Surely you do not imagine it is because I ran away from your home?" She giggled again. "I can assure you it is not. Your wife is vexed because I eloped with her favorite. Wickham told me so. You should keep watch on Harriet, Colonel."

Keeping his face blank, Fitzwilliam watched Jane and Lizzy rush Lydia out of the library before she said more. Darcy followed the sisters out of the room. Fitzwilliam turned to Forester. "Colonel, it is evident Mrs. Darcy did not commit this crime. Whom do you suggest we question next?

Colonel Forester turned, his flushed face set in a rigid expression. "I am not convinced Mrs. Wickham is free from suspicion, gentlemen. But as we must still question Miss King, I thought it best to let the issue rest for now."

Chapter Ten

Ohhh!" Lizzy cried, stopping halfway up the stairs, and turning to look back at Jane. Lydia had jerked her arm away and rushed on ahead so only Darcy and Jane heard Lizzy's outburst.

"Lizzy, what is the matter?" Jane rushed up the stairs, bringing her level with Lizzy. "Are you unwell?" Yet even as she said the words, Jane noted Lizzy's squinted eyes and red face. She recognized the expression from their childhood. Lizzy was sick, but not physically. Jane glanced at Mr. Darcy as he stood beside his wife.

Lizzy followed Jane's gaze and attempted a smile to ease her husband's concern. "I am fine, Darcy. Only I need to speak with Jane. Please, do go ahead to check on Georgiana and Miss Brown."

"Miss Brown seems nice," Jane murmured as they climbed the stairs, giving Mr. Darcy time to outdistance them. "I regret that she was the one to discover the body."

"She is nice." Lizzy's brow wrinkled. "She is kindness itself to Georgiana, and always willing to do her wishes, if circumstances permit." Lizzy turned a thoughtful look on Jane. "Miss Brown reminds me of someone. But I cannot think who it is."

"That cannot be what vexed you so."

Lizzy stopped on the stairs and turned as Jane paused beside her. "Ohhh, that man is impossible." Eyes flashing, she continued through gritted teeth. "How can he speak to me in such a way? And Fitzwilliam, Darcy's own cousin, said nothing to help."

"But Lizzy, Colonel Fitzwilliam could not come to your aid and do his job fairly."

"Oh, Jane, as usual you are correct, but why does Colonel Forester dislike me so much? If he were to speak in such a manner to Lydia, I could understand, but I hardly know the man."

"It does seem strange that he was so determined to make you appear guilty." Jane paused, soothing chatter from the ballroom filled the air, but here, they could speak their thoughts and not be overheard. "It almost seems as if he is protecting someone by making you appear guilty of the crime."

"You have voiced my opinion perfectly. I could not put my finger on what was troubling me, but you are correct." Lizzy stepped close to Jane and lowered her voice. "I can not imagine who he is protecting, but we must discover their identity."

"Lizzy, you cannot!" Jane caught Lizzy's arm and stopped her as she rushed to the top of the stairs. "You must do nothing. Involving yourself in this situation further could only may you seem guilty."

"But I am involved. Colonel Forester," Lizzy inhaled a shuddering breath, "tried to make me sound guilty of murder."

"Indeed he did and that is why you must keep your distance from this situation." Jane whispered intently. She stared in Lizzy's eyes, willing her to understand. "Think what would happen if you discovered the identity of the real murderer. The colonel, with his attitude, could still accuse you of the crime and laying the blame on someone else. Please, Lizzy, I insist you stay visible in the ballroom at all times. You must allow Bingley and I to search out the truth. I beg you agree for your own safety."

"Bingley?" Lizzy rolled her eyes. "I am sorry, Jane, but Bingley is much too nice to act as my defender. If I am in danger, I need to discover the facts for myself or have the help of someone with Darcy's nature."

"Lizzy, you must hear me out."

Lizzy stopped mid-step and turned to stare at her sister. This authoritative tone from her dear, easy-going Jane was something she had not heard before in all her life. Whatever had happened to her calm, cool sister's disposition? "Jane, I appreciate —"

"You narrowly escaped this last session with the colonel. What do you suppose he intends next? Indeed, if he is protecting someone as we assume, you must remain as distant from any details as possible." Jane took a deep breath and struggled to regain her composure.

"I know only too well how this goes against your nature, but in this instance I am certain what I say is correct. Do you trust me, Lizzy?"

"Jane, do you need ask? I would trust you with my life, but—"

"Is it Bingley you—"

"Jane, please, do not speak the words."

"How can I not? Your life is at stake—"

"Oh, Jane!" Lizzy flung her arms around Jane and hugged her tight. "My dear, Jane, do you not realize that other than Darcy, I love you more than anyone in the world? However, my future is threatened by lies, and I fear your sweet nature cannot withstand the challenge needed to prove me innocent. Bingley is too nice, by far, for such a task. Poppa even commented on Bingley's easy nature. To clear my name, I need someone willing to fight for my honor."

"Do you suppose for a minute I would not?" Jane stood tall with her shoulders squared. Heat filled her cheeks but she would not be dissuaded. "Do you imagine I have no knowledge of Bingley's true character? Have you never considered why Darcy regards Bingley as his friend? If he has so little regard for Bingley, why are they as close as brothers?"

"Jane, I—"

"Pray, do forgive my outburst. This evening's events have caused me to loosen my tongue in a most unbecoming manner."

"Or perhaps there is more stiffness in your backbone than you allow us to observe. Seeing you now, Jane, with sparks in your eyes and fire in your cheeks, I can well believe you will defend me as well as Darcy could."

"I will not fail you, Lizzy. You have my word. Bingley and I will help to find the answers and discover the murderer. Bingley is attending the questioning sessions. He has knowledge of what occurs there. Pray, assure me you will do nothing to cast further blame on your head."

Lizzy stared at the guests mulling around in the ballroom and frowned. Darcy barely escaped a close encounter with the colonel's questions earlier in the evening. She dared not put him at risk by complaining about the colonel. Again, Jane's suggestion of using caution proved to be the best choice. Lizzy needed to remain visible and stay removed from all suspicion to protect Darcy and Georgiana.

"Oh, Jane, what would I do without you? Your goodness and calm keep me sane. Forgive my quick temper, for I know you will never fail me."

CR80

Denny arrived in the library after Mr. Darcy passed on the colonels request for his presence.

"Lt. Denny, how well did you know Mr. Wickham?" Colonel Fitzwilliam asked pleasantly.

Recalling Carter's warning, Denny kept his tone calm. "I would say as well as a brother, Colonel. Before Wickham left Brighton, we were almost inseparable."

"When you went gaming and drinking with friends?"

"We liked a game of chance," Denny admitted with a smile, "and a pint better than we should." His face sobered, "Else, we did, before tonight."

"The news of Wickham's death saddened you?" Colonel Fitzwilliam asked.

"It did," Denny purposely turned away from the blood staining the rug where Wickham fell, "I feel bad for Lydia, uh, Mrs. Wickham. She was crazy about Wickham from the day they met."

"When you give voice to the word crazy—"

"She was besotted with Wickham and could not stand for him to be out of her sight." Denny gazed at the fire. "I often wonder how it would feel to be loved in such as way."

"Would you describe Mrs. Wickham as jealous?" Colonel Forester stepped forward as he asked the question.

"Colonel, you saw Lydia...Mrs. Wickham at socials. She was not averse to having a flirt, but she never had eyes for anyone but Wickham."

"You did not answer the question, Denny. Was Mrs. Wickham jealous of Mr. Wickham's attention to other women?" Colonel Forester demanded in the no nonsense tone he used with the regiment.

"I have no answer to that question, Colonel."

"Because you will not or—"

"Lydia never did anything that led me to form such an opinion." Denny avoided the colonel's stare and looked instead at Colonel Fitzwilliam. "We all enjoyed socials and having a good time together."

"Perhaps you are being too kind to your friend's widow. Remember, Mr. Wickham is dead. Could his wife be the murderer?" Colonel Forester stood so close Denny was forced to raise his head to meet the colonel's stare.

"Lydia would never harm Wickham. Of that I am certain." Denny ran a finger inside his collar.

"Very well, soldier, who would want to harm Mr. Wickham?"

Denny swallowed and stared at his boots for long seconds before lifting his gaze to Colonel Forester. "I know of no one, sir."

"Yet Wickham owed debts to all he knew. I suspect there is not a man in the regiment but who loaned him coin." Colonel Forester turned away and walked to the fireplace. "Are those men not angry over losing their money?"

A sheepish grin covered Denny's face. "Colonel, you know how Wickham was." Denny glanced over to Colonel Fitzwilliam. "He could talk the fleas off a dog. We knew he was all talk and no pay."

"Much as I hate to admit, Denny, I am not removed from rumors of Wickham's behavior." Colonel Forester moved to stand over Denny again. "For this reason I must ask if you were annoyed with Wickham over something to do with your family?"

Color rushed to Denny's face. He glanced toward the door before he met the colonel's stare. Clearing his throat, he admitted, "Months ago, it is true, I was displeased with Wickham. But we worked things out and were on friendly terms when he moved up north."

"What was the nature of your disagreement?"

"It was a personal matter, sir."

"Ah, so you say." Colonel Forester paced a few steps then turned back to face Denny. "You have a sister, perhaps?"

"Wickham intended no harm, Colonel. My sister is young and not familiar with the actions of men in the militia. Once I explained their habits to her, things went back to normal."

"What are you concealing, Denny?"

Bingley watched as Denny stared past the colonel's shoulder instead of meeting his gaze. "My sister married her beau and settled down to married life. All is well."

Bingley recalled the whispers he had heard about Wickham and Miss Darcy, and later, his supposed elopement with Lydia Bennet. Without intervention, he had no doubt Wickham would not have married Lydia. Had Wickham misled Denny's sister? Bingley suspected his actions were less than honorable, and Denny did seem to be hiding something. Had Wickham stirred more trouble than Denny wanted to admit? Was Denny hiding details of his disagreement with Wickham because he had taken measures into his own hands?

"You settled your differences with Wickham before he moved

north?" Colonel Forester asked again.

"We are friends, least, we were before his murder." Still, Denny avoided Colonel Forester's gaze.

"Did you speak with Mr. Wickham after he arrived at the ball?" Colonel Forester demanded.

"Only in passing," Denny shrugged, "Lydia's family crowded around before we could exchange more than greetings, but we were going to meet in the garden."

"Ah," Colonel Forester rocked back on his heels, "so it was Wickham you had arranged to meet. Not some female whose identity you are keeping secret?"

"I planned to meet Wickham." Color tinted Denny's cheeks. "We could converse without any need to watch our language if we spoke outside.

"Did your meeting with Wickham occur?"

Color deepened in Denny's cheeks. "I am afraid not, sir."

"I am surprised, young Denny. Why did you not meet Wickham as planned? Some other distraction, perhaps a woman, kept you away?"

Despite his heightened color, Denny held his head high. "When I arrived, Wickham was already speaking with someone. Then I heard Lydia's voice in the dark and went off to find her."

"If you could not meet with Mr. Wickham, his wife was a suitable distraction?"

"Colonel, as you are well aware, Lydia is my friend same as Wickham was. I thought only to keep her from learning her husband was meeting another woman."

"Who was the woman with Mr. Wickham?" Colonel Forester asked in a low tone.

Both Colonel Fitzwilliam and Bingley moved a step closer to hear the identity of a woman who might lead them to the murderer.

"It was Miss Bingley, sir."

"Caroline?"

"Caroline Bingley?" Colonel Fitzwilliam demanded over Bingley's exclamation.

"Yes, sir," Denny said as he returned the stares of the three men. "Mr. Bingley's sister."

૯෴

After asking Denny to send Captain Carter to the library, the men waited in silence until the door closed behind him. Colonel

Fitzwilliam whirled to face Colonel Forester. "That gives us nothing. We already knew that Miss Bingley met with Wickham."

"It confirms her whereabouts, though I cannot think why she met with Wickham." Bingley said.

"Perhaps we were too quick to discard Miss Bingley as a possible suspect." Colonel Forester offered.

"Now, wait—"

"You wished to speak with me, Colonel?" Captain Carter's arrival interrupted Bingley's objection.

"Captain, have a seat." Colonel Forester continued without a pause. "Speaking as an officer, Captain, what did you think of Mr. Wickham?"

Captain Carter lifted a broad shoulder. "I have found we learn the true measure of a man when we fight beside him. I did not serve in that role with Wickham. He was a friend."

"Would you say you were as close to Wickham as Mr. Denny?"

"Colonel, I am sure you are aware rank puts distance in relationships, as it must."

"Yet, you looked upon Wickham as a friend." Colonel Forester paced across the rug, stopped beside the bloodstain on the floor and stared down at it for long seconds. "Admitting friendship seems to indicate you condoned Wickham's behavior."

"Not at all, Colonel, Wickham was always ready for a game of cards and willing to while away a night drinking pints, but that does not mean I agreed with his choices."

"Explain yourself, Captain." Colonel Forester walked over and stared at Carter. "Which of Wickham's actions did you disapprove of?"

"His treatment of females comes to mind, sir. Wickham paid little heed to what damage he might do a woman's reputation as long as he achieved his aim."

Captain Carter kept his tone level, but observing him, Bingley detected emotions as deep as those Darcy kept hidden. Evidently, Colonel Forester sensed as much, as well, because he studied Carter for long moments before turning to glance at Bingley and Fitzwilliam.

"Are you speaking of any female in particular, Captain Carter?" Colonel Fitzwilliam asked in a calm tone.

"Most any female he spent time with, sir. Several of those women are here tonight, as a matter of fact."

"Captain, are you including Mrs. Wickham in that group?" Colonel Forester's soft tone put Bingley on alert.

"Of course, sir," Carter met the colonel's stare, "Wickham dropped his attachment to Miss Lizzy Bennet for Miss King, and shortly after, dismissed her to run off with Lydia. Tonight he met another woman in the garden with Mrs. Wickham here at the ball."

"Ah, yes," Colonel Forester sighed. "We know of his meeting with Miss Bingley. We were hoping you could inform us of someone we did not know."

Captain Carter studied each of them in turn, and then faced Colonel Forester. "I cannot think what more you wish me to say, Colonel. Wickham used his charm with your wife same as he did all the women he met. You know as well as I do what mettle of man he was, but he was my friend and will be missed."

"He borrowed from you?" Colonel Forester asked in a mild tone that did not match the color in his face. Captain Carter acknowledged the question with a slight nod, and Colonel Forester continued. "Yet you harbored no ill will for Wickham not paying his debt?"

Captain Carter lifted a shoulder. "To know Wickham was to know he never repaid a loan, but sometimes men of pleasant company are worth the risk of a bad loan."

Hands clasped behind his back, Colonel Forester pursed his lips for a long moment, then said. "You say he charmed Mrs. Forester. When was this?"

Captain Carter sent Bingley and Colonel Fitzwilliam a keen glance and slowly straightened in the chair to full alert. "I cannot say, Colonel. I only mentioned it to imply that knowing Wickham was present was to acknowledge that he could charm any female in the room."

"No women in particular, then?" Colonel Forester asked in a deceptively soft tone.

"If you insist on names," Captain Carter glanced at Bingley and Colonel Fitzwilliam, before turning back to Colonel Forester, "he was in the garden with Mrs. Hurst."

"Mrs. Hurst? Are you certain it was not Miss Bingley?" Colonel Forester demanded as he glanced at Bingley and Fitzwilliam.

"I am not mistaken, Colonel."

"Thank you, Captain. When you return to the ballroom would you ask Mr. Hurst to join us please?" Colonel Fitzwilliam waited until the door closed, and then turned to the other two men. "This is unbelievable. No sooner do we find uncover a hint, but the next breath reveals we are mistaken."

"Why do you not consider this to be a reasonable clue, Colonel?" Forester demanded.

"Because," Bingley responded before Colonel Fitzwilliam could, "the Colonel will tell you that my sister and Mr. Wickham were acquainted. We met Wickham when we visited Darcy at Pemberley. Of course Louisa would stop to speak if she encountered Wickham in the garden."

"Very well, Mr. Bingley, then you will have no reason for concern when we question your sister."

ᆵ

In the ballroom, Captain Carter resorted to informing Mrs. Hurst that her husband was needed in the library, as Mr. Hurst was snoring loudly, and turned to find Denny almost on his heels. Before he could offer any words of reassurance, Mrs. Forester was upon them.

"Captain Carter, do enlighten us." Mrs. Forester leaned close and fluttered a scrap of lace in front of her face so only her bright gaze was revealed. "Was my husband very harsh with his questions?"

After a cautioning glance at Denny, Carter smiled. "Not bad at all, ma'am. As you are well aware, Colonel Forester is a gentleman."

"Nonsense, Captain. But then of course you must say complimentary things of your commanding officer." She sent a sly glance toward Denny. "I am certain he asked if you had seen me in the garden?"

"As a matter of fact, Mrs. Forester, he did not." Carter noted the flash of disappointment in her eyes and wondered if he had been mistaken all along. Perhaps she was only trying to get her husband's attention and not really interested in flirtations with other men in the militia.

"Come, Denny, let us fetch some punch. The good Captain is going to keep his own council as always." She grabbed Denny's arm, and fluttered her eyes as they walked away.

Carter frowned. Perhaps he was mistaken. It seemed his first assumption was correct after all.

"Ah, Captain Carter, you survived the questions I see." Miss King smiled as she reached his side.

"Aye, but barely with my hide," Carter said. He returned her smile and noticed lines around her eyes. Not from the late hour, even though it would soon be dawn, but from worry, he suspected. "Miss King, are you quite certain you made the right choice when you decided to keep your relationship with your cousin concealed?"

"I cannot be disloyal to Maggie, Captain." Mary King glanced around but they could not be overheard. "You have been kindness itself through all this trouble, and I thank you, sir. Only a good friend would keep our confidence as you have, but, now more than ever, it is imperative that I remain silent. My cousin's future is at stake. With Wickham's death, our last hope of gaining support from the child's father is gone, but now an even greater threat hangs over our heads."

"Of what are you speaking, Miss King?"

"Surely you realize the danger, Captain. My cousin is the one who discovered the body, but what if it became known that she and Wickham—"

"Ah, now I see. You fear she would be charged with murder." Carter frowned as he studied her delicate features and firm chin. "Have you considered the risk if the truth is uncovered? Are you ready for such an occurrence?"

"I have tried to plan for that event, Captain, but I must confess I am at my wit's end. If only I could be confident I have done what is fair to all."

⋉⋊

Across the ballroom, Jane listened to the soothing voices of Aunt Gardiner and Aunt Phillips as they tried to calm her mother, and prevent another attack on her nerves. However, her interest soon focused on Captain Carter's return to the ballroom.

Upon the captain's arrival, several people moved in his direction. As the Captain paused to speak to Mr. Hurst, Denny advanced from his left and Mrs. Forester appeared from his right. At the same time, Miss King crossed the center of the room and moved toward the captain.

Denny reached the captain first and seemed anxious to speak with him, but Mrs. Forester joined them. Jane watched Denny's shoulders slump as his colonel's wife fluttered her eyes at the captain. A few heartbeats later, Mrs. Forester, too, seemed ready to stomp her foot. Then she whirled away and pulled Denny toward the table of refreshments.

Miss King arrived and Captain Carter greeted her with a slight bow and a smile. As they gazed at each other, Jane observed their posture and recognized their unspoken words from their expressions. Had she not looked much the same when she first met Mr. Bingley? Could this be a match waiting to blossom, or was she mistaken, and this was only about the murder investigation?

As Jane continued her observation of the pair, Miss King's countenance flashed with worry and doubt. Again it occurred to Jane that she might have found an ally in Miss King. No sooner had that thought occurred, when she observed Mrs. Hurst approach the captain in an agitated state. Jane moved toward them before she had time to contemplate her actions. She was the hostess, but more importantly, she had promised Lizzy she would try to discover the identity of the murderer. Perhaps this was her chance to find a hint of who it might be.

As she approached the group, Jane studied the frustration on Louisa's face as she spoke with Captain Carter. Uncertain of the cause of Louisa's unrest, Jane forced her voice to remain calm as she asked. "Louisa, is something wrong?"

"Why would you imagine that, Jane?" Louisa's face twisted in fury as she glanced at Jane. "Captain Carter has brought word the colonels want to question Hurst downstairs, but he is dead to the world. What am I expected to do?"

Jane studied the lines of strain in her sister-in-law's face and spoke quickly. "He needs coffee. Can you wake him enough to drink?"

Louisa stomped her foot. "I tried to rouse him, but he spent half the night refilling his cup with punch."

"If you like, I will assist your efforts, Mrs. Hurst." Captain Carter took her elbow and guided her toward the chairs where Mr. Hurst lay sprawled in his chair and sound asleep.

Jane turned to Miss King and put her hand on her arm. "May I have a word, Miss King?" Pausing to send one of the staff to fetch hot coffee, Jane turned to her companion. "I must speak frankly. Miss King, after this night's events, I am convinced we share more than our wish to be accepted by local society."

"I beg your pardon?" Miss King attempted a smile that did not reach her eyes.

Jane watched shadows play across her expressive face and said half to herself. "Lizzy was right. You do remind me of someone I have met."

"Mrs. Bingley, pray do not speak such words."

"Oh, but I am certain I am right, Miss King, and I believe we should work with each other instead of going our separate ways."

"I am uncertain of what you mean, Mrs. Bingley. How can we help each other?"

Jane paused to study the young woman at her side for a long heartbeat before she continued. "We both have good reason to discover who murdered Mr. Wickham."

"Pray tell me why you would suggest such a thing, Mrs. Bingley?"

"You are a suspect, Miss King, as everyone here tonight is. But I think you are worried about more than your own welfare."

"Mrs. Bingley—"

"I am not concerned about being accused, because I did not leave this ballroom," Jane continued, ignoring Miss King's attempt to speak, "but most of my family and Bingley's have been questioned. Some quite harshly, I believe. After observing your reactions, I have reached the conclusion that we should work together to discover answers about this night's events. Do you not agree, Miss King?"

"As you quite rightly mentioned, Mrs. Bingley, all the guests are suspects. So why should I be more concerned than any other guest?"

"Perhaps because Mr. Wickham led you on and tried to form an attachment—"

"Oh, but it was I who called off our connection."

"Do you suppose the colonels would believe you? Mr. Wickham is not here to confirm or deny your words. What if they suspect you are a spurned lover?"

"Mrs. Bingley, please—"

"I am not convinced you have cause to worry on that account, Miss King. However," Jane paused and gazed across the room, "when it comes to your relationship to Miss Brown, I am not so certain."

Miss King gasped, then tried to recover and stammered. "Whatever can you mean, Mrs. Bingley?"

Jane pursed her lips as she studied Miss Brown, then returned her attention to Miss King. "I do not believe you to be sisters. Your likeness does not lead to sudden awareness, though in truth, my sisters and I hardly resemble one another. I suspect you must be cousins, perhaps?"

"Mrs. Bingley, I beg you not—"

"Miss King, I have no wish to disclose your secrets. I mention the subject only to make you aware of my understanding. It it my belief that you wish to discover who committed this murder as much as I do."

In spite of Jane's soothing tone, Miss King cast a glance about the room. The skirts of her gown moved as if she was readying herself to flee, but her level gaze studied Jane. Finally she inhaled deeply and flung her shoulders back, as if visibly gathering herself for a struggle. "Am I to assume you have a suggestion, Mrs. Bingley? For I must tell you even before you make the suggestion, I cannot betray my cousin by disclosing our relationship."

ᨏᨀ

Meanwhile, the men in the library barely heard the noise of the soft knock. Bingley noticed the sound and moved to open the door, but could hardly contain his reaction. Of all the people he might have suspected to be standing in the hallway, the murderer included, he was not prepared for the sight of his household cook.

"Really, Mrs. Doud, whatever the matter is, I am quite certain Mrs. Bingley, or my sister will be happy to assist you."

"Mr. Bingley, begging your pardon, sir, but it is you that I must speak with." The cook backed her rounded form away from the door, allowing room for Bingley to step into the hall.

"What is it? What is the matter? There are important issues —"

"It concerns the Mistress, sir."

"My wife? What is wrong? Has something happened to her?"

"No, sir, but Mrs. Bingley came to the kitchen a while back and requested I rouse the staff to cook food for the guests." The cook paused, her ample bosom heaving as she fought for breath.

"I can find no fault with that. My wife is quite conscious of the comfort of our guests."

"I agree, sir, and I did her bidding, but she said more." The cook gulped and continued in hurried speech. "Mrs. Bingley said we must keep watch for anything out of place around the house."

"Good idea and I suggest you get on with it."

"That's the trouble, sir. We did as Mrs. Bingley asked and found this." Mrs. Doud lifted her hand, revealing a napkin wrapped around a long slender object. She unfolded the cloth, exposing a bloody letter opener in the white folds of linen."

"Good heavens, woman." Bingley reached for the napkin, but paused. "Better bring this inside and show the colonels what you have found." Bingley shoved the door open and urged the reluctant woman to enter the library. "Gentlemen, look at this."

Colonel Fitzwilliam and Colonel Forester stared at the cook as they came forward.

Bingley said, "Mrs. Doud, reveal to them what you found."

"T'was not me that found it, sir."

Both colonels released an exclamation as they stared down at the brass blade covered in blood. From tip to handle, the blade was at least a hand's length. Elaborate carvings covering the silver handle were filled with dried blood. All told, the item would reach from a man's wrist to his elbow.

Bingley had used the letter opener many times. In fact, if he remembered correctly, he had used it the day before the ball, so he was certain the letter opener had been in the library. "I believe we have the murder weapon, gentlemen. Where was this found, Mrs. Doud?"

"When maid went to dust to the dining room first thing this morning, she spotted this thing in potted plant. She turned plumb lightheaded when she saw the blood, I can tell you."

"The discovery was a shock, I am certain." Bingley turned to the other men. "Gentlemen, anything more you wish to ask of Mrs. Doud?"

"Thank you," Colonel Fitzwilliam nodded to the woman, "but that is all for the time being."

Mumbling as he stared at the letter opener in his hand, Colonel Forester returned to stand in front of the fireplace. "This would do the deed, no doubt, but uncovering the murder weapon seems somewhat convenient."

"Only to the uninformed, sir," Bingley replied as he approached the colonel. "It seems my wife alerted the staff to be on lookout for any thing out of place in the house." Bingley paused. "Do you doubt this sharp object, covered in blood, is the murder weapon, Colonel?"

"But this is a county area, and the blood could be from a chicken or cow. The cook most likely has both on hand, and handled the letter opener after cleaning raw meat." Colonel Forester mused as he continued to stare at the letter opener.

Colonel Fitzwilliam spoke into the persisting silence that followed. "The blood is dried. What reason is there to doubt this letter opener is the cause of Wickham's injury? There is no possible reason the kitchen staff would have the item or bring the thing to our notice if it was not out of place."

"Unless one of the staff is the murderer," Colonel Forester said as he met their questioning stares.

"Sir, this is outrageous —"

"Of course it is. I quite agree this is the murder weapon. I was only offering a suggestion before we leapt to a conclusion." Colonel Forester laid the napkin and the letter opener on the desk, "Now, to find who hid this letter opener in the plant."

Suddenly the door swung open and banged against the wall and Mr. Hurst lurched into the room, with Louisa and Caroline on either side, holding his arms. "I am present as requested, gentlemen." Mr. Hurst slurred the words as he stumbled to a wingback chair and fell into the seat with a thump.

Mrs. Hurst let go his arm and turned to glare at Bingley. "I am not at all sure what you imagine you can learn from him, but I will not leave his side."

"Really, Charles, Louisa is quite correct. You are aware of his state when Hurst has a few nips." Caroline glared at her brother, and then turned her glowering gaze on the colonels. "Would either of you gentlemen care for coffee?"

"Not now. If you would depart, please, so we might speak with Mr. Hurst." Colonel Forester's tone left no doubt this was an order.

"I am not leaving my husband." Mrs. Hurst flounced to a near-by chair, plopped down, and turned a questioning gaze on her sister. "Caroline?"

"Unlike you, Louisa, I am not Mr. Hurst's keeper." Miss Bingley swept to the door with a rustle of her silk gown. "Gentlemen, if you change your mind, Charles can ring for coffee."

The door closed with a click and silence filled the room as the occupants stared at one another. Only Mr. Hurst was unaware of the silent battle of wills going on around him.

After one last glare at Mrs. Hurst, Colonel Forester shrugged his shoulders, then cleared his throat with a deep rumble. "Perhaps we should commence with the questions."

"I should hope you have no plans to dawdle about any longer than necessary after insisting we return to this room and the horrible odor. I must say, Colonel, I am not at all impressed with the way you have handled this affair." Mrs. Hurst announced.

"Begging your pardon, ma'am," Colonel Forester bowed to Mrs. Hurst. "Now, Mr. Hurst, how well did you know Mr. Wickham?"

"Um, ah, yes, Wickham," Mr. Hurst blinked, "fine fellow. Fine fellow, indeed, and always up for a game of cards if no pretty ladies are about."

"Ah, so you played cards with him often?"

"What say you? Often, nay, fellow's not around much, is he?"

"Mr. Hurst, would you like some coffee?" Colonel Fitzwilliam offered.

"Coffee? Nay, the wife poured a jug of that stuff down my throat. What I really need is —"

"Hurst, pay attention to the Colonel's questions."

Mr. Hurst leaned forward and wagged his finger at Colonel Forester. "She's sharp, that wife of mine. Nothing gets by her. What'd you say, wife?"

"Mr. Hurst, did you see Mr. Wickham while you were in the garden?" Colonel Forester's voice was loud as he leaned toward Mr. Hurst.

"Wickham in the garden? Why'd he go out there? It's damned cold outside." Mr. Hurst yawned. "Ah, I recall now, but he was alone when I talked to him."

"You spoke with Mr. Wickham? Was he waiting for someone?" Colonel Forester demanded.

The only sound in the room was the crackling of the fire and the rustling of Louisa's skirts as she shifted in her chair. Seeing Louisa's strained expression, Bingley stood rigid, waiting for his brother-in-law to respond. He doubted Hurst would recall, but perhaps Louisa could give them some idea of the time Hurst and Wickham talked. If only...

"Jovial fellow, that Wickham is, always genial. Sorry to speak harsh words to him, but a man has to protect his family."

Gasps filled the room, but other than the loud expulsion shock, no one made a sound. It was as if they were afraid of startling Mr. Hurst into silence. They waited in silence for several loud ticks of the clock. However, they need not have bothered. Mr. Hurst opened his mouth wide in a mighty yawn, flung his head back against the chair, and closed his eyes. In two heartbeats, his snores filled the silence of the room.

"Mr. Hurst? Can you hear me? Wake up, Mr. Hurst." Colonel Forester raised his voice with each word, but to no avail. Mr. Hurst snored contentedly while the occupants of the room fidgeted with agitation. The colonel expelled a sound of disgust and turned to Mrs. Hurst. "What did he mean, Mrs. Hurst? Why was he speaking to Wickham? What is this about protecting his family?"

Her head angled high, in her usual manner, Louisa replied, "I'm afraid I have no notion. Hurst goes on so, I rarely listen when he speaks."

With a sniff, she stuck her chin out and glared at them.

It was a pose Bingley had observed times too numerous to count and his gut warned they would get not another word out of her. Yet he knew her too well to be deceived. The colonels might not notice the color tinting her cheeks, but Bingley knew Louisa was vexed and he was curious as to why. Had the questions or perhaps her husband's inebriated state, offended her? On the other hand, perhaps there was a more serious reason. Perhaps she knew what Hurst referred to and wished for the matter to be kept silent. Whatever the cause, Bingley was aware that his sister was not telling the truth.

"Mrs. Hurst, did you overhear the conversation between Mr. Wickham and your husband? Was Mr. Hurst angry when he approached Wickham?"

"How can I respond if you disgorge questions with every breath, Colonel?" Though it seemed impossible, Louisa's chin lifted even higher. "I walked with Caroline and heard nothing of the conversation. Though, if want my opinion, Hurst was making reference to a senseless custom of his family that he tries to maintain when he plays cards."

"What sort of custom? Would this be a matter that would vex him?"

"Some rubbish about always winning the fifth game of cards." Louisa turned a wide-eyed glance on Bingley. "You must remember the details, Charles. Perhaps you can explain."

Fighting to keep all expression from his face as her pleading gaze bored into his, Bingley shrugged. What was she asking of him? He could not be disloyal to his own sister, yet how could he proceed without further explanation. He needed to speak with Jane. "I know nothing of the rules of the game, Louisa. If you recall, I have no head for playing cards." Louisa's furious expression distorted the hours she had spent on her looks before the ball, and warned him of consequences to come. "It is as my sister said," Bingley met the intense stares of both colonels, "when Hurst starts prattling, my thoughts wander."

"As you see, Colonel, the remark meant nothing." Louisa gave an elegant shrug, drawing attention to the low cut neckline of her gown. "Same as most words that leave my husband's mouth."

Colonel Forester exchanged glances with Fitzwilliam and expelled a heavy sigh. Then he turned back to Louisa. "Very well, madam, you may go."

"Charles, do assist me in getting Hurst to his room." Louisa demanded as she rose from her chair.

Not bothering to refuse her barely disguised order, Bingley helped her to wake Mr. Hurst and pull him upright to stand on his feet. Once he staggered out the door, with Louisa's help, Bingley sent the colonels a questioning glance. "Gentlemen, what now?"

Colonel Fitzwilliam shook his head. "None of our questions have revealed suspicion of any of the guests."

"Ah, begging your pardon, Colonel, there is the matter of Mrs. Darcy and Miss King, if you recall."

"Colonel Forester, I beg to differ. Do you not recall we discharged claims against Mrs. Darcy?"

"Perhaps we were too hasty in that matter. And there is still the King woman's rejection by Mr. Wickham to contemplate."

"So, we have nothing to go on and the messenger should be close to London by now." Colonel Fitzwilliam shook his head. "I had hoped we could have the crime solved by the time the authorities arrive in the morn, but here we are with no further clues. Perhaps we need some fresh air. Mrs. Hurst was correct. There is a foul stench in this room."

As one, they turned to stare at the bloodstain on the rug.

"Is it such a bad thing if we don't solve the crime? Can the authorities not proceed with the information we present them?" Bingley asked as he turned away from the sight.

"I see it as a matter of honor," Colonel Fitzwilliam said in a thoughtful tone. "As the local magistrate put his faith in us, I feel honor bound to discover who committed this murder."

"I agree," Colonel Forester nodded, "and we cannot keep your guests contained much longer."

"That is a growing difficulty and one reason Sir William turned to officers in the militia, not to mention that he admitted he had no stomach for such business." Colonel Fitzwilliam said. "I would not like it said we were incompetent, as well."

Bingley was the first to speak. "The officials should arrive soon after first light so there is still time to reach a conclusion. Perhaps you could do with some refreshment as the night grows long. Jane arranged a display of foodstuff for those who are hungry."

"Right," Colonel Forester headed for the door, but turned back, "we shall take repast and return with questions for Miss King and Mrs. Darcy."

Colonel Fitzwilliam marched past Bingley and murmured, "Will that man never stop?"

Bingley followed after them, but his sister's willingness to draw him into the fray cautioned him to keep his mouth closed.

Chapter Eleven

With caution ringing a warning in his head, Bingley recalled his sister's request and rushed past both colonels to the stairs. Just in time, he grabbed hold of Mr. Hurst's arm as he swayed, nearly tumbling he and Louisa backwards.

After the colonels passed, giving room for them to stand three abreast, Bingley helped Louisa haul her husband up the stairs. Once in the ballroom, they eased Mr. Hurst's sagging weight into a chair.

Quiet descended all about them as Colonel Forester raised his voice and demanded attention. Reactions varied as the colonel announced everyone should remain in the ballroom until he and Colonel Fitzwilliam solved the murder.

When guests started talking again, Bingley turned to his sister and in a low voice asked, "Louisa, why did you imply I knew of Hurst's whereabouts?"

"You are my brother, are you not?" Louisa muttered, flinging Mr. Hurst's limp arm away from her. Straightening from his slouching form, she turned a glittering glare on Bingley. "Of course, I expected you to confirm my words."

Bingley took a deep breath and surprised himself almost as much as his older sister when he continued to question her. "Why were you in the garden?"

"Really, Charles, what a senseless question." Louisa stomped to a nearby chair and flounced down as she aimed another stinging glare at him. "What reason do I need other than the crowd and warmth in this room?"

Bingley spared a moment to consider how happy Jane was to have the entire county attend her first ball. She had not stated as much, but he knew from the troubled expression in her usually calm eyes, she was greatly concerned for the success of this event. "Even so, why did you not ask Caroline to walk with you, or Hurst, even?"

"Hurst? Walk anywhere?" Louisa emitted an unladylike snort. "Look at him, Charles. Do you suppose I want to spend more time in his company when he is in such a condition?"

"Louisa, did you arrange to meet anyone in the garden?"

"Assuming I was meeting someone, what business is it of yours, little brother? Married women have some freedoms, you know." Louisa sniffed. "Now that you have married your precious Jane, you should be alert, Charles. She appears quiet, but she might hide an attraction to men exuding a sense of danger and excitement. Neither of which describes you, my dear." Louisa heaved a sigh as her gaze roamed about the guests clustered around the room. "Marriage gets boring after a while as you will find soon enough."

ψω

"Sorry, Will, but the news is not good." Colonel Fitzwilliam glanced around the ballroom as he stood beside Darcy. The scene looked somewhat shabbier than when he arrived hours earlier, and now gave the impression of a wilted bouquet. Women's gowns were crumpled. Men's collars hung loose and they wore the glassy expression of too much drink. Even the light from the many candles seemed dim as tapers burned low and smoke hung like heavy fog over the guests. "Colonel Forester seems determined to accuse Lizzy or Miss King of the murder."

Standing a step away, Mary overheard the colonel's comments and went rigid with fear. She did not linger on the outskirts of the group around the Bennet family to learn more. With a quiet word to Lady Lucas, who was more interested in listening to Mrs. Bennet repeat the details of her last session in the library, Mary drifted away from the group.

Not for the first time this evening, she was relieved the food and drink table was located at the far end of the room. Several strolls to the table, in pretense of securing a sip of punch, had given her time to consider the bits of conversation she had overheard from other guests.

Yet none of those remarks was as troubling as Colonel Fitzwilliam's latest comment. Did the colonels actually think she might have murdered Wickham? Filling two cups with lemonade, Mary made her way over to Georgiana's side. "Miss Darcy, you have been so kind to sit with Miss Brown, my heart goes out to you. For I suspect you would like nothing more than the prospect of spending time with Mr. Darcy and his wife at a time such as this. Do allow me to sit with your companion while you reassure yourself in their presence, and perhaps discover the latest news."

"How thoughtful of you, Miss King, but I must not leave Maggie after the shock she has experienced."

"Oh, please go converse with your dear brother, Miss Georgiana." Maggie Brown smiled at her charge. "I am certain you will soon feel restored from being in his presence and I feel much more myself after my time of rest."

"Do take a leave from your task, Miss Darcy." Mary smiled at the young woman. "Miss Brown was so kind to me when I arrived, I wish to show my appreciation and keep her company, now."

"If you are quite certain, Miss King." Miss Darcy cast a longing glance toward her brother and his wife. They were standing where Mary left them, talking with Colonel Fitzwilliam. "I will not be long."

"Do not rush your visit on my account." Mary said as she perched on the edge of the chair Miss Darcy had vacated. "Truthfully, I am happy for a chance to sit. I fear we have not yet heard the end of this night's events."

As Miss Darcy walked away, Mary passed a cup to Maggie. For a startled moment, as she watched the girl's light step, Mary longed to again be as young and unburdened as Miss Darcy. However, she knew all was not as it seemed for Maggie had made her aware that Miss Darcy's life was not lacking in unrest. She now knew Wickham had tried to ruin Miss Darcy's life as well, and turned to her cousin with renewed determination. "Maggie, why did you not did tell me you were to meet Wickham in the garden?"

Maggie's hand froze with the cup halfway to her mouth as she returned Mary's gaze. "How did you learn of my plan?"

"I tried to follow you. I had no choice if I intended to keep you free from harm."

"It was not me." Maggie lowered the cup with a trembling hand and looked into Mary's eyes. "I went only as far as the library."

"Do you mean to say you arranged a meeting with Wickham in the garden and backed out? When I think of all the pricks and scrapes I obtained from trying to remain close to the figure I thought was you, and not bump into some other guest, I could..."

Mary paused. Her eyes grew wide as she stared at her cousin. A new and very frightening thought occurred to her and she managed to say. "Pray tell me you did not arrange to meet Wickham in the library."

Chewing her lip, Maggie gave a nod. "It is true. That is why I stayed in the library after Miss Bingley pounced on me for using the room so freely."

"Upon my word, Maggie, how could you!" Memory of the evening's events chased through Mary's head. Colonel Forester's questions, Miss Bingley's knowing glances, and Lydia Wickham's accusations. Staring into Maggie's eyes, Mary whispered urgently. "I beg you not to reveal this information to anyone. Colonel Forester believes I am the one guilty of this murder. It would do us both a great deal of harm if your meeting was discovered."

"I did not murder him." Maggie's whisper was so low Mary could barely hear the words, but Maggie's tone was too intense to ignore. "I could never —"

"I know, but gather yourself, please." Mary gave Maggie's arm a gentle squeeze. "Some good came from my outing, for I met Captain Carter in the dark." Mary sent Maggie a smile but her cousin's lips wobbled. "Please do not trouble yourself, Maggie. You must maintain your composure. We cannot have guests asking how I upset you. It would not do for them to think I asked you about the murder."

"Did you, Miss King?" Colonel Fitzwilliam demanded, giving both of the women a start as he stopped beside their chairs.

"I beg your pardon, Colonel Fitzwilliam." Mary brushed at the lemonade she sloshed on her skirt when she jumped and frowned. "You appeared so suddenly, I spilled my drink. Now, you were asking if I did what?"

"I made reference to your last words as I approached." Colonel Fitzwilliam watched as Mary and Maggie tried to dry the punch from their laps. "My apologies for startling you, but I fear you were speaking to Miss Brown of the murder."

Mary managed to gather her wits and send him an innocent look. "Why would you suggest such a thing, Colonel?"

"Very simple, Miss King. As I approached, I clearly heard the word murder."

"Oh, now I understand." Mary waved a graceful hand. "Colonel, surely you must know the more you strive to avoid mention of a subject, the more it seems to fall from your tongue." Mary glanced at Maggie. "I urged Miss Brown to drink her lemonade and try to keep her spirits up. I think my words were, 'If you do not, people will think I am asking you about the murder.' Of course, that is what everyone is speaking of, but I was only trying to distract Miss Brown, not revive her memory of those terrible moments."

"As you say, the recent murder is the topic of discussion, but I would prefer you not speak of the matter to Miss Brown."

Chin high, Mary straightened in her chair, and sent him a guileless stare. "Why ever not, Colonel, if it would make Miss Brown feel better to talk about the event."

"Does this mean you were asking her questions?"

"Now you are putting words in my mouth. I am merely stating a fact. Speaking of the event might rid Miss Brown of the horror of her recollections." Mary arched a brow and sent him a challenging glance.

Colonel Fitzwilliam was not intimidated. "More to the point, Miss King, when we next question Miss Brown, I would rather her answers be fresh, and not something rehearsed from numerous telling."

Maggie stiffened to alert and found her voice. "Must I answer more questions?"

It was a good thing Maggie spoke, because Mary's mouth went so dry she could not move her tongue. More questions for Maggie must mean the colonels intended to start the questioning over again. Would this night never end? How many more hours must they wait before the murderer was discovered? Or the London authorities arrived?

ꙮ

After his intense discussion with Louisa, Bingley shared his concerns with Jane and urged her to seek other suspects as she circulated among the guests. His plan was to distract Jane from worrying over the blame aimed at her sister, Lizzy, but after his exchange of words with Louisa, he worried his own sister was as much at risk as Jane's. The only way he could prove members of their family were innocent was to discover who murdered Mr. Wickham.

"Jane, as hostess of this ball nothing will appear unusual if you move about the guests. They will assume you are concerned with their comfort, and perhaps, by doing so, you will overhear some remark that might reveal the person guilty of this crime."

"But Charles," Jane turned a wide, concerned glance on her husband, "I have been doing that very thing all evening and I have yet to hear a word worth repeating."

"We must try, Jane. Colonel Forester is convinced the murderer is one of the guests. And now, my sisters and Lizzy are suspects." Bingley frowned. He found it hard to imagine Caroline or Louisa capable of such violence. In truth, before this night's events, he was not aware they had more than a passing acquaintance with Wickham. Had Jane known his sisters were familiar with the man? He dared not think how would Jane react if she learned his sisters were carrying on a flirtation with Lydia's husband.

Come to that, he had never contemplated that Louisa might seek amusement outside her marriage. He was aware married women in London frequently had secret liaisons, but here in the county, where the society was closely connected, he never imagined such occurrences. Nor had he considered that Louisa would stop looking down her nose at people in the county long enough to allow such an attraction to take place.

What other secrets might this night reveal?

αβɔ

"Jane," Lizzy clasped Jane's arm tightly and urged her to step away from Bingley, "what am I to do?" Lizzy glanced back at her husband. "Darcy insists I not get involved, but how can I twiddle my thumbs and wait to be accused of murder?"

"Lizzy, we settled this earlier." Jane cast a worried glance in Bingley's direction, and recalled his concerns for their sisters, "It is not your usual response to leave matters of other to settle, but I fear in this instance you must heed Mr. Darcy's wishes." Bingley was in deep conversation with Darcy, and Jane drew in a breath to settle her wits as she turned back to her sister. "Mr. Darcy is right. Anything you do now might make you look guilty. You must trust us to find the solution—"

"But Jane—"

"Lizzy, prove what you often when I delay reacting is true. You must not act first and regret it later, this time. Please, heed what Mr. Darcy says." For once, Jane was the sister with the firm tone. She found she liked the assurance such an attitude gave her. "He cares for you. How can you not adhere to his advice?"

"I know —"

"Did I not promise you I would find the answer?" Jane managed a slight smile. Bingley's recent comments made her question her ability to keep her word, but for Lizzy's sake, she must. "After all, my instructions alerted the staff to search for the weapon. I will not fail you, Lizzy, though I fear I failed my expectations for this ball."

"Oh, Jane, you had no cause to expect Wickham would be murdered at your ball."

Jane expelled a deep sigh. "I must confess, I was thinking of my failure to find our sisters and Caroline a love match, not of Wickham's demise."

"Oh, Jane," for the first time in hours, humorous lights danced in Lizzy's eyes, "do you mean to say you planned this ball to find Kitty and Mary a match? Our Mary? My dear, Jane, your heart is too good for the rest of us to measure. Pray, do not berate yourself for this eve. You and Bingley made a match on the first meeting, but Darcy and I took much longer to attract each other. Surely you of all people realize matching Kitty and Mary will take time?"

☙❧

Lydia, with her usual fluctuating emotions, seemed to have overcome her shock, but not her need for attention. "Oh, why are the colonels taking so long to eat? I am tired of sitting here with nothing to do."

"It is said —"

"Mary Bennet, if you share one more of your quotes, I will —"

"Girls, do watch your tone." Mrs. Bennet raised her voice over Lydia's. "Can you not see everyone is looking at us." Mrs. Bennet fluttered her handkerchief better than any female could a fan, and stared at her offspring. "Do you not realize that after events of this night, there are three of you. You must not sit here quarreling."

"I am not quarreling, Mamma," Kitty offered brightly. "I have said not a word."

"I cannot believe Wickham is dead." Lydia wailed as if suddenly reminded that she should be sad. "What will I do without him?"

"When I was your age," Mrs. Bennet rolled her eyes, "if anything had happened to your father, I know what I would have done."

"Then we are fortunate you are not Lydia's age, are we not my dears?" Mr. Bennet said. He sat two chairs away, yet, he peeped over the top of his book and with a bright-eyed glance, joined the conversation. "For we would have none of the daughters we have now, if my numbers are correct, because we were not married yet, when you were Lydia's age."

"Oh, Mr. Bennet, if you are trying to vex me —"

"Why would I do so, my dear? After all, you have just reminded our daughters that we are the focus of all attention this night. Why would I take the chance you might suffer a fit of your nerves?" Mr. Bennet cast a calm glance at his wife, not bothering to hide the twinkle in his eyes.

"Oh, you know what I mean." Mrs. Bennet fluttered her handkerchief and huffed. "Before tonight, we had three married daughters, and now I must start the search all over again."

"Not for me," Mary replied, "for it is said —"

"Oh, Mary, do be quiet." Mrs. Bennet snapped.

"Not for me, either" Lydia sniffed.

"Come, child, it is early yet. You cannot mean what you say. Come the morrow, you will have a change of heart." Mrs. Bennet's tone softened as she studied her youngest daughter. "Did you not enjoy being married to Mr. Wickham?"

"Of course I did, but now I think I shall enjoy being a merry widow as well." Lydia's emotions took another turn. "Just imagine all the things I can do now, and there is no one to tell me I cannot."

Mrs. Bennet's eyes widened as she stared at her favorite daughter. Indeed, she understood Lydia's words better than most people might. Before she could respond, however, Colonel Fitzwilliam joined them.

"It sounds as though you plan to enjoy widowhood, Mrs. Wickham."

"I must amuse myself somehow, Colonel." Lydia stood, "Can you not find who killed my husband?"

"After the comments I just heard, perhaps we need look no further than his wife," Colonel Fitzwilliam murmured as he studied Lydia.

Lydia stomped her foot. "Oh, do be serious, Colonel. I want this night to be over so I can leave. I must purchase widow's weeds if I am to look decent when I appear in public."

"Fashion is not our priority, Mrs. Wickham, and I must caution you to appear less happy and more distraught if you expect people to think you actually miss your husband." Colonel Fitzwilliam glanced at each of the Bennets and turned back to Lydia. "I came to check on how you are holding up in the circumstances, but I see I need not be concerned."

Lydia stomped her foot again as Colonel Fitzwilliam gave a slight bow and walked away. He was not as good looking as Darcy or as wealthy, but his father was an earl. He would be a good catch for any woman wanting a husband, and she was accustomed to being married to a man in uniform. Yet he sent her only a cool glance as he departed. Oh, bother him. Just when she needed to practice acting like a widow, she slipped into old habits and, clearly, Colonel Fitzwilliam was not impressed.

Flopping back in her chair, Lydia wailed, "If we are not to dance, why can we not just go to bed?"

"We must stay together because, Colonel Fitzwilliam said the murderer could be in the house." Kitty offered helpfully.

"I have heard it said that we are safer in a group than in separate rooms." Mary replied.

Lydia turned a glare on her sisters and silently challenged them to utter another word. It was only the first night, and she had already failed to be a charming widow, and they were not helping. Oh well, Colonel Fitzwilliam was not the only eligible man here tonight. Denny and Captain Carter were still available. She glanced around the room and almost ground her teeth at what she observed.

Captain Carter was in deep conversation with that redheaded Mary King. Surely he did not find her attractive. Wickham had chased after her once, but after they were married, he assured Lydia he was only interested in Miss King's inheritance.

Nevertheless, Carter's interest in Mary King did not trouble Lydia nearly as much as the sight of Denny standing with that...oh! She could not even say the woman's name. Denny looked quite content as he conversed with Colonel Forester and that wife of his. She had heard rumors when she and Wickham were in Brighton and she knew Harriet Forester better than most. Had she not learned a trick or two from the woman?

Still, even with Harriet's skill at luring men to her side, Denny need not appear so willing to do Harriet's bidding. After they moved north Wickham had received missives from friends informing him such happenings were going on in Brighton, but she had not believed it was true. Surely Denny would not give Harriet a second glance. Yet the evidence before her eyes proved it was true and she shuddered with rising anger. She could not lose Denny to that woman's grasp.

She would take steps to see it did not happen.

When she next she was questioned by Colonel Fitzwilliam, she would tell all she knew. Her brow wrinkled. Colonel Forester would be present and undoubtedly he would dispute her words, but she tossed her head at the imagined slight. Well, let the colonel deny what was fact. She knew what Wickham had told her, and the colonel might as well face the truth. She had been forced to do so, for her Wickham truly was dead.

ᏣᏯ

"How are you holding up, my dear?" Colonel Forester passed a plate of food to his wife. "Do you have someone to talk with, for I imagine Lydia and the Bennets are engaged with other matters?"

"Oh, stuff," Mrs. Forester snapped. "As if Lydia is the only one who will miss Wickham." She sniffed into a scrap of lace. "He was my friend, too, and I did not imagine Lydia could be so cold to me. But it is her loss." She peered at her husband through her lashes. "Would it not be droll if she was found to be Wickham's murderer?"

"You must have something to eat my dear, for you must maintain your strength."

"Why," Mrs. Forester moaned, "a ball without music and dancing is too boring to discuss."

"You did not say who you keep company with while I am away."

"Oh, this one and that," Mrs. Forester said as she chewed. "People are friendly until they learn I know no more about what you are doing than they do."

"Patience, my dear," Colonel Forester cautioned. "All questions will be answered in good time."

"Tell me, husband, who do you think did this deed?"

"My dear, I must not—"

"Oh, do tell me, husband." Mrs. Forester turned pouting lips for his to see. "You are off with the men and I am stuck with nothing to do."

"Has no one talked with you the whole night?" He asked again.

"Well, Miss King conversed with me for a time, and so did Miss Bingley. But that sister of hers looked at me as if I were something stuck on her shoe." Mrs. Forester paused for another bite. "Mrs. Bingley is nice, much nicer than Lydia ever was. Oh, and Denny and Captain Carter came over to talk, as well."

"My dear, you do not sound lonely, but you best be aware of men in the militia."

"We cannot dance, husband. All we are left to do is talk. And since we are all staying at Lucas Lodge, it is only natural that we share our thoughts."

"Fear not, my dear. This will soon be over and you shall have your entertainment restored."

"Too bad Wickham had to get himself killed and ruin the party." Mrs. Forester sighed. "Tell me, husband, who do you think did the deed?"

"Now, my dear—"

"Oh, stop 'my dearing' me, husband," Mrs. Forester snapped. "I am your wife. Surely, you can tell me what you think. Who would I repeat your words to since I have broken with Lydia?" But she gasped and whirled to face him so fast she almost upturned the plate of food she held. "Is that why you keep silent? You say nothing because you suspect Lydia murdered poor Wickham. Oh, how could she? That wicked girl, I knew she was trouble when she came to stay with us, but this is beyond repair. Poor, charming Wickham did not deserve to die."

"Calm yourself, my dear." Colonel Forester implored as she blinked tears from her eyes. In an exasperated tone, showing his need to regain her good nature, he added. "Lydia is not the one I suspect most."

"Oh, do tell me who it is, husband." Mrs. Forester latched a hand on his arm and stared devotedly into his eyes. It was one of her favorite habits and always won his favor. "Who do you think is guilty?"

"You must not say a word, wife."

"Of course I will not. But just think of the help I can be to you. While you are out asking questions, I can watch all the people you suspect." She wheedled in the little girl voice that he favored.

"Umm, that might be helpful, actually." Colonel Forester paused to glance around the room. "My top three suspects are Mrs. Darcy, Miss King and of course, Lydia."

Mrs. Forester gasped. "Mrs. Darcy!" She convulsed in a fit of giggles. "How droll that is, husband. Lydia's own sister. Oh my—"

"You must not speak the names aloud, my dear."

"Of course not, husband." Mrs. Forester attempted to regain control of her laughter. "Now eat, for you will need your strength my colonel."

"I should hope so, my dear," Colonel Forester murmured as his gaze caressed her face, "and soon."

Coloring prettily under his warm gaze, Mrs. Forester tossed curls that started the evening in an artful arrangement and squeezed his arm. "Now, husband...Oh, Denny, do join us."

"Denny," Colonel Forester said as he turned to the younger man with a questioning glance. "Are you standing strong? I recall that you and Wickham were close."

Chapter Twelve

*F*itz, what is this madness," Mr. Darcy demanded as he turned to his cousin.

"Ah, so you heard Bingley's account to his wife about our problem?" Colonel Fitzwilliam showed no surprise at the question. That he expected as much was the reason he stopped to speak to Will on his way back to the library. "I am certain Bingley relayed an accurate account. Forester seems convinced Miss King or your wife committed the crime."

"Lizzy could no more murder a man than could I."

"The investigation is not over. I have every confidence we will uncover a hint to steer us in the right direction. I have no expectation it will concern Lizzy."

"Your opinion means a great deal to me, Fitz, but what of Forester? He is outspoken and domineering —"

"Qualities of a true commanding officer —"

"That may well be, but this is not the militia. My wife's character will suffer from Forester's insinuations even though she is not guilty. What matter of man is he to focus his attention on Lizzy?"

Fitzwilliam shook his head. "Bingley and I are in agreement with you on that score, but Forester is convinced this was a crime of passion, and he believes Wickham broke Lizzy's heart."

"What utter nonsense —"

"I must depart. Forester is standing in the door, motioning for me." As he walked away, Fitzwilliam realized he had not broached the second point of his concern with Darcy. And that worry was the source of his unrest as he followed Forester down the stairs to the library.

As they descended the stairs, Fitzwilliam heard the groans of activity coming from the kitchen, as if the house were just awakening for the day. Yet that was not true on this morn. Neither guests nor staff had been to bed since the discovery of Wickham's body.

Another of his senses kicked into alert. The closer they came to the first floor, the stronger the scent of cooking grew. Usually, the aroma of cooked pork stimulated his hunger, but unlike other occasions when he had been up all night, on this day the odor of greasy food added to the weight of the murder on his mind and his stomach churned.

CRSO

As Mary King stood a few paces away, in a group of women, with Lady Lucas, she overheard the conversation between Colonel Fitzwilliam and Mr. Darcy. The mention of her name caused unrest to choke air from her lungs. She was certain she was on Colonel Forester's list because of blame voiced by Lydia Wickham's hysterics upon hearing of her husband's death. Had those men not considered Lydia's state of mind at the time?

Mary glanced at Wickham's widow, confirming that Lydia seemed quite content to bask in the attention bestowed on her, at present. Still, Mary was not convinced that Lydia's calm manner would last if she tried to speak with her. All evening, Mary had tried to stand near the group around Lydia, waiting for a chance to offer her condolences, even though, experience warned her to stay far away from Lydia Wickham.

The situation left Mary with only one option. She information to remove suspicion from her name. Therefore, she must speak with someone who had reason to feel bitter toward Lydia, but who? Obviously, the local residents would not give forth any damaging comments. Lydia was one of their own and had been robbed of her young husband. This meant Mary would learn nothing from most of the guests.

Mary gazed about the room, mentally compiling a list of possibilities. Mrs. Gardiner, one of the most pleasant women Mary had ever met, was Lydia's aunt. Mrs. Phillips was also an aunt and, far from being as good-natured as Mrs. Gardiner, but though she had softened some during the long night, that lady made no effort to hide her impression of Mary.

Since none of the Bennets was unlikely to give her the information she needed, Mary considered speaking to the Darcys. Yet, she was reluctant to approach Mr. Darcy as his wife was Lydia's sister. That left Georgiana Darcy, and while Mary had made amiable conversation with Miss Darcy when trying to get close to comfort Maggie, she doubted Miss Darcy knew little, if anything, of Lydia's actions.

Mary tried to stifle her growing unease as she searched faces of guests in hopes of inspiration. She needed to speak with someone local. Someone who might disapprove of Lydia. Mr. Bingley's sisters came into view and Mary paused. Did she dare approach them? Caroline Bingley seemed more vocal, though both of Mr. Bingley's sisters seemed ready to pass judgment on anyone beneath their gaze.

This observance caused Mary to contemplate how someone as pleasant as Mr. Bingley could have sisters with such good opinions of themselves. Still, she might use their distaste of local society to her advantage, so she must attempt to engage in conversation with Caroline Bingley. However, she was not eager to attract their scorn upon her person at present.

A burst of laughter drew her gaze toward Lydia. As Mary viewed the group around Lydia, she caught the disapproving glances Lady Lucas sent in Lydia's direction. Now there was a possibility. Mary recalled earlier comments from her visits to Lucas Lodge.

Lady Lucas, despite her friendship with Mrs. Bennet, made no secret of her dismay that the Bennet sisters attracted the attention of eligible bachelors in the county, while her daughter failed to do so. Even the sudden marriage of her eldest Lucas daughter had not softened Lady Lucas' opinion of the Bennet sisters.

Yet, Lady Lucas was her host, and Mary was reluctant to mention any topic that might create tension. She needed Sir William and Lady Lucas's approval to establish her acceptance in the county. They had shown nothing but kindness to her, making her reluctant to risk the loss of their good will. They were good hearted and generous to her as well as the officers currently staying at Lucas Lodge.

Thinking of officers startled a gasp from Mary's lips. Why had she not realized sooner? She knew the perfect person to ask about Lydia Wickham. A fellow houseguest at Lucas Lodge and one she had not considered, until now. Most likely, she overlooked Mrs. Forester because she did little to encourage friendship with other females, while basking in the attention of the young officers also staying at the Lodge.

Mary tilted her chin. She had more to worry about than Mrs. Forester's preference for male companionship. Actually, Mrs. Forester's preference of companionship might work in Mary's favor. Deciding to act before she could change her mind, Mary murmured an excuse to the group. But the women around Lady Lucas were so busy chatting, they hardly noticed as she left to seek out Mrs. Forester.

And what Mary found was much as she expected., Mrs. Forester was huddled in a quiet corner with Denny. Though Mary admitted Mrs. Forester's actions were not surprising. After all, perhaps she and Denny were more comfortable in each other's company than with local guests.

Conversing with those of whom you knew little was a manageable feat at a ball, but much more difficult after long hours with no dancing. However, it appeared to be no hardship for Mrs. Forester and her companion to carry on a conversation. Mrs. Forester leaned close to chat and her features glowed with warmth, hinting at a close association between the two or too many trips to the punch bowl.

Perhaps even both possibilities were correct, though Mary recalled other occasions when she had observed the two of them in easy conversation. Pausing in mid-step to consider her options, Mary glanced back at the group of women standing near the young widow that she had just left.

Yet it was the frown on Lydia Wickham's face that captured her attention, for Lydia was staring at Denny and her former friend. At least Mary assumed they were estranged, given Lydia's comments to Mrs. Forester when she learned of Wickham's death.

Lydia had spared no one when her accusations erupted. The Foresters were targets of Lydia's ill temper the same as Mrs. Darcy and Mary were. For that reason, Mary decided to act on her earlier suspicions and continued her approach toward the couple in the corner.

"Mrs. Forester, Denny, I trust you are recovering from the shock, as Mr. Wickham was a good friend to you both."

After exchanging a glance with the woman at his side, Denny stepped back and said. "Ah, Miss King, indeed we are attempting to grasp the situation. I was inquiring if Mrs. Forester would care for coffee to restore her calm. I believe the brew has been refilled for the aroma is strong and the night has been long."

"Indeed it has. I have danced many a night until dawn, but I declare this night more exhausting than all those events pinned together." Mrs. Forester announced as she smiled at Denny. "Do fetch coffee for us, Denny for I am quite certain Miss King also suffered a loss with Wickham's death and craves a sip of the restorative brew as much as I do."

"Coffee sounds agreeable if you can manage three cups." Mary smiled at Denny, unable to contain her delight at having a chance to speak to Mrs. Forester alone. As Denny walked away she said, "Such pleasant manners, do you not agree, Mrs. Forester?"

"Oh, my yes," Mrs. Forester twitched at her skirts as she sat down in a chair pushed against the wall, "without Denny and Captain Carter's company this eve, I am not certain what I would do. They are a great distraction in Brighton, as well. We have known them longer than dear Mr. Wickham."

"Such a loss," Mary eased down onto the edge of the chair next to Mrs. Forester, "and so young to die."

"Age is not relevant." Mrs. Forester sighed. "I fear being attached to the regiment teaches one that lesson. But Wickham's loss is particularly painful." She blinked rapidly and sniffed. "We were all such close acquaintances, you understand. Facing the risk of death each time there is a battle with the enemy makes one live every moment to the fullest, I have found."

"Such a situation must be very demanding on one's constitution," Mary said in a tone filled with commiseration as she watched Mrs. Forester's gaze follow Denny. Suspicion of their involvement grew as she observed emotions flash in the woman's eyes. "Being the wife of the commanding officer of a regiment must be difficult. I expect you are needed to offer support to grieving widows, as well."

Mrs. Forester straightened her shoulders as her startled glance turned to Mary, but her tension visibly eased when she saw nothing but sympathy in Mary's gaze. "It is difficult, but I admit I leave most of that sort of thing to my husband and the other officers. For I am young, you see, and not as experienced in dealing with the harsher realities of life."

Mary managed a soothing tone, "How stressful your role must be. I am not certain I could respond in the appropriate manner."

"I can deal with the social events of my husband's position. After all, where else would I have attendance from so many handsome, young men?" Mrs. Forester turned a glittering glance on Mary. "You thought Mr. Wickham very handsome at one time, as well, I believe."

"Indeed, I did," Mary said and tried not to expose her dismay at the topic. She needed to get some information before Denny returned. "As did many other women in this room. I believe you did as well, Mrs. Forester, did you not?"

Mrs. Forester's brow furrowed as she gazed into the distance. "Wickham was an intriguing mix of charm and danger which makes a woman's heart flutter." Her gaze turned back to Mary. "I must admit I am curious, Miss King. You had an opportunity many women long for and yet you turned away. Tell me, exactly why did your understanding with Wickham end for you were the focus of his attentions before he turned his sights on Lydia, I believe."

"Alas, my uncle's advisor was very outspoken," Mary sighed and forced her fingers to relax the grip on the folds of her dress, " and for some reason, he took a dislike to Mr. Wickham."

Mrs. Forester gave a soft snort. "For reasons I fail to understand, men do not appreciate the charm Mr. Wickham possessed." She leaned forward to confide, "My own husband is one such man. For all his experience with men in the militia, he seemed less able to note Wickham's worth than that of other men in his command."

"Oh, indeed, and how did his reluctance come to your attention?"

"Well, take the incident with Lydia, for instance. The silly girl came to Brighton as my companion, you understand. With her inexperienced ways and total disregard for manners, she was quiet popular with the regiment. I cannot think when I have had more fun than when she was with us, but that was all before she ran off with Wickham. Yet would my husband listen when I warned him that trouble was brewing? I cautioned him that Wickham could spin a spell around the heart of a young girl such as Lydia."

"Yet she fell for his charm despite the age difference?"

"Wickham was not old," Mrs. Forester snapped. "Not nearly as old as my husband in any case, but yes she succumbed to his smooth speaking ways. And I must admit I was not surprised."

"So, it was true affection on Lydia's part, not just some ploy to gain freedom from her parents?"

"Upon my word, I tell you Lydia spoke of nothing but Wickham for weeks before they eloped. I declare, it was so constant I even fancied myself infatuated with him from just listening to her carry on about him endlessly. It was definitely a love match on Lydia's side, though I cannot think the same for Wickham." Her eyes widened as her gaze fastened on Mary. "I have no need to explain his ways to you, for you were attached to Wickham, as well."

"I do wonder though," Mary said, trying to keep the flush from her cheeks as she recalled her brush with Wickham's attentions. Taking a deep breath, she attempted to steer the conversation back to Lydia. "Is it possible Lydia might have discovered Wickham's easy manner with women and attacked him in anger?"

"What nonsense!" Mrs. Forester said. Then she smoothed the skirt of her gown as if to calm her emotions as she continued. "What I mean to say, is why would Lydia care if Wickham charmed other women? He married her did he not?" Brow wrinkled, Mrs. Forester continued in a determined tone. "Besides, as much as I loathed Lydia's lashing out and accusing the colonel and me of killing Wickham, I distinctly remember seeing her in the garden the whole time I was there. And now that I recall her whereabouts, I am certain Lydia did not murder Wickham." Mrs. Forester's cheeks flared with color and sparks glittered in her eyes. "But I am hopeful whoever murdered Wickham will hang."

Startled by the depth of emotion ringing in Mrs. Forester's words, Mary attempted to keep her face free of any expression. Shocked as she was by Mrs. Forester's sharp words, Mary was certain of one thing, at least. Lydia Wickham did not murder her husband.

But she considered the possibility of Mrs. Forester's involvement with renewed interest. Her emotional reaction concerning Wickham's death seemed to indicate more than friendship existed between Wickham and his colonel's wife. Mary took a deep breath. Had she discovered the suspect guilty of Wickham's murder?

Mary considered the possibility that Mrs. Forester's reactions were those of a scorned lover. It was a possibility she must give careful consideration. It could be that Mrs. Forester was only lashing out because she and the colonel were accused of Wickham's murder. However, with Lydia no longer under suspicion, Mary needed a new suspect, and Mrs. Forester's behavior with Denny certainly gave the impression that she was, indeed, a possible candidate.

ᓚᗷᓗ

"Captain Carter," Colonel Fitzwilliam paused in front of the fireplace, "you were closely acquainted with Mr. Wickham's associates and Mrs. Wickham, I believe."

"That is correct, sir." Captain Carter replied from his seat in a wing-backed chair near the hearth. "I was friends with Lydia...Mrs. Wickham and Denny before I met Mr. Wickham."

"How did your acquaintance begin?"

"Denny and I were in the militia together before we arrived in Meryton. Denny met Lydia and Kitty Bennet in town and introduced me after they became friends. Then Wickham arrived in Meryton to take his commission and he became one of the group."

"What can you tell me about Wickham's other friends?"

"Colonel, Wickham could spin yarns that lured people to his side. I never met them all."

"Did he have enemies?"

Captain Carter stared at the flames blazing in the fireplace for a heartbeat. "Not that I recall, Colonel, but he had many debtors."

"Mr. Wickham borrowed funds from his friends?"

Captain Carter expelled a bark of laughter. "Wickham could extend his debt to any merchant in town and leave the shopkeeper smiling. As to his friends, everyone knew loaning Wickham funds was the price for sharing his company."

"Did any one person loan Wickham more than they could afford? Mr. Denny, perhaps?"

"Denny's pockets are not deep, and he loaned Wickham more than he should, in my opinion."

Colonel Forester snapped upright from where he was leaning against the mantel. "You did not approve of Wickham borrowing money?"

Captain Carter shrugged. "I cautioned Denny not to put his credit on the line by extending loans to Wickham."

"Did Denny listen to your advice?"

"Colonel Forester," Captain Carter angled his chin high. "That is a question you must ask Denny."

"Very well, Captain," Colonel Fitzwilliam glanced at Colonel Forester as he said, "Will you ask Denny to join us?"

"I like Carter," Colonel Forester said as the door closed behind the captain. "He is a fine officer, yet I suspect he is not revealing the entire truth."

"On what do you base your observation, Colonel?" Fitzwilliam stood by the corner of the mantel and waited for the response.

"Years of dealing with militia men," Colonel Forester said with a shrug. "Or perhaps it was the way his posture went rigid when you asked the question."

ᘓᘔ

"You wanted to see me, Colonel?"

"Ah, Denny," Colonel Forester turned to the door as Denny walked in, "come have a seat."

Denny chose the chair Captain Carter had vacated, but then most people would. What little warmth was left in the room, after the chill of the long night and lowering the blaze to keep down the stench, radiated little farther than the wing-back chair.

"Have you had any sleep, Mr. Denny?" Colonel Fitzwilliam inquired.

Denny snapped to alert. "No sir, mostly we have talked and nibbled on refreshments."

"Would you say your head is clear, not clouded by punch?"

Denny's shoulders relaxed as he laughed. "Sir, I make it a practice to stay alert around the ladies. I have no wish to end up with a wife because I was so far in my cups I spoke without thought and proposed marriage."

"Any chance you have plans to marry soon, Denny?" Colonel Forester demanded.

Appearing startled, Denny responded. "Not that I plan, sir."

"Ah, spoken like a man free of ties," Colonel Forester replied.

"Yes, sir." Sensing the note in the colonel's voice, Denny squared his shoulders and sat up straight as he waited for the next question.

" Indeed," Colonel Forester cleared his throat, "well, back to the reason we requested your presence, Denny. I fear we must repeat our earlier question. Who did you see in the garden?"

Denny ran a finger inside his collar. "Well. Almost everyone, sir."

"Indeed," Colonel Forester snapped. "Name the guests you encountered, if you please."

"Um, well, I saw you, Colonel, and Mrs. Forester, Captain Carter, Lydia, Mrs. Darcy, Miss Bingley, Mr. Hurst and his wife," Denny paused and wrinkled his brow. "I believe that is everyone, sir."

"You failed to mention Mr. Wickham." Colonel Forester inserted in a quiet voice. "Did you see him in the garden?"

"Well, no sir, but I heard his voice." Denny frowned and glanced at the door as if he wanted to escape, "Oh, and I saw Kitty and Miss King, as well."

Fitzwilliam noticed the tension in Denny's voice and said. "Tell us about the gambling debts Mr. Wickham owed you."

"It was just a gaming debt, sir." Denny shrugged as he looked from one officer to the other. "Most of my friends owe debits from playing cards. Wickham was no different."

"You were not distressed over his failure to repay you?" Colonel Forester asked.

Denny lifted a shoulder. "My pockets are not deep, Colonel, but Wickham had taken a wife. Since Lydia and Wickham were friends, I was fine with Wickham's delay in repaying the debt."

"Ah, so because of Mrs. Wickham, you allowed Wickham to abuse your agreement. I believe you knew her before Wickham arrived in Meryton?"

"I met Lydia soon after the regiment arrived in Meryton, but Wickham was my friend before I met Lydia. She had nothing to do with our gambling debits."

"Was there a rivalry between you and Wickham for Lydia's affections?" Colonel Forester demanded. "Before you reply, Denny, do recall that my wife was privy to Lydia's confidences for some time before her marriage, so please respond truthfully."

Color tinted Denny's cheeks, highlighting his youth and boyish handsomeness, as he stared at his superior officer. "Very well, Colonel. It is true that I had thought to speak for Lydia's hand when my fortunes improved, but that seemed a very distant future."

"Then Mr. Wickham arrived and stole her heart from you?"

"No, Colonel Forester," Denny spoke in a firm even tone. "Wickham arrived and won the hearts of all the females in his association. Even women with husbands were susceptible to his charm. So there was no contest between us, if that is what you mean to imply."

"That is my point exactly, young Denny." Colonel Forester said in a stern tone. "I believe there was competition. There is always gambling among young militia men concerning the ability to win the attentions of the unmarried ladies."

"'Tis true," Denny's shoulders slumped, making him seem even younger, "there were bets on who will win the most hearts, but nothing like that occurred on my part concerning Lydia. She was but a friend."

"You say you did not see Mr. Wickham in the garden, but you heard him?" Colonel Fitzwilliam said in an attempt to steer the conversation back to the murder. "Did you hear him argue with anyone, inside the house or out?"

"No, sir. Though, I heard a man's angry voice speak Wickham's name in the garden." Denny frowned. "And now that you make mention of it, earlier in the evening, I heard Wickham snap at one of the servants."

"Really," Colonel Forester's voice dripped with satisfaction, "can you identify the man you heard speak in anger?"

"No, he was too far away. I only heard the angry tone of his voice."

"Denny," Colonel Forester stared from under lowered brows, "do you recall which servant you heard Wickham reprimand?"

"Yes, sir," Denny gave an eager nod, "it was the woman who found the body. Miss Brown."

◌ॐ◌

"Miss Brown, take your time, and tell us again, what happened in this room before you discovered the body."

Miss Brown's voice trembled as she related the same details she had described earlier, and Colonel Fitzwilliam could find no reason to think she was being anything but truthful. "Very well, Miss Brown. But why did you not tell us you had spoken to Mr. Wickham in the hallway upon his arrival?"

"Oh, well I forgot after the shock of finding him dead. Snd it was a matter of no importance, in any case."

"Perhaps you hoped to conceal the matter as he spoke harshly to you?" Colonel Forester said.

"Not at all, sir. It is true, Mr. Wickham's tone was abrupt, but I thought him cold and hungry, not angry."

"As he had only just arrived, Miss Brown, why did Mr. Wickham snap, do you suppose?" Colonel Fitzwilliam tried to keep his tone mild so as not to frighten the young woman, after Colonel Forester's harsh tone.

"I am positive Mr. Wickham was just in need of rest after the long trip, Colonel. Mrs. Wickham was complaining about all that had gone wrong on their journey, and Mr. Wickham stopped me to ask directions to their room. But I did not know and that is when he used a sharp tone."

"That is all? Why use an abrupt the tone with you?"

"I was the only person he saw," Miss Brown lifted a shoulder, "and I am not familiar with this house. The Wickhams were cold and hungry, and I did not know the way to their room."

"Very well," Colonel Fitzwilliam gave a nod, "you may return to the ballroom for now."

The door closed behind Miss Brown with a sound loud as a gun shot. Colonel Forester was first to voice his frustration. "All this time and we have nothing. What are we to do?"

Chapter Thirteen

*A*s soon as Captain Carter returned to the ballroom, Mary King approached him. "Captain Carter, have you managed to return unscathed by all the questions? Perhaps you are in need of some food to restore your strength after your ordeal."

"How considerate of you to make the suggestion, Miss King," Captain Carter was swift to reply. He took hold of her arm and turned toward the table at the end of the room. "But I will only take nourishment if you will join me."

As they joined the line circling the buffet table, Mary arched a brow as she glanced at him. "Tell me, Captain, do you not enjoy Mrs. Forester's company?"

"Ah, so you noticed she was headed in our direction," Captain Carter sighed. "After dodging questions from her husband for the past hour, is it any wonder I wish to avoid her company?"

"You shock me, Captain, and make me very curious. Why avoid the colonel's questions when he thinks only to discover who murdered Mr. Wickham?"

"You believe this to be so, Miss King?"

"Of course, what other reason could the colonel have but to solve this crime? You should answer his questions truthfully, Captain."

"Aye, Miss King, but you would respond likewise if the answers would cast suspicion on your best mate."

"'Tis true, I am sure, but have you considered the possibility of his guilt, Captain?" Mary dipped a spoon in a dish of scrambled eggs. The texture and odor were not to her liking, but few foods appealed to her at four in the morning.

"He is as guilty as any in this room, Miss King, but not of Wickham's murder. Still, if I revealed details that would clear Denny of murdering Wickham, I am quite certain the colonel would murder Denny."

"Whatever can you mean, Captain?" Mary stared at him from wide eyes. The piece of bread in her hand suddenly felt weighty enough to use as a weapon.

Captain Carter returned her stare and considered his next words carefully. He glanced around the table to confirm they could not be overheard, but still, he delayed. He should keep the words to himself, yet he had reached the end of his patience with keeping Denny's assignations quiet. In fact, he was quite certain Colonel Forester suspected him of hiding something after the questions he endured. Colonel Fitzwilliam probably had his suspicions, as well. Though, truth be told, had Colonel Fitzwilliam been the one asking the questions, he would have explained his actions to the fullest. Instead his responses made him appear as guilty as the murderer and he was weary of covering for Denny.

"At the time of the murder, Denny was in the bushes snuggling with Mrs. Forester. He could not have committed the crime."

"Oh, no," Mary exclaimed in a voice heavy with disappointment, "that means neither could Mrs. Forester be guilty."

Carter stared at her, surprised by her reaction, and clenched his fingers on his plate. He had expected a giggling response or probing questions about Denny's involvement with the colonel's wife, but not this forlorn look on her face. "Miss King, had you reason to suspect Mrs. Forester?"

"How could I not," Mary stirred in the bowl of fried potatoes as she spoke, at least she thought the strong scent of onions and crusty brown blobs were fired potatoes, "after what Mrs. Wickham said when she first heard her husband was dead."

"Pray, do not give any thought to Lydia's outburst. She is like a kettle and expels steam when her anger runs hot. Give her a chance to regain her composure and she will be laughing before you can turn around."

"Oh, if only I could, Captain, but Colonel Forester and Colonel Fitzwilliam's questions were quite intense. I fear they took Mrs.

Wickham's words seriously."

"Why would they do so? After her stay with the Foresters in Brighton, Colonel Forester is well aware of Lydia's disposition." Carter lifted a lid on a dish and quickly replaced it. "In fact, I suspect he holds Lydia responsible for his wife's behavior, but that is unfair. Mrs. Forester was a flirt long before she became friends with Lydia."

"How can you say such things when we are not long acquainted?" Mary dropped the spoon back into the bowl of jelly and turned to face him. "Do you not care for Mrs. Forester, Captain?"

"Miss King, I have no wish to seem forward, but I have noticed you from a distance for some time, and tonight's events have made us close acquaintances, has it not?"

Heat warmed Mary's cheeks as she smiled. To discover the captain shared her feelings of being connected was more than she had hoped for at this time. Yet she dared not think ahead until she was free of blame in Wickham's murder. "I am pleased with your words, Captain, but much depends on your opinion of Mrs. Forester."

"Then let me speak plainly, Miss King. I care about my friends, but care not for how Mrs. Forester takes advantage of them. Because she is the colonel's wife, they dare not refuse her advances. Even Wickham rushed to do her biding. Now, poor Denny cannot tell one foot from the other when she is near."

"I must say, Captain, your opinion of her character is not very flattering," Mary offered.

"Indeed it is not. Nothing of this night leads one to look for the best in a person, present company excluded, of course, Miss King."

"Captain, I —"

"I say no words lightly, Miss King. But I have observed your kindness to others since before we met. Tonight, you have gone out of your way to console Miss Brown after her shock of discovering Wickham's body. I also observed your frequent attempts to speak with Lydia, even after she aimed her wrath at you and blamed you for killing Wickham for all to hear. I have no doubt but that you would offer comfort to Lydia, as well, had she allowed you to speak."

"Captain, you bring me to blush —"

"I am but a man, Miss King, but these are facts. I have no wish to offer you flattery, only a sincere estimation of your character from what I have observed."

Mary's face filled with heat. How could he say such words when all she had done this night was to search for proof she was not a murderer. Yet a part of her blossomed under his intent gaze. "You appear to have observed me for some time, Captain. Were you not distracted by Mrs. Forester's ploys as were Wickham and Denny?"

Captain Carter stood tall and studied the plate of food in his hand, as if he knew not from where it came. "My attentions were never temped by false promises of one woman when I could observe the true character of another." He looked deeply into her eyes as he said. "I would not speak of such things, Miss King, but this night has made me very aware that counting on the morrow can be futile. I ask nothing but to be thought of in a kind manner and promise to do the same in return."

"Captain, your kind words have stolen all sensible thought from my head."

"You need say no words, Miss King, but allow me to be considered as an acquaintance. That is all I ask."

"Oh, but you see, Captain, I wish for more, and I dare not turn away any offer of friendship. The possibilities are in too short supply. As for asking nothing, kind sir, I wish...I so hope that you want more."

"Then I must speak the truth, Miss King. Since the moment, I first saw you on the night you met Wickham at Mrs. Phillips gathering, I have thought of little else. However, as an officer in the militia, I have little to offer. A friendly countenance and occasional smile is all I have any right to expect."

"As greatly as I value the friendship you so kindly offer, Captain, you have so much more to offer, but I fear I am undeserving of your attentions."

"Then I must say again, Miss King, I ask for nothing."

"Captain," Mary closed her eyes as thoughts muddled in her head, then someone behind them coughed, indicating they should move. Mary stepped away from the table and walked to the middle of the floor. As Captain Carter joined her, she looked up to meet his gaze. "Your words deserve recognition and honesty. And I am very much afraid my actions have deceived you."

"You could not, Miss King. I have observed your acceptance of condescending comments with no retaliation of your own. Your character is one of the reasons why I cannot ignore my inclination to speak."

Mary moved a step closer to him, until their toes touched and looked up. "Captain, I return your high regard, and have done so for some time now. So please consider the confidence I am about to place in you as well deserved. If you choose to ignore your inclinations after you hear what I have to say, I will understand, but your kindness tonight will never leave my heart. For that reason, I must tell you that what you credit as my kindness, was in truth prompted by what I fear you will consider a selfish need. For you see, Captain, Mrs. Wickham accused me of murdering her husband, and in my effort to prove otherwise, I found myself unable to reveal that Miss Brown is my cousin. Pray, do not think badly of me —"

"Carter," Lydia said in an impatient tone as she flounced to a standstill beside the captain, "I do believe you have been ignoring me," Lydia cut her eyes toward Mary, "and spending too much time with others."

"Mrs. Wickham," Captain Carter seemed to struggle to find words, "would you care for a plate of food?" He offered her the plate in his hands, as he glanced at Mary.

Staring at the plate he offered, Lydia shook her head. "No, I want to select my own. Do they have ham? Come, Carter, you must go with me to collect a plate for I am not yet used to being on my own." With a whirl of her skirts, Lydia turned away.

Carter sent Mary a long glance and slowly followed.

Mary stood in the middle of the ballroom, the filled plate in her hands, and watched them walk away as fear washed over her. He did not need to speak of his reluctance. Mary knew he had no choice but to do as his friend asked. Yet in her need to prove she was of good character, she had revealed details to Captain Carter that could seal her own fate and Maggie's. Could she trust the captain to keep her confidence, or was his connection to Lydia and Wickham so strong he would reveal all?

☙❧

Jane circulated among the guests and listened to conversations around her. As she expected, the main topic was Wickham's murder. She paused to confer with the housekeeper on the food offerings and then moved on to speak to Bingley's sisters.

"Well, Jane," Caroline's tone dripped honey as Jane came near, "how does it feel to be hostess at your first ball."

As Jane stood before Caroline's chair, with Louisa only a few seats away, she recalled receiving reprimands from her parents years ago. Yet unlike those times, when her skin turned the color of clotted cream, then flushed the color of a rose in full bloom, Jane angled her chin and smiled at Caroline as she would any other guest. This was her home, her ball, and these were her guests. "Well, I plan to not have a murder occur at my next ball, Caroline, but other than that, things seem as they should."

Caroline twittered with pretended mirth. "Jane, after this murder, I suspect you will have no cause to ever host another ball."

"Do hush, Caroline," Louisa commanded in her elder-sister tone, "how can Charles expect to move up in society if Jane does not give balls?"

"Pray tell me who would attend such balls," rolling her eyes, Caroline said. "Only those wishing for the latest gossip would dare step foot in any event Jane hosted."

"Does that mean you would not attend?" Jane asked in her most innocent tone.

Caroline appeared startled for a breath, then she leaned forward and said, "Listen, Jane, this nonsense must end. Colonel Forester as much as accused Hurst of Wickham's murder. You must do something."

"What shall I do, Caroline?" Jane motioned to the roomful of guests. "Request the real murderer step forward and confess?"

"Do stop being ridiculous and take this seriously, Jane. Our brother's reputation, and your own, are at stake. You must do what you can to discover who murdered Mr. Wickham."

"As you are so adamant, Caroline, I wonder that you have made no effort to reveal the truth yourself."

"Jane, you must hear what I say —"

"I was not in the garden as you were, Caroline, so I cannot speak for the innocence of those who were."

"Even though your precious Eliza, Lydia and Kitty were in the garden, as well?" Caroline arched a darkened brow. "Believe what I say, Jane, you must discover who killed Wickham."

"Yet you warned me against such actions earlier."

Caroline's expression tightened. "That was before the colonels accused Hurst. Whatever would Louisa do without her husband?"

"You seem certain of Mr. Hurst's innocence, Caroline. So who do you think did this deed?"

"I am sure I do not know such a person. It was not Mrs. Forester, of that I am certain. For I saw her hiding in the bushes with my own eyes, and quite occupied with young Denny." Caroline smirked as she glanced at Louisa.

Jane managed to keep her mouth from dropping open, but shocked as she was, she could not ignore the strained look on Louisa's face at hearing Caroline's words. What was troubling Louisa? Surely she was not worried the colonels really believed Mr. Hurst was guilty. For one thing, he was never steady enough on his feet to undertake the murder of a younger man. And he never strayed far from a source of refreshment, for another. "I will make inquires, Caroline. That is all I can promise."

Jane sighed as she walked away. Louisa's discomfort sent uneasy thoughts raging through her head as she considered Caroline's warning. Troubled by the possibilities Caroline hinted at, Jane experienced a moment's relief when her gaze encountered Miss King.

Her unease returned, however, when she noticed Miss King was standing in the middle of the ballroom with Captain Carter and Lydia. That Miss King's interest in Mrs. Forester uncovered no hint as to the identity of the killer seemed disprove Caroline's claims, and Jane mentally crossed one name off her list as she paused to wonder when she would next have a chance to consult with Charles.

 CB80

After Denny departed from the library, Colonel Forester joined Colonel Fitzwilliam in front of the fireplace. Bingley stepped closer, as well, but after a glance at of each of the colonels, he turned to stare into the flames. The long night was almost over and still they had no hint as to the identity of Wickham's murderer.

"Well, Colonel," Colonel Fitzwilliam studied his fellow officer, "I suggest we take leave of this room and break bread to restore our energy. The morn is nigh and we have realized little of what we have been charged to accomplish."

"Aye, 'tis true, but after hearing from Denny and Captain Carter we have discarded all doubt of Mrs. Wickham committing the crime."

"I am of the same mind on that point." Colonel Fitzwilliam turned to his host. "How say you, Bingley? Is Mrs. Wickham free of suspicion?"

"I never considered otherwise," Bingley blinked as he looked away from the fire, "and not because she is my wife's sister, but because she was in the company of her sisters while she was in the garden. And I can vouch for her deep affection for Mr. Wickham."

"Ah! Yet that is the very reason we could not overlook the possibility she was guilty. Indeed, strong emotions can oft be at the root of such deeds as this," Colonel Forested replied. "Yet, I do not believe Lydia Wickham guilty of this murder." He continued with a sigh. "Much as it pains me to speak ill of a fellow guest, and someone I shared a meal with on many occasions at Lucas Lodge, I am convinced we again contemplate the possibility of Miss King's guilt."

"Why would you believe such?" Bingley demanded. Jane had defended Miss King, and even gone so far as to offer her friendship. Bingley dreaded Jane's response if her good opinion of their guest proved wrong.

"What is the meaning of your strong defense of someone not related to you, Bingley?" Colonel Forester demanded. "Even for your own sisters you did not reveal such emotion."

Heat warmed Bingley's face as he looked from one officer to the other. "My concern is for Jane. She is convinced Miss King is of a kind heart and warm disposition."

"Mr. Bingley, need I remind you that an innocent face can cloud your judgment?" Colonel Forester sent Bingley a hard stare as he spoke. "We can forgive your wife for a lack of reasoning, for I have found women do not think as clearly as men when it comes to such matters." Releasing an impatient breath, he glared at Bingley. "Have Miss King's actions gone unnoticed by you this night?"

Bingley's jaw tightened. "Jane is a good judge of character—"

"Begging your pardon, Bingley, I fear we must hear Colonel Forester out." Colonel Fitzwilliam frowned as he studied each man in turn. "I overheard bits of two conversations about the murder between Miss King and Miss Brown. Perhaps we should examine further Miss King's motive for spending time with Miss Darcy's companion. As one of her guardians, I would be remiss in my duties if I did not delve further into associations with my ward."

"Miss King is conversing with guests other than Miss Brown." Colonel Forester rocked on his heels. "Have you not noticed how she roams about the ballroom, but rarely contributes to discussions? She moves from group to group and listens."

"Perhaps she refrains from making remarks because she has yet to feel accepted by county society." Bingley stared at the two colonels.

"Indeed, this could be a fact," Colonel Forester nodded, "but if that be the case, why put herself forward to join strangers in conversation, if not to gather information?"

Bingley knew why Miss King was circulating among guests. He and Jane discussed the matter, and Miss King's motives seemed the same as their own. "Perhaps, she is searching for answers as we are. After all, Lydia did accuse Miss King of murdering Wickham."

"All the more reason for us to question Miss King again." Colonel Forester nodded. "We should not underestimate Miss King."

Chapter Fourteen

Tense silence greeted Bingley a short time later as he accompanied Miss King to the library. After a glance at the two officers, Bingley motioned toward the chairs grouped near the fireplace. "Please, Miss King, make yourself comfortable."

With a questioning glance at the officers, Miss King settled on the edge of the nearest chair.

Colonel Forester stopped pacing to stare down at her, "Miss King, why do you suppose Mrs. Wickham blamed you for her husband's murder?"

Miss King glanced at both officers before responding. "Mrs. Wickham received distressing news. I was merely in her line of vision."

"She looked at you after learning her husband was dead. Why would she do so?"

"Mrs. Wickham was distraught with grief and unaware of what she was saying."

"Yet, Mrs. Wickham loudly accused you and Mrs. Darcy of murdering her husband."

"I should think Mrs. Wickham's claims that four different people murdered her husband would be reason enough to assume she was speaking out of her head." Miss King angled her chin and returned his stare. "You and your wife were accused of the murder, as well, Colonel. Are we to take those words seriously?"

A grim expression settled on Colonel Forester's face as tension filled the room until it felt almost visible.

Bingley met Colonel Fitzwilliam's glance. By reminding Colonel Forester that he and his wife were accused, as she had been, she was certainly making it difficult for Colonel Forester to blame her for the murder. Indeed, considering her tone and calm manner, it appeared Jane was correct in her belief of Miss King's innocence. Why else would she confront her accuser with reminders of Lydia's claims of his own guilt?

After long ticks of the clock, Colonel Forester cleared his throat loudly. "You are correct in your statement of facts, Miss King. I am sure you understand how easy it is to delve into a problem and forget one is involved."

A collective seemed to escape the room as Miss King tilted her head and said, "But of course, Colonel."

Yet any release of tension was short lived. Colonel Forester planted himself directly in front of Miss King and asked in a tone better suited for addressing one of his men. "Now, can you enlighten us as to why you ended your attachment to Mr. Wickham? You were one of several young women who enjoyed his attentions, yet he offered you a marriage proposal. Why end your arrangement?"

"I must ask why is the ending of my engagement of any importance in solving this crime, Colonel. My connection to Mr. Wickham was short-lived and long past. Mr. Wickham had since married another woman."

"Precisely my point, Miss King. Perhaps you were a spurned lover intent on gaining revenge regardless of how long it took to accomplish your aim."

"Does that make Mrs. Darcy a spurned lover, as well, Colonel? Or, perhaps, even Miss Bingley is one, for that matter?" Miss King sent Bingley a glance full of apology before she continued, "Surely, Colonel, you are grasping for theories in your attempt to solve this murder."

Colonel Forester frowned. "Why make mention of Miss Bingley? We have no cause to believe there was a connection between her and Mr. Wickham."

Miss King lifted a shoulder and focused her gaze on his face. "Miss Bingley spoke to Mr. Wickham in the garden, and as you seem intent on questioning the simplest of connections, perhaps you should speak with her."

Colonel Forester assumed the fierce glare of an officer displeased with his men as he replied. "Indeed, we must consider all possibilities, Miss King. Now, perhaps you will explain why you spend so much time speaking with Miss Brown?"

"It has been a long night, Colonel, and meaningless conversation grows more tedious by the hour. As I had nothing else to do and Miss Brown seemed distressed over her discovery of Mr. Wickham's body, I tried to distract her." Miss King's cheeks flushed as she glanced at each of them and continued in a low voice. "It has not been long since I lost my uncle. I only sought to offer comfort to another."

Colonel Fitzwilliam spoke for the first time. "Miss King, I find your kindness in relieving my ward of the care of her companion commendable, but each time I approached, you and Miss Brown were speaking of the murder. I find the occurrence strange if, as you say, you were only offering her comfort. Can you give an explanation of your conversation?"

"You are quite correct, Colonel, but you only heard a part of our conversation. I was merely seeking to relieve the thoughts weighing on Miss Brown's mind and I have found it helps to put into words those things we fear most."

"On the contrary, Miss King, I believe you were examining Miss Brown's memory in an effort to discover if she recalled anything pointing to your guilt." Colonel Forester announced. "Therefore, Miss King, I hereby accuse you of the murder of George Wickham."

The silence following Colonel Forester's statement was deafening. No one moved. Only the crackling blaze in the fireplace penetrated the stunned silence of the library.

The four occupants of the room stared at each other with mixed reactions. Miss King's mouth opened in a gasp but she never made a sound. Bingley stared at the two officers. Colonel Forester's face glowed red and veins in his neck bulged as he stared at Miss King. His brow winkled, Colonel Fitzwilliam turned and stared at Colonel Forester.

Finally, Miss King made a choking sound and her face turned the deep red color of her hair. Bingley rushed to pour her a glass of water from the tray.

Miss King gasped for air until her complexion returned to normal, and then she rushed into speech. "I did not murder Mr. Wickham. I could never do such a thing. However, as you insist on exposing all that is personal in my life for public scrutiny, I will tell you all the facts. I wished to keep this information to myself, but I cannot keep silent under charge of being a murderer. It was I who broke off the relationship with Mr. Wickham, not the other way around."

"So you implied before, but I must why you would end the engagement?" Colonel Forester demanded. "What young woman wanting a husband does such a thing? Is it not the goal of all single young ladies to find a husband as soon as possible so they may boast of their conquests?"

Miss King sent him a reproachful glare. "Colonel Forester, must I explain what seems obvious to everyone else in the county? Mr. Wickham was only interested in wealth. Though I must confess, until Captain Carter told me that Mr. Wickham borrowed money from all his friends, I had no idea of the true extent of his debt."

"Females of marrying age are not usually deterred by the fact that a young man borrows money." Colonel Forester stated.

"To what age do you refer, Colonel? Do you mean to imply that I am past the first flush of youth and therefore desperate for any match I am offered?"

"Your spoken words, Miss King, not my own."

"I see that I must explain." Miss King's sigh sounded loud in the stillness of the room. "The executor of my uncle's estate made inquires and discovered tales of Mr. Wickham's habits. After hearing the information, I considered Mr. Wickham's sudden interest and realized he was focused only on my inheritance. When next I saw him, I ended our arrangement."

"Still, I believe you were reacted to the insult from his lack of affection and his focus on your fortune." Colonel Forester's tone rang with the determination of a military man refusing to give up on a battle.

"I disagree, Colonel." Colonel Fitzwilliam said. "I am of the opinion that Miss King should feel relieved at her narrow escape rather than harbor anger at the loss of Mr. Wickham's attentions. Therefore, I can determine no reason she would wish him ill will."

"This is my reaction as well," Bingley added. "I have experience at observing these affairs and my sisters expressed relief at being rid of fortune hunters."

"Yet, Miss Bingley met with Mr. Wickham in the garden," Miss King blurted.

The room fell into silence for long moments as the men considered her words. Then Colonel Fitzwilliam said, "Miss King, on one point I am unclear. Why did you go about the room and ask so many questions about the murder?"

"I fear I must confess I was uneasy, Colonel. Mrs. Wickham accused me of the murder, and I wanted proof that I had not committed the crime. It was to that aim, and nothing more, that I asked questions. Even though I felt sympathy for Mrs. Wickham's distress, I was unnerved that she should blame me for the deed."

"That is the cause of all your questions? You were only trying to solve the murder?" Colonel Forester demanded.

"But of course that is all, Colonel. What other reason could I have? My only intent was to prove my innocence."

Frowning thoughtfully as he studied her, Colonel Fitzwilliam said. "If that be the case, then perhaps you will share with us what you have discovered?"

"Colonel," Colonel Forester roared, "have we not wasted enough time without now pausing to consider speculations from every guest in attendance."

"I agree too much time has passed with little results, Colonel," Colonel Fitzwilliam said as he turned back to Miss King. "However, we accused Miss King of this crime and I believe we must hear what she has learned. Miss King, if you please?"

"I fear I must disappoint you, Colonel, for I found no answers, only more questions."

"Such as?"

Miss King shrugged. "The first matter to cause me concern was the number of people who arranged to meet with Wickham in the garden."

"I should think the answer to that question was simple," Colonel Forester barked. "Wickham planned to meet every female he could lure into the dark. Yet the fact remains, that his murder occurred in this room, not in the garden. So as you see, Miss King, the more important question is, who met Mr. Wickham in the library."

◇◈◇

"Captain Carter?" Reluctantly, Mary approached the captain as he stood with Denny and Mrs. Forester. "I am instructed to ask you to report to the library."

Captain Carter turned to her and studied the expression on Mary's face, then gave a slight nod and turned toward the door of the ballroom without saying a word.

Dismayed as she was, Mary skipped to keep pace with him.

"Captain, I am so sorry for I fear the cause of your summons falls on my head." Captain Carter paused in mid-step and Mary rushed to explain. "You see, the colonels accused me of murdering Mr. Wickham. Well, to be perfectly clear, it was Colonel Forester who made the declaration. But in my rush to prove my innocence, I mentioned you said Wickham owed money to all his friends."

"Miss King, do not concern yourself on my behalf," Captain Carter gave a polite bow, "for you have only spoken the truth."

C×80

As soon as Captain Carter closed the library door behind him, Colonel Forester launched into speech. "Captain, I am most disappointed in you."

At the same time, Colonel Fitzwilliam said, "Captain Carter, tell us more about Mr. Wickham's debts."

Choosing to respond only to the comment he had cause to defend, Captain Carter turned to Colonel Fitzwilliam. "Colonel, considering what I have recently heard about Wickham's relationship with Mr. Darcy, I am confident Wickham's debt to all his acquaintances is no shock to you."

"Be that as it may, Captain," Colonel Fitzwilliam gave a nod of assent as he continued, "but the question remains as to why you did not see fit to mention this debt at our first conversation?"

Captain Carter straightened to his full height, making him as tall as Colonel Fitzwilliam and half-a-head taller than Bingley. "Wickham's death at a ball, instead of in the midst of battle, came as a shock, Colonel. Considering Mrs. Wickham's distress, I had no wish to speak ill of Wickham."

"Your sentiments are duly respected, Captain. Now, kindly enlighten us—"

"Stop this sentimental nonsense at once, Captain. Who did Wickham owe money, and why did an officer in my command fail to reveal relevant information about a former member of the regiment?"

Captain Carter kept his stance and stared straight ahead. "I am not in possession of that information, Colonel."

"This is not a damned national secret, Captain," Colonel Forester barked. "Tell us of what you are aware."

"Sir, I am not—"

"Captain," Colonel Fitzwilliam kept his voice low as he interrupted Carter, "Could you reveal the extent of Wickham's debt to

Mr. Denny?"

"I would rather —"

"Are you refusing to cooperate, Captain?" Colonel Forester demanded.

"I would prefer you to ask Denny about the matter, Colonel."

"A man of honor," Colonel Fitzwilliam gave Captain Carter a nod of approval, "very well, I suggest we speak with Mr. Denny."

Chapter Fifteen

After Captain Carter left the ballroom, Mary King allowed her gaze to roam over the guests. After the long night and with dawn approaching, the sparkle and shine had worn off even the most calculated expressions. Neck cloths drooped under chins of men looking more disheveled by the hour. And the women faired no better, as their gowns now looked wrinkled beyond repair. Their hair, so carefully styled upon arrival, now hung in forlorn tumbles. Their faces looked drawn by lines of fatigue, telling of the long night of tension and no sleep.

Mary's gaze settled on Maggie, who now looked more composed as she attended to Miss Darcy's needs. Comfort seemed in short supply while they were obliged to remain in this room to avoid risk of being murdered in their beds. Mary made an effort to renew her own energy, but she needed little effort as she was still reacting to her narrow escape from being charged with murder. Still, as she glanced about the room, she felt the need to discover a solution to this crime.

What frightened her now that she had narrowly escape a charge of murder, was her worry over how the colonels would react if they discovered she and Maggie were cousins. Her fear increased as she imagined both she and Maggie being blamed for the murder. It seemed that now, more than ever, her freedom relied on finding who had murdered Wickham. Yet to this point, all she had discovered was more questions.

Why had Caroline Bingley snapped at Maggie earlier in the

evening in the hallway and then again in the library? Mary was convinced she was missing something important as she searched faces of the guests. After confirming Miss Bingley's location in the opposite end of the room, she turned her attention to her cousin. Had Maggie angered Miss Bingley in some way when Mr. Bingley and his sisters were visiting Mr. Darcy? But how? She must find the answer.

"Are you asleep on your feet, Miss Darcy?" Mary tried to appear as if she had drifted aimlessly toward the chairs where Maggie and Georgiana sat in a corner. Miss Darcy seemed exhausted and Mary regretted she must endure these events. She was too young for exposure to the harsh realities of a murder, and truthfully, Maggie seemed in little better shape. She had suffered the misfortune of discovering Wickham's body, and Mary knew better than anyone how much that incident pained her cousin. "Perhaps a cup of tea would revive you, Miss Darcy. Shall I fetch it for you?"

"You are most kind, Miss King," Georgiana offered a shy smile, "but what I would like more than tea is to hear your news. As you just returned from talking with the colonels, you can tell us all that is happening." Georgiana sent a doubtful glance toward Maggie, "Or perhaps good manners should have prevented me from referring to your ordeal."

To refuse a timid request in that sweet tone would take more effort than Mary could manage at such an early hour before day. How was it that dancing the night away was not as exhausting as sitting around waiting for a murderer to be discovered? Settling in a chair facing Maggie and Georgiana, Mary smiled at Miss Darcy. "Manners are somewhat in conflict with the situation we find ourselves in, do you not agree?"

"Oh, indeed, Miss King, I have broken many of Miss Brown's rules this night and yet," Georgiana smiled at her companion, "she has not complained to my brother, once."

"Then let us distract your Miss Brown yet again," Mary returned the girl's smile, "and I will tell you of my time in the library. Though I fear you will be disappointed, for I have no new revelations to add to the questions put forth by the colonels."

Georgiana leaned forward. "Do tell who you think committed this deed, Miss King."

"Miss Georgiana—"

"It is quite all right, Miss Brown, for I have asked myself the same question." Mary tapped her chin as she considered her response. "Actually, Miss Darcy, you know the people here tonight better than do I. Who do you think committed the murder?" Mary ignored Maggie's gasp and kept her gaze on Georgiana's expressive face. Perhaps this young girl's outlook could give a different account of the events.

Georgiana sat straighter and looked about the room. When she turned back to Mary, her eyes held a glow despite her lack of sleep. "I cannot select one person I would credit with such a crime. It is my guess that a highwayman slipped into the house and did the deed. He could have followed the coaches and entered the library when we were in the ballroom. Mr. Wickham danced for quite a while, you know."

Not even trying to conceal her surprise, Mary replied, "What a splendid thought, Miss Darcy. I wonder if the colonels have considered such a possibility."

"I have heard no such account from my brother, but I will inform Colonel Fitzwilliam of my opinion when next he comes for sustenance." Georgiana turned a cheerful gaze toward Maggie. "At the mention of food, I find I suddenly feel quite famished. I could use some refreshment if you would be so kind as to collect it for me, Miss Brown." Miss Darcy turned to Mary and smiled. "I could get my own plate, but I do not care to do so with everyone watching."

"Oh, my dear, I know the feeling. You cannot make a move without feeling as if daggers are piercing your back. Though I suppose we can place no blame when we all wonder who the murderer is," Mary smiled at the young girl. "In fact, I believe I will accompany Miss Brown. She only has two hands and I feel quite thirsty after answering all the questions asked by the colonels."

"Oh, Miss King, I am so sorry —"

"I did not mind your queries, Miss Darcy, for I take pleasure in conversing with you. Your Colonel Fitzwilliam, however, is quite demanding."

"He is indeed, Miss King, you cannot imagine how exacting he is as a guardian."

"We will return shortly, my dear. Pray do not fall asleep while we are gone." Maggie said to her charge as they stood and straightened their gowns. But once they were out of earshot of Miss Darcy, Maggie hissed for Mary's hearing alone. "How could you discuss the murder in such a manner in front of Miss Darcy?"

"Wickham's murder is known by all present in this room, and

Miss Darcy was made aware of the realities of life, as we all were on this eve. I understand how she must feel, but is it not better to speak of events than to allow them to weigh on our mind?" Mary cast a glance about to assure they were out of hearing for others as she said. "What are you hiding from me, Maggie?"

Color filled Maggie's cheeks. Looking flustered, she grabbed a plate and stared unseeingly at the table loaded with food. "Whatever do you mean, Mary? Why would I keep secrets from my own cousin?"

"I asked myself the same question each time I encounter glares from the colonels. Surely you are aware that I want only to help you in any way I can. Please, can you not tell me what I have over-looked?"

"Mary, you are weary from discovering the man you had once promised to marry was murdered and answering all the questions from the colonels. And so you should be. But pray do not concern yourself any more on my behalf."

Mary laid her hand on Maggie's arm and forced her cousin to meet her gaze. "Say what you will, Maggie, but Wickham was also the man who fathered your child."

Maggie gasped in alarm and jerked a serving spoon out of a bowl of cooked apples, forcing Mary to let go her arm. "Mary, I beg you not to say such words in this room. The harm done by the wrong person overhearing such matters is not to be considered."

"Then you must tell me all, Maggie. For I am the person in this house who knows you almost as well as I know myself, yet I cannot understand the animosity between you and Caroline Bingley."

For long heartbeats, Maggie turned her attention to filling Georgiana's plate and remained silent. Finally, with a swift look about the room to make certain they were alone, she mumbled, "Miss Bingley happened upon us in one of the corridors at Pemberley." Maggie cast Mary an imploring glance. "Pray, do not say the words I see written on your face. It should never have happened. But of all the people in this room, Mary, you are more aware than most of the charm Wickham possessed, and I could not resist him."

⧉

Mary finished her tea in the company of Miss Darcy and Maggie then took her leave. To pretend all was as it should be, after hearing Maggie's words, put a strain on her conversation. She excused herself from their company, with claims that she needed to walk to stay awake. But in truth, she could not endure mindless chatter when her head was filled with questions about Maggie's guilt in Wickham's death.

It was time she spoke with Caroline Bingley. Though the intent seemed simple enough, managing such a conversation would be difficult, for Mary was quite reserved in her manner. Nevertheless, her future and the safety of her cousin and the infant were at risk, leaving Mary with no other choice.

She approached Mr. Bingley's sisters and the sleeping form of Mr. Hurst with a polite smile on her face. "Mrs. Hurst, Miss Bingley, are you as weary of this night's events as am I?"

Caroline Bingley was so startled by Mary's approach she jerked around and almost fell off her chair. However, Mrs. Hurst sent Mary a glare so scathing it would sear a slab of bacon. Nevertheless, Mary could not allow their reaction to discourage her and kept her attention on the younger sister.

Caroline snickered as she sent Louisa a glance. "My dear Miss King, I sincerely doubt we share your state of fatigue, as you have been up and down the stairs to the library repeatedly to answer questions."

"Oh, but climbing stairs is good for the constitution, do you not agree, Miss Bingley? Speaking of which, as we are closed in this ballroom," Mary struggled for an innocent expression, "I wonder if you would accompany me on a stroll around the room? At this late hour, not yet day or night, it is difficult to keep one's senses alert, do you not agree?"

Arching her brows, Caroline sent Mrs. Hurst a speaking glance before responding. "Perhaps you have a point, Miss King. Let us move about the room, if you so wish."

ദൈ

Mr. Bingley entered the ballroom and went straight to Jane's side. Before he could say a word, however, Jane said. "Oh, my dear, did you observe of what is happening?"

Frowning, Bingley turned his gaze upon the room to find the cause of Jane's unease. "I notice no cause for alarm, my dear. This night has gone on too long. You must be weary."

"It is Caroline and Miss King. They are strolling about the room together. Miss King approached Caroline after sitting with Miss Darcy and Miss Brown. I wonder why." Jane glanced toward the far end of the room at Caroline's tall slender form beside the slight figure of

Miss King. In other circumstances, Jane might have smiled at the contrast in their appearances, but on this night a sense of dread filled her. "Do you suppose Miss King discovered some clue to the identity of the murderer and thinks Caroline is involved?"

"I know not," Bingley studied the two women with a frown, "but I must take the opportunity to ask Louisa some questions while Caroline is out of hearing." With a look of regret, Bingley left his wife and joined Louisa. Taking the chair Caroline had recently vacated, he ignored Louisa's glare as he spoke. "Hurst has slept through the night, then?"

Louisa snorted. "So would you if you emptied the punch bowl with no assist from other guests."

"Is marriage to Hurst so tiresome, Louisa? You have never said as much, but since acquiring a wife, I am aware of how the habits of another can affect you on a daily basis."

"Are you quite well, Charles?" Louisa demanded. "I am married to Hurst these many years, yet this is the first time you paid notice to such matters."

"As I said, my recent marriage opened my eyes to your situation. Has your married state been a disappointment to you?"

"Not as much as you assume," Louisa sounded weary, but Bingley noticed rigid way she held herself as she said, "When Hurst is in his cups, I do much as I please."

"Does that mean involving yourself in indiscretions, Louisa?"

"Charles, I am astounded you would ask such a thing." Louisa said. She leaned close and peered in his face. "Are you brought to flush, brother dear?" Then with a familiar roll of her eyes, she tossed her head and sniffed. "Do not concern yourself in my affairs, Charles. If my husband has no complaint, neither should you."

"I insist you take my question seriously, Louisa. We are searching for a murderer."

"You believe I am capable of such an act, Charles? What inspired you with that thought?"

"I did not—"

"I have a less than alert husband, Charles, but I control my emotions and no man has yet to drive me to the heights of passion needed to commit murder."

"You consider Wickham's death an act of passion?" Bingley frowned. "Why would such a thought occur to you?"

"Really, Charles, you are such a pleasant sort," Louisa sniffed, "but did you never notice Wickham's manner?" Louisa rolled her eyes again and laughed. "Can you name one man who exhibits the amount of charm and the easy manner Wickham did? I think not. Look about this room. Did you notice the women in tears at the news of Wickham's demise? How can his death be anything but the result of passion?"

CR80

After Mr. Bingley left the ballroom with Denny, Jane joined her family.

"Lizzy," Jane put a hand on Lizzy's arm and urged her away from the group around the Bennets, "we must have a conversation with Lydia."

"What is the matter, Jane? You are as pale as a nightdress."

"Lizzy, I fear I must speak with Lydia on an unpleasant topic and I need your help."

"I am not certain I can be of assistance, Jane. I tried to speak with Lydia earlier tonight, in the garden, and my comments were not received very well at all." Lizzy glanced toward their younger sister. "If anything, she seems more stubborn now than before her marriage."

"Perhaps she has good reason for her attitude." Jane sighed and then relayed the results of Bingley's conversation with Mrs. Hurst.

"Come, Jane," Lizzy frowned, "surely you cannot think Wickham would stoop so low in the short time since they married."

"It is not a pleasant thought, but you must admit he showed no steadfastness in any of his previous relationships." Jane sighed and turning from Lizzy, went to call Lydia to their side.

"So what is this matter of such great importance, Jane?" Lydia glared at Lizzy. "Has Lizzy told you of our conversation in the garden? Well, I stand by every word, especially now. With my dear Wickham dead, I must depend on support from my family more than ever."

"Lydia, this is another matter, entirely." Jane sighed. "I wish I need not ask, but I must if we are to discover who killed Wickham." Jane looked in Lydia's eyes and said, "Do you believe Wickham was faithful to you?"

Lydia's mouth dropped open. Then she gave a snort and stomped her foot. "How can you say such a thing now of all times?"

"Please believe it was not easy for me to do so," Jane said. She glanced at Lizzy, wondering at her silence, and then a thought occurred to her. Lydia was still jealous of Wickham's attention to Lizzy, so perhaps that was why Lizzy was keeping quiet. "However, things have been said during the questioning in the library. The colonels think this might be a crime of passion. For that is the reason I must ask you to recall events and tell us of anyone you think Wickham might have been involved with recently."

Lydia's wailing response expressed enough pain to break even the hardest of hearts.

Chapter Sixteen

Colonel Fitzwilliam stood with his back to the door as he said. "Mr. Denny, how would you describe your relationship with Mrs. Wickham? I assure you I ask only in the interest of discovering who murdered her husband. We have no wish to judge your actions."

Denny gave a slight tilt of his head. "I appreciate your words, Colonel, but my friendship with Mrs. Wickham is no secret. We were friends even before Wickham arrived in Meryton."

"And that is all, there was no secret longing on your part?"

"I considered Lydia too young at the time, Colonel."

"Very well, Mr. Denny, I believe that is all we require of you at this time." As the door of the library closed behind Denny, Colonel Fitzwilliam studied the expressions of his two partners in the investigation, and addressed them in a firm tone. "Gentlemen, we learned nothing from Mr. Denny but what we had already heard from Captain Carter. I suggest we take a short time to rethink our plan. The sun is not yet up, but soon we must decide if we are going to request the guests remain any longer."

"Good thought, Colonel, I fear the men have tired of keeping watch. And I find myself in need of nourishment." Mr. Bingley responded eagerly. "Let us return to the ballroom. Jane has organized a selection of foods." Bingley turned to the man standing guard of the fireplace. "Colonel Forester, will you join us? Or shall I send a maid with your coffee?"

"What? Oh, ummm, of course I will accompany you. I must confer with my wife as to her welfare. She feels abandoned at this event." Colonel Forester turned grim, red-streaked eyes on Bingley. "If you will pardon me for saying so, Bingley, your wife's family has not made Mrs. Forester feel very welcome at this ball."

Bingley straightened his shoulders. "Colonel, I am most distressed to hear of your wife's discomfort. But you must admit my wife's family suffered greatly when their daughter disappeared from the safety of your home in Brighton."

"She did not vanish, sir." Colonel Forester's face filled with color. "She left a note stating her intentions to run off with that scoundrel Wickham."

"Be that as it may, Colonel," Colonel Fitzwilliam stopped on his way to the door and turned to face Colonel Forester, "you must concede the fact that the Bennets had reason for concern until Mr. Wickham and Lydia were found safe and married."

After a rough clearing of his throat, Colonel Forester said in a lower voice, "I never heard details of that situation. When, exactly, did Wickham marry Lydia Bennet?"

Bingley stepped forward to open the door and gave a slight bow as he waved the colonels through. "Colonel, that is a question you must ask the Bennets. The information you seek is not mine to tell."

☙

After obtaining a cup of coffee, Colonel Fitzwilliam joined Darcy. Nourishment would be welcome, but he dared not indulge for fear of falling asleep before he discovered the answers he needed to identify the murderer.

"How goes it, Fitz?" Mr. Darcy greeted him.

"Not very encouraging, I fear." Fitzwilliam sipped from the hot, restoring brew in his cup. "We can not find enough information to identify the culprit. To be quite frank, Will, I question the good sense behind our actions since this investigation started."

"Surely you had no expectation that identifying the killer would be an easy task." Mr. Darcy lifted a shoulder as he glanced around the room. A gray tinge to the windows announced the coming of dawn as did the lines of exhaustion on faces of the guests. "After all, a person capable of murder must be conniving enough to hide his identity, do you not agree?"

"Sensible as always, Will, but I must confess I have no thought of how to make progress from this point, and, the passing hours only make the task more difficult. Colonel Forester is not the most jovial fellow at the best of times, and hours of questioning guests have added nothing to his disposition."

"You did not serve with him in the same regiment?"

"There is no previous acquaintance between us, if that is what you are asking, cousin." Fitzwilliam lifted his cup. "Though, I must confess, after this night I am relieved over the lack of a former connection. Colonel Forester's familiarity with some guests and the victim has taken a toll on his bearing."

Darcy nodded, "It must be a strain to question men in your command when you are aware you might send one of them to hang. Leading men into battle, when all are in danger would be easier, I believe."

Fitzwilliam drank from his cup and glanced around the room. Bingley stood nearby, holding a cup and saucer as he talked with his wife. Bingley met Fitzwilliam's gaze and lifted his cup in greeting. Fitzwilliam gave a nod in return. "I must confess, cousin, Mr. Bingley is the most even-tempered man I have ever encountered. Without his presence, some of the guests might have taken offense at the questions we were forced to ask."

"'Tis a fact, cousin, I believe Bingley's disposition and good humor to be second only to my own." With a sly grin at Fitzwilliam, Darcy took a drink from his cup.

Fitzwilliam coughed to keep from choking on the coffee he was swallowing. "Will Darcy, I spent half a lifetime thinking you were without humor, and you chose a time such as this to express levity. And before the sun has taken to the sky, as well."

"You appeared in need of some lighthearted words, cousin." Darcy studied Fitzwilliam with a practiced glance. "I fear responsibility weighs too heavy on your countenance this early hour."

"How right you are, cousin." Fitzwilliam stared across the room as Colonel Forester leaned protectively over his wife. Yet her stiff posture and the pout on her full lips did not bode well for the colonel. "I must confess to feeling concern for Forester's health. He turned almost purple when Bingley made a comment he did not appreciate."

෦෫

A short time later the three men returned to the library. As the door closed behind them, Fitzwilliam said, "Colonel Forester, before we make inquires of the other guests, perhaps we should discuss your relationship with Captain Carter and Mr. Denny."

"May I inquire as to what brought this topic to mind, Colonel?"

"Only concern for your welfare, sir," Fitzwilliam injected quickly. "It occurred to me that asking questions of your own men must be quite a strain, considering one of them could hang if found guilty."

"That is a fact, sir." Colonel Forester responded in a blustering tone. "Was this the subject you were discussing with Mr. Darcy when the two of you were looking so intently in my direction?"

"I do beg your pardon, Colonel. Actually, Darcy and I did mention your name. My cousin commented on how tired we appeared. And as I could not see my own face, I turned to examine yours." Fitzwilliam paused. "Darcy expressed his sympathy for the fact that you must question men with whom you are so closely acquainted."

"Rightly so, but not the words I expected at all."

"How very interesting." Fitzwilliam studied the other man as he continued. "May I ask what pronouncement were you expecting, Colonel?"

"One never knows when attending gatherings such as this. My wife took note of your interest in our presence, as well. She suggested I should take care to protect myself in your company."

"Come now, Colonel—"

"I am quite certain the concern is only for your well-being, Colonel Forester." Bingley rushed into speech.

"Be that as it may, Colonel, I could only assume you were making some observation on my conduct. Perhaps even suggesting I showed partiality to my men."

Fitzwilliam made note of Colonel Forester's defensive posture and considered this matter needed further examination. Indeed, if they found a man in the militia guilty of the crime, he would insist the magistrate hear the evidence. Then Sir William could determine if the man was guilty. "On the contrary, Colonel, you have my sympathy as you might find it necessary to send one of your men to his death."

Colonel Forester lifted his chin even higher. "It is no less than he deserved if he is guilty of this murder. Do you not agree, Colonel Fitzwilliam?"

Tension seemed to permeate the room. After a long pause, Fitzwilliam disregarded the colonel's tone as he spoke in a low voice. "I agree, and much as I am loath to do so, I fear we must speak with Mrs. Wickham again."

"Colonel, are you quite certain that is necessary?" Bingley asked.

The first rays of sunlight showed through the tall windows of the library, but the candles still provided the needed light. "Mrs. Wickham is overcome with grief, and this room appears the same as when she saw Wickham's body on the floor. Could we not — "

"Get on with fetching her, sir. I agree with the Colonel." Colonel Forester's voice rose over Bingley's objections. "We must speak with the widow if we are to sort this out."

Bingley caught back further words of protest before they escaped his mouth, but he objected to the tone Colonel Forester used when he said the word widow. Lydia Bennet...Wickham had not invited this situation upon her head, and Colonel Forester was in error if he imagined otherwise.

Reluctant though he was, Bingley followed the colonel's orders. And there was no doubt in his mind it was an order. The colonel's commanding tone made it clear. Bingley might be the host, but Colonel Forester considered himself and Colonel Fitzwilliam to be in charge.

That suited Bingley's frame of mind for he was sorely exhausted by the turn of events and facing Lydia's sharp tongue was the last thing he wished.

Arriving in the ballroom, he approached Lydia and his reception was much as he had expected. Lydia balked at his request that she return to the library. Perhaps she wanted only to avoid another round of questions, or maybe she was opposed to returning to the scene of the murder. Bingley could not be certain of what made her refuse his request. However, after much persuading from Jane and Lizzy, over Mrs. Bennet's loudly voiced objections, Lydia agreed to accompany him to the library.

Lydia stomped down the stairs at a fast pace, stalked into the room, and burst into speech before Bingley could close the door. "Really, Colonel Forester, how unkind of you to insist I return to this room."

"Try to avert your line of sight, Mrs. Wickham." Colonel Fitzwilliam advised when she paused for breath. "We regret the need to inconvenience you at a time such as this, but I am certain you understand our chances of catching the murderer are slipping past and you are in possession of facts no one else can know."

"The murderer could be half way to town for all the time that has passed since my poor husband was murdered, and I have answered enough questions from Jane and Lizzy. Why must I answer more?" Lydia flounced over to a chair and plopped down. "I had nothing to tell them, and I have nothing more to reveal to you."

"Interesting," Colonel Forester paced in front of Lydia's chair, "what questions did your sisters ask, Mrs. Wickham?"

"How droll of you, Colonel." Lydia snickered before she continued. "They asked about Wickham if you must know."

"Perhaps you could repeat their questions and we will not make the mistake of asking the same things."

Colonel Fitzwilliam sent Colonel Forester a glare and turned to Lydia. "Mrs. Wickham, I am afraid we must ask again, on the off chance that you have recalled some detail you failed to mention earlier. Can you think of anyone who wanted to harm your husband?"

Lydia turned wide eyes on Fitzwilliam. "I just realized, Colonel, you and Mr. Darcy are cousins, but neither of you possess the measure of charm my Wickham had. I expect that is reason enough for some men to wish him dead. Women noticed my husband, you know. And that made other men envious."

"Did the interest women showed Mr. Wickham concern you, at all?" Colonel Forester asked.

Lydia rolled her eyes. "How can you think that, Colonel? Every woman wants a husband other women envy." She lowered her eyes and peeped at him through her eyelashes. "Harriet discussed this topic with me many times when we were alone."

"Had Mr. Wickham disagreed with anyone recently?" Colonel Forester demanded in the tense silence that followed her words. "Perhaps he had words over a card game, or encountered the husband of one of the women you referred to?"

Lydia turned to Colonel Forester with glare of dislike. In fact, had Colonel Forester been the one murdered, after seeing Lydia's expression, Bingley could almost imagine she would be a suspect in the colonel's murder.

"We arrived late, thanks to poor travel arrangements and useless public transport." Lydia snapped. "Poor Wickham hardly had time to change before the ball. There was no opportunity for a disagreement to develop. Mind you, even had there been time, any dispute could not be blamed on Wickham. It was not in his nature to fight."

"Of course he would fight. He was in the military." Colonel Forester raised his voice. "And we're well aware of the fact that your husband owed money to all he knew. Can you not see how his debts could result in ill feelings, Mrs. Wickham?"

Lydia snorted. "Wickham's friends all borrowed money, as well. How else can these men live? They struggle to survive while men such as Darcy and Bingley have more than they need. But do they share? Did they offer to help? I think not. So do not blame debt as the cause of my poor Wickham's death, Colonel."

"Very well, Mrs. Wickham, who do you blame for your husband's death?"

Chapter Seventeen

*B*ingley and the colonels returned to the ballroom after their wasted interview with Lydia. The long hours and endless questioning were wearing on their energy. They needed liquid for their throats and food for energy. "Jane, my dear, I mean no harm, but I must say, speaking with your sister is mindful of turning in circles. There is no sense or reason to half what she says and you go no where. But perhaps it is just me."

"Oh, my dear Bingley, of course it is not you. Lydia has had a stubborn streak since the day she was born. And truthfully, Lizzy and I often puzzled over what was in her head other than the desire to have things her own way. Yet her disposition is sweet as honey if you do not cross her."

"Not vexing her takes effort," Bingley admitted as he glanced about the room. "Now I must speak to Caroline if you will excuse me, my dear."

Bingley was not looking forward to this conversation, but it was his duty. Caroline was his sister. Therefore, he was her protector. Not that she needed protection. More often than not, he felt obliged to protect the target of her tongue, rather than her. Even after being up all night her eyes flashed daggers as he approached. "Caroline, you are still awake I see."

"What do you expect, as we are confined to this room like prisoners? Surely, Charles, you have learned enough to catch the murderer by now, for it is nearly morn."

"Ah, but you are mistaken, my dear. For you, two hours after sunrise might be nearly morn, but for one who enjoys the outdoors, such myself, three hours have gone wasting since the start of day, and still we cannot identify the person guilty of this crime."

"What nonsense, Charles. Can you not use the militia men to frighten the truth out of the guilty person? Do something. Anything to get us out of this wretched ballroom. Between the odors of cold food and bodies too long without a bath, I fear I am on the verge of having a fit of vapors like Mrs. Bennet does. Do you know she has enjoyed at least four such fits since we first heard of the murder?"

"Caroline, do try to be kind to Jane's family."

Caroline gave a snort. "After events of this night, I dearly wish never see any of them again, including Eliza." Caroline turned to stare at Lizzy and Darcy. "Now there is a candidate for your murder, Charles. Poor Eliza never got over Wickham's marriage to Lydia."

"Pray how could that be when she won Darcy? You are mistaken, Caroline. However, I feel you should be aware your name has been mentioned as a possible suspect."

"What utter nonsense do you speak, Charles." Caroline let loose a twitter of laughter as she glanced toward Louisa, but her sister had finally succumbed to the hour and closed her eyes. "What reason could I possibly have to harm Wickham? I barely knew the man."

"You were seen leaving the library a short time before his body was discovered."

"Ah, it sounds as though your colonels are desperate to make an identity, Charles. Yet it is true that I stopped by the fire in the library to warm my hands. But you and the colonels are forgetting a one point. I found that servant of Darcy's making free use of the library when I arrived. Perhaps Miss Brown is your guilty party."

"Caroline, do stop calling Miss Brown a servant. And that reminds me, why did you confront her earlier in the hallway?"

"Did I?" Caroline focused her gaze on the wrinkles in her skirt and tried to smooth them with a shaking hand. "I cannot recall."

"Earlier in the evening, before the ball, you encountered Miss Brown and —"

"Really, how you do go on, Charles. Do you expect me to make time to speak when I pass a servant in the hallway?" Caroline rolled her eyes and gave a snort. "Is this what marriage to one of the Bennet girls has done for you, Charles? For I must tell you it is not in the least bit flattering."

CR&O

After Bingley left to go speak with Caroline, Jane noticed Denny standing at the table of refreshments and quickly moved to join him. "Denny, I have had not an occasion to speak with you since hearing of the murder. Please accept my condolences for I recall how close you and Mr. Wickham were."

Denny bowed. "Your memory is correct, Mrs. Bingley. Wickham was a splendid friend, even when he borrowed my last coin."

"Oh, was it that bad? I understood he had debts —"

"No reason to fret yourself, Mrs. Bingley. After all, what are friends for, if not to be there with a loan when needed?"

"Spoken as the true friend I know you were, Denny. I still cannot believe this happened. Do you recall anyone who wished Mr. Wickham harm?"

"Only a list as long as my arm of men he beat at cards or charmed away their ladies," Denny said with a laugh.

"He left no discontented connections behind when he left Brighton?" Jane picked up a plate and pretended an interest in the food. Their cook had outdone herself on the offerings, but most of the dishes were cold by now and did not appear as appetizing as when hot from the kitchen.

"Wickham borrowed money and charmed the ladies," Denny shrugged, "but he did not engage in matters of anger. He used his charm against his opponents, rather than pistols or swords."

"Yet someone was unhappy with him," Jane said as she selected a piece to toasted bread for her plate. "And vexed enough to commit murder."

"Begging your pardon for speaking ill of your sister's husband, Mrs. Bingley, but knowing Wickham's ways, I would bet money on a woman being the cause of his murder." With a slight bow, Denny turned and walked away.

Jane stared at the table as she mulled over Denny's comment. Much as she disliked the idea, she realized that Denny's parting words could well be the cause for Wickham's murder. Now, if she could just determine which female Wickham was in pursuit of before his death.

Poor Lydia would be vexed if Denny's suggestion proved correct, but the murderer must be caught. Still Jane paused. For as much as she wanted the truth revealed, it occurred to her that Denny's words could also be used against members of her family. Lizzy could be described as being beside herself with jealousy over Wickham having, yet another, lover. Papa might be blamed for defending his daughter's honor, though Jane knew the physical act was not in his nature. That left Lydia to act as the jealous wife and new fear blossomed in Jane's heart.

She knew her youngest sister well. Lydia expected to get her way. And everyone in the area knew she had a temper. Lydia was spoiled and thrilled at being Wickham's wife. She would not take the news of Wickham having an affair lightly.

Jane stared about the room as tension built inside her. What should she do? How could she discover the truth? Because spoiled as she was, Jane could not find it in her heart to believe Lydia would commit murder. Stomp her foot and yell, she would do, but not murder. Not when she was besotted with Wickham.

◌ৡৈ◌

Mary King watched Mr. Bingley engage his sister in conversation. That Caroline Bingley disliked his words was easy to perceive from the expression on her face. The first thing Mary noticed about Bingley's sisters was their very expressive features. With one withering look, or roll of their eyes, and they made a person feel as unimportant as a twice worn ball gown. Mary considered what it would be like to possess such confidence and yet, she could not imagine treating another person with such disregard.

With that thought foremost in her mind, Mary turned her attention to Jane Bingley. She watched Jane approach Mr. Denny, and her senses prickled with curiosity. Mary knew little of Mr. Denny, for Wickham had wasted none of their time together speaking of his friends. Indeed, she shuddered at thinking of the pace at which he pushed their relationship. Yet she had escaped better than dear Maggie had, but that thought brought to mind another worry.

Mary was certain there was a connection between Caroline Bingley and her cousin, but what could it be. Mary sighed for Maggie had left her with little choice. She must confront her cousin. Acknowledging the enormity of what she was about to do, and the damage it might cause to their relationship, Mary angled her chin higher. She must uncover the truth of Maggie's involvement with Wickham if she was to prove they were innocent of his murder.

She crossed the room to the corner where Maggie sat with Miss Darcy. By chance, as she approached, Georgiana rose from her chair beside Maggie and crossed the room to join Mr. and Mrs. Darcy. Covering her sigh of relief, Mary studied her cousin's drooping face as she stopped in front of Maggie's chair. "Are you well, Maggie?"

Maggie managed a slight smile as she looked up. "Do sit down, cousin, for you must be as weary as am I."

"Have you managed to calm your nerves?" Mary asked as she settled in the chair beside her cousin. "The fright of your discovery was most startling, especially considering your situation."

Maggie's eyes filled with tears as she looked at Mary. "How can I find any peace? When I am with Miss Darcy, I must appear calm for her sake. She knew Wickham as a child, if you recall." Maggie gulped. "But my heart aches with a sadness I can hardly contain. Oh, Mary, I so hoped—"

"My dear Maggie, I understand this is difficult for you, but you must consider the situation. Mr. Wickham took another woman as his wife. What hope did you have that he would return your affections or offer to care for your child?"

Maggie drew in a shuddering breath. "But can you not see, Mary. If I gave up hope, what else did I have? What reason to wake each day?" A sob escaped her pinched lips. "It is true Wickham married another, but even to see a smile from him made my day brighter. I hoped...and prayed, once he saw his son, he would come to me—"

"Without the benefit of marriage, or any assurance he would support you and his child? Oh Maggie, how could you think so little of yourself? Or ask for so little for your own child?"

Maggie shoved Mary's hand off her arm and sat stiffly erect as she glared at her cousin. "Mary, pray tell me, what you know of love? I speak of a love so strong it makes you go against all you know is right, just so you can share the little your lover is willing to give." Maggie gulped a breath. "You were engaged to Wickham, but you never loved him. I could see it in your face. You enjoyed having a handsome suitor, but when it came to choosing Wickham or your inheritance, which did you choose, Mary? You chose the inheritance and your security." Maggie stared at Mary, with all the hurtful anger and frustration inside her showing clearly on her features. "Do you suppose I would ever have made your choice? I could not, for I loved him. From the first time he came to visit you, I looked in his eyes and felt I had met the man my heart was made for."

Shocked by the sudden burst of emotion and the depth of Maggie's feelings for Wickham, Mary could only sit and stare at the cousin she thought she knew as well as she knew herself. Yet Maggie's words proved her wrong. Where once she had thought Maggie a soft, soothing person, there now sat a woman willing to give up all she had for the man she loved. This new side of Maggie and her single minded determination, frightened Mary more than words could describe.

Had Maggie loved Wickham enough to kill him rather than share him with another woman? Pondering that possibility, Mary looked away from her cousin's face and drew a shuddering breath. Icy shivers raced through her body. She had to discover whether Maggie's emotions were strong enough that she could murder because of them. Yet how could she be certain when all this time she had believed she and Maggie were alike? Believed they were both easy going and hiding a desire to be loved. Maggie's words confirmed the part about wanting love was correct. Yet she had also revealed her resolve to achieve that love at any cost, and that admission added to Mary's questions.

Did Maggie have something to do with Wickham's murder?

Maggie's opinion of her true emotions concerning Wickham were, as well. Much as she wanted to deny Maggie's claim that she had not loved him, she could not. Since she sent Wickham away, she often worried that her emotions did not run deep enough to allow her to experience true love. If she had loved Wickham, as Maggie had described love, would she have refused his advances? Yet listening to Maggie speak of her feelings for Wickham, Mary questioned what might have happened if she, too, had loved him with the intensity her cousin had described.

"Why did you not tell me of your feelings for Wickham?" Mary stared at Maggie, as if she had never seen her before. Indeed, she felt she had never known her cousin's character at all, and that suspicion left an aching pain in her heart. "All the times he came to visit, you never said a word. And what of the time since I ended our agreement? You could have poured out your heart to me, but you remained silent. Why did you not reveal your feelings?"

"What purpose would doing so have served? You agreed to marry him. What was I to say? Oh, please do not marry the man I love? What manner of person would that make me?"

"But Maggie, my actions made you suffer —"

"Do not flog yourself on my account, Mary. I made my choice, not you. I returned to work for the Darcys, if you recall."

Mary's eyes opened wide as the obvious truth occurred to her. "You knew!" Her thoughts tumbled too fast for words. "You were aware you would see Wickham if you worked there...is that why?"

Maggie's head jerked in a nod and tears filled her eyes. She brushed at her cheeks and turned to a slight smile on Mary. "I had him for a while, at least." Maggie sat tall and her expression turned to stone. "Even while he was courting you, he came to me, Mary. Think hard of me if you must, but I loved him."

"Miss King?"

Relief rushed over Mary as she turned to find Jane Bingley standing at her side. "Mrs. Bingley, how may I be of service to you?"

"Perhaps you would walk with me, Miss King, so we might speak?"

CʒꙅꙨ

Jane and Bingley had watched the exchange between Miss Brown and concluded they should speak plainly with Miss King. Any reluctance on their part had eased as they observed Miss Brown's expressions while Miss King spoke.

Still, as Miss King rose from her chair, Jane turned in Bingley's direction to seek reassurance. She must keep her voice calm, despite her unease. "Miss King, forgive me, but I must speak bluntly. My husband and I would like to have a word with you."

Miss King's apprehension was obvious to Jane as she watched expressions chase across her guest's face. Still, she headed toward her husband, confident Miss King would follow. She needed to have Miss King's attention and her cooperation.

"Ah, Miss King, so kind of you to join us," as Bingley spoke, he produced three cups of steaming tea from the tray at his side. "Do forgive the dramatics, but my wife and I would like to have a conversation in private with you."

Chapter Eighteen

*J*ane and Bingley were not the only ones to observe Mary King's conversation with Miss Brown.

"I say, Colonel," Colonel Forester approached Fitzwilliam as he stood by the table of refreshments, "did you by chance notice Miss King's choice of companion for the past while? I mention this because of my wife's comment about how often our fellow house-guest seems to converse with the woman who discovered Wickham's body."

Fitzwilliam glanced toward the corner where Miss Darcy usually sat with Miss Brown and observed his ward was not there, but Miss King was in deep conversation with the woman. "Miss King's habit of seeking out Miss Brown does make one question her reason for doing so."

"Could we have the person guilty of this crime?"

Colonel Fitzwilliam frowned. "How do you suggest a female as small as Miss King could take a man of Wickham's size by surprise and murder him?"

"It might not be as difficult as you assume, Colonel." Colonel Forester's enthusiasm for the topic added a note of excitement to his tone. "Perhaps she allowed Wickham's advances to reach more intimate familiarity than society deems appropriate."

"That seems unlikely, as their attachment is long past."

"Not so distant, Colonel, and, as you have heard, Wickham never sheathed his charm, even when he was with women who were married."

"Have you any proof of this matter, Forester?"

"My own wife will confirm what I have said, sir." Colonel Forester's nostrils flared at Fitzwilliam's show of doubt. "After several social events, she has commented on Wickham's tendency toward familiarity."

"Perhaps we should converse with your wife, again, Colonel."

"To what end, Colonel? Why waste the effort. I believe we should question Miss Brown."

"All in good time, Colonel." Fitzwilliam's brow wrinkled as he glanced toward his ward's companion. "I am of the opinion we give Miss Brown time to gather her nerves after the shock of finding a body."

Colonel Forester expelled a sound like a bull stomping the ground, ready to attack. "Very well, then I suggest we call Miss King back to the library and review her relationship with Wickham. Now, if you will excuse me, I must deliver this plate to my wife."

Fitzwilliam watched him stomp off and wondered at the emotional outburst. In his opinion, Colonel Forester was more rattled by this murder than he wanted to reveal. Wrinkling his brow even more, Fitzwilliam could not help but wonder why. Had the colonel and Mr. Wickham been better friends than the officer implied?

ༀༀ

"Ah, Mrs. Bingley, I regret we seemed to have spoiled your event, but may I congratulate you on providing substance of such generous proportions to your guests during this trying night." Colonel Fitzwilliam said as he approached the Bingleys and Miss King. He had observed their intense expressions with curiosity, especially since Miss King spent so much time with Miss Brown.

"You are too kind, Colonel," Jane tilted her head in a polite nod. In the past, she would have allowed the conversation to flow around her and said nothing more, but this night had changed her in ways she had yet to understand. She had an inner strength and a need for answers that she never recalled experiencing before the events of this night. "Can you give our concern of harboring a murderer any relief? Perhaps you have discovered clues, and will soon reveal the person who committed this deed?"

"I fear I can offer no such comfort at this time." Colonel Fitzwilliam bowed. "However, you are correct in part of your observation. We must continue searching for any information we can discover. To that end, Bingley, I suggest we return to your library." He paused and allowed his gaze to settle on the third member of their party, who had remained conspicuously silent during their exchange. "Miss King, might I request your presence for a brief discussion."

"Of course, Colonel," Miss King said and with a polite tilt of her head, she turned her steps toward the door.

Bingley's glance trailed from the departing figure of Miss King to mingle with his wife's gaze for a long heartbeat, before he turned to Colonel Fitzwilliam. "I am at your service, sir."

"One question before we go, Bingley." Colonel Fitzwilliam glanced from Miss King's departing figure to the Bingleys. He studied them one at a time, noting the open honesty of each face and voiced his question reluctantly. "I am confused as to how well you are acquainted with Miss King."

"Oh, not at all before this night," Mr. Bingley replied eagerly.

"I first met her at my aunt Phillips's social, but I can hardly claim to know her. When Mr. Wickham chose her company instead of Lizzy's that same evening, we had no further encounters until Miss King arrived with Sir William's party tonight." Jane replied. "But if you refer to frequent conversations we have exchanged this eve, Colonel, I admit to a keen interest in Miss King's acquaintance and her opinions."

Colonel Fitzwilliam's brow wrinkled. "I beg your pardon, Mrs. Bingley, but I am confused by your response. You appear to think Miss King is in possession of some information you wish to learn. Are your referring to Wickham's murder?"

"That may be the case, Colonel, but only because it is the topic all the guests are speaking of, with little mention of anything else." Jane held his gaze. "What interests me is Miss King's attempt to make her way in local society, same as I must do now that I am married and wish for acquaintances to view me in a different light. We share the need to make a good impression on local society, and that is all."

"I see," the colonel acknowledged with a slight bow, "I will retreat to the library. Will you join me, Bingley?"

As they watched Fitzwilliam walk toward Colonel Forester, Bingley lowered his head and spoke for Jane's hearing alone. "That is not our only interest in Miss King, my dear, and I must admit I have rarely observed you use subtlety to this extent."

"Oh, pray do not think harshly of me, Charles, but I admit I feel protective of Miss King. I could not stand here and allow Colonel

Fitzwilliam to assume the worst of her when all I have observed is her kind nature. Do not be vexed with me, husband."

"I could not, my dear, but now I fear I must follow the colonels and commence with this next review."

୬୫୨

Increasingly agitated at the turn of events, Mary descended the stairs with a firm tread, but halfway to the bottom, a sense of caution slowed her steps. There was no way of knowing if the murderer still lurked in the shadows of this great house, or if that person had escaped into the night after killing Wickham. Nevertheless, whichever the case might be, proceeding at her clipped pace would be reckless if she cared for the safety of her person.

When no shadows lurched out of the dim light on the lower stairs and the front hallway, Mary approached the door to the library. But try as hard as she might, she could not exert the effort to lift her hand to the brass handle and enter the room alone. Memory of Wickham's enduring charm, and his body on the floor in a pool of blood, held her rigid.

The night they first met at Mrs. Phillips' social, she had been flattered when the most handsome man in attendance focused his attention on her. She was little Mary King, fresh from her country upbringing and unschooled in the ways an heiress should act. When he spoke to her, Wickham rested his gaze on her features, as if she were the only woman in existence. She knew there were other dancers on the floor, but her feet executed the steps of the dance without conscious effort on her part, and her heart thundered in her chest, leaving her breathless.

By the end of the evening, the power of his charm coaxed her natural caution into silence, and the expression in his eyes held her spellbound. Chills chased along her nerves, even now, when she remembered how Wickham's request to call on her had overcome her natural reserve. Perhaps if her uncle's legal advisor had not intervened, they might have married. But to what misery?

Wickham's interest in her proved to be only her inheritance and not her as person. That she first assumed he was as attracted to her as she was to him was proof of her poor judgment. In the past hour, Maggie's words revealed the unhappiness she would have endured had she not broken their engagement.

How could she justify such poor judgment? Could she credit her inexperience and youth, or must she accept that she could not give a good estimation of another person's character? In truth, Maggie's revelations left her mind reeling with all she might have faced, and the worst was not Wickham's betrayal of her emotions. He had known her but for a few weeks and acted as any poor young man, of a handsome countenance and empty pockets, might have done upon learning of her wealth. It was not that she excused his behavior, but, rather, she understood his actions.

What she could not understand or justify was the behavior of her cousin.

Mary stood with her back against the wall and shifted her weight from one foot to the other. As she waited for the colonels to come down to the library, she tried to examine her emotions. If she had fallen under Wickham's spell, would she have reacted as Maggie had? Or was Maggie right, and she had never loved him at all?

Maggie insisted Mary had not, or she would never have sent him away. Still, Mary could not believe she would have acted as Maggie had done. She could not imagine continuing an affair with her cousin's future husband. Yet Maggie had done just that. What troubled Mary even more, and made matters worse, Maggie admitted some of her encounters with Wickham occurred under Mary own roof.

Mary twisted her hands as memories filled her head. While she had acted the proper young lady, and kept her distance from her promised husband, Maggie had given her all to a charmer like Wickham. Yet Mary could not hold back the question burning in her head. Did she lack the qualities needed to hold a man's attentions? Was she less of a woman for keeping control of her emotions, in her efforts to protect all she held dear? Was she cold hearted and uncaring? Was Maggie weak and immoral?

Then again, why place blame. They were both victims of a master charmer, but did it matter, now that Wickham was dead?

Mary tapped her toe on the floor and gazed about the rays of light beginning to brighten the hallway. Dull clangs and thuds told of activity in the distant kitchen. The scent of cooked meat hung heavy in the air. That odor and the fear that she was misguided in her protection of Maggie made her stomach roil.

She could not accept that Maggie had wronged her, even after learning of the affair with Wickham. If Mary had married him, she had no doubt he would have continued with Maggie and any other willing female in his path. That fact exposed Maggie's weakness and confirmed Mary's opinion that Wickham had not changed since their arrangement had ended.

Instead of holding on to her sadness over Maggie's betrayal, she should examine others who might have fallen victim to Wickham's charm. She might discover the murderer. Before she could pursue that thought further, the colonels came down the stairs, followed closely by Mr. Bingley.

Colonel Fitzwilliam opened the door and motioned for her to enter. "Miss King, please forgive our delay."

Mary paused inside the door, allowing Colonel Forester to proceed farther into the room, before she moved to sit in a chair facing away from the bloodstain on the floor. Despite the passing hours, the air hung heavy with the scent of decay and the sickening odor of blood.

It would be a wonder indeed, if she kept her mind on questions, while remembering events that occurred just feet away this very night. Except now it was morning, and the sun's rays were shining through the windows to add light to the room. Yet the passing of hours meant little as thoughts of Wickham's murder were still fresh in her mind.

"Miss King, we regret the need to trouble you yet again, but your actions in the ballroom have not gone unnoticed." Colonel Fitzwilliam said as he stood several feet away and waited for her response.

Mary stared at each of the three men, two in uniform and as different as night and day, and Mr. Bingley, the most pleasant of them all and possibly her cohort in trying to solve this crime. "Ask what you will, gentlemen, for it is of no bother. Yet I must admit I am puzzled as to what actions you refer to with such a statement."

"Your constant efforts to associate with Miss Brown makes us question why you would do so, Miss King." Colonel Forester's lack of patience was evident in his sharp tone.

"Colonel, you must forgive me for saying so, but since this event occurred you seem focused on insulting my character, and I am at my wits end as to the reason that would be so." Mary flung out her hand. "I was a target for a woman distressed by news of her husband's death, as were you, but you continue to question my integrity. Even after I explained earlier that I was only offering comfort to Miss Brown, you still doubt my word.

"Miss Darcy thanked me for relieving her from the stress of

dealing with Miss Brown's anguish, but you appear to think I am guilty of some crime." Mary stared at the shocked expressions on the men's faces as she paused for breath.

"Well, here is one more point you can claim I am guilty of, if you wish." She watched as if observing of a play, as the men all but leaned closer to hear what she might say. "I have a deep concern for Miss Brown's welfare because she is my cousin."

Their gasps told her all she needed to know about the weight of her admission.

Colonel Forester's face turned beet red, as he stood in front of the fireplace, staring down at her. Standing at the end of the sofa across from where she sat, Colonel Fitzwilliam merely arched his brow. Mr. Bingley could not keep his surprise from showing on his expressive face.

Watching them, Mary drew in a deep breath and wondered what would happen next.

Colonel Fitzwilliam was the first to recover. "Miss King, I am most appreciative of your efforts to take some of the worry from my ward. Miss Darcy is quite fond of Miss Brown, but she is young and inexperienced at handling situations such as this."

"Colonel, can you not see this information adds to the possibility that Miss King may indeed be guilty of the crime, and with Miss Brown's assistance?" Colonel Forester rocked on his heels as he delivered the words in a satisfied tone.

"Colonel—"

"Explain yourself, Colonel," Colonel Fitzwilliam spoke over Bingley's protest.

"As you said yourself, Colonel, one small woman would have difficulty overtaking a man of Wickham's size. However, now we have two females. Together they could overpower a man and stab him."

"Really, Colonel, that is hardly believable," Mr. Bingley protested.

"Why conceal the fact that Miss Brown is your cousin, Miss King?" Colonel Fitzwilliam asked in a mild tone.

"Think about our situations, Colonel." Mary turned to face Fitzwilliam as she twisted her fingers in the folds of her gown. "My cousin insists on providing for herself, regardless of my new-found wealth. It is a matter of pride for her, and, while I admire her determination and respect her wishes, it would never do for our relationship to become public knowledge. People in this social circle would not understand, and trust me, it is difficult enough to gain acceptance in society without making it common knowledge that my cousin is a servant in Mr. Darcy's household." Mary stressed her words, knowing she might embarrass him, but she was desperate to clear her name.

"Mr. Darcy does not consider Miss Brown a servant."

"Perhaps Mr. Darcy is more open-minded than some other members of society. Still, Maggie wished our connection to remain a secret once we discovered we would both be attending this event." Mary waited, expecting another claim against her character.

"I say, this still does not ring true —"

"Colonel, I do not share your objection." Colonel Fitzwilliam's commanding tone left no doubt of his opinion.

"Now, see here, Fitzwilliam —"

"Enough, Colonel Forester. This constant casting of blame and chasing false leads has lasted the entire night, and still we are no closer to learning who murdered Wickham. It is time we stopped harassing helpless females and completed the job we were ask to do." Colonel Fitzwilliam turned to Bingley. "How do you stand on this, Bingley? You have heard all when we were questioning your guests."

Bingley stepped forward, "I must agree with you, Colonel. I fear we have exhausted our leads in this issue."

Colonel Fitzwilliam stared at his counterpart for a long minute. Finally, Colonel Forester gave a sharp nod of his head and tucked his chin into his chest. Colonel Fitzwilliam turned to Mary. "Miss King, please accept our apologies for any humiliation we might have caused you on this occasion. I believe we all agree you are free of any suspicion in Mr. Wickham's murder."

Chapter Nineteen

ingley returned to the library with Mr. Bennet, Sir William, and Mr. Darcy. As they sat in chairs facing the fireplace, where the two colonels were standing, Colonel Forester said, "The news is not to our liking, gentlemen. We have no suggestion as to who committed this murder."

The new arrivals exchanged looks, shifted in their chairs, and studied the two officers with stares registering their displeasure.

"Not even a suspicion after hours spent with questioning guests?" Mr. Darcy's tone was mild, but his was intense.

"The situation is not as simple as you might suppose, Darcy." Colonel Fitzwilliam's use of Darcy's name showed his irritation after a night of wasted efforts. "We spoke with all who were acquainted with Wickham and found nothing."

"Um, well, that is often the case when a crime is committed —"

"Yes, yes, Sir William, but this is a contained crime." Mr. Bennet interrupted before his friend could begin a long-winded speech as was his habit. "The murder happened under this roof and the guests were in this house. This is not some crime on the street."

"Still, there are limitations." Colonel Forester insisted. "We have only the weapon, not a reason for such a crime. We have agreed that our inquiry proves a stranger committed this crime."

"Such a possibility is not acceptable," Mr. Bennet's ire was obvious by his raised voice.

Bingley had not heard his father-in-law speak in anger since meeting him. And from the expression on Darcy's face as he stared at

Mr. Bennet, Bingley concluded Darcy, too, showed disbelief at Mr. Bennet's firm tone.

"Be that as it may," Sir William blustered, "we must accept the facts. These gentlemen have done as we requested. If they found no cause to name the killer then I believe we must conclude the murderer is not one of the guests."

"Nonsense, how can that be?" demanded Mr. Bennet. Despite their surprise at his insistence, it was obvious he had more emotional involvement in this crime than anyone in the room. With Wickham's murder, Mr. Bennet now had an extra female to provide for rather than just the two daughters still unmarried.

"Mr. Bennet, you were not in this room to suffer through the long hours of questioning." Colonel Forester's tone failed to hide his contempt for the objections. "You gentlemen sit there and condemn our failure, but you experienced none of the unpleasantness we faced this night."

"Have you not come face to face with enemies on the battlefield, Colonel Forester? Then do explain how the search for a murderer could be more difficult." Mr. Darcy rested against the back of his chair as he waited for Colonel Forester to respond.

The room went silent. Even the small blaze left in the fireplace emitted not a crackle or pop to disturb the tension filling the room.

"The blame lies outside this room, I believe —"

"Quite correct, Mr. Bingley," quick to back up Bingley's defense of their efforts, Colonel Fitzwilliam bowed to Bingley as he continued, "we have done all than we can —"

"You did not identify the murderer." Mr. Bennet's firm tone filled the room.

"Not all is lost." As soon as the words tumbled out his mouth, Bingley regretted speaking. Jane had her own reasons for wanting this crime solved quickly. He understood those reasons, but these men would not. Even Mr. Bennet, her own father, would not understand Jane's need to prove she was worthy of being his wife. Now, with a few careless words, he might have exposed her unease to others and he doubted she would forgive him for the betrayal.

"What is this nonsense you speak, Bingley? Have you not heard all the interviews and agreed we found nothing?" Colonel Forester demanded.

"Indeed, I have heard all, but there are other sources of information we should consider." Reluctantly, considering the disquieted atmosphere of the room, Bingley disclosed the fact that he and Jane had tried to discover evidence on their own.

"My wife and I have a keen interest in solving this crime, both for her sister's sake and because it occurred in our home. As host of the ball, Jane was in a position to move about and converse with guests. She hoped to discover some detail that would assist in solving the murder."

"I say, Bingley, pray explain why Mrs. Bingley thought to intrude on conversations of her guests in such a manner." Colonel Forester demanded. "I would expect any hostess to be far too distracted in seeing to her guests to have the time to listen to their conversations in such an underhanded manner."

"I consider Mrs. Bingley's actions anything but underhanded, Colonel." Mr. Darcy's voice rang with authority as he stared at Forester. "In fact, Charles, I find your course of action exceptionally clever."

"As the matter concerns Jane's family and mine, we considered it our duty to try to help." Bingley explained after receiving the nod of approval from Mr. Darcy.

"Then by all means, tell us what have you discovered?" Colonel Forester's tone barely concealed his disapproval of their actions.

Bingley paused for some length before admitting, "Not a great deal, I fear. After keen observation, we found no indication that anyone at the ball smokes a pipe." Everyone in the room turned to stare at the table where the pipe was found. "However, we discovered another guest was also making attempts to uncover the identity of the killer."

After much discussion, following Bingley's disclosure, the men agreed they should again request Miss King's presence in the library. But this time they wanted to ask for her assistance in this matter, rather than blame her for the crime.

C�ಲO

"Please, do take a seat, Miss King." Colonel Fitzwilliam said as she entered the library. All eyes turned on her, as Miss King selected the wing-backed chair nearest the door, and not a breath escaped until Colonel Fitzwilliam continued. "Mr. Bingley has informed us of your attempts to clear your name. I understand you made an effort to collect evidence to that end, and we need to inquire as to any progress you made."

Mary studied the faces around her as she considered how she

should reply. She could not reveal Maggie's private details for fear of harming her cousin. Deep in her heart she was certain Maggie would never harm Wickham. With her lips sealed on that information, all she could speak of was what she had observed with her own eyes. "When I returned from the garden with Captain Carter, we saw Miss Bingley slip out of the library."

"That is not possible. Caroline—"

"Not so fast, Bingley," Colonel Fitzwilliam commanded. "I recall Captain Carter making mention of this detail when we quested him earlier. We must reconsider all facts as we do not know the exact time Wickham was murdered. Miss King, please continue."

"I can tell you no more than what I saw."

"Perhaps you know more than you are aware of, Miss King," Colonel Fitzwilliam said in a thoughtful tone. "Why, for instance, do you use the word 'slip' to describe how Miss Bingley left the library? Did she act as if she had some reason for not wanting to be observed?"

Sending Mr. Bingley a contrite glance, Miss King replied. "Not as I recall, Colonel. In fact, I am quite certain she was in a temper."

"Are you implying she was displeased for some reason? To say you saw her slip out of the room implies she moved quietly, as if wishing to be unseen. Now you say she was in a temper. Explain yourself." Colonel Forester demanded.

"From the way Miss Bingley stomped up the stairs, Colonel, I would describe her as being in a temper." Chin lifted high, Miss King stared at Colonel Forester. "But when she came out of the library, she closed the door softly. I can only assume she did not care for other occupants of the room to know of her agitation."

"Who was in the library, Miss King? This is the first mention you have made to another occupant."

No one in the room made a sound as they waited for her response to Colonel Forester's question. The colonels and Bingley knew the answer from questioning Miss Brown, but this moment concerned what Miss King knew.

"I have no knowledge of that fact to share with you, Colonel. Miss Bingley closed the door. I could see nothing, and as Captain Carter and I were chilled, we continued up the stairs at a discrete distance behind Miss Bingley."

"You did not consider stopping in the library to warm your hands by the fire?"

"Indeed not, Colonel. As you might recall, I am a guest in this house. I knew nothing of a warm fire in this room. But I was well aware of the warmth in the ballroom."

"Miss King, we were led to believe you have information that might assist us to catch the person who murdered Mr. Wickham." Colonel Forester snapped.

"I fear I have no answers, Colonel, only more questions. Perhaps you should speak with Miss Bingley if you wish to learn more."

"Why did she say that?" Bingley demanded of Darcy as the door closed on Miss King's hasty exit.

"I know not, Charles, but we must assume your sister is in possession of some detail we need. Bring her quickly. Let this be done before full day," Darcy said in a low tone.

CR80

Caroline Bingley entered the library with the air of a queen bestowing favor on her lowly subjects. With a calm glance at the waiting audience, she said, "Ah, Darcy, I wondered where you had disappeared to."

"Miss Bingley," Colonel Forester spoke with authority, "we are not here to be sociable. This is a matter of grave concern. Someone murdered Mr. Wickham in this room, and you were observed leaving the room, about the time we believe the crime occurred. Therefore, I will speak bluntly. Did you murder Mr. Wickham?"

"Colonel, I must insist—"

"Colonel," Caroline's twittering laugh sounded over Bingley's outburst, "how entertaining of you." Far from being disconcerted by his blunt question, Miss Bingley seemed to enjoy the attention. "You must suffer from the lack of sleep if you imagine such a thing is possible." Opening her eyes wide, she continued, "You are asking questions of the wrong sister, I fear. I am not the one who stayed in the garden long after my drunken husband returned. Perhaps you should question why Mr. Hurst troubled himself to go outside when all he usually does is keep close to the punch bowl?"

"Caroline—"

"Oh, Charles, do stop worrying." Caroline snickered. "This is far more entertaining than any parlor game."

"Do you mean to imply your own sister committed this crime?" Colonel Fitzwilliam asked in a mild tone as he sent Bingley a silencing glance.

"Well, of course not," Caroline batted her eyelashes with the skill of a demure female. "Why would I consider such an act from my dear sister? I am merely suggesting you examine her husband's activities."

"Caroline, think of what you are saying." Bingley demanded. "You are as much as accusing Hurst of committing this murder."

"Oh, do be serious, Charles." Caroline rolled her eyes. "I am merely curious as to why he exerted such effort to wander about the garden."

"Do you believe Mr. Hurst had reason to harm Mr. Wickham?"

Caroline glared at Fitzwilliam. "You must ask Mr. Hurst that question, Colonel. I fear I do not have the answer."

Colonel Fitzwilliam returned her stare for several long heartbeats. "Very well, Miss Bingley, perhaps you can tell us why you entered the library instead of returning upstairs to the ballroom."

Caroline arched a brow as she stared at the colonel with a half smile on her lips. "Well, to warm myself in front of the warm fire, of course. Really, Colonel," Caroline made a snickering sound, "surely you do not think I came to read a book on the night Jane and Charles were hosting their first ball?"

"Did you see anyone else in the room when you entered?" Colonel Forester's words roared loud in the quiet room.

"Only that servant making herself welcome to the books." Caroline sniffed and eyed the colonel as if he were on a level with the offender in her opinion.

Recalling how easily Caroline became vexed, Bingley waited for the scathing comments he was certain would follow. No one escaped with the last word when disagreeing with Caroline, except Louisa. However, neither of the two colonels seemed to pay any notice to the glitter in his sister's eyes.

"Are you referring to Miss Brown?" Colonel Fitzwilliam asked in a mild tone. "Did she leave the library after your conversation with her?"

"Quite the opposite if you must know," Caroline snapped.

Colonel Fitzwilliam exchanged a glance with Colonel Forester, and turned to Bingley. "Mr. Bingley, if you would be so kind, please request your sister and Mr. Hurst to join us." He paused and looked around the room. "Perhaps we will finally get some answers."

❧

That Mrs. Hurst did not welcome the summons to return to the library was evident. She stormed in as if being forced to associate with a roomful of servants. "Really, Charles, can you not gain control this situation so your guests are not inconvenienced?"

Mr. Hurst stumbled along behind his wife and fell into a chair with a loud sigh. "Ah, there you are. What say you, Bingley?"

"Mrs. Hurst—"

"Colonel, I am aware that a certain amount of discussion is necessary, but must we have others present for the event? Why is Caroline here? Did you not finish questioning her?"

"Just listen, Louisa—"

"Mrs. Hurst," Colonel Fitzwilliam interrupted Caroline, "please describe the events of last evening so we can clear your sister of any suspicion of murder."

"Caroline? Commit a murder?" Louisa gave a mocking laugh. "Surely you are not serious, Colonel. My sister hardly knew Mr. Wickham and she is certainly not capable of committing murder."

"I say, Colonel, my wife is right on that account," Mr. Hurst's thoughts and speech seemed unhindered for a change. "In fact, between the two of them, I would venture to say Louisa has more of the temperament needed—"

"Really, Hurst, what you are saying?" Louisa's face turned the dull red of fine wine, but her husband kept speaking as if she had not said a word.

"But my wife could not have done the deed because she was in the garden with me." Mr. Hurst leaned back in his chair with a satisfied nod of his head. Only those who knew him well could detect the extra wobble that passed for a nod, Bingley decided.

"You are certain she was with you the entire time?" Colonel Forester demanded with a satisfied glance at Colonel Fitzwilliam. "If that be the case, then we are left with no one to speak on Miss Bingley's behalf."

"Now that you make mention of the fact, I seem to recall, m'wife walked to the house with Caroline. But she came back to tell me to come inside." Mr. Hurst pursed his mouth and gave an affirming nod of his head. "I had too much punch to drink, you see. Damn wicked stuff that punch is, too. Hits a blow before you figure out it is loaded."

"Mr. Hurst, are you quite certain Mrs. Hurst escorted you and Miss Bingley back to the house?"

"Aye, 'tis true," Mr. Hurst flapped his hand, "did I not just say as much?"

Colonel Forester turned to Mrs. Hurst. "Madam, did you see Mr. Wickham while you were in the garden?"

"Of course," Louisa responded in her usual clipped tone, "Caroline was speaking to Mr. Wickham when Hurst and I bumped into her in the dark."

"Your husband says you then left the garden with your sister. Was Mr. Wickham still there when you quit the garden?" Colonel Fitzwilliam asked.

Bingley heard Fitzwilliam's low tone and watched the colonel's expression change, sensing he was observing a hunter approaching his prey. Fear raced through him, for both his sisters were in the colonel's sights.

"He was in fine form, Colonel, and still conversing with my husband when I returned to the a short time later to urge Hurst to come inside."

"He was there, as well." Mr. Hurst blurted as he pointed a wobbling finger toward Colonel Forester. "Ask him. I am not certain he can vouch for Wickham's presence, but he almost trampled over me in the dark, he did."

"Sir, you are mistaken." Colonel Forester's face filled with color. "Perhaps you saw my wife and assumed I was there as well. However, I assure you I was not."

Colonel Fitzwilliam straightened to his full height as all eyes turned to rest on him. Finally, frustration heavy on each word, he said, "Mr. Bingley would you be so kind as to request the presence of all the guests we have previously questioned."

⚘

A short while later, Mrs. Forester, Captain Carter, and Denny entered the library. Miss Brown and Miss Darcy followed behind them, with Lizzy, Jane, and Miss King on their heels. Mrs. Bennet entered next, with Lydia, Kitty, and Mary close behind her.

Mrs. Bennet's entrance was all one would expect of a woman so in tune with her nerves. She wasted not a moment on polite behavior but rushed into speech. "Colonel, if you are going to put questions to my dear Lydia again—"

"Wife, come sit by me," Mr. Bennet said. "Colonel Fitzwilliam is only doing what we asked of him."

With a loud sniff, Mrs. Bennet settled down beside her husband. "You asked the colonel to prolong events surrounding poor Wickham's murder? Oh, Mr. Bennet, how could you!" Mrs. Bennet waved a hand holding a scrap of lace. "You are willing to expose my poor Lydia's nerves to the terrible events of this night all over again? It will not do, Mr. Bennet, think of her nerves. Dear Lydia is sensitive to the events around her, just as I am. She cannot bear this strain, I tell you."

Then, noticing that Kitty and Mary were hovering nearby, Mrs. Bennet said, "Oh, Kitty, Mary do stop lurking about and find a seat. You know I cannot catch a breath of air when you stay close as a shadow."

Mr. Darcy stood from his chair so Lizzy could sit. His sister perched on the arm of the chair to remain close. Jane sat in a chair nearby, with Mr. Bingley standing beside her. They all turned their attention to Colonel Fitzwilliam as he looked about the room, and then started to speak.

"This day started with little hope we would discover who murdered Mr. Wickham. However, that puts us all at risk, and I refuse to leave this matter without resolution. Therefore, I must ask the questions again. This time each of you will hear the responses. Take note if anyone gives information you know to be untrue, and speak aloud to guard your own safety." He gazed at the shocked expressions on the faces before him and continued. "Let us begin with a simple question. Who was the first person to leave the ballroom?"

Silence followed as everyone looked around at other guests. After the silence lasted several heartbeats, Captain Carter said. "I believe Wickham was first out of the ballroom."

"That sounds possible. He never liked being confined." Denny murmured.

Colonel Fitzwilliam gave a nod. "Very well, and who left the room after Wickham?"

Another silence followed, and then Mrs. Forester spoke in a timid voice, "I went out for a breath of fresh air, though I cannot be certain it was after Mr. Wickham left, for I did not see him."

Following her declaration, Denny and Captain Carter exchanged glances, but neither spoke.

"I saw my wife leave the ballroom so I broke off my conversation with Sir William and followed to ensure her safety." Colonel Forester added.

Frowning at hearing the claim, Colonel Fitzwilliam said. "I do not recall your departure being mentioned in earlier questioning, Colonel."

"It seemed of no importance." Colonel Forester shrugged. "I heard Wickham's voice, but did not pay any mind. I was intent on protecting my wife in the darkness, not encounter a murderer."

"And yet, a murder occurred last evening." Colonel Fitzwilliam turned. "Mrs. Forester, were you not uneasy at walking alone in the dark?"

Mrs. Forester lifted her chin, "Really, Colonel, I am married to a commanding officer of the militia. I cannot show fear of a little thing such as a dark garden."

"At least we can confirm Mr. Wickham was in the garden, inasmuch as you heard him speak, Colonel." Colonel Fitzwilliam paced a few steps, and turned back. "Who left the ballroom behind Colonel Forester?"

"I followed Mrs. Forester," Lydia said as she glared at her former friend. "I wanted to speak with Harriet in private."

Denny cleared his throat and spoke up. "I followed after Wickham so we could have a chance to talk."

"Was there anything of consequence intended by your desire for conversation, Mr. Denny?"

"Only time to converse with an old friend, Colonel," Denny said with a shake of his head. "We had no chance to make conversation because we were dancing, and I thought to spend some time with him. Yet once I reached the garden, it was so dark I could not find Wickham."

"Colonel, I left the ballroom after Denny," Captain Carter said, "but it was so the dark I could not find Denny or Wickham."

Ignoring the distraction of Captain Carter's comment, Colonel Fitzwilliam turned back to Denny and said. "Mr. Denny, were you intending to demand payment for the gambling debt Mr. Wickham owed you, by any chance?"

Shrugging, Denny gave a reluctant nod. "In part, but we were friends, and it seemed a good time to talk over times since we last met."

"Yet you were observed conversing with Mr. Wickham in the ballroom before he left to go outside. Did you not have enough of each other's company?"

"Colonel, before Wickham left Brighton to join a northern regiment, we spent most of our days in each other's company. A few words between dances did not compare. We arranged to met outside." Denny held Colonel Fitzwilliam's gaze without blinking.

"Colonel, if you must have all the details or threaten us with claims of being a murderer," Caroline drew her words out with exaggerated slowness, "I observed Captain Carter leave the ballroom and followed him to secure an escort for a stroll in the garden to cool off."

"Yet you made no mention plan when we spoke earlier, Miss Bingley." Colonel Fitzwilliam said. "Did you meet with Captain Carter in the garden? I ask because of all the other claims of not being able to see in the dark."

"I am afraid I did not." Caroline waved an elegant hand. "It was too dark and even though others said they left before I did, I saw only Mr. Wickham."

"Ah," was Colonel Fitzwilliam's only response before he turned to his fellow officer. "Any questions you wish to ask, Colonel Forester?"

"As I am not of a mind as to your reasoning, Colonel, carry on if you will." Colonel Forester lifted a shoulder and stepped closer to his wife.

"Several guests are still unaccounted for," Colonel Fitzwilliam said as he looked around the room. "Who left the ballroom after Miss Bingley?"

"I followed Caroline," Mrs. Hurst said. "I thought to accompany her as it was dark and I, too, wished to get some refreshing air. I was not aware of her plan to meet with Captain Carter."

Caroline rolled her eyes. "There was no plan, Louisa. I simply saw the Captain leave and wanted to walk with him for safety."

"Aye, but I had a plan." Mr. Hurst blurted. "My wife left the room so I quit the group I was talking with and followed her. Wanted to make certain she was not in the dark alone."

"Alone, Mr. Hurst, or did you suspect your wife was meeting someone?" Colonel Fitzwilliam asked.

"Why the dickens would you say that?" Mr. Hurst demanded. "Easy to tell you have no worry of a wife, if you can come up with such ideas as that."

"Forgive my plain speaking, Mr. Hurst, but you would have us believe that, even after you drained a goodly portion from the punch bowl, you still gave conscious thought to protecting your wife?"

"'Tis a fact, sir." Mr. Hurst puffed out his chest and raised his chin high. "Makes no matter the amount I drink, m'wife deserves protection. Moreover, I vouch for what Forester said. It was darker than Hades in that garden. Why the Colonel there almost trampled me in the dark, and him a trained militia man."

"Um, very well, as you say it was a dark night. Who left the ballroom after Mr. Hurst?" Colonel Fitzwilliam asked.

Kitty raised a trembling hand and said, "I might have done."

"Or it could have been me, for I paid no notice of Kitty leaving, but I wanted a private word with Lydia." Lizzy said.

"So, Mrs. Darcy followed her sister, Lydia," Colonel Fitzwilliam frowned as he turned to Kitty. "And who did you follow, Miss Bennet?"

Kitty's face filled with rosy color as both her parents turned to stare at her, but she angled her chin and replied in a firm tone, "I followed Denny. Since Lydia is married, I thought he might notice me."

"Kitty Bennet —"

"Miss Bennet, did you find Mr. Denny when you arrived in the garden?"

"No, but I saw Miss King lurking about in the shadows after I lost sight of Denny."

Colonel Fitzwilliam turned to Miss King, "Miss King, we have no mention of you leaving the ballroom."

"I followed Captain Carter." Color filled Miss King's face as she met Colonel Fitzwilliam's probing stare. "I wished a quiet word with him as we are both staying at Lucas Lodge."

Colonel Fitzwilliam rubbed his chin as a frown wrinkled his brow. Lips pursed, he studied Miss King for a several long heartbeats, before turning back to Kitty. "Miss Bennet, after you observed Miss King in the garden what happened?"

"I, uh, I heard loud voices in a far corner of the garden and stopped walking. It was very dark, you see, and I was frightened."

"Did you recognize the voices?" Colonel Fitzwilliam asked in a low voice.

Kitty glanced about her then rushed into speech, "It was Mr. Hurst and Wickham."

"What say you, girl?" Mr. Hurst thumped the arm of his chair as he stared about the room. "What is the meaning of this?"

Mrs. Hurst placed her hand on his arm. "Do be quiet, Mr. Hurst. You were full of punch at the time. Pray say no words you might regret."

"Good advice, Mrs. Hurst, but I am curious as to why you feel it necessary to caution your husband to mind his words." Brows lifted,

Colonel Fitzwilliam waited for Mrs. Hurst to respond, but her husband finally rallied his senses and burst into speech.

"Madam, why do you say such? I was in complete control of my faculties and I would appreciate it if you did not make me sound out of my head."

Colonel Fitzwilliam turned a questioning glance on Mrs. Hurst, but her only response was a sniff as she pinched her lips tight and angled her chin. Lifting one shoulder to show his resignation at her lack of response, the colonel turned back to Kitty. "Miss Bennet, if you please, tell me again, did you overhear the conversation or just the noise?"

Chewing her lip, Kitty darted a glance at her parents, then rushed to say, "Mr. Hurst warned Wickham to stay away from his wife."

"What the—"

"Stay away from his wife?" Mrs. Bennet's voice rose. "What nonsense is this you speak, Kitty? Wickham had a wife so why would he bother with another woman?"

Colonel Fitzwilliam exchanged a glance with several men in the room. Then with a bland expression, he turned to the man in question. "Indeed, Mr. Hurst why did you see fit to warn Mr. Wickham to stay away from your wife?"

"Colonel, pray pay no mind to what Hurst says. He consumes too little food and too much drink, and then talks out of his head." Mrs. Hurst blurted.

"Quite right, wife, but my head was not muddled by drink and I was not in my cups when I last spoke to Wickham."

As everyone in the room had observed the condition of Mr. Hurst the evening before, Colonel Fitzwilliam ignored the man's claims and turned back to Kitty. "What happened next, Miss Bennet?"

Kitty's face lost color as she glanced about her. Then, after an obvious struggle, she regained the ability to speak. "I was shocked by what Mr. Hurst said so I turned to run inside and bumped into Lizzy."

"Was Mrs. Darcy alone?"

"What? Oh, yes, she was looking for Lydia."

"Do you have any thought as to why Mrs. Darcy wanted to find Mrs. Wickham?"

"There is no need to badger Kitty. I will answer that question,

Colonel." Lydia turned to glare at Lizzy. "Lizzy said I should to stop Wickham from asking Darcy for money." Lydia expelled a sound of ridicule mixed with humor. "Can you imagine, with all of Darcy's fortune, Lizzy claimed he has done enough for Wickham."

After a long thoughtful study of Lydia, Colonel Fitzwilliam turned his attention back to Kitty. "Miss Bennet, did you tell Mrs. Darcy what you had overheard?"

"No. I wanted to, but when I bumped into Lizzy, she was with Lydia. As I had no wish to start a row, I kept quiet until I could speak with Lizzy alone. But I think my sisters were arguing when I bumped into them."

Colonel Fitzwilliam studied the three sisters and finally turned back to Kitty. "Do you have any thoughts as to why they were quarreling?"

Kitty shrugged. "Same as Lydia said, I suppose. Lizzy's always going on about how we should behave, and since Lydia married Wickham, she is always complaining about not having enough money."

"Very well, Miss Bennet, I will repeat my first question. Why did you follow Mr. Denny to the garden?"

"Because...because I wanted to talk to him." Kitty's cheeks filled with glowing color. "Lydia was vexed when she arrived at the ball and spared no time for me. Lizzy and Jane were talking or with their their husbands and I was lonely. Denny is entertaining so I thought perhaps, now that Lydia is married, he might show interest in me."

"How did Denny respond, Miss Bennet?"

"Please, Colonel," Jane raised her voice and spoke for the first time. "Kitty has answered enough questions. Clearly, she had nothing to do with the night's events. Can you not turn your attention from her wishful thoughts and proceed?"

"I'll have you know I found Denny in the dark." Kitty snapped as she glared at Jane, then she turned to the colonel. "No one else could find who they were looking for, but I did." She turned to face the Colonel. "And for your information, Denny had no interest in speaking to me. He was too intent on following Mrs. Forester."

"Kitty Bennet, watch your tongue," Lydia snapped.

"Really, Miss Bennet, how you do go on," Mrs. Forester replied in a fluttering tone. "Surely, Colonel, you will pay no regard to this young girl's observances."

"I tell you, I speak the truth." Kitty glared at the people staring back at her. "Ever since the guests from Lucas Lodge arrived, Denny has hovered around Harriet Forester as if she were the only woman in the room. And it's not fair." Kitty's voice rose. "Harriet is married. Yet she makes eyes at other men right in her husband's face. If you think I am mistaken, look how she paid attention to Wickham before he married Lydia. Maybe she continued after he married Lydia, for all I know. Then tonight, here comes Denny trailing after Harriet, ignoring me, and I am unmarried."

Silence settled over the room as the guests stared at Kitty when she finally stopped speaking. Despite the shine in her cheeks and a need for air, Kitty did not shrink from the weight of their attention. Rather, she seemed to grow taller and lifted her chin in a defiant angle. "I speak only the truth."

"My poor Kitty," Mrs. Bennet sniffed as she watched her daughter with a compassion usually in short supply.

"Child, come here," Mr. Bennet said as he motioned for Kitty to sit on the arm of his chair.

Yet the loudest response came from across the room. The sound rose high enough to cover the concerned murmurs from Kitty's parents, and all heads swiveled to stare at the speaker.

"Kitty Bennet, how can you say such vile things? I believed us to be friends," Mrs. Forester cried. "I am married to the commanding officer the regiment. I must appear friendly with men in his command—"

"Not as friendly as you get," Lydia snapped. "Pray, do not forget, I was there. I know you fancied Wickham before the regiment moved to Brighton."

"What is this nonsense?" demanded Colonel Forester. "More claims from a woman gone mad with grief at losing her husband?"

"Let us focus on the murder investigation," Colonel Fitzwilliam raised his voice to be heard and then turned to Mary King. "Miss King, why did you wish to speak with Captain Carter?"

"My reasons were of a personal nature, Colonel, and I cannot think why you would ask me to expose them to common judgment."

"Colonel," Jane raised her voice over continued whispers about the room, "Miss King wishes to keep her reasons to herself, as is her right. But in the interest of discovering who murdered Mr. Wickham, I believe I can answer your question." Jane paused to study Mary King for a long heartbeat. Finally, after an obvious battle of wills, Miss King tilted of her head in agreement, and Jane turned back to the colonel. "I believe Miss King wished to obtain Captain Carter's assistance in a personal matter."

Colonel Fitzwilliam glanced from Jane to Miss King and back. "Even so, I fear I cannot leave the matter unheard. I must ask for an explanation, Mrs. Bingley."

"Then I must request Miss King's consent to continue." Jane's glance returned to Miss King. After a pause, Mary turned a questioning glance to Miss Brown. Long ticks of the clock later, Mary received a slight nod from her cousin.

Miss King met the colonel's questioning gaze. "Are you certain this is necessary, Colonel? I assure you this is a personal matter that has nothing to do with Mr. Wickham's murder."

"For the sake of all concerned, I must insist on an explanation, Miss King."

"Very well, Colonel. I followed Captain Carter because I wished to gain his assistance in forcing Mr. Wickham to acknowledge the birth of his son."

Shocked gasps filled the room.

"No!" Lydia jumped up from her chair and stomped her foot. "Not one word she says is true. My Wickham would not — "

"How can you say such a thing about dear Wickham at a time like this?" Mrs. Bennet cried. "Has my poor Lydia not suffered enough."

"What is the meaning of this assertion," Mrs. Forester demanded. "I would know — "

"Young lady, I know not what you hope to gain by discrediting my daughter's husband with this claim." Mr. Bennet's voice rose over Mrs. Forester's objections and caught the attention of all who believed they knew him to be a man of a mild disposition.

However, one set of eyes in the room aimed not at Mr. Bennet, but at the raging Mrs. Forester. That Colonel Forester was vexed by his wife's outburst was obvious from color tinting his face to match his uniform.

Yet even with all the unsettled emotions aimed in her direction, Miss King did not withdraw her claim as she returned their stares.

Chapter Twenty

$\mathcal{W}$hat of the good name of my cousin, sir? Have you no compassion for the woman your daughter's husband wronged?" Miss King rose out of her chair and stood tall as she confronted Mr. Bennet.

"Once society discovers she gave birth to a child without benefit of marriage, what future will she have? How can she provide for her child when she is turned away from work?" Miss King's voice filled with emotion. "I did not make this claim lightly. But my cousin was treated poorly and all she did wrong was to give her love to the wrong man."

"I will not hear such words," Lydia wailed. "My Wickham did not father that woman's child. He loved me! I know he did." She gasped for breath as she turned a fierce glare on Miss King. "You wanted Wickham from the night you first met. Before he loved me, you stole him from Lizzy and not a word of what you say is true."

"Oh, my poor Lydia, do calm yourself, child. Ignore this woman's claim. She will receive her just due, for I am certain dear Wickham would never look at a female with such red hair." Mrs. Bennet said.

"Wickham's child is that of my cousin, Maggie, not my own, Mrs. Bennet."

"So you say, but how can we believe your words? Dear Wickham never mentioned a child. Why would we believe you about this cousin when it is obvious you make these claims to protect your own reputation?"

"Your words imply that you accept Wickham has fathered a son, else why would you accuse me of protecting my reputation." Miss King said in a level tone.

Mrs. Bennet opened her eyes wide as she stammered, "Why, I never said such a thing. Oh!" Mrs. Bennet flapped the bit of lace handkerchief in front of her face. "Oh, Mr. Bennet, say something."

"I believe you have said enough for the both of us, my dear." Mr. Bennet's usual placid demeanor was back in place. "Do calm yourself, my dear."

A new voice spoke into the growing disquiet of the room. The slight quiver in Miss Brown's voice silenced the whispers Mrs. Bennet's tantrum started.

"It is not Mary's reputation she is attempting to protect, but mine." Miss Brown met the stares aimed in her direction. "And that of my son, Wickham's child."

"How can such a claim be correct," Mrs. Hurst demanded in the stunned silence following Miss Brown's words. "Mr. Wickham moved up north, did he not?"

"How could my husband know you? Before this ball, I have never seen you." Lydia cried.

"Mrs. Wickham, I am deeply sorry for your loss and the pain this night brought upon you, but I am Miss Darcy's companion. Wickham was a frequent visitor at Pemberley, while he tried to ruin that young girl's reputation. That is how we met."

"This cannot be," Lydia insisted. "We have known Wickham for two years, at least. How old is the child you claim as his?"

"My son is but an infant," Miss Brown stated in a stronger tone. "Not yet eight months born."

"Eight months?" Lydia's gasp sounded loud in the sudden silence. Even she could work out the meaning of such a claim. Miss Brown's connection with Wickham occurred before Lydia claimed his interest. She whirled to Miss King. "This happened while he was betrothed to you."

Miss King's face drained of all color as she clamped her lips together. Miss Brown glanced at her cousin, and then gave a nod to acknowledge Lydia's words were true. "Much as it pains me, I am forced to admit this is true."

Lydia let lose one of her bursts of uncontrollable laughter. "So, Miss King could not keep Wickham's interest, even with her large inheritance." She doubled over with laughter. "I could not imagine how Wickham could admired that red hair —"

"Miss Brown," Colonel Fitzwilliam sent Lydia a frown as he interrupted her careless remarks, "I must agree with those who question the plausibility of your claim and ask that you enlighten us as to how this happened."

Miss Brown turned to speak to Mr. Darcy and Georgiana. "I regret this matter came to light in such a public manner, Mr. Darcy. But while Mr. Wickham was visiting Miss Georgiana at Pemberley, my feelings for him led to my poor judgment."

"Speak as you must, Miss Brown. It is past time for Wickham's total disregard of decent behavior to come to light," Darcy said.

"What is the meaning of this, Darcy? Why are you not defending Wickham? Why have you turned against him?" Lydia demanded. Then she turned her irritation on her sister. "This is your fault, Lizzy. You turned Darcy against Wickham."

"Lizzy, how could you do such a thing to your sister and her only just married to Wickham?" Mrs. Bennet demanded.

"Do hush, wife, and you as well, Lydia. None of this has to do with Lizzy. This all lands at the feet of that charmer Lydia insisted on having for a husband," Mr. Bennet announced with a nod. "Let this woman speak."

"You tell me to hush when my heart is broken?" Tears rolled down Lydia's face as she faced her father. "You always take up for Lizzy, even when my Wickham is dead."

Mr. Bennet rose from his chair and moved to Lydia's side. Placing an arm around her shoulders in a fatherly hug, he murmured, "Calm yourself, child. You suffer now, but this display of emotions helps nothing. We must discover who murdered Wickham."

Miss Brown's face crumpled in reaction to the emotional display. "I betrayed my cousin and myself. I wanted only for Mr. Wickham to acknowledge his son. I would never harm him."

"I believe we have solved the question of who murdered Mr. Wickham, do you not agree, Colonel Fitzwilliam?" Colonel Forester wore a satisfied smile as he turned to the distressed woman. "We have proof Miss Brown and Wickham were in this room and the letter opener was in plain view, according to Mr. Bingley. Miss Brown we find you guilty of murder."

"No! This cannot be." Miss King jumped back to her feet. "Maggie could never harm the man she loved. She betrayed her personal beliefs and the relationship we shared. She gave up any chance of having a future and she did all this because she loved Wickham. She would never harm him."

"What you say is understandable, Miss King, but so is the fact that we have found no other suspects. That being the case we are left with one conclusion," Colonel Fitzwilliam's tone rang with reluctance.

"I beg to disagree, Colonel Fitzwilliam. Think of all you have heard in this room." Miss King waved an arm. "What of the other two women who were quick to defend Wickham? Both are married women, and either one of their husbands could have murdered Wickham out of jealousy."

Colonel Fitzwilliam met the plea in Miss King's gaze as he pondered her words.

Colonel Forester snorted. "Nonsense. We discovered all we need to prove your cousin is guilty of murder."

"A moment if you please, Colonel." Colonel Fitzwilliam held up a staying hand. "Surely there is no need to rush to a conclusion. We have been this long, perhaps we should hear what Miss King has to suggest."

Miss King looked at the people staring at her and continued. "It is my belief that you should interrogate Mr. Hurst and Colonel Forester."

"Very well," Fitzwilliam gave a nod to acknowledged her suggestion and turned to the guests in the room. "Mrs. Hurst, did you arrange to meet Mr. Wickham in the garden?"

Mrs. Hurst gasped and turned the color of clotted cream.

Bingley sprang forward to defend his sister, "Colonel, is this necessary — "

"This is outrageous," Colonel Forester objected loudly, interrupting Bingley's courteous tone.

"Gentlemen, if you please," Colonel Fitzwilliam aimed a forceful glance at each man. "I will ask these questions in an attempt to discover the truth." Then he returned his attention to Mrs. Hurst and demanded, "Madam, if you will respond, please?"

"I simply followed my sister out for a refreshing breather after the smoky, stale air in the ballroom, Colonel. Perhaps Caroline arranged to meet Wickham, but I did not."

Colonel Fitzwilliam turned away without a response and said, "Mr. Hurst, you were heard issuing a threat to Mr. Wickham. What brought about the confrontation?"

"There was no confrontation. I said what I said and I stand by it. A man must defend his own, Colonel. As a man in uniform you should understand that."

"It is a fact, the militia defends our rights, Mr. Hurst, but I am not so quick to agree to such in personal matters." Colonel Fitzwilliam turned to Caroline. "Miss Bingley, why did you meet Mr. Wickham in the garden?"

"Really, Colonel, a female would understand why any woman would want to be with Mr. Wickham." Caroline twittered.

"Why is she saying such things about my Wickham?" Lydia wailed as she looked at her father.

Mrs. Bennet's cheeks flushed as she turned a bright glance on her daughter.. "Hush, child. You should understand such opinions after being married to dear Wickham."

Mr. Bennet studied his wife's flushed complexion and rolled his eyes. "Never mind, child. We must allow Colonel Fitzwilliam to deal with this matter."

Colonel Fitzwilliam arched a brow and leveled his glance on Caroline. "Miss Bingley?"

"If you must know, I wanted to speak with Wickham to ask for his help," Caroline snapped. When Colonel Fitzwilliam lifted his brow higher, she huffed. "I wanted to ask him to flirt with me when the dancing resumed."

"Why—"

"I am confused," Colonel Fitzwilliam said as he sent Lydia a sharp glance to stop her words. Then he turned back to Caroline. "Miss Bingley, why did you ask a married man to act in such a manner?"

"I had my reasons, and they are none of your concern, Colonel. They are in no way connected to this murder."

"Perhaps your request led someone to murder Mr. Wickham." Colonel Fitzwilliam replied as he held her stare.

"Very well, if you must know, Colonel." Caroline rolled her eyes and a hint of color tinted her cheeks as she rushed to say, "I wanted Wickham to flirt with me to make Darcy jealous."

"Make Darcy jealous?" Colonel Fitzwilliam tried to conceal a laugh as he sent Darcy a glance. Then he returned his attention to Caroline. "Explain yourself, please."

Color deepened her cheeks, but Caroline angled her chin high and shrugged one shoulder. "If a man as handsome as Mr. Wickham found me desirable, I believed Darcy would realize what he gave up when he married Eliza Bennet. And before you ask, Colonel, if Wickham had refused to help, I intended to ask Captain Carter's assistance."

"Did Mr. Wickham refuse to act as you wanted? Did you murder him in anger?"

A snort escaped Caroline. "Really, Colonel, you have been in the military too long. Perhaps you failed to notice, but I carry no weapon." Caroline lifted a shoulder and sighed.

"Perhaps you picked up this letter opener from the desk and stabbed him." Colonel Fitzwilliam turned a grim gaze on her.

"It is true that I knew of the letter opener, but why do I not have blood on my gown? This is only wasted conjecture, Colonel, for I missed the chance to speak to Wickham when my sister appeared quite unexpectedly."

"Can you give an account of events after your sister arrived?"

"There was nothing to cause interest, if that is what you are implying. Before we could exchange two words, Hurst came blundering down the path and accused Louisa of arranging to meet Wickham. Louisa and I left Hurst staggering around Wickham's shadow and made a hasty retreat."

"Did Mr. Hurst have time to murder Mr. Wickham after you departed?"

"What nonsense. Hurst was so far in his cups he could hardly stand. How could he move a body? And Louisa's conscience stopped her departure, before we were halfway back to the house. She returned to fetch Mr. Hurst back inside, so I entered the house alone."

"Mrs. Hurst, when you returned to your husband, did you find Mr. Wickham free of harm?"

"Of course, my husband had since departed, and Mr. Wickham was quite healthy."

Colonel Fitzwilliam paused to consider the gushing tone of Mrs. Hurst's reply. Then he asked, "Did you immediately seek out your husband's whereabouts?"

Louisa blinked rapidly, then sent the colonel a catlike smile. "Really, Colonel, you must realize married women sometimes find themselves weak in the presence of such charm as Mr. Wickham possessed. Surely you are aware of such things, being a man in uniform."

"Ohoo! Why does she say such things about my husband?" Lydia wailed.

"Mrs. Hurst, if you will please confine your comment to what occurred last evening? We are searching for a murderer. To the best of your knowledge, was Wickham alive and free of injury when you last saw him?"

"Colonel, I assure you Mr. Wickham was in fine form when last I saw him." Her words caused not a few snickers in response, as well as sniffs of disapproval.

"This is not fair!" Lydia wailed amid gasps of shock and muffled comments. "Wickham was my husband. Why can she not chase after her own husband?"

Colonel Fitzwilliam met Bingley's distressed gaze, then turned his attention to the task at hand. "Mrs. Forester, I believe you enjoyed a close relationship with Mr. Wickham, as well."

"Now, see here, Fitzwilliam," Colonel Forester roared.

"Husband, I will respond to this, if you please." Mrs. Forester glanced at her husband's set expression, angled her chin, and turned a hard glare on Colonel Fitzwilliam. "Colonel, as wife of the commanding officer, it is my duty to associate with his men and assist in keeping morale up in these troubled times."

"Is this account written in some manual of wifely-duties, Mrs. Forester, or a goal of your own undertaking?"

Lydia snickered, as did several other occupants of the room.

"Really! Colonel, I am quite certain I have not a thought as to what you imply."

"Then perhaps I should speak bluntly." Fitzwilliam met Colonel Forester's furious glare and continued, "Mrs. Forester, exactly how well acquainted were you and Mr. Wickham?"

"Well enough, sir, especially as he and Lydia were a special friends of mine." Mrs. Forester lifted a shoulder. "For that reason, it is possible we spent more time in Mr. Wickham's company than with other members of the regiment. But, of course, our association ended when Lydia and Wickham moved to a northern regiment."

"Do we have your word that this is a forthright description of your connection with Mr. Wickham?" Colonel Fitzwilliam demanded. As Mrs. Forester slowly tilted her head, Colonel Fitzwilliam turned to her husband. "Colonel Forester, are you in agreement with your wife's portrayal of her dealings with Mr. Wickham?"

"Of course, my wife gave an apt account of her relationship to Wickham. Now, Colonel, I suggest we question the real murderer and obtain details from Miss Brown."

"Colonel Fitzwilliam, I beg you to think again of this claim, before you make such a charge against my cousin." Miss King's eyes glowed green with emotion as she continued. "Maggie could never kill anyone, and especially not the father of her child."

Colonel Fitzwilliam studied Miss King in the sudden quiet that followed her words. Then, with a deep sigh, he straightened his shoulders and turned to his ward's companion.

"Miss Brown, were you angered by Mr. Wickham's interest in your cousin after he had lured you into an indiscretion?" Colonel Fitzwilliam paused and then added, "Before you respond, I will state that most women I know would be extremely upset if they discovered the father of their child had plans to marry another woman."

Tears rolled down Miss Brown's face as she turned a saddened glance on Miss King. "Much as I wish to deny it, the colonel speaks the truth, Mary. I was angry and hurt, but you never said an unkind word to me, even when I arrived at your door with a newborn child in my arms." Miss Brown turned wide eyes on Colonel Fitzwilliam. "But I did not hurt him, Colonel. I could never harm Wickham or Mary. I told her nothing about the father of my child until she ended her betrothal to Wickham."

"If I understand the situation correctly, Miss Brown, you had other reasons to be envious of your cousin. Perhaps you wished to hurt her by forming the relationship with Wickham. Were you not vexed to discover she inherited a fortune? Did you wish to ruin her relationship with Wickham by claiming he was the father of your child?"

"No! Colonel, I could not!"

"Is it even true that Wickham fathered your child, Miss Brown?"

Miss King gasped, outraged at the cruelty of the question, and whirled on Colonel Fitzwilliam ready to defend her cousin. "Colonel, how could — "

"Hush, Mary," Miss Brown said as she reached for Mary's hand. Tears rolled down her cheeks as she looked in Mary's eyes. "The colonel is right. I have been hiding the truth from you and I have suffered the pain of my dishonesty these past months. I beg you. Please do not be furious with me — "

"You carried on an indiscretion with Mr. Wickham," Caroline announced over Miss Brown's halting confession, "for I discovered you snuggling in the hallway at Pemberley."

"It is true. I fell for Wickham's charm, while he was trying to lead Miss Georgiana astray." Miss Brown swallowed a sob and turned to her cousin. "How foolish is that, Mary? I tried to gain his favor, even then, but to no avail. Then you formed an attachment with him, and next I knew, you announced plans to marry him. You were going to marry the man I loved."

Not a whisper of sound disturbed the room, except for Miss Brown's gasps for air.

Mary pulled her hand from Maggie's grip and leaned back to stare at her cousin in surprise. "But, what sense does this make? I had no knowledge of your feeling for him when I agreed to marry Mr. Wickham. Yet you had the child. How can you now claim it to be a lie?"

"Oh, Mary, I am so sorry. But the lie is my claim of being a mother, for I was false with you from the start on that matter." Miss Brown leaned close to force Miss King. "I planned not of this. Please believe me."

"But...how can this be, Maggie? How can I believe a word you say now?" Miss King stared out of a face pale as porcelain. "The child is under my roof even as we speak."

"Do you recall sending for me when your uncle fell ill? It was on the trip home that this all started. A young girl in the coach was heavy with child. When she fell into childbirth, being the only woman available, I had to assist in her delivery. It was a most difficult birth and the mother very young. Not long after birthing a healthy son, she died." Miss Brown glanced down as she twisted her hands in her lap.

"After assisting with the babe's entry into the world, I felt a duty to the infant when his mother died. So I agreed to take the unwanted child when none of the other passengers wanted to help. On the journey home, I realized what I had done. I was unmarried and appearing with a babe would bring shame upon my head. It was then that I realized I now had found a way to force Wickham to turn his attention back to me."

"Maggie! How could you allow me to think you had committed such an indiscretion when none of it was true? And the poor babe? What is to become of him now that he is not needed in your ploy to capture Wickham's interest?"

"Did I not tell you?" Lydia cried. "I knew Wickham did not father another woman's child."

"That is why I found you lounging about the library last evening?" Miss Bingley demanded. "You hoped to meet Wickham? But to what end as he already had a wife?"

"I made no plan but to fill the time while Miss Georgiana was at the ball." Miss Brown glanced toward Miss Darcy. "I asked permission to look for a book to read while she attended the party. The room was so warm, I curled up in that chair to read." She pointed to a wingback chair on the far side of the room.

"What is this nonsense?" Colonel Forester demanded. "Why should we listen to more of this drivel when the woman admitted, with her own words, that she lied?"

"Even so, Colonel, we must discover what she knows." Colonel Fitzwilliam turned and, asked in a low voice, "Miss Brown, what occurred next?"

After only a slight hesitation, Miss King reached for Miss Brown's hand and gave it a squeeze. The cousins exchanged a long glance.

Then Miss Brown continued. "Miss Bingley came in and was quite disturbed at finding me in the room. After making her displeasure known to me, she left the room and I returned to reading my book, but I must have fallen asleep."

Mrs. Hurst made a loud sniff. "Any servant worth her salt would have taken leave of the room before Caroline finished speaking."

Colonel Fitzwilliam silenced Mrs. Hurst with a frown and said, "Miss Brown, please, continue."

Miss Brown's voice quivered as she lifted her head and looked at the colonel. "A noise at the door alerted me that I was not alone. After the previous encounter, when my presence brought Miss Bingley's ire upon my head, I remained quiet. Not that I felt I was doing anything wrong by reading in the library, but I was not eager to suffer another lecture. So I kept quiet in the warmth of the room and allowed the newcomer to do the same."

"Well, stop all this dithering, woman and tell us who came in," Mrs. Bennet exclaimed.

"I saw no one." Miss Brown's gaze was steady as she met the stares aimed in her direction.

"How can that be?" Miss Bingley demanded. "When I entered, it was obvious you were aware of my presence. Perhaps this is another of your lies."

"Caroline, please—"

"Stop the prattle and allow Miss Brown to speak." Colonel Fitz-william's command. Bingley's protest was interrupted by

"Colonel, it is as Miss Bingley suggested, I stayed out of sight behind the wing of the chair. But I heard footsteps cross the room toward that chair in the far corner." Miss Brown pointed to the chair beside the table where Bingley had found the pipe. "I knew of the location because I had considered curling up in that comfortable looking chair when I arrived. But the shadows around the chair would not allow me to read and the chair I picked was comfortable."

"Your comfort is of no importance," Lydia exclaimed. "Who came into the room?"

"I saw no one. I stayed quiet and kept out of sight. After a time, I smelled the scent of pipe tobacco. Considering the heavy footsteps I heard earlier, I believed the other occupant was a man and felt I had even more reason to remain quiet. He remained silent, as well, and after observing how some guests behave at parties, I believed he must be waiting for a woman. So I filled the silence by trying to guess who he was, until finally, curiosity got the better of my good judgment. I peeped around the arm of the chair."

"All this blathering about nothing is very trying for my nerves." Mrs. Bennet fanned her face with her handkerchief.

"Wife, your nerves become active at the most inconvenient times. Do give them a rest and let the poor woman continue."

After aiming a glare at Mrs. Bennet, Colonel Fitzwilliam said, "Do continue, Miss Brown."

"The man was but a shadowy figure as he leaned back in the chair and smoked his pipe."

"What nonsense is this?" Colonel Forester exclaimed.

Mrs. Forester sent her husband a warning glance, then turned to Miss Brown and demanded. "Were you not frightened at being closed in the room with a stranger, and so far from the guests?"

"Indeed, I was. My heart was thudding so loudly I was certain he would hear. But I strained hard to view the man's features so I might identify him if need be."

"Whatever did you expect?" Mrs. Hurst demanded. "That some man might take offense at you making free use of the house belonging your employer's host?"

Caroline Bingley sniffed. "I am of the opinion that servants should stay in their rightful place."

"What place do you refer to, Miss Bingley?" Lizzy demanded. "Miss Brown secured permission to use the books in this room."

"Miss Brown is my sister's companion and in no way considered a servant." Mr. Darcy's voice rang with a finality that told all within hearing the matter was not to receive mention again. After a pause, while he stared at each guest in turn, Mr. Darcy turned to Miss Brown. "Please continue."

"I was interested in seeing only a man I knew. My cousin was certain Wickham would be a guest at this event. So I made an effort to see through the shadows and smoke to discover if this might be him. Though, I confess I had little hope, for I did not recall ever seeing him smoke a pipe."

"I cannot bear to hear more of this nonsense," Lydia wailed. "She has no right to speak of my husband in that familiar manner."

"I agree with Mrs. Wickham, for once." Colonel Forester's voice rang loudly in the room. "Why waste time listening to a woman who is most likely the murderer? I say we turn her over to the magistrate and be done with this madness."

Colonel Fitzwilliam ignored the interruption and returned his attention to Miss Brown. "Was Mr. Wickham the man you observed?"

"Much to my sorrow, it was not. When the man leaned forward to put his pipe on the table, his features were easily visible."

"Who was it? Stop your blathering and speak." Mrs. Bennet said.

Colonel Fitzwilliam took a step closer. "Miss Brown, please continue."

"The man was a stranger to me. Since it was not Wickham, I leaned back in my chair, out of his view, and mulled over my disappointment." Miss Brown cleared her throat. "Why had I expected the man I wanted most to meet would be easy to make contact with? In my world, men take advantage of women who seek employment to support themselves. There is only a meeting between them if that is what the man wishes. I learned this to be true, to my sorrow, and yet I hoped things would be different if only I could speak with Mr. Wickham."

"A load of poppycock and empty hopes, if you ask me," Mrs. Hurst tossed her head. "Had you not put yourself forward in such a manner, this would never have happened."

Carol Hutchens

"Are you giving a lesson in morals, Mrs. Hurst?" Lizzy demanded. "Can you forget the lecture and allow the identity of the murder to be disclosed?"

Mrs. Hurst tossed her head with an energy promising ill for someone in the near future, but Lizzy ignored her and turned to Miss Brown. "Please do continue, Miss Brown."

"There is no proof this man is guilty," Colonel Forester insisted before Miss Brown could open her mouth to speak.

"All the more reason for us to hear what Miss Brown has to say, do you not agree, Colonel?" Fitzwilliam returned his attention to Miss Darcy's companion. "Please continue, Miss Brown."

"With the warmth of the room, and the need to remain quiet, I must have drifted off to sleep, for the next thing I recall is the sound of the door opening. The noise must have startled me awake and then I heard someone enter the room. At first, I thought it was the man with the pipe leaving. Then I heard a man speak."

"Was it Wickham? Who was he speaking to?" Lydia slipped to the edge of her seat. "Or was it you who murdered my husband?"

"I am not the murderer, Mrs. Wickham, but it was Wickham who entered the room. I know for I would recognize his voice anywhere."

"What did he say?" Mrs. Bennet demanded.

Miss Brown blinked rapidly. He said, '*So, you are waiting in the dark for me?*' and my heart almost stopped. The sound of his voice and his casual tone sent shivers over my body. You see, I recalled his expert use of his voice, as he charmed me into doing his will." Miss Brown stared at Colonel Fitzwilliam with a plea in her eyes. "W-when I first heard him speak, I thought...I hoped with all my heart...he was speaking to me. That somehow he had discovered my hiding place and come to find me."

"No, he would never—"

"Oh, really, this is too much. Stop the hysterical details and speak of what happened next." Miss Bingley's voice rose over Lydia's broken voice.

Colonel Fitzwilliam eyed the two women for a heartbeat, then sent Miss Brown a reassuring nod to continue.

Miss Brown drew a shuddering breath, making a visible effort to pull herself together as she continued. "The man with the pipe said, '*If I am, I have had a long wait. And judging from the twigs attached to your uniform, I would hazard to guess you have not suffered the cold night*

258

air, all alone.'"

"Why does she speak of such things about my Wickham?" Lydia demanded in a tone heavy with emotion, but all eyes in the room were focused on Miss Brown.

Voice lowered, Colonel Fitzwilliam urged her to continue. "What did you hear next, Miss Brown?"

"Mr. Wickham said, *'No, sir, I have not.'* And he laughed."

"Is that when you murdered him?" Colonel Forester demanded.

"Colonel, please allow Miss Brown to finish before you rush to a conclusion." Colonel Fitzwilliam turned a kind glance on Miss Brown. "How did you feel after hearing Mr. Wickham admit he had conducted a liaison in the garden with another woman? Were you vexed?"

"I suppose I should have been —"

"Why? Wickham was not your husband. He was mine, and my Wickham did not meet another woman in the garden. I know he would not —"

"Hush, child," Mr. Bennet said with all the compassion of a father wanting to ease his daughter's pain. "Best to hear all that happened and be done with the pain."

Colonel Fitzwilliam said, "Were you vexed, Miss Brown?"

"Given more time, perhaps I might have worked up a temper, but I recalled the sound of his laugh so well, nothing else mattered." Miss Brown leaned forward. "You see, I loved —"

Gasps escaped from several locations in the room.

Miss Brown paused.

All the guests gathered in the room searched for the source of the uncontrolled emotion. That Lydia was one who reacted was obvious from the livid color of her pinched lips, but who else?

Miss Brown frowned as her gaze searched faces around her but she returned her attention to Colonel Fitzwilliam as she continued. "I loved Wickham's charming smile, and easy manners. He was confident he could win any battle of wills and believed that he could."

"Must we sit here and listen while this woman makes my daughter's husband sound like a character out of one of those new novels people whisper about? This is most unseemly." Mrs. Bennet sent Miss Brown a withering look.

"I fear we must, Mrs. Bennet if we are to discover who murdered Mr. Wickham." Colonel Fitzwilliam said. Then he turned to Miss Brown as he asked, "Nothing seemed remiss to you? Mr. Wickham sounded the same as when you last met?"

"Not really, for I heard a note of tension underlying his words when he spoke."

"Did you make yourself known to him and ask if anything was wrong?" Lydia demanded. "Perhaps you offered to comfort him and he turned you away."

"I had no chance for the man in the chair spoke before I could." Miss Brown turned to Colonel Fitzwilliam, "The man with the pipe said, *'Ah, Wickham, no doubt you were entertaining yourself with another man's wife, but you had better pray to the heavens it was not mine.'*"

"Wickham said, *'Sir, you under estimate your –'*"

"*'Wickham, when it comes to you, I learned anything is possible.'*"

"Wickham replied, *'Sir, you underestimate your wife's loyalty to you and do her dishonor by assuming she would find another man's attentions welcome while married to you.'*"

"*'Ah, but you see, Wickham,'* the other man rose from his chair for I heard it creak, *'I know of my wife's ability to betray me between the sheets, and to my disgust, so do you.'*"

Miss Brown shuddered as she recalled the details and covered her mouth to hold back a sob. Then, voice quivering, she continued. "All I could think about was Wickham in the arms of that man's wife. Was there no end to his betrayal of me? He declared his undying affection for me, and next I found him charming Miss Georgiana. But I could not fault her for believing in his charm. I held him responsible for my pain. I believed him and succumbed to his charms and his lies, and he betrayed me."

"You murdered him!" Lydia cried as she jumped to her feet. "I loved him and you murdered him."

"A woman scorned!" Colonel Forester nodded. He rocked on his heels as his gaze bored into Colonel Fitzwilliam. "Did I not tell you this was a crime of passion?"

"No! I could not move. I slumped back in my chair, lost in misery." Ignoring Colonel Forester, Miss Brown responded to Lydia's outburst. "I could not hurt Wickham. I loved him." She paused to catch her breath. "Then I heard a loud thump. Consumed as I was by pain, I had missed the rest of the conversation. When I looked past the back of my chair, I saw a man leaning over a body on the floor." Her lips trembled and tears rolled down her cheeks. "Wickham was crumpled on the floor."

"Why did you not call for help, Miss Brown?" Colonel Fitzwilliam asked in a soft tone.

"I was frightened. I had no wish to be murdered. I stared at the body of the man who ruined my life, but I could not move. He was dead. Wickham was dead. Before I could regain my senses, the other man whirled around and rushed out the door."

"Did you then call for help?" Colonel Fitzwilliam demanded.

"To my shame, I did not." Miss Brown shook her head. A curl escaped and hang down along side her face.

"You did nothing!" Lydia sobbed loudly. "My poor Wickham collapsed on the floor and she did nothing."

"It shames me to admit, but fear kept me rooted my chair. What if the murderer came back? He could murder me, as well." Staring at nothing, emotions flashing on her face as if she were reliving the event again, Miss Brown whispered. "Wickham was dead."

"Maggie, don't—"

"You as good as murdered my husband, for you did not help him." Lydia cried.

"Mary," Miss Brown twisted around to face her cousin, "Wickham stole my heart and promised me his in return. He left my bed and my life but I never wished him dead. How could I? All my hopes of rectifying that one mistake died when I saw him on the floor. He ruined my life, and before I could beg him to make amends, he was murdered. But not by me."

"See here, Fitzwilliam, what more proof do you need? That woman clearly had a reason to murder Wickham, and emotions strong enough to do the deed." Colonel Forester's booming voice shattered the shocked silence of the room. "We have found the person guilty of this crime and the case is closed."

"Not so fast, Colonel," Colonel Fitzwilliam held up a hand, "Miss Brown, can you identify the man who smoked the pipe?"

"I could not at that time, Colonel. I can now." Her shoulders were shaking with sobs, and her voice wavering, Miss Brown raised her hand and pointed. "It was him that I saw. It was Colonel Forester."

Lydia and Mrs. Forester made squawking sounds of disbelief as gasps filled the air. All eyes turned to stare at Colonel Forester.

"You claim such nonsense because I saw through your story from the start," Colonel Forester huffed. "We know you are the murderer. Anyone sitting in that chair," he pointed to the chair in the corner, "could have seen you if indeed, you were sitting there as you claimed."

"You can be assured she was sitting where she claimed. I found Miss Brown sitting here in the library." Caroline Bingley said. "But I left and cannot speak for what she did later."

"Be that as it may, I am convinced Miss Brown is the murderer." During Miss Brown's description of events, Colonel Forester had moved to a position near the door. Now, with people staring and waiting for his explanation, his face turned a color to match his uniform. Tone blustering, he glared at the guests gathered in the room, "That woman clearly is not in her right mind. You heard her words. Wickham used her and tossed her aside for her cousin. If anyone had reason to murder Wickham, it was she."

"Colonel, you are quite correct when you say Wickham treated her badly." Colonel Fitzwilliam gave a reluctant nod of agreement.

"No, this is all lies, I tell you." Lydia screeched. "Wickham would not look at a servant. I do not believe a word she said."

"Hush, daughter," Mr. Bennet said softly into the quiet surrounding them. "Allow the colonel to speak."

With a nod to Mr. Bennet, Colonel Fitzwilliam turned to study Colonel Forester's ruddy complexion. "Yet I must ask, Colonel, can you offer any reason why Miss Brown would make such a claim against you?"

"I know of none, Fitzwilliam," Colonel Forester said as he glared at Miss Brown. "Before this night I have never seen the woman."

"A fact that appears to be in your favor, Colonel, and we all agree she could make the claim out of anger over you naming her as the murderer."

"Right, again, Colonel," Colonel Forester's rigid stance seemed to relax, "I have thought all along that passion was at the root of this crime. Now, it seems Miss Brown's words prove me right."

"Um, 'tis true, Miss Brown had reason to wish Wickham harm." Colonel Fitzwilliam frowned. "Yet I noticed a shinny spot on your right pocket. From something rubbing against your uniform, I suppose, Colonel?"

"What the blazes?" Colonel Forester stared down at his right side, then lifted his head and glared at Fitzwilliam. "Does the state of my uniform matter, when we are attempting to solve a murder, Fitzwilliam?"

"Perhaps it matters not at all, Colonel." Colonel Fitzwilliam turned his attention to Mrs. Forester, who was sitting there gaping at him with an open mouth. "Yet I must ask, Mrs. Forester, does Colonel Forester smoke a pipe?"

Amid the shocked gasps filling the room, Mrs. Forester turned a frightened glance to her husband. What she saw in his expression turned her face an even more alarming shade of pale. Eyes wide, she turned back to Colonel Fitzwilliam. Her head tilted forward. as if she were a puppet attached to a string. "Yes, but that does not —"

"What complete nonsense," Colonel Forester roared. "Now see here, Fitzwilliam, smoking a pipe does not mean I murdered Wickham. You could smoke a pipe, for all we know, and before you ask, yes I came in this library earlier tonight. To be quite honest, escaping the noise and heat of the ballroom appealed to me, and I found the quiet in this room most welcome." Colonel Forester inhaled noisily. "I will even admit I stood over Wickham's body. However, my only intention in so doing was to confirm he was actually dead. If one sees a body on the floor, is it not a natural reaction to check on it?"

"Exactly, Colonel, and what you say is all well and good, if that is what actually happened. Yet you did not sound the alert to inform others of Wickham's death." Colonel Fitzwilliam's tone was one of a man well versed in his authority, as he waited for his fellow officer to respond.

"Ah, for the very reason you are thinking now, Colonel. I was aware my wife had been tumbling in the bushes with Wickham. And you know as well as I, if the husband knows of such affairs, everyone else knows the fact, as well."

"This is nothing but lies! Wickham did not fancy Harriet!" Lydia cried as she jumped to her feet again. "After we married, he had nothing to do with her."

"Mrs. Wickham, please —"

"Ohhoo, I will never really be Mrs. Wickham again," Lydia wailed. She turned to face her family. "What am I to do?"

"Mrs. Wickham, please. We must focus on the murder —"

"Say please all you want, Colonel, but you will not stop me from speaking the truth. You and Darcy are just alike. Your noses are so high, you cannot see in front of your face." Lydia snarled. "You were all envious of my Wickham's ability to attract women, and I will not allow you to discuss him in this manner now that he is dead."

"Daughter, hush —"

"Papa, pray do not speak to me as if I am a child," Lydia turned on her father, "for I am a married woman, and... and you never liked

Wickham—"

"My poor, dear Lydia," Mrs. Bennet cooed, "of course we liked dear Wickham. Have you not heard me say he reminded me of a uniformed man from my youth? I would not say such words if he were not special. Do sit down, my dear. It is your nerves making you spout such nonsense. Here, use my salts."

With a loud sob, Lydia collapsed in her chair. Kitty stepped closer, obviously wanting to offer comfort, but reluctant to move her hand closer to Lydia for fear of becoming a target of her sister's anger. Mary eased closer to Kitty and they stood staring down at their younger sister.

Colonel Fitzwilliam spoke with authority. "Colonel Forester—"

"Use some sense, Fitzwilliam," Colonel Forester roared. "Wickham's own wife admits he charmed women. Wickham made fools of half the men in this room, including your own cousin, Mr. Darcy. Why would I be the one who murdered him?"

"Miss Brown," Colonel Fitzwilliam turned away from the colonel's outrage, "did you see Colonel Forester—"

"I am a respected Colonel in the militia, trusted with the responsibility of my own regiment. Who will believe a servant's word against mine?" Colonel Forester demanded.

"Miss Brown, did you see Colonel Forester murder Mr. Wickham?"

Miss Brown stared at the two men, then slowly shook her head. "No, but I heard Wickham fall and when I looked, not much time had passed."

"Did you hear the door open or close before you looked? Or hear footsteps of anyone else entering or leaving the room?"

"No."

"Colonel Forester—"

"What would you do, Fitzwilliam, tell me that at least? We have worked all our lives to achieve this rank. I know I did and then a scoundrel like Wickham comes along, and charms my own wife right under my nose. Yet the worst part was the men in the regiment snickering behind my back. Even after I refused to have Wickham in the regiment, and he was forced to move north, it continued." Colonel Forester's face turned dark as his voice grew louder. "How can I command a regiment when the men have no respect for me? Wickham ruined my life, my marriage, and my career."

With that last shout, Colonel Forester turned on his heel and ran out of the library.

"Should we go after him?" Captain Carter asked in a shock loaded voice?

"No, the authorities will arrive soon." Sir William announced in a surprisingly firm tone.

Mrs. Forester made a loud whimper and collapsed in a fit of tears.

Denny paused for a moment to stare at Lydia, then he rushed to Mrs. Forester's side.

Kitty watched as Denny tried to comfort the colonel's wife and stomped her foot. "This is not fair. Denny cheated."

Lydia watched her former friend console the wife of the man who murdered her husband and started wailing. Her cries grew even louder when Kitty and Mary tried to sooth her.

Mrs. Bennet glanced from her daughters to Mr. Bennet and said in a loud voice for all to hear, "I never liked that Denny. He always seemed too friendly to suit me."

"Then, wife, I expect it is just as well you have a husband already." Mr. Bennet said. His words offered no comfort for Mrs. Bennet for she started wailing loud as Lydia.

Captain Carter moved to Miss King's side, as she tried to soothe Miss Brown. "Do stop crying before you make yourself ill, Maggie, dear. You must pack your bag and come home with me, and this time I intend to win the argument. If you insist you must work to support yourself and the baby, then you can act as my companion, but you and the child will always have a home with me."

Miss Brown lifted a tear streaked face. "Oh, Mary, I cannot for how will you ever find a husband with me in tow?"

"Ah, Miss Brown," Captain Carter bowed, "much as happened this long night, and not all of it for the worse. I gathered my courage and offered my heart and my love, such as it is, to Miss King. And much to my delight, she has accepted my offer of marriage."

"Mary, can this be true?" Miss Brown stared at them both. "For you said not a word."

"Oh, yes, Maggie it is true and now that we are not accused of murder, I am beside myself with happiness."

A short distance away, Miss Darcy burst into tears after all the unrest of the past few hours. Lizzy and Mr. Darcy huddled around her and offered comfort. She had known Wickham all her life and his death unsettled her youthful emotions.

Caroline Bingley tried to catch Captain Carter's attention, but then she became aware he had no notice of anyone except Miss King. Caroline shrugged and walked away. As she moved past Jane and Bingley, she paused. "Jane, when next you plan a ball, pray give me notice so I might make other arrangements." With a twittering laugh, she turned and followed Louisa and Mr. Hurst out of the library.

Her exit turned out to be a timely, indeed. For had Caroline not observed the Hursts holding hands with her own eyes, as they climbed the stairs ahead of her, she would never have believed it possible.

After Caroline departed, Bingley and Jane joined Colonel Fitzwilliam and Sir William in front of the fireplace.

"Well, Colonel, what action do you take next? Do we organize a party to go after Colonel Forester?" Bingley asked.

Colonel Fitzwilliam and Sir William exchanged glances. Colonel Fitzwilliam turned back to Bingley as he said, "I think not. Sir William will report our findings to the proper authorities and they will deal with Forester."

"'Tis the best plan for all." Sir William said as he hooked his thumbs in the pockets of his waistcoat. "The colonel tells me you and Mrs. Bingley deserve credit for uncovering his deception."

"Really, it was mostly the work of Jane and Miss King." Bingley smiled down at his wife. "But I must ask, Colonel, how did you discover Colonel Forester was the murderer?"

"Your wife tipped me off, Bingley."

"What did I do?" Jane asked with an arched brow.

"Among other things, it was your casual comment about the state of his uniform that alerted me." Fitzwilliam shook his head. "I knew he acted the jealous husband, but I considered him guilty of no more until Mrs. Bingley commented that it was a shame the militia could not replace our uniforms when they showed the wear. She gave the example of the shiny pocket on Forester's coat."

"Aye, the ladies notice such things." Sir William said.

"Indeed they do," Colonel Fitzwilliam said as he bowed. "Now, if you will excuse me, Bingley and Mrs. Bingley, I must return to my regiment."

CR80

A short time later, and much faster than either expected it to happen, Jane and Bingley watched their guests prepare to depart. Standing to one side of the large front door, and out of the midst of the activities going on around them, Bingley leaned down and whispered for Jane's hearing alone, "Soon, wife, we will have the house to ourselves."

"My dear Bingley, I will be so glad. But our ball was a disaster. Nothing happened as I planned." Jane forced her mind from his comment while their guests straggled about, and still needed her attention. For she knew when the house was empty of the last of their guests, her eagerness would match his. "I wanted to find love matches for our sisters, but I fear I failed miserably."

"Be that as it may, my dear, you did not fail as a host."

"Oh, Charles, how can you say so, when a murder happened and I allowed three eligible men to slip away without any interest in either of our sisters? Yet, to add to my disappointment, two of those men found love matches at our ball and neither of them looked twice at our sisters." Jane expelled a deep sigh as she watched her mother order her father about to gather their cases.

Bingley glanced around the large front hall. Colonel Fitzwilliam was saying his farewells to Darcy, Lizzy, and Miss Darcy. The Bennets were intending to depart as soon as Lydia stopped complaining about needing widow's weeds, before she could venture out the door. "I confess, I am confused. Of what matches do you speak, my dear?"

"I had thought Colonel Fitzwilliam might be a possible match for Caroline. However, after observing them together, I am now aware their temperaments would never suit. And, I hoped Denny and Captain Carter would make a match with Kitty and Mary, but obviously that is not going to happen, after events of the past hour."

"There is always a chance they will show interest at our next ball, my dear." Bingley smiled, hoping to relieve the worry from Jane's expressive face.

"I fear not, Charles. I believe poor Denny is lost to Mrs. Forester, and surely you noticed how Captain Carter and Miss King send out sparks when they look at each other."

"Ah, I did notice Captain Carter seemed quite taken with Miss King and that is good. But never fear, my Jane, for when it comes to making a match, you are perfect for me."

"Oh, Charles, I do so love being your wife."

"Then make me one promise, my dear. No more balls for at least a year. I wish to concentrate on starting our nursery."

Jane flushed prettily, as well brought up females tend to do at the mention of private time spent in the arms of their husbands, and smiled. However, the promise of her interest was in her eyes, as she returned Bingley's adoring gaze.

Then, abruptly, they both turned their attention to the needs of their guests and became efficiency itself as they quickly eased their beloved family members and friends on their way.

Epilogue

"Do hurry, Denny," Mrs. Forester urged as they rushed down the back stairs.

"Hold up, Harriet." Denny glanced back at the stairway. "We have some time for privacy here before Sir William's coach leaves."

"We are not going back by Sir William's coach, Denny. Now, hurry. We must go to the stables for horses and make our own way back to Lucas Lodge so I can pack my things before Lady Lucas and Sir William return." Mrs. Forester resumed her headlong rush down the steps to the back entrance of Netherfield Hall.

Once they were in the stables, Denny looked around the stalls and frowned. "Why are we doing this? Sir William's coach is the latest in comfort and we can not take horses without permission."

"Of course we can," Mrs. Forester snapped as she searched for a bridle. "Sir William will see to the return of the horses."

"But why the rush? I don't—"

"We must leave the area before my husband comes to his senses and returns to defend his honor. We will go back to our lives in Brighton. The colonel would not dare show up there for fear of being caught."

"Why must we run? We did nothing wrong."

"Oh, Denny! Why did you not go with me into the library last night when I insisted on checking to discover why my husband left in such a rush?"

"You told me to wait—"

"If only I had not...you might have stopped me." She rushed to Denny's side and clutched his coat in both hands. "I was beside myself at seeing Wickham snuggling in the bushes with another woman. I lost my head."

"What are you speaking of, Harriet? What did you do?"

"Oh, Denny! Can you not see? Forester thought he killed Wickham, but he only wounded him. But I was so incensed, when I saw him on the floor, I did not think. I just grabbed the letter opener from the floor and pierced the blade deeper into Wickham's wound."

Denny backed away one step and then another. "You mean — that is why you insisted on hiding that letter opener? But you said the colonel —"

"Yes, my dear, what did you tell young Denny?" The colonel stepped out of the dark shadows in the back of the stables. "I tried to figure out which of our fellow guests had done the deed. And all along it was it you, wife."

"Husband! Whatever are you thinking? You must run. If they catch you, they will hang you."

"Ah, that is what I thought at first, my dear, but now...I have Denny here as a witness to my innocence."

"No, husband. You cannot take the risk. You would not —"

Harriet let out a squawking sound as the colonel took hold of her upper arm. "Husband, let me go. Denny help me. Colonel, think of your position. You must run."

"Stand back, young Denny. You cannot win, even if I walked away. Knowing what she is capable of, you would end up sleeping with one eye open, waiting for her to tire of you."

"Oh, Denny, pray do not listen to him. I could never hurt you," Harriet begged. Tears gathered in her eyes, as her husband pulled her toward the back of the stable. "Please, Colonel, husband, where are you taking me?"

"You are right about one thing, wife. I should leave the area before I am hanged and I do not intend to make the journey alone."

"Denny! Help me."

Colonel Forester turned back from the door at the rear of the stables. "I said all along it was a crime of passion, Denny. Go back to the Lodge with Sir William. Get on with your life. And the next time you are tempted by a married woman, walk away."

Mouth hanging open, feet anchored to the floor, Denny watched in stunned silence, as Colonel Forester lugged his wife through the field to a waiting carriage. A minute later, they disappeared down the dirt lane.

Who Murdered Mr. Wickham?

ABOUT THE AUTHOR

A reader of romance since her early teens, Carol spent many hours doing chores and making up her own romance stories. College brought interesting conflicts, one being whether to major in biology or home economics. Both majors were heavy with science classes but the creative side of home economics won her over.

A teaching career followed, with marriage to her own hero and two wonderful sons. Yet, the stories in her head would not be still. When she retired from teaching, Carol started putting her dreams on paper and this book is one of the results.

Other Books by Carol Hutchens:

The Redbud Romance Series
THE SUBSTITUTE BRIDE #1
A BRIDE FOR MR. RIGHT #2
WHERE THE HEART IS #3

The Cupid Dog Romance Series
WHEN A DOG PLAYS CUPID   Book #1
HERO'S BALL...Book #2

Other Romances
THE BEST MAN

Medical Romance
DR'S SURPRISE TRIPLETS, WIFE NEEDED
HOW CAN THE HEART FORGET

Mystery
FLAMES OF DECEIT
WHO MURDERED MR. WICKHAM [historical]

Dear Reader,
Thank you for reading my book. The words used in this novel were researched in Samuel Johnson's Book of Words, Vol. I and Vol. II., 1753 edition. All phrasing was intended to resemble the style used in Pride and Prejudice, and all mistakes are mine.

If you liked the story, please leave a review on line. If you'd like to read more books similar to this one, please check out the titles listed above.

I started this journey in my teens by reading every romance novel I could get my hands on, so readers are very precious to me.
All the best,
Carol

Happy Reading!

www.ingramcontent.com/pod-product-compliance
Lightning Source LLC
Chambersburg PA
CBHW031302170626
46807CB00001B/277